HOPE TO DIE

ALSO BY LAWRENCE BLOCK

THE MATTHEW SCUDDER NOVELS

THE SINS OF THE FATHERS • TIME TO MURDER AND CREATE • IN THE MIDST OF DEATH • A STAB IN THE DARK • EIGHT MILLION WAYS TO DIE • WHEN THE SACRED GINMILL CLOSES • OUT ON THE CUTTING EDGE • A TICKET TO THE BONEYARD • A DANCE AT THE SLAUGHTERHOUSE • A WALK AMONG THE TOMBSTONES • THE DEVIL KNOWS YOU'RE DEAD • A LONG LINE OF DEAD MEN • EVEN THE WICKED • EVERYBODY DIES

THE BERNIE RHODENBARR MYSTERIES

BURGLARS CAN'T BE CHOOSERS • THE BURGLAR IN THE CLOSET • THE BURGLAR WHO LIKED TO QUOTE KIPLING • THE BURGLAR WHO STUDIED SPINOZA • THE BURGLAR WHO PAINTED LIKE MONDRIAN • THE BURGLAR WHO TRADED TED WILLIAMS • THE BURGLAR WHO THOUGHT HE WAS BOGART • THE BURGLAR IN THE LIBRARY • THE BURGLAR IN THE RYE

THE ADVENTURES OF EVAN TANNER

THE THIEF WHO COULDN'T SLEEP • THE CANCELED CZECH • TANNER'S TWELVE SWINGERS • TWO FOR TANNER • TANNER'S TIGER • HERE COMES A HERO • ME TANNER, YOU JANE • TANNER ON ICE

THE AFFAIRS OF CHIP HARRISON

NO SCORE • CHIP HARRISON SCORES AGAIN • MAKE OUT WITH MURDER • THE TOPLESS TULIP CAPER

KELLER'S GREATEST HITS

HIT MAN • HIT LIST

OTHER NOVELS

AFTER THE FIRST DEATH • ARIEL • COWARD'S KISS • DEADLY HONEYMOON • THE GIRL WITH THE LONG GREEN HEART • MONA • NOT COMIN' HOME TO YOU • RANDOM WALK • RONALD RABBIT IS A DIRTY OLD MAN • THE SPECIALISTS • SUCH MEN ARE DANGEROUS • THE TRIUMPH OF EVIL • YOU COULD CALL IT MURDER

COLLECTED SHORT STORIES

SOMETIMES THEY BITE • LIKE A LAMB TO SLAUGHTER • SOME DAYS YOU GET THE BEAR • EHRENGRAF FOR THE DEFENSE • ONE NIGHT STANDS

BOOKS FOR WRITERS

WRITING THE NOVEL FROM PLOT TO PRINT • TELLING LIES FOR FUN & PROFIT • WRITE FOR YOUR LIFE • SPIDER, SPIN ME A WEB

ANTHOLOGIES EDITED

DEATH CRUISE • MASTER'S CHOICE • OPENING SHOTS • MASTER'S CHOICE 2 • SPEAKING OF LUST • OPENING SHOTS 2

HOPE TO DIE

A MATTHEW SCUDDER NOVEL

LAWRENCE BLOCK

HarperLargePrint

An Imprint of HarperCollins*Publishers*

HOPE TO DIE. Copyright © 2001 by Lawrence Block. All rights reserved. Printed in the United States of America. No part of this book may be used or reproduced in any manner whatsoever without written permission except in the case of brief quotations embodied in critical articles and reviews. For information address Harper-Collins Publishers Inc., 10 East 53rd Street, New York, NY 10022.

HarperCollins books may be purchased for educational, business, or sales promotional use. For information please write: Special Markets Department, HarperCollins Publishers Inc., 10 East 53rd Street, New York, NY 10022.

FIRST HARPER LARGE PRINT EDITION

Printed on acid-free paper

Library of Congress Cataloging-in-Publication Data

Block, Lawrence.
    Hope to die : a Matthew Scudder novel / by Lawrence Block.
      p. cm.
  ISBN 0-06-019832-X (Hardcover)
  1. Scudder, Matt (Fictitious character)—Fiction.
  2. Private investigators—New York(State)—
New York—Fiction. 3. New York (N.Y.)—Fiction.
  I. Title
  PS3552.L63 H66 2001
  813'.54—dc21   2001030454
ISBN 0-06-621400-9 (Large Print)

01 02 03 04 05 RRD 10 9 8 7 6 5 4 3 2 1

**This Large Print Book carries the
Seal of Approval of N.A.V.H.**

This one's for
JOHN B. KEANE

Life is a narrow vale between the cold and barren peaks of two eternities. We strive in vain to look beyond the heights. We cry aloud—and the only answer is the echo of our wailing cry. From the voiceless lips of the unreplying dead there comes no word. But, in the night of Death, Hope sees a star, and listening Love can hear the rustling of a wing.

—Robert Green Ingersoll,
at the grave of his brother,
Ebon Clark Ingersoll,
June 1879

Hope is the only universal liar who never loses his reputation for veracity.

—Robert Green Ingersoll,
speaking at the Manhattan Liberal Club,
February 1892

ACKNOWLEDGMENTS

The author is pleased to acknowledge the considerable contribution of the Ragdale Foundation, in Lake Forest, Illinois, where this book was written.

HOPE TO DIE

ONE

It was a perfect summer evening, the last Monday in July. The Hollanders arrived at Lincoln Center sometime between six and six-thirty. They may have met somewhere—in the plaza by the fountain, say, or in the lobby—and gone upstairs together. Byrne Hollander was a lawyer, a partner in a firm with offices in the Empire State Building, and he might have come directly from the office. Most of the men were wearing business suits, so he wouldn't have had to change.

He left his office around five, and their house was on West Seventy-fourth Street between Columbus and Amsterdam, so he had time to go home first to collect his wife. They may have walked to Lincoln Center—it's half a mile, no more than a ten-minute walk. That's how Elaine and I got there, walking up from our apartment at Ninth and Fifty-seventh, but the Hollanders lived a little further away, and may not have felt like walking. They could have taken a cab, or a bus down Columbus.

However they got there, they'd have arrived in time for drinks before dinner. He was a tall man, two inches over six feet, two years past fifty, with a strong jaw and a high forehead. He'd been athletic in his youth and still worked out regularly at a midtown gym, but he'd thickened some through the middle; if he'd looked hungry as a young man, now he looked prosperous. His dark hair was graying at the temples, and his brown eyes were the sort people described as watchful, perhaps because he spent more time listening than talking.

She was quiet, too, a pretty girl whom age had turned into a handsome woman. Her hair, dark with red highlights, was shoulder-length, and she wore it back off her face. She was six years younger than her husband and as many inches shorter, although her high heels made up some of the difference. She'd put on a few pounds in the twenty-some years they'd been married, but she'd been fashion-model thin back then, and looked good now.

I can picture them, standing around on the second floor at Avery Fisher Hall, holding a glass of white wine, picking up an hors d'oeuvre from a tray. As far as that goes, it's entirely possible I saw them, perhaps exchanging a nod and a smile with him, perhaps noticing her as one notices an attractive woman. We were there, and so were they, along with a few hundred other people. Later, when I saw their photographs, I thought they looked faintly familiar. But that doesn't mean I saw them that night. I could have seen either or both of them on other nights at Lincoln Center or Carnegie Hall, or walking in the neighborhood. We lived, after all, less than a mile apart. I could have laid eyes on them dozens of times, and never really noticed them, just as I very possibly did that night.

I did see other people I knew. Elaine and I talked briefly with Ray and Michelle Gruliow. Elaine introduced me to a woman she knew from a class she'd taken several years ago at the Metropolitan, and to a terribly earnest couple who'd been customers at her shop. I introduced her to Avery Davis, the real estate mogul, whom I knew from the Club of Thirty-one, and to one of the fellows passing the hors d'oeuvres trays, whom I knew from my AA home group at St. Paul's. His name was Felix, and I didn't know his last name, and don't suppose he knew mine.

And we saw some people we recognized but didn't know, including Barbara Walters and Beverly Sills. The occasion was the opening of New York's summer music festival, Mostly Mozart, and the cocktails and dinner were the festival's thank-you to its patrons, who had achieved that status by contributing $2500 or more to the festival's operating fund.

During her working years, Elaine made a habit

of saving her money and investing it in rental property around town. New York real estate has been a can't-lose area even for people who do everything wrong, and she did most things right, and has done very well for herself. She was able to buy our apartment at the Parc Vendome, and there's enough income generated by her apartment houses in Queens so that, as far as money is concerned, neither of us needs to work. I have my work as a detective, of course, and she has her shop a few blocks south of us on Ninth Avenue, and we enjoy the work and can always find a use for the money it brings in. But if nobody hired me or bought paintings and antiques from her, we wouldn't wind up missing any meals.

We both like the idea of giving away a certain amount of what comes in. Years ago I got in the habit of stuffing ten percent of my earnings into whatever church poor box came along. I've grown a little more sophisticated in my giving since then, but I still find a way to get rid of it.

Elaine likes to support the arts. She gets to more operas and gallery openings and museum shows than I do (and fewer ball games and prizefights) but we both like music, classical and jazz. The jazz joints don't hit you up for contributions, they just call it a cover charge and let it go at that, but every year we write out a lot of checks to Lincoln Center and Carnegie Hall. They like to encourage us with perks of one sort or another, and this evening was one of them—drinks, a sit-down dinner, and complimentary orchestra seats to the opening concert.

Around six-thirty we went to our assigned table, where we were joined by three other couples, with whom we exchanged names and chatted amiably throughout the meal. If pressed, I could probably recall the names of most if not all of our table mates, but what's the point? We haven't seen them since, and they don't figure in the story. Byrne and Susan Hollander were not among them.

They were at another table, which I later learned was on the other side of the room from us. While I might have seen them earlier, it's unlikely that I laid eyes on them during dinner. Their seats for the concert were just two rows in front of ours, but at the extreme right of the center section, while we were toward the left. So, unless we bumped into each other on the way to the rest room during intermission, I don't suppose we would have seen them at all.

The meal was pretty good, the company at dinner pleasant enough. The concert was very enjoyable, and, true to its stated theme, leaned toward Mozart, including one of his piano concertos and the **Prague** Symphony. There was an orchestral suite of Antonín Dvořák's as well, and the program notes drew some connection between him and Mozart, or perhaps between him and Prague, Dvořák being a Czech. Whatever it was, I didn't pay too much attention to it. I just sat there and enjoyed the music, and when it was done we walked home.

Did the Hollanders walk home? It's hard to know one way or the other. No cab driver came forward to report driving them, but neither did anyone recall seeing them on the street. They could have taken a bus, but no one reported witnessing that, either.

I think they probably walked. She was wearing heels, which might have lessened her enthusiasm for a half-mile hike, but they were both in good shape, and it was a perfect night for a leisurely walk home, not too warm, not too humid. There are always a lot of cabs after a concert, but there are even more people trying to flag one, even when the weather's good. It certainly would have been simpler for them to walk, but there's no way to say with certainty just how they got home.

When the concert ended, when the conductor had taken his last bow and the musicians walked off the stage, Byrne and Susan Hollander had something like an hour and a half to live.

Though, as I said, I can't know this, in my imagination they are walking home. They talk some— about the music they've heard, about something outrageous one of their dinner companions said, about the pleasures of walking on a night like this in a city like theirs. But they are silent much of the time, and the silences are companionable, of the sort known to long-married couples. They have been close enough for long enough so that a shared silence is as intimate as a shared thought.

Crossing the avenue, he takes her hand, even as she is reaching for his. They hold hands most of the way home.

Their house is a brownstone on the downtown side of Seventy-fourth Street, near the middle of the block. They own the house, and occupy the upper three floors; the ground floor and basement are leased to an upscale antique dealer. When they bought the place twenty-six years ago with the proceeds of an inheritance, it cost them a little over a quarter of a million dollars, and the antique shop rent was enough to cover their taxes and running costs. Now the property is worth at least ten times what they paid for it, and the store rent is currently $7500 a month, and covers a whole lot more than their tax bill.

If they didn't already own the house, they are fond of saying, they couldn't possibly afford it. His earnings as a lawyer are substantial—he was able to put their daughter through four years at a private college without taking out a loan, or even dipping into savings—but he couldn't go out and buy a three-million-dollar house.

Nor would they need that much space. She was pregnant when they bought the house. She lost the baby in the fifth month, got pregnant again within the year, and gave birth to a daughter, Kristin. Two years later their son, Sean, was born, and when he was eleven years old he was killed playing Little League baseball, hit in the head accidentally with a bat. It was a senseless death, and it stunned both of them. His drinking increased over the next year, and she had an affair with a friend's husband, but time passed and the wound healed and his drinking normalized and she ended the affair. That was the first real strain on their marriage, and the last.

She is a writer, with two novels and two dozen short stories published. Her writing is not profitable; she writes slowly, and her stories wind up in magazines that pay in prestige and contributor's copies instead of dollars, and her two novels, respectfully reviewed, had modest sales and are now out of print. But the work is satisfying beyond the rewards it brings, and she is at her desk five or six mornings a week, frowning in concentration, reaching for the right word.

She has an office/studio on the top floor where she does her writing. Their bedroom is on the third floor, along with Kristin's bedroom and Byrne's home office. Kristin, twenty-three, resumed living with them after she graduated from Wellesley. She moved in with a boyfriend after a year, then came back when the relationship ended. She often stays out overnight, and talks about getting a place of her own, but rents are sky-high and decent places hard to find, and her room is comfortable, convenient, familiar. They're happy to have her there.

The lowest of the floors they occupy, the second

floor, is what brownstone residents know as the parlor floor, with larger rooms and higher ceilings than the rest of the dwelling. The Hollander house has a large eat-in kitchen, and a formal dining room that they have converted into a library and music/TV room. And there's the living room, with a large oriental carpet on the floor, Arts and Crafts furniture that's more comfortable than it looks, and a working fireplace flanked by floor-to-ceiling bookshelves. The living room faces out on West Seventy-fourth, and the heavy drapes are drawn.

Behind those drapes, one in a large oak frame chair upholstered in tobacco-brown leather, the other pacing back and forth in front of the fireplace, the two men are waiting.

The men have been in the house for over an hour. They entered just about the time Byrne and Susan Hollander were reclaiming their seats after the intermission, and they'd finished going through the house by the time the concert ended. They were looking for things to steal, and didn't care how much of a mess they made in the process, spilling drawers, overturning tables, pulling books off shelves. They found jewelry in a dresser drawer and a vanity, cash in a locked desk drawer and on a closet shelf, silver tableware in a chest in the kitchen, and objects of some value throughout the house. They filled a couple of pillowcases with what they'd selected, and these are in the living room now. They could have shouldered them and left before the Hollanders came home, and now, as one sits and the other paces, I can imagine them thinking of doing just that. They've already done a good night's work. They could go home now.

But no, it's too late now. The Hollanders have arrived, they're climbing the half-flight of marble steps to their front door. Do they sense an alien presence within? It's possible that they do. Susan Hollander is a creative person, artistic, intuitive. Her husband is more traditionally practical, trained to deal in facts and logic, but his professional experience has taught him to trust his intuition.

She has a feeling, and she takes his arm. He turns, looks at her, can almost read the thought written on her face. But all of us get feelings all the time, premonitions, vaguely disquieting intimations. Most of them turn out to be nothing, and we learn to ignore them, to override our personal early warning systems. At Chernobyl, you may recall, the gauges indicated a problem; the men who read the gauges decided they were faulty, and ignored them.

He has his key out, and slips it into the lock. Inside, the two men hear the key in the lock. The seated man gets to his feet, the pacer moves toward the door. Byrne Hollander turns the key, pushes the door open, lets his wife enter first, follows her inside.

Then they catch sight of the two men, but by now it's too late.

I could tell you what they did, what they said. How the Hollanders begged and tried to bargain, and how the two men did what they'd already decided to do. How they shot Byrne Hollander three times with a silenced .22 automatic, twice in the heart and once in the temple. How one of them, the pacer, raped Susan Hollander fore and aft, ejaculating into her anus, and then thrust the fireplace poker into her vagina, before the other man, the one who had been sitting patiently earlier, out of mercy or the urge to get out of there, grabbed her by her long hair, yanked her head back forcefully enough to separate some hairs from her scalp, and cut her throat with a knife he'd found in the kitchen. It was of carbon steel, with a serrated edge, and the manufacturer swore it would slice through bone.

I would be imagining all of this, just as I imagined them holding hands as they crossed the street, even as I imagined the two men waiting for them, one sitting in the tobacco-brown chair, the other pacing before the fireplace. I have let my imagination work with the facts, never contradicting them but filling in where they leave off. I don't know, for example, that some inner prompting warned either or both of the Hollanders that danger waited within their house. I don't know that the rapist and the knife-wielder were different men. Maybe the same man raped her as killed her. Maybe he killed her while he was inside of her, maybe that increased his pleasure. Or maybe he tried it out, thinking it might heighten his climax, and maybe it did, or maybe it didn't.

Susan Hollander, sitting at her desk on the top floor of her brownstone, used her imagination to write her stories. I have read some of them, and they are dense, tightly crafted constructions, some set in New York, some in the American West, at least one set in an unnamed European country. Her characters are at once introspective and, often, thoughtless and impulsive. They are, to my mind, not much fun to be around, but they are convincingly real, and they are clearly creatures of her imagination. She imagined them, and brought them to life upon the page.

One expects writers to use their imaginations, but that portion of the mind, of the self, is as much a part of the equipment of a policeman. A cop would be better off without a gun or a notebook than without an imagination. For all that detectives, private and public, deal in and count on facts, it is our capacity to reflect, to imagine, that points us to solutions. When two cops discuss a case they're working on, they talk less about what they know for a fact than what they imagine. They construct scenarios of what might have happened, and then look for facts that will support or knock down their constructions.

And so I have imagined the final moments of Byrne and Susan Hollander. Of course I have gone much farther in my imagination than I have felt it necessary to recount here. The facts themselves go farther than I've gone here—the blood spatters, the semen traces, the physical evidence painstakingly gathered and recorded and assessed by the forensic technicians. Even so, there are questions the evidence doesn't answer unequivocally. For example, which of the Hollanders died first? I've suggested that they shot Byrne Hollander before they raped his wife, but it could have been the other way around; the physical evidence allows for either scenario. Perhaps he had to watch her violation and hear her screams until the first bullet mercifully blinded and deafened him. Perhaps she saw her husband killed before she was seized and stripped and taken. I can imagine it either way, and have in fact imagined it every possible way.

Here is how I prefer to imagine it: Almost as soon as they are inside the house and the door is kicked shut, one of the men shoots Byrne Hollander three times, and he is dead before the third bullet enters his body, dead before he hits the floor. The shock alone is enough to induce an out-of-body experience in his wife, and Susan Hollander, disembodied, hovers somewhere near the ceiling and watches, emotionally and physically disconnected, while her body is abused on the floor below her. Then, when they cut her throat, that body dies, and the part of her that has been watching is drawn down that long tunnel that seems to be a part of all near-death experiences. There's a white light, and she's drawn into the light, and there she finds the people who loved her and are waiting for her. Her grandparents, of course, and her father, who died when she was a child. Her mother, who died just two years ago, and her son, of course, Sean. There's never been a day that she hasn't thought of Sean, and he's there now, waiting for her.

And her husband's there, too. They were only apart for a few minutes, really, and now they'll be together forever.

Well, that's how I prefer to imagine it. And it's my imagination. I guess I can do as I please with it.

TWO

Their daughter Kristin found the bodies. She'd spent the evening with friends in Chelsea and was going to stay over at a girlfriend's apartment in London Terrace, but that would have meant wearing the same clothes to work in the morning or else running home first to change. A man she'd just met offered her a ride home, and she took it. It was a few minutes after one when he pulled up and double-parked in front of the house on West Seventy-fourth.

He was going to walk her to her door, but she stopped him. Still, he waited while she crossed the sidewalk and mounted the steps, waited while she used her key, waited until she was inside. Did he sense something? Probably not. I suspect it was habit, the way he was brought up: when you see a woman home, you wait until she's safely inside before you take your leave.

So he was still there, just about to pull away, when she reappeared in the doorway, her face a mask of horror. He killed the ignition and got out to see what was the matter.

The story broke much too late for the morning papers, but it was the lead item on the local news, so Elaine and I learned about it at breakfast. The gal on New York One reported that the victims had attended a concert at Lincoln Center that evening, so we knew we'd been there listening to the same music with them; what we didn't know then was that they'd been at the patrons' reception and dinner as well. It was unsettling to think we'd been in the same concert hall with them, along with several thousand other people; it would be more unsettling later to realize that we'd all been part of a considerably more intimate gathering.

The double murder was more than front-page news. It was, in journalistic terms, a wonderful story. The victims, a prominent attorney and a published writer, were decent, cultured people, murdered brutally in their own home. She'd been raped, always a bonus for the tabloid reader, and subjected to a second violation with the fireplace poker. In a less outspoken time than ours, that last detail would have been veiled. The police generally hold back something like that, to make it easier to screen false confessions, but this time the press got hold of it. The **Times** left it unreported, perhaps out of decency, and the TV news hinted at a further violation without getting specific, but the **News** and the **Post** showed no such restraint.

A police canvass of the area turned up a neighbor who had spotted two men leaving a house, probably the Hollander house, sometime after midnight and before one. She noticed their departure because each had a laundry bag slung over his shoulder. She didn't regard the sight as suspicious, never thinking they might be burglars, assuming instead that they were roommates, headed for the twenty-four-hour laundromat around the corner on Amsterdam. She remembered thinking that it was a shame young people had to work such long hours these days, and the only time they had to do their laundry was in the middle of the night.

The description she furnished was vague, and a session with a police artist led nowhere, as she had never gotten a clear look at their faces. They were, as she recalled, neither tall nor short, neither fat nor thin. She thought, although she couldn't swear to it, mind you, that one of them might have had a beard.

Forensics thought she might be right. They'd recovered a couple of hairs that had almost certainly come from a man's beard, and you didn't need a DNA check to know they weren't Byrne Hollander's, as he was clean-shaven.

According to the woman, it was possible that one of them limped. She remembered there was something awkward about his walk, attributing it at the time to the weight of the sack of laundry he was carrying. And maybe that's all it was, but maybe he'd been limping. She couldn't say for sure.

When you luck into a story that sells papers, you keep it on the front page whether or not there are any new developments. The **Post** showed the most imagination, actually running a sketch of the suspect with the headline HAVE YOU SEEN HIM LIMPING? It showed a man with a Mephistophelian beard and generally demonic facial features, a sack slung over his shoulder, furtively slouching. Toward Amsterdam Avenue, I suppose, if not Bethlehem. The implication, of course, was that this was a police sketch, but it was no such thing. Some staff artist at the paper had cobbled it up to order and there it was on the front page, with the **Post**'s readers urged to come up with a name to go with the imaginary face.

And, of course, dozens of them did, flooding the police tip line, the number of which the paper had been considerate enough to furnish. When someone phones in a tip in a high-profile case, you can't dismiss it out of hand, even when it's the result of some journalist's fantasy. There's always the possibility that the tip's legit, that the caller's using the sketch as an excuse to point the police toward someone of whom he has reason to be suspicious. Every call gets checked out, not because those checking expect results, but because they know how they'll look if the tip they overlook turns out to be on the money. The first thing you learn in the NYPD, on the job if not in classes at the academy, is to cover your ass. And the job keeps on teaching it to you, over and over.

One caller said the cops ought to take a look at a guy named Carl Ivanko. It wasn't that the sketch looked like him, exactly, because Carl's face was sort of lopsided, as well as longer and narrower than the face in the sketch. And the caller didn't know if Carl had a beard. Facial hair was sort of an on-and-off thing with him, and it had been a while since the caller ran into Carl, and if he never saw him again, well, that would be fine.

So it was more the description than the sketch, really, that had brought Carl to mind, although there was something about the sketch that had triggered his action, even though it didn't bear much resemblance to Carl. The thing was, Carl had something wrong with his hip, and it gave him an awkward walk some of the time. It wasn't a limp, not exactly, but what it came down to was he walked funny.

But then a lot of guys have a bum hip or a trick knee, and maybe had a beard once. What made the connection, see, was the poker, and that wasn't based on anything that happened, not as far as the caller knew. It was what he'd said, Carl, and he'd said it more than once. Of a woman who'd failed to reciprocate his interest, and of another woman who'd caught his eye on the street. What I'd like to do, Carl said, I'd like to take a hot poker and shove it up her cunt.

Or words to that effect.

No one was hugely surprised to learn that Carl Ivanko had a sheet. His juvenile record was sealed, but since then he'd been arrested twice for burglary. He pleaded out on both occasions, drawing a suspended sentence the first time and doing three years upstate for the second charge. He'd also been picked up once for attempted rape, but the charges were dropped when the victim couldn't pick him out of the lineup.

The last known address for him was his mother's place on East Sixth Street, four flights up, with an Indian restaurant on the ground floor. That was the block between First and Second, where almost every building had an Indian restaurant on the ground floor. Mrs. Ivanko didn't live there anymore, and no one in the building knew who Carl was, let alone what had become of him.

There are lots of ways to find someone when you want to badly enough, but Carl turned up on his own before they could try most of them. Brooklyn police officers responding to a complaint of a bad odor emanating from a locked ground-floor apartment in the 1600 block of Coney Island Avenue broke in to find two male Caucasians, ages twenty-five to thirty-five, who had apparently been dead for several days. Documents on the bodies, later confirmed by fingerprints, identified the two men as Jason Paul Bierman and Carl Jon Ivanko. Bierman's wallet held a driver's license with the Coney Island Avenue address. Ivanko didn't seem to have a driver's license, but a generic Student ID card in his wallet supplied some information. It was the kind you can buy in souvenir shops, and gave Ivanko's college affiliation as "Mean Streets University" and his address as "the Gutters of New York." There was a space for someone to notify in case of accident or serious illness. "The City Morgue" was Ivanko's suggestion.

Both men had died of gunshot wounds. Ivanko, sprawled full-length on the uncarpeted floor, had been shot twice in the chest and once in the temple, in a manner more or less identical to Byrne Hollander, and, ballistics later established, with the same .22-caliber automatic. The cops didn't have to look hard for the gun; it was still in Jason Bierman's hand. He was sitting on the floor in the corner of the room, his back against the wall, his gun hand in his lap. He had apparently put the barrel in his mouth, tilted it upward, and fired a single shot through the roof of his mouth and into the brain. Professional killers are supposed to favor .22s for head shots because the bullet typically caroms around inside the skull, with fatal results a strong possibility. It had worked for Bierman, but it might have worked whatever gun he used. Cops, drunk or depressed or both, have used their service revolvers in this manner for years; the .38-caliber slugs may not bounce much, but they do the job.

Both of the pillowcases from the Hollander bedroom turned up in the Bierman apartment, one empty and wadded up on the floor, the other half full of stolen goods on the unmade double bed. The wooden chest of sterling silver, service for twelve, rested on top of Bierman's chest of drawers. Kristin Hollander was able to identify it, along with several pieces of her mother's jewelry and other articles taken from her home.

Forensic analysis established that the facial hairs found at the crime scene were from Carl Ivanko's beard, and the semen recovered from Susan Hollander's anus was his as well. Posthumous x-rays of Ivanko revealed deterioration of the hip socket that would account for the limp the witness had reported and the caller confirmed.

I didn't know all of this at the time, although it was all reported at considerable length on television and in the papers. By then I had something else on my mind.

Besides sending in a contribution, Elaine typically orders tickets to around a dozen concerts during the month-long Mostly Mozart festival. I keep her company more often than not, and when business or inclination keeps me away, she can always find a friend to use my ticket. Last year she took T J to one performance, a countertenor singing with a small orchestra of period instruments. I'd have enjoyed it myself, but I had a case I had to work. It was T J's first classical concert, as far as we knew, and she said he seemed to like the whole thing, music and all, but not to expect him to run out and buy a whole batch of CDs.

We went to the opening concert on Monday night, and our next tickets were for Thursday night, a sold-out affair with Alicia de Larrocha at the piano. By then we'd learned that the Hollanders had not only attended Monday's concert but had been at the patrons' dinner as well. The killers had not yet been found, and Avery Fisher Hall was buzzing with the story. As far as I could tell, it was all anyone was talking about.

I made a point of heading for the patrons' lounge during intermission, more for the conversation than the free coffee and Toblerone bars they give you. One couple we see there often enough to nod to asked if they hadn't seen us at the dinner, and if we'd seen or known the Hollanders. We said we hadn't known them, and we might or might not have seen them there, that it was impossible to say.

"That's just it," the woman said. "We sat with three other couples we didn't know. We could as easily have been seated with Byrne and Susan Hollander."

"We could have **been** Byrne and Susan Hollander," her husband said. He meant they could have suffered the Hollanders' fate. How convenient it had been, after all, for the killers to know that the Hollanders were out for the evening, and when they could be expected to return home. Was it impossible that they'd had a list of people expected to attend the patrons' dinner? And couldn't they have just as easily selected any of the names on that list?

It was a stretch, but I knew what he meant and how he'd gotten there. Any disaster—a crime or an earthquake, anything at all—has a lesser or greater impact upon us in proportion to the likelihood that it could have happened to us. The Hollanders were people like us, we might but for the luck of the draw have been seated next to them at dinner, and was it impossible that it was precisely what we shared with them that had gotten them killed? It was not impossible, so it could have been us instead of them—and we shivered with the odd blend of terror and relief that is so often the consequence of a narrow escape.

The patrons' lounge was full of people who were glad to be alive—and the least bit afraid to go home, because who could be certain the killers were finished?

That was Thursday. Saturday morning the cops kicked the door in on Coney Island Avenue, and a few hours later the media had the story and the city—especially that part of it that lived on the Upper West Side and went to concerts—breathed a sigh of relief. The killers were no longer at large, which was wonderful, and in fact they were dead, which was even better. The story would still be interesting enough to sell newspapers for several more days, maybe even a week, but it was already beginning to fade into the past. It wasn't scary anymore. Burglar alarm sales, which had spiked during the week, would drop back to normal. Women could leave the can of pepper spray home, after having gotten in the habit of tucking it in their purse on the way to a concert. Men who'd told their lawyers to find out just how hard it was to get a carry permit could now decide it was more trouble than it was worth.

I was no less interested in the story now, listened to the news reports, and read whatever appeared in print. On Monday I had lunch with Joe Durkin. It was social, I wasn't working on anything, but our relationship had been strained a year or so ago when I had some work that cost me my PI license. I could live fine without a license, I'd done so for twenty years, but I couldn't get along without some of the friendships I'd built up with people in and out of the police department. So I made it a point to get together with Joe now and then, and not just when I needed a favor.

He's a detective at Midtown North, so it wasn't his case, or even his precinct's, but it was part of our lunchtime conversation as it was part of so many others, with or without a professional interest in the subject. "The crime rate's down," he said, "but I swear the guys who are out there are trying to make up for it by being twice as nasty. When did burglary become a contact sport, for Christ's sake? A burglar was always a guy who wanted to avoid human contact."

"A gentleman jewel thief," I suggested.

"Not too many of those, were there? But your professional burglar acted like a pro, took what he could use and left the rest, got in and got out in a hurry, and your run-of-the-mill break-in was the work of some smash-and-grab junkie who kicked the door in, grabbed a portable radio, something he could get ten bucks for, and ran like the thief he was. These fucks stole all they could, tore the place apart, and then sat down to wait for the folks to come home. You know what it was? It was a cross between a burglary and a home invasion. A home invasion, you don't go in unless you know the vics are in the house, because you want the confrontation."

"Drug dealers."

"A prime target," he agreed. "'Tell us where the money is or we cut your kid's head off.' Which they'll probably do anyway, the cocksuckers. These two went in, tossed the place, and waited for it to turn into a home invasion. Why? More money?"

"Could be. Maybe they didn't find as much as they expected."

"I guess it's a line of work where you live in hope. Maybe they saw a picture of the lady and decided they wanted to make her acquaintance."

"Or they already knew what she looked like."

"Either way. I'll tell you, Matt, gentleman jewel thief or junkie with a monkey, rape never used to be part of the game plan. Now it happens all the time. She's there, she's cute, what the hell, might as well. Hey, if there's something you like in the fridge, wouldn't you grab a bite?"

"It's not supposed to be sexual," I said.

"That's what they keep telling us. It's hostility toward women, or some such crap."

"Well, I'd say a guy has to be the least bit hostile to do what this one did with the poker."

"The son of a bitch. Yeah, of course, no question. I mean, it's never a loving act, is it? Raping a woman. But how the hell can they claim it's not about sex? If sex has nothing to do with it, where did the son of a bitch get his hard-on from? What, did somebody sprinkle Viagra on his cornflakes?"

"And somehow they only feel this hostility toward the ones they find attractive."

"Yeah," he said, "isn't that a coincidence? He does her, he gets off, you'd think he'd be feeling grateful if he's feeling anything at all. So he shows his gratitude by doing her with the poker, and then he cuts her fucking throat. I swear, one like this makes me wish we had the death penalty."

"We do have the death penalty."

He gave me a look. "Makes me wish we had the death penalty the way Texas has the death penalty. You know what I mean."

"Anyway, there's no need for it in this case. They're already dead."

"Yeah, and thank God for that. No lawyer's gonna get 'em off and no parole board's gonna decide they've learned the error of their ways. The one prick, Bierman? The shooter? At least for once in his life he did the right thing."

"I wonder why," I said.

"Who knows? Who knows why they do anything? And, when you come right down to it, who gives a shit? They're off the board. They're not gonna do it again."

That night I walked up Ninth Avenue a couple of blocks and went to an AA meeting in the basement of St. Paul the Apostle. Early on, when I left my wife and sons and the New York Police Department and moved back to the city, I got in the habit of stopping at St. Paul's, sitting for a few minutes in the stillness, lighting the odd candle for people I wanted to remember, or couldn't seem to forget, and stuffing the poor box with my curious largesse. I was always paid in cash in those days, and so my tithing was in cash, and anonymous. I can't say what my contributions amounted to because I never kept track of what I earned, and what difference does it make now? I do know the Paulist Fathers never invited me to a patrons' dinner.

Now my AA home group has its meetings there, one flight down from the sanctuary where I once lit my candles and gave away my money. I like the coincidence of that, but I've been going long enough for the irony to have worn thin. I've been sober eighteen years, a day at a time, and that sometimes astonishes me. That's more years than I was a cop, and almost as many years as I drank.

Early on I went to meetings every day, and sometimes two or three. Now it's more like two or three a week, and there have been weeks when I haven't gone at all. It's not uncommon for attendance to lessen with time. On the contrary, it's the usual pattern, although there are some stalwarts twenty or thirty years sober who still get there seven days a week. Sometimes I envy them, and other times I figure it's what they do instead of having lives of their own. The program, after all, is supposed to be a bridge back to life. For some of us, as my sponsor occasionally pointed out, it's just a tunnel to another meeting.

It's been a couple of years since my sponsor died, and it seems to me I went to more meetings before then. He was killed, shot dead in a Chinese restaurant by a hired gun who mistook him for me. The man who shot him is dead now, just about everybody involved wound up dead, and I'm still alive and, more remarkably, still sober.

They're pretty clear on what you should do if your sponsor dies or drinks or runs off with your wife. First you get your ass to a meeting, and then you find yourself another sponsor. That's the conventional wisdom, and I have no quarrel with it, but it's generally honored in the breach by those of us who've been sober more than ten years or so. For my part, I couldn't see anyone taking Jim Faber's place in my life. Early on he'd been a tower of strength and a source of essential counsel, but over time he became more of a friend and less of an adviser. Our standing date for Chinese food every Sunday night was a time for us to talk about anything and everything. I'm sure it helped me stay sober, and be comfortable in my sobriety, and I suppose that was the point. But there'd been a lot more than that to the relationship, and I've never felt inclined to hunt for a replacement.

I've sponsored people myself over the years, on and off. A year ago I had two sponsees, one sober a few years, one fresh out of rehab. Neither one looked to me like the beginning of a beautiful friendship, but sponsorship's a practical relation-ship, designed to help both parties stay sober, and I'm sure I went to more meetings and stayed more active in the program because of the role I played. But one of my sponsees—the new one—drank and disappeared, and the other one moved to Califor-nia, and no one had turned up to take their place.

I could search actively for somebody else to sponsor, I suppose, but I haven't felt the need. When the pupil is ready, the mystics say, the teacher will appear. And I would guess it ought to work as well the other way around.

There are people who quit going to meetings and stay sober. All you have to do, when all is said and done, is not drink. I sometimes wonder what would happen if I stopped going, but I haven't let myself entertain the thought. My time's not that valuable. I figure I can afford a couple of hours a week.

We had concert tickets that night, but there was a soprano on the bill, and I'm generally happier when they stick to instrumental music. So Elaine was at Lincoln Center with her friend Monica, and I was at a meeting. I got myself a cup of coffee and said hello to the people I knew. I used to know almost everybody, when I was more active and went to more meetings. I took a seat at the back and thought about this, and looked around the room and realized that I'd been sober longer than anybody else there.

That happens now and then. Eighteen years isn't forever, and there are plenty of men and women with twenty and thirty and even forty years without a drink, and the meetings in retirement communities are probably swarming with them. In a church basement on Ninth Avenue, however, eighteen years is a pretty long time.

The speaker told a story with a lot of cocaine in it, but he drank a lot, too, enough to qualify him as an alcoholic. My mind wandered, but I got the gist of it. He'd been drunk and now he was sober, and sober was better.

Well, amen to that.

When the meeting was over I helped stack the chairs, and thought about joining people for coffee at the Flame. I went straight home instead. Elaine wasn't home yet, and I checked the answering machine and found a message from Michael, my elder son.

He said, "Dad, are you there? Pick up if you're around, will you? I guess you're out. I'll try you again later."

No request to call him back, and not a clue what it was about. I played the message back a couple more times, trying to divine something from the words and the tone. He sounded strained, I decided, but a lot of people do when they have to talk to a machine. Still, he probably left messages all the time. He had a good position with a firm in Silicon Valley, he made sales calls all the time, spent half his life on the phone.

Of course it's probably different when you're calling your father.

It was a few minutes past ten, and three hours earlier in California. I looked up his number and dialed it. It rang four times and I got his machine, rang off without leaving a message.

I went and played back his message again. Sat there frowning at the answering machine.

I went into the kitchen and made a pot of coffee, and I was drinking a cup when Elaine came home with Monica in tow. I poured a cup for Monica and put the teakettle on for Elaine, who only drinks coffee in the morning. I fixed her a cup of chamomile tea and the three of us sat around and talked about the concert, and about the Hollanders. I would have mentioned the phone message, such as it was, but it could wait until Monica went home.

When the phone rang Elaine was closer to it, so she picked it up. "Oh, hi!" she said, sounding delighted, but that didn't give me a clue to the caller's identity. She always responds that way, even when it's a telemarketer trying to get her to switch her long-distance service to Sprint. "How's California? Oh, you're here? That's wonderful! But listen, your dad's right here," she said. "I'll let you talk to him."

I stood up and took a step toward the phone, but her face clouded and she held up a hand to warn me off. She said, "Oh? Oh, no. Oh, Michael, that's awful. I'm so sorry. How did it happen? God, I'm so sorry. Here, I'll put your father on."

She lowered the receiver and held her hand over the mouthpiece. "He wants to talk to you," she said, "but I think he wanted to tell me first, so I could tell you."

Tell me what? That his marriage was in trouble, that his child was sick—but why was he in New York? What bad news would have sent him rushing east?

"It's Anita," she said. That's Mike and Andy's mother, my ex-wife. "She had a heart attack. She's dead."

THREE

It must have been a very grand house in its day, a country estate of fieldstone and half-timbered stucco built when Syosset was a tiny village surrounded by potato fields. Since then a ton of development houses have been thrown up where they used to grow potatoes, and few of the big old houses are still private residences. Some have been pulled down, while others survive as nursing homes or office suites.

Or funeral homes, like this one on Albemarle Road. I drove past it the first time. I hadn't missed it, Michael's directions were good and there was a big sign on the front lawn, but I guess I must have been reluctant to arrive. I circled the block, and, halfway around, I turned left instead of right and found my way to our old house.

It looked smaller, and the lot larger, than I remembered. It was what they used to call a ranch house, and maybe they still do—three bedrooms, a living room, dining room, and kitchen, all on one floor, all on a quarter-acre suburban lot. Someone had added an enclosed breezeway connecting the house and the garage, and someone else (or the same person, for all I knew) had replaced the casement windows in front with a big picture window. The shrubbery in front had filled in, or died and been replaced, and there was a tree I had planted, then a spindly white oak sapling, that now towered over the house. There was another tree on the front strip that hadn't been there when I lived there, and a clump of white birch that I'd put in was gone. Maybe a subsequent owner hadn't liked the birches, maybe his kids had stripped the bark to make a canoe.

Or maybe the trees had simply died. Birches, I seemed to remember, were relatively short-lived trees, and it had been thirty years since I'd lived in that house, say thirty-three or thirty-four years since I planted the birches. That doesn't seem like a very long time for a tree, even a short-lived tree, but things don't always last as long as you expect them to.

Marriages fail, people die. Why should trees be different?

When I got to the funeral home a second time I pulled into the lot and found a place for my rental car. In a mortician's house are many mansions, and a fellow who looked a little heartier than the circumstances called for was waiting in the entrance hall to steer me in the right direction. He asked for the name of the party I was there for, and without thinking I gave my own. It had been hers for years, and I guess on some level it still was, as far as I was concerned.

His face, professionally noncommittal, registered first that there was no Scudder funeral on the books, then that he recognized the name; the sons of the deceased bore it, and he would have met them. Before he could say anything I corrected myself. "I'm sorry," I said. "That was her name when I knew her. It's Thiele now."

I let him point me down a hallway and followed it to a room flooded with afternoon sunlight. I found a seat in the last row. The service had already begun, and a man in a black suit was talking in the unmistakable tones of a clergyman about the frailty of human life and the durability of the human spirit. He didn't say anything I hadn't heard before, or anything to which I could take exception.

While the words washed over me, I looked around the room. In the front row I saw a man I took for Graham Thiele; I'd never met the fellow, but that could only be him, seated next to two girls who had to be his daughters. He was a widower when Anita met him, with two girls living at home; her own sons were out of the house by then, and she'd moved in with Thiele and helped him raise his daughters.

I saw other people I recognized—Anita's brother and his wife, both of them suddenly middle-aged, and heavier than when I'd known them, and her sister, Josie, who'd hardly aged at all. On the other side of the center aisle sat my two boys, Michael and Andrew, with June, Michael's wife, seated between them. Michael and June have a daughter, Melanie, and a year ago Elaine and I flew out for a long weekend in San Francisco, in the course of which we drove to San Jose for a look at my granddaughter. June is third-generation Chinese-American, slim and exquisite, and Melanie is one of the more powerful arguments for interracial marriage.

I didn't see Melanie. She was what, two? Certainly no more than three, and too young for a funeral.

But then so was Anita.

Her birthday's in November," I'd told Elaine. "She's three years younger than me, three and a half. That makes her fifty-eight."

"God, that seems young."

"She had a heart attack. I thought men got heart attacks."

"So do women."

"She wasn't heavy, she didn't smoke. Although

what the hell do I know about it? Maybe she weighed three hundred pounds and chewed cigars. I'm trying to remember the last time I saw her. I can't. I spoke to her on the phone when that lunatic Motley was on the loose, killing any woman he could find who was somehow connected to me. I told her she might be in danger and to get out of town for a while."

"I remember."

"She was pissed off. How dare I interfere in her life? I told her it wasn't by choice, but I have to say I could see her point. You divorce a guy and move on, you don't want to have to run and hide because he got himself on somebody's shit list."

"You must have talked to her since then."

"I did. I remember now, I called to congratulate her when Melanie was born. Wait a minute, that's wrong. I called, all right. But I got him instead, Thiele, and he said Anita had flown out to see the kid for herself."

"And you called Michael's house, and she answered the phone."

"That's right. I remember she kept telling me how beautiful Melanie was, as if she was telling herself as much as she was telling me. It bothered her when Michael and June got married."

"I didn't know that. Because she's Chinese?"

"Uh-huh. So Michael said. Because it would be difficult for them, coming from different cultures, di dah di dah di dah. That's how she put it, but I think all it was was she didn't want a Chinese daughter-in-law, or grandchildren with slanted eyes."

"But she got over it."

"Oh, sure. People do. And Anita was never mean-spirited, or particularly narrow-minded. It was just that she didn't know any Asians. Then her son married one and she got used to it."

"How do you feel, baby?"

"About June? I think she's the best thing that ever happened to Michael, with the possible exception of Melanie. But that's not what you mean."

"No."

"I'm not sure how I feel," I said. "Like I've lost something, but what? She hasn't been in my life for years."

"Maybe you've lost part of the past."

"Maybe. Whatever it is, I feel sad."

"I know."

We were silent for a long moment, and then she asked me if I wanted another cup of coffee. I said I thought Monica got the last cup, and anyway I didn't figure I needed any more coffee.

"She died Saturday morning," I said. "The boys flew in Sunday. I don't know where Andy's living now. It was Denver last I heard, but that was a while ago. He doesn't stay anyplace for very long."

"Gathers no moss."

"They flew in yesterday," I said, "and called me tonight." I let that hang in the air, and then I said, "The funeral's tomorrow. Out in Syosset."

"You'll go, won't you?"

"I suppose so. Pick up a car from Avis and drive out. It's at two in the afternoon, so I'll miss the rush hour going out, and probably coming back, too." I looked down at my hands. "I can't say I'm looking forward to it."

"I think you should go, though."

"I don't think I've got much choice."

"Do you want me to come? Because I will if you want, and I won't feel hurt if you don't."

"I think maybe not," I said.

"Or I could keep you company and wait in the car, so you won't be parading Anita's replacement in front of all her friends. Or, as far as that goes, T J would be glad to keep you company."

"He could wear a chauffeur's cap," I said, "and I could ride in the back seat. No, I'll drive myself, I think, and keep myself company. I don't know that I'll mind the solitude. I'll probably have things to think about."

So I sat there in the last row and thought about things, and when the service ended I walked up the aisle and mumbled something to Graham Thiele, something about how sorry I was, and he mumbled something back, assuring me it was good of me to come. We could have phoned it in, both of us. Then I turned to Michael and Andy. They were both wearing suits and ties, of course, and they looked good dressed up like that, my two big handsome sons.

"I'm glad you could come," Michael said. "The service was okay, don't you think?"

"It seemed fine," I said.

"Are you going to ride out to the cemetery? I could see if there's room in the limo with us, or you could just join the parade, except they don't call it that. What's the word?"

"Cortege," Andy supplied.

"And afterward we're all going back to Graham's house. Uh, their house."

"I think I'll pass," I said. "On the house, and on the cemetery. I think I'd be out of place."

"Well, that's up to you," Michael said. "Strictly your call."

Andy said, "Whatever, we've got a job to do." He was pulling on a pair of black silk gloves. "We're pallbearers," he said. "It's hard to take it all in, you know?"

"I know."

"They're going to close the casket. If you want to take a last look at Mom . . ."

I didn't much want to, but then I hadn't really wanted to come out to Syosset, either. There are things you just do, and the hell with what you want or don't want. I went over and looked at her and was immediately sorry I had. She looked dead, waxen, looked as though she had never been alive in the first place.

I turned away and blinked a few times but the image was still there. It would stay with me for a while, I knew, and then it would fade, and eventually I would remember the woman I used to know, the woman I'd married, the woman I'd fallen in love with once upon a time.

I looked for my sons and there they were, both wearing the black pallbearer's gloves now, both with expressions that were hard to read. "Maybe we could meet someplace afterward," I suggested. "It's what, two years since I last saw you, Mike? And I can't remember the last time I saw you, Andy."

"I can," he said, "because it's the last time I was in New York. Four years ago, and I met Elaine for the first time, and the three of us walked to a restaurant and had dinner."

"Paris Green."

"That's the one."

"Well, is there a place here in Syosset where we can meet? A coffee shop or something? After the cemetery, and after you've had a chance to see people back at the house."

They exchanged glances. Michael said, "Once we get back to the house, I think we have to stay there. There's a lot of people who'll be dropping in, and I think we'd be missed if we slipped out."

"Mom had a lot of friends," Andy said.

"Maybe between the cemetery and the house," I said. But they'd be riding in the limo, Michael said, and Andy said the limo'd bring them back here, that was the plan, and they'd get their own cars.

"So June can drive your car back," he said, "and I'll run you and me over to Hershey's."

"God, not the Hershey Bar," Michael said. To me he said, "It's a beer bar, it's all high school and college kids, it's crowded and noisy. You wouldn't like it. As far as that goes, I wouldn't like it."

"You used to," Andy said. "Before you turned into an old man. Anyway, it's an afternoon in the middle of the week. How rowdy do you think it's going to be?"

"Jesus, the Hershey Bar," Michael said.

"Well, pick someplace better, if you can think of one."

"I can't, and they're waiting for us, so I guess it's the Hershey Bar." He gave me quick directions and then the two of them let one of the mortuary staff guide them to their places on opposite sides of the now-sealed casket. Anita's brother, Phil, had the spot behind Andy, and there were three other men whom I didn't recognize.

I left them to their work.

I drove out to the cemetery after all. I hadn't planned on it, but somehow my car wound up queueing along with the others, and I sat there and followed the car in front of me. We had a police escort, so we didn't have to stop for traffic lights, and

I told myself the cops out here had it easy, with nothing to do but take an occasional run out to the cemetery. But I knew better. They have crime on Long Island, and people selling drugs and other people using them, and men who batter their wives and abuse their children, and others who drive drunk and plow head-on into a school bus. They don't have Crips and Bloods and drive-by shootings yet, not that I've heard, but they probably won't have long to wait.

I stayed in my car at the cemetery while everybody else walked over to the graveside for the service. I could see them from where I was parked, and as soon as the service was over I started my engine and found my way out of there.

I hadn't paid close attention to the route to the cemetery—you don't when all you have to do is tag along after the car in front of you—and I took a few wrong turns on the way back, and a few more finding my way to the Hershey Bar. I parked and went in, expecting my sons would already be there, but the place was empty except for the bartender, a blue-jawed skinhead in a Metallica T-shirt, its sleeves rolled up to show health club muscles, and his sole customer, an old man in a cloth cap and a thrift-shop overcoat. The old fellow looked like he belonged on a bar stool at the Blarney Stone or the White Rose, but here he was at a college kids' bar in Syosset, drinking his beer out of a heavy glass mug.

There were college pennants on the rough wooden walls, and beer steins hanging from the exposed beams, and the bar and tabletops held bowls of miniature chocolate bars. Hershey bars, of course, in several varieties, along with foil-wrapped Hershey's Kisses. It was consistent with the name of the joint, to be sure, but why would anyone want to nibble chocolate as an accompaniment to beer? I could think of several bars that used to set out complimentary bowls of peanuts in the shell, and I remembered the chickpeas at Max's Kansas City, but who'd want to pair a Dos Equis or a St. Pauli Girl with a Hershey's Kiss?

The bartender was looking at me, eyebrows raised, and I didn't want a beer or a chocolate bar. I wanted bourbon, better make it a double, straight up, and leave the bottle.

I patted my pockets as if I'd lost something— my wallet, my car keys, my cigarettes. "Be right back," I said, and got out of there and sat in my car. I turned the key so I could play the radio, and I found a station that featured what they called Classic Country, which Elaine would call a contradiction in terms. But they played Hank Williams and Patsy Cline and Red Foley and Kitty Wells, and then Mike and Andy pulled in and got out of a gray Honda Accord. When they reached the entrance Mike said something, and Andy gave him a poke in the shoulder and held the door open, and the two of them disappeared inside.

I waited for the last notes of "It Wasn't God Who Made Honky Tonk Angels." Then I went in after them.

FOUR

Mike ordered a Heineken's and I said I'd have a glass of Coke. The bartender asked if Pepsi would be all right, and I said it would be fine. Neither one was what I wanted, but I wasn't going to have what I wanted, and the fact was I didn't really want it anymore. The urge had been strong enough to get me the hell out of there, but wanting a drink is a world away from having one, and now the wanting had passed. A Coke would have been fine, and a Pepsi would be fine, and so would a glass of water, or nothing at all.

Andy said, "What the hell, we're on Long Island, right? I'll have a Long Island Iced Tea."

They thought that one up after I stopped drinking, so I never learned what's in it, but I gather it contains a mix of liquors, and that tea's nowhere to be found. The name's ironic, and I suppose it's a reference to rum-running during

Prohibition, which would make it doubly ironic, since the kids who get wasted on it can't even remember Vietnam.

The drinks came. Andy sipped his and pronounced it a stupid drink. "Who thought this up?" he wondered. "It's supposed to have a kick like a mule but it doesn't taste like anything at all. I suppose that's the point, especially if you're nineteen years old and looking to get your girlfriend drunk." He took another sip and said, "It grows on you. I was going to say this is my first Long Island Iced Tea and it's going to be my last, but maybe not. Maybe I'll finish it and have six more of them."

"And maybe you won't," his brother said. "Gray needs us back at the house."

"Is that what you call him? Gray?"

"It's what Mom called him," Andy said. "I never had much occasion to call him anything, really. Just if he answered the phone when I called, or the couple of times I visited."

"Which would have been four years ago," I said.

"Plus once since then."

"Oh?"

"I guess it was last Thanksgiving. I never did come into the city, I just visited here for a couple of days and flew straight out again." He looked at his glass. "I called you a few times," he said unconvincingly. "I got the machine every time I called, and I didn't want to leave a message."

I said, "He seems like a nice enough fellow, Gray."

"He's all right," Andy said.

"He was good for Mom," Michael said. "He was there for her, you know?"

Unlike some people. "I never thought I'd see this day," I said, surprising myself with the words, evidently surprising them as well from the looks on their faces. "I always assumed I'd go first," I explained. "I didn't think about it much, but I guess I took it for granted. I was older by three years and change, and men generally die first. And all of a sudden she's gone."

They didn't say anything.

"Everybody says that's the best way," I said. "One minute you're here and the next minute you're gone. No pain to speak of, no long-drawn-out illness, no standing at the brink and staring out at the abyss. But it's not what I would want for myself."

"No?"

I shook my head. "I'd want time to make sure I wasn't leaving a mess. My affairs in order, that sort of thing. And I'd want time for other people to get used to the idea. A sudden death may be easier on the victim, but it's harder on everybody else."

"I don't know about that," Michael said. "June's got an aunt with Alzheimer's, she's been hanging on for years. Be a lot easier on all concerned if she stroked out or had a heart attack."

I said he had a point. Andy said when it was his turn he wanted to be lowered into a vat of lanolin and softened to death. That seemed funny, but not funny enough to laugh at, given the mood at the table.

"Anyway," Michael said, "we had a warning. Mom had a minor heart attack about a little over a year ago."

"I didn't know that."

"I didn't hear about it right away. She and Gray didn't exactly call a press conference. But she had diabetes and high blood pressure, and—"

"I didn't know that, either."

"You didn't? I guess she developed diabetes about ten years ago. I don't know about the blood pressure, how long she had that. I believe you can have it a while without knowing it. The diabetes was mild enough so she didn't need injections, just oral insulin, but I guess it affects the heart, and so does the high blood pressure. She had the one heart attack, and it was just a question of time until she had another one, but I didn't expect it this soon."

"I thought she'd beat it," Andy said. "She seemed fine at Thanksgiving, and she and Gray were full of plans. There was this riverboat cruise through Germany they were going to take."

"It's next month," his brother said. "They were going to leave right after Labor Day."

"Well, I guess that's out," Andy said. "Maybe you can use their tickets, you and Elaine."

There was an awkward silence, and then he said, "Sorry, I don't know why I said that." He picked up his glass and looked at the ceiling light through it. I thought of all the times I'd done that myself, though never with a glass of Long Island Iced Tea. "This stuff ought to come with a warning label. I'm sorry."

"Forget it."

"Anyway, I don't suppose Elaine would want to go to Germany, would she?"

"What do you mean?"

"Well, she's Jewish, isn't she?"

"So?"

"So she might not be that crazy about going to Germany. She might be worried about getting turned into soap."

Michael said, "Andy, why don't you shut up?"

"Hey, it was just a joke, okay?"

"A stupid joke."

"Nobody likes my jokes," Andy said. "Soap, lanolin, I can't win. Nobody likes my jokes today."

"It's not a great day for jokes, bro."

"Just what is it a great day for, bro? Will you tell me that?"

"I guess you guys'll want to get back to the house," I said, not knowing what they wanted to do, not caring much, knowing only that I wanted to get the hell out of there. "Gray can probably use you for the next few hours."

"Gray," Andy said. "You ever meet him?"

"Just now, at the funeral."

"I figured you were old friends, calling him Gray and all."

I turned to Michael. "I think you'd better drive," I said.

"Andy's all right."

"Whatever you say."

"He's upset, that's all."

"Talking about me like I'm not here," Andy said. "Can I ask a question? One fucking question?" He didn't wait for permission. "Where do you get off having the long face, talking about how you thought you'd be the first to go? I mean, where in the hell does that come from? Who appointed you chief mourner, for God's sake?"

I could feel the anger, moving up my spine like an army. I kept a lid on it.

"You didn't give a shit about her while she was alive," he went on. "Did you ever love her?"

"I thought I did."

"But I guess it didn't last."

"No," I said. "The two of us weren't very good at being married."

"She wasn't so bad at it. You were the one who left."

"I'm sure I wasn't the only one who thought of it. It's easier for a man to leave."

"I don't know," he said. "Past few years, I've run into a few women who didn't find it so goddam hard. Pack a bag, walk out the door, easiest thing in the world."

"It's not always as easy as it looks."

"Especially if there's kids involved," he said. "Right?"

"Right."

"I guess we didn't count, me and Mikey."

I didn't have anything to say to that. And the anger I'd felt before was gone now, stuffed wherever that sort of thing gets stuffed. If I felt anything it was an almighty weariness. I wanted this little talk to be over and I knew it was going to go on forever.

"Why'd you come, anyway?"

"Because your brother called me up and told me about it," I said. "Not Saturday, when he found out about it, and not Sunday when you both got here, but late last night." I turned to Michael. "That was considerate," I said. "That way I didn't have a long period of agonizing before the funeral."

"I just—"

"In fact," I said, "with any luck at all I'd have made plans it would have been too late to cancel, and I wouldn't be here at all. Just your luck I'm a guy who hasn't got too much to do these days."

"I was afraid to call," he said.

"What were you afraid of?"

"I don't know. How you'd take it, what you'd say. That you'd come, that you wouldn't come. I don't know."

"I couldn't not come," I said. "I won't pretend I wanted to be here, but there's no way I could have stayed away. I had to be here for you two, even though you might have been happier if I'd stayed in the city. And I had to be here for her." I took a breath. "She was a good woman, your mother. I couldn't have stayed married to anyone, the kind of man I was. She did the best she could. Jesus, I guess we both did the best we could. That's what everybody does, the best they can, and that's all anybody does."

Andy wiped away tears with his sleeve. He said, "Dad, I'm sorry."

"It's all right."

"I'm sorry as hell. I don't know what got into me."

"Six different kinds of booze," Michael said, "all in one drink. What the hell did you expect?"

What did any of us expect?

I'm afraid you won't get to see any of them this time around," I told Elaine. "Mike and June fly home tomorrow morning."

"What did June do, leave Melanie with her parents?"

"They brought her along," I said, "but I didn't get to see her. June thought the funeral would be too much for her, so she stayed at the house. I don't know whether they hired a sitter or some family member stayed with her."

"And you didn't get to see her at all?"

"I could have, if I'd wanted to go to the house, but I decided I'd rather come straight home."

"I don't blame you. What about Andy? He has to go straight home to Denver?"

"Tucson."

"Tucson in the summer? It's like an oven."

"Well, I guess he figures he'll enjoy the winters. If he's still there."

"Your rolling stone."

"Not mine," I said. "Not anymore. They're neither of them mine anymore, honey. I don't know if they ever were."

"You're saying that because of the kind of day you've just had."

"That's only part of it. Oh, I'm still their father, and they're still my sons. Otherwise we wouldn't get on one another's nerves the way we do. We'll get calls and cards at Christmas, and Andy may even keep us up to date on address changes. And they'll call if they happen to be in the city. Maybe not every time they come here, but some of the time. Of course they won't come to the city all that often."

"Baby—"

"And when I drop dead," I said, "they'll fly in for the funeral, and they'll show up wearing suits. They both look good in suits, I have to say that for them. They'll help carry the box, they got in practice for that this afternoon, although they'll have more weight to deal with next time."

"Unless you waste away," she said.

"Aren't you something," I said. "You won't let me get away with a thing, will you?"

"Would you love me more if I did?"

"I don't see how I could. They'll be decent to you, incidentally. They were decent to Gray. That's what they call him, Gray."

"So you said."

"Oh, I mentioned that? Gray. Big, good-looking fellow with one of those open, honest faces. Looked like he might have played football in school. Linebacker, maybe. Put on some weight since then but stayed in pretty good shape."

"You're in pretty good shape yourself."

"For a guy on the verge of wasting away. Right now they resent you some, but right now they resent everybody. When the time comes, they'll stand up."

"That'll be a comfort."

"Incidentally," I said, "just for the record, when the time comes I want a closed casket."

"I'll take care of it," she said. "Unless I go first."

"Don't you dare," I said.

We went to bed around eleven-thirty, and it didn't take long for me to realize I wasn't going to be able to sleep. I tried to slip out of bed without waking her but she sat up and asked me where I was going.

"I'm wired," I said. "I can catch the midnight meeting, most of it, anyway."

"That's probably not a bad idea."

I got dressed. At the doorway I paused and said, "I might be late."

"Say hello to Mick for me."

"I'll do that," I said.

When I first got sober there was a midnight meeting every night at the Moravian church on Lexington Avenue. They lost the meeting place years ago, but AA meetings are like hydra's heads, and two sprang up in its place, one downtown on Houston Street in what used to be a fairly notorious after-hours, and the other, my destination tonight, at Alanon House, an AA clubhouse on West Forty-eighth. Ordinarily I'd have walked, but I was late as it was; a cab pulled up just as I hit the sidewalk, and I held out a hand and flagged it.

They were reading the Preamble when I got there. I took one of the few empty seats and realized this was my second meeting in as many days. I had the thought that I might go every day for a while, and my next thought was that I probably wouldn't go to another meeting for a week. I didn't know what the hell I was going to do, and that, when you came right down to it, was why I was in that room listening to a skinny little girl with sharp features and blotchy skin tell how she'd started raiding her parents' liquor cabinet at eleven, how she was a crack whore at seventeen, and how now, at the ripe old age of twenty-three, she had high hopes, eight months of sobriety, and HIV.

You get a slightly different crowd at the midnight meetings. In the old days at the Moravian church it wasn't all that rare for an active drunk to start throwing chairs until a couple of members teamed up to throw him out. You see a lot of tattoos at the midnight meetings, a lot of leather, a lot of body piercings. On average, the people who show up at that hour are younger and more newly sober, squeezing in one last meeting to keep from picking up a drink. By the time it's over, all the liquor stores will have closed. Of course the bars can stay open until four, and delis sell beer around the clock, but by one in the morning there's a chance you can go to bed sober and actually get to sleep.

Along with the new and the desperate, the late meetings draw the people whom temperament or circumstance has made creatures of the night. And there are those, some long sober, who prefer a meeting with more of an edge to it, one where you might see someone pull a knife, or throw a chair, or have a **petit mal** seizure.

I sat there with all my years, sixty-two of them, eighteen of them sober, feeling different from the younger, newer, wilder people around me.

But not that different.

When the meeting ended I thanked the speaker, helped with the chairs, and went out into the night. The air was thick and heavy as wet wool. I walked through it, west and then north, and wound up at the southeast corner of Fiftieth and Tenth and went into Grogan's Open House.

Mick Ballou owns Grogan's, although his name

can't be found on the lease or the ownership papers. In the same unofficial way he owns some other businesses around town. He used to own a farm in the Catskills, where he fattened a few pigs and kept chickens for eggs, but when the farmhouse burned down he walked away from it. The owner of record died that night, along with his wife and a lot of other people, and I suppose the nominal owner's son wound up with what was left of the farm. Mick, I know, hasn't been back to see. He won't go anywhere near the place.

The farm was never designed to turn a profit, but he probably makes money at Grogan's, and with his other businesses. They could lose money, though, and it wouldn't matter much, as his real money comes from criminal activity of one sort or another. He robs drug dealers, and hijacks legal and illegal shipments, and lends money to people whose arms and legs are their only collateral. I'm an ex-cop, a once-licensed private detective, and this career criminal is my closest friend, and I have long since given up trying to explain it.

Past lives, Elaine says. We were brothers once. And that's a better explanation than any I can offer.

The bartender gave me a nod. I knew his name was Leeky, but I didn't know how he spelled it, two e's or e-a, for the vegetable or a plumbing problem or some Gaelic word unknown to me. He was fairly new, one of those close-mouthed lads who turn up at Grogan's fresh off the plane from Belfast. Ireland has more people entering than leaving these days, the result of the economic turnaround they like to call the Celtic Tiger. But Mick's visitors don't get to ride the tiger. They've got jail sentences hanging over them, or men looking to kill them, so they get the hell out and wind up dodging the INS, living in the Bronx or Woodside, and working, behind the stick or on the street, for Mick Ballou.

Who was at his usual table with a pitcher of water and a bottle of the twelve-year-old Jameson he favors. His face lit up at the sight of me, which put him very much in the minority that day. I stopped at the bar for a cup of coffee, then went over to where he was sitting and took the chair opposite his.

"A fine night," he said, "and thank God for air conditioning. Have you been out? But of course you have or you wouldn't be here. Is it any better?"

"It's cooled off some," I said, "but the air's pretty bad."

"You don't know whether to breathe it or eat it with a spoon. But you've things on your mind heavier than the air."

"You never met my first wife, did you?"

"I never knew you then."

"I buried her this afternoon," I said, but that sounded wrong. It never sounds entirely right, unless the speaker wielded the shovel himself, but in this case it struck me as particularly inappropriate. "Other people buried her," I said. "I sat in my car and watched them do it."

"Ah, Jaysus," he said, and took a drink, and I sipped my coffee, and we talked.

We talked for a couple of hours, and I don't remember what we said, but it was easy conversation, with long speeches and long silences. I know we talked about the Hollanders, and of the two men who'd murdered them, and who'd outlived them by mere days.

"Good job they're dead," he said of the killers.

Sometimes we make a full night of it, staying on after closing hour, with all the lights out but the one shaded bulb over our table. Sometimes we're still at it when the sun comes up, and Mick puts on the butcher's apron that's all he has left of his father, and we go down to Fourteenth Street for the butchers' mass at St. Bernard's. Sometimes we have breakfast afterward in a diner on West Street, or at Florent on Gansevoort.

But this time either we didn't need to do all that or we lacked the energy for it. The last customer staggered out around three-thirty, and Leeky locked the door and shut down the bar. He was half through with putting the chairs up on the tables, prepping for the man who would sweep it out first thing in the morning, when I got him to let me out.

I walked home. The air seemed clearer now, but that may have been my imagination.

FIVE

Late Saturday morning I was drinking a second cup of coffee and looking at the TV listings, planning my day, trying to decide between the third round of a golf tournament on ESPN or the Mets game on Fox. The evening was set, there was a welterweight bout scheduled on HBO, but I still had the afternoon to take care of.

The phone rang, and it was T J. "Time you get off the phone and out the door," he said. "I be at the Morning Star, waiting to have breakfast with you."

"I already had breakfast," I said.

"That case, come sit across the table an' keep me company. It be good for your heart."

"How's that?"

"Elaine always says it does her heart good to watch me eat. Don't figure it can hurt you none."

"You're probably right," I said, and poured the

rest of my coffee in the sink. Ten minutes later I was across the street at the Morning Star with a fresh cup of coffee that wasn't half as good as the one I'd discarded. Although I'd talked to him a couple of times on the phone, it had been a week since I'd seen T J, and I hadn't realized how much I missed him.

"Sorry 'bout your wife," he said. "Ex-wife, I mean."

"Elaine told you?"

He nodded. "Said you went out to the funeral. I ain't been to many."

"The longer you live," I said, "the more you get to go to."

"Something to look forward to," he said. He had a plate of eggs and sausages and home fries in front of him, and he ate as he talked. I don't know that it did my heart good to watch him, but I can't say it did it any harm.

He put down his fork, took a long drink of orange juice, and wiped his mouth with his napkin. "Girl I'd like you to meet," he said. "Real nice, real pretty, real smart."

"She sounds terrific," I said, "but what would Elaine say?"

He rolled his eyes. "Might be a little young for you," he said. "Goes to Columbia."

"That's where you know her from."

"Uh-huh. Been going to this history class she's taking, but that's not her major. She be majoring in English."

"That case, she probably be speaking well."

"Wants to be a writer," he said. "Like her aunt."

"Who was her aunt, Virginia Woolf?"

He shook his head. "One more guess," he said, "and don't be wasting it on Jane Austen."

Something clicked. I looked at him and he looked back and I said, "Susan Hollander."

"Figured one more guess was all you'd need."

"Susan Hollander was her aunt? What's the girl's name?"

"Lia Parkman. Her mama and Susan Hollander was sisters. That makes Susan her aunt, and Kristin her cousin."

"And you'd like me to meet her."

"Be good if you did."

"Why?"

"She thinks somebody murdered her aunt and uncle."

"Well, I wouldn't be surprised if she's right," I said, "seeing that everybody else on the planet shares her opinion. A pair of punks named Bierman and Ivanov murdered the Hollanders, and—"

"Ivanko, Carl Ivanko."

"What did I say?"

"Said Ivanov."

"Close enough," I said, "since it's a name we can all forget, and the sooner the better. He's dead, along with his partner, so it's too late for him to hire Johnnie Cochran and wriggle off the hook. It's not emotionally satisfying this way, with the bad

guys dead and gone before anybody can catch up
with them, but at least it's wrapped up, over and
done with." My coffee cup was empty, and I
looked around for the waiter. "If your friend Lisa
thinks those two clowns didn't do it—"

"Lia."

"How's that?"

"Name's Lia," he said. "Spelled like Lisa, but
without the S."

"That would do it."

"Well, it coulda been L-E-A-H, but there's
some pronounce that Lay-a."

I still couldn't find the waiter, and decided the
coffee wasn't good enough to have more even if I
could. "The evidence is pretty strong," I said. "No
matter how bright your friend is, I'd say the cops
got it right this time. Bierman and Ivanov killed
her aunt and uncle."

"Sounds like."

"Ivanko, I mean. I said it wrong again, but I
meant Ivanko."

"I know."

"You heard me say it wrong again, but this time
you decided not to correct me."

"You never know," he said. "Detecting don't
work out, I might want to go in the diplomatic
service."

"So you're practicing. Probably not a bad idea.
A little diplomacy never hurts. If she's as smart as
you say, she knows they did it, Bierman and his
friend."

"She knows."

"Though maybe it's a stretch calling him Bierman's friend, since Bierman wound up punching his ticket. She thinks somebody else was involved."

"Uh-huh."

"Fingered the burglary for Bierman and his friend, set it up to come out the way it did, with both the Hollanders dead. And then took out the two of them and set it up to look like thieves falling out, like murder and suicide."

"She didn't take it that far." He polished off his orange juice, wiped his mouth. He turned his head, and the waiter hurried over with the check, as if he'd been hovering offstage waiting for just that cue. T J left it where the waiter set it down and said, "Lia didn't get into the how. Just the who and the why."

"And what would they be?"

"Be best if she told you herself."

"It's a police case," I said, "and it's closed. I don't see how it's anything for us to mess with."

"Probably isn't."

"But what can it hurt to talk to the girl? Is that what you were going to say?"

"Figured it went without saying."

"It'll be a waste of time. How much do you like this girl?"

"It ain't a romance, if that's what you mean."

"There's no case to take, but if there were, could she afford to hire us? Has she got any money?"

"Don't guess she's swimming in it. Girl's maxed out on student loans."

"This sounds better and better," I said. "A girl with no money wants to hire us to beat a dead horse. She goes to Columbia, that means she's on the Upper West Side. Or does she live with her parents?"

"Be a tough commute. Her mom's in Arizona and her daddy's in Florida."

"And she didn't go home for the summer."

"Stayed for summer session. She's just taking this one course, 'The French Revolution and Napoleon.' "

"And that's where you know her from."

"It's pretty interesting stuff. Those dudes had something, but it got away from 'em. Lia's taking the one course and waiting tables at this fake Irish pub. You know it ain't a real Irish pub 'cause they got food." He took a breath. "She's off today. She's living in student housing, got three room-mates. I thought we'd meet her in a coffee shop up on Broadway and a Hundred Twenty-second."

"Today?"

He nodded. "One o'clock's what I told her. We leave now, we be right on time."

"And if I said no?"

"Then I show up alone," he said, "and say how you was tied up lookin' for Judge Crater and the Lindbergh baby."

"But you figured I'd come."

"Thought you might."

"I was going to watch TV," I said. "There's golf and there's a Mets game."

"Tough call, which to watch."

"Either one's better than wasting time in a coffee shop on Upper Broadway." The check was still on the table, and I sighed and reached for it. "I'll get this," I said.

"Figured you would," he said. "Seein' we on a case, you can expense it."

TJ's a street kid I ran into on Forty-second Street some years back, before they went and turned the Deuce into Disney World North. He appointed himself my assistant, and I liked his company enough to put up with him. Then I found out how useful he could be. He's a natural mimic, moving effortlessly from hip-hop jive to the Queen's English, turned out one day in baggy shorts and a Raiders cap and the next in a Brooks Brothers suit.

For a while we didn't know where he lived, and I suspect his beeper number was as close as he came to a permanent address. Then one Christmas I gave him the hotel room I'd occupied ever since I moved out of the house in Syosset. I was married to Elaine by then, and living at the Parc Vendome, but I'd held on to my old room across the street at the Northwestern as a combination office and bolthole, and because it was rent-controlled, and nobody in New York gives up a rent-controlled space except at gunpoint. I figured it could go on being

my office, but he could live there and run it for me.
The other half of his Christmas present was a
computer, and he ran that for me, too, pulling information off the Internet as if out of the ether.
By now Elaine had a computer of her own, and she
and T J e-mailed each other across the street, like
two kids with a pair of tin cans and a piece of
string. She told me she could teach me how to use
the thing in about fifteen minutes. One of these
days, I said.

I find things for T J to do, legwork and desk
work, and try to keep him out of harm's way.
That's usually not hard—my work's not terribly
dangerous—but he took a bullet once, and it didn't
seem to dull his enthusiasm. He helps Elaine at her
shop, where his manner, superior yet deferential,
would make you think he trained at Sotheby's.
And lately he's been spending a lot of time at Columbia, where he dresses in khakis and polo shirts
and just walks into any class that looks as though it
might be interesting. You can't do that, not without registering and paying an auditor's fee, but it's
a rare professor who's got a clue as to who does or
doesn't belong in his classroom, and the few who
do catch on are tickled at the thought that someone
wants to hear what they have to say even if he's not
getting academic credit for it.

Elaine, on learning how he was spending his
free time, had offered to pay his way through
school. The idea horrified him. Twenty-five, thirty
thousand a year so he could sit in the same class-

rooms and listen to the same lectures? And all so he could parrot it all back to them and wind up with a diploma? Where was the sense in that?

On the way to the subway, I said, "Ivanko or Ivanov, it's really the same name. One's Russian and the other's Ukrainian, but they're both just fancy ways of saying Johnson."

"Why I like this job," he said, "is I be learning something every day."

"Uh-huh. It's Kristin, right?"

"Say what?"

"That she figures set the whole thing up. The daughter, her cousin. Kristin. That's who she's looking at, isn't it?"

"Well," he said, "it ain't Jane Austen."

SIX

Years ago, in the late Fifties and early Sixties, there were two artists, husband and wife, whose popular success was exceptional, if brief. Their name, if I remember correctly, was Kean. He painted waiflike children with enormous eyes, and she painted waiflike pubescent girls, similarly big-eyed. It seemed to me that her paintings had an erotic element lacking in his, but my judgment may be subjective, and a pedophile might have seen it the other way around.

The Keans had a few spectacular years, with young couples all over the country buying reproductions of their paintings and hanging them in the living rooms and finished basements of their suburban starter homes. Then something happened—Woodstock, maybe, or Altamont, or the Vietnam War—and all the folks who'd been buying the Keans' work and marveling at the way the eyes followed you all around the room suddenly decided the stuff was pure crap, trite and saccharine and mawkishly sentimental.

Down came the Keans, banished to attic crawl spaces, eventually donated to church rummage drives or trotted out for garage sales. The artists disappeared from view. Elaine's guess was that they'd changed their names and started painting sad clowns.

Over the past few years, she'd snapped up every thrift-shop Kean she saw, and we now owned forty or fifty of them, all tucked away in her locker at Manhattan Mini Storage. They'd cost her from five to ten dollars apiece, and she was sure she'd get ten or twenty times that when the time was right.

"Two years into the next Republican administration," she said, "and I'll sell out overnight."

Maybe, maybe not. The point is that Lia Parkman could have modeled for Kean—the wife, the one who painted teenagers. She had the long Modigliani neck, the slim hips, the attenuated fingers, the straight ash-blond hair, the translucent skin, and, inevitably, the enormous eyes. And she had that waif quality, the aching vulnerability that had sold the paintings in the first place and then turned them so cloying in a few years' time.

She was waiting for us in a corner booth at the Salonika, a Greek coffee shop not unlike the one we'd just left. She had a cup of tea in front of her, the tea bag pressed dry in the saucer, a wedge of lemon floating in the cup. There was a book on the table next to her teacup, library-bound, with its title and author and Dewey decimal number stamped on the spine. **The Reign of Terror**, by Bell. A pair of eyeglasses with perfectly round lenses rested on top of the book.

T J introduced us and slid into the booth opposite her. I sat down next to him. She said, "I tried to call you."

He took his cell phone from his pocket, looked at it, put it back. "Didn't ring," he said.

"I said that wrong," she said. "I didn't actually try to call, because I didn't have your number with me. But I wanted to call."

"Whatever you wanted to say," he pointed out, "you can just tell me, 'cause here I am."

"Well, that's it," she said. "What I wanted was to save you the trip. I made a mistake, T J."

"And now you wish you never said what you did."

She nodded. "I think it was the shock," she said. "And maybe this"—she tapped the book—"had something to do with it. Robespierre, Danton, the Committee of Public Safety. Everybody going crazy and acting out."

"Marat takes a bath," T J said, "and she goes and stabs him."

"Charlotte Corday. Anyway, I was horrified by what happened to Aunt Susan and Uncle Byrne, and I guess I couldn't accept the obvious explanation, that burglars chose their house at random and killed them because they picked the wrong time to come home." Her eyes found mine. "It just seems so arbitrary, Mr. Scudder. You don't want to believe things happen like that, just out of the blue, for no reason at all. But I guess they do, don't they?"

"You were overwrought," I said.

"That's right."

"And shocked, and deeply saddened. So it's not surprising your mind produced an alternate scenario, one in which things happened for a reason."

She was nodding, grateful to me for helping her out.

"Tell me about it," I said.

"I beg your pardon?"

"Your scenario. Let's hear it."

"But it's ridiculous," she said. She might have said more, but the waitress was hovering. By now I was hungry enough to order a cheeseburger and a cup of coffee. T J said he'd have the same but make it a bacon cheeseburger with a side of fries, and make them all well-done, the burger and the fries both, and instead of the coffee a glass of milk'd be good, or did they happen to have buttermilk? They did, and he said that's what he'd have.

He never gains an ounce, either.

Lia started to say she was fine with the tea, then changed her mind and ordered the spinach pie, the appetizer, though, not the full dinner. The waitress left and she picked up her teacup and looked at it and put it down again.

"It's ridiculous," I prompted.

"Oh. Well, it really is. I don't think I should even say it out loud."

"Because it's not fair even to think such things, and saying them is worse."

"That's right."

"On the other hand," I said, "we came all the way uptown, and there's food coming, so we'll be here awhile. And we might as well talk about something."

"I wanted to call you—"

"But you didn't," T J said, "and even if you did, we probably would have come anyway."

This surprised her. "Why?"

"To make sure it was what you really wanted," I said, "and that nobody was holding a gun to your head."

"You think—"

"I don't think anything. I'd have come uptown to get some idea what to think. That's generally worth an hour and a couple of subway tokens. But it's beside the point, because you weren't able to call us and here we are, and we might as well cut to the chase. You think your cousin set up your aunt and uncle."

"But I don't think that. I told you—"

"I know. You don't think it, but you did, even if you'd like to pretend you didn't. It's just a thought, Lia. Best thing you can do with it is bring it out into the open."

"Otherwise it'll go bad," T J said.

She took a breath and nodded and picked up her

teacup, and this time she drank from it before setting it back in its saucer. "She inherits everything," she said.

"Kristin."

She nodded. "That was the first thing I thought of. Not 'Poor Kristin, she's an orphan, she's alone in the world.' The first thing I thought was she's a rich girl now."

"How rich?"

"I don't know. But even if all there is is the house, it's worth a fortune. A brownstone in the Seventies? There was one somebody was talking about the other day, West Eighty-fourth Street I think it was, and they were asking two-point-six. I don't know, maybe that's not a fortune anymore, maybe it's pocket change if you're one of the dot-com people, but it still seems like a lot of money to me."

"Could be mortgaged," I said.

"Uncle Byrne said it was free and clear. He was proud of that, how they'd paid the house off years ago, and now it was worth so much money. He said how much better an investment it turned out to be than any of his stocks, so that means there must be stocks, too, don't you think?"

"But not very good ones."

"Still, they'd have to be worth something, wouldn't they?"

"Sure."

"And I'm sure there was insurance. And there

were the things they owned, Aunt Susan's jewelry, the silverware, the paintings. They took the jewelry and silver, but it was recovered, wasn't it?"

"I believe so."

"And what wasn't would be covered by insurance. Oh, God, what's the matter with me, sitting here adding up their assets in my head like, I don't know, a vulture or something. I mean, they're **dead**. What difference does the money make? It's not as if they got to keep it. They were **murdered, they're dead**."

There was a silence, and it lasted awhile because the waitress turned up with the food. T J picked up a french fry and made a face at it, indicating it wasn't as well-done as he'd hoped, but he didn't send anything back, or leave anything on his plate, so I guess it wasn't too bad. My cheeseburger tasted fine, and the coffee was better than the Morning Star's.

Lia took one bite of her square of spinach pie and put her fork down. "I envied her," she said abruptly. "Kristin. That's what it was. I envied her when they were alive, having two wonderful parents who loved her and loved each other. My parents—no, forget it, I don't want to go there."

"All right."

"Uncle Byrne and Aunt Susan kept inviting me over for dinner. I begged off about half the time because I didn't want to take advantage. And I couldn't help feeling like a poor relation, which I was right to feel, really, because that's what I was. I'm on scholarship, otherwise I couldn't afford Columbia in a million years, and even with a scholarship it's not easy."

Her hands were busy as she talked, gesturing, touching her hair, brushing away imaginary crumbs. When her nails caught the light I saw she was wearing colorless nail polish on them. I decided she was painstaking enough to protect her nails but disinclined to embellish them. She wasn't wearing lipstick, and I wondered if she'd used colorless lip gloss. Was there a pattern here, and what could I make of it?

"You envied Kristin," I prompted.

"When they were alive. And when I heard what happened, after the initial shock wore off, or maybe it hadn't worn off, not really—" She paused for breath, looked away, then met my eyes. "I thought, well, now she's rich. And I envied her all over again."

"And you figure that makes you a horrible person."

"I don't think it makes me a candidate for sainthood. Do you?"

"I haven't met a lot of saints," I said, "but then I've lived a sheltered life. I don't think less of you for envying your cousin, before or after the murder, and I certainly don't think less of you for owning up to it. But what I think of you isn't very important, either. How do you feel?"

"How do I feel?"

"Right now."

She frowned, thinking about it. "I feel okay," she said, surprised.

"Good. How'd you get from envy to suspicion?"

"From envy to—oh, right. Suspicion's an overstatement, really. I wouldn't call it suspicion."

"We'll find something else to call it. How'd you get there?"

"The burglar alarm," she said.

"They had a burglar alarm?"

"And it didn't go off."

"Maybe they forgot to set it."

"That's what it said in the papers, that they owned a burglar alarm but neglected to set it that night. But they always set it. They had a break-in the first year they owned the house, someone came in through a window and took some cash and a portable TV, and after that they got the alarm system. It was connected to the front door and to all the windows on the first floor, and the store downstairs from them had its own alarm system, and that was set, too."

"Maybe they just set it most of the time."

She was shaking her head. "Both of them, Aunt Susan and Uncle Byrne, they would set it before they went down to the corner to mail a letter. It was automatic. On their way out they would key in the number to set it, and the minute they walked in the door they keyed it in again to turn it off.

They'd been doing it for twenty years. They wouldn't suddenly quit and get robbed the same night."

"If the keypad was by the front door—"

"It wasn't. It was inside the coat closet."

"That's better," I said, "but it's still the first place a burglar would look."

"Why would he look anywhere?" T J wondered, and answered his own question. "The metal tape on the windows. Tip 'em off in a heartbeat."

"Tape on a window doesn't mean there's an alarm system, or that it's set," I said. "But if I was breaking into a house it would be enough to make me take a quick look around. I might do that even if I didn't see tape on the windows. Especially if I spent a little time checking the place out first, in which case I might have known about the alarm system before I got anywhere near the front door."

Lia said, "But they'd need more than that, wouldn't they? There's a four-digit number you have to enter in order to deactivate the alarm."

"There are other ways," I said, "if you happen to know them. You can rewire the system and bypass the alarm. But that would show up later on. What was the number, do you happen to know?"

"Ten-seventeen," she said. "One-oh-one-seven. It was their wedding anniversary, they got married on the seventeenth of October. I forget the year."

"Well, you wouldn't need to know the year to deactivate the alarm."

"No," she said, and her eyes widened. "You don't think . . ."

"That you were the set-up person? Why, were you?"

"Of course not!"

"Good, we can cross you off the list. And you can relax, because you were never on it. How'd you happen to know the number?"

"Aunt Susan told me."

"So you would feel like a real member of the family?"

Her eyes welled up, making her look that much more waiflike. "We went shopping," she said, "and she had her arms full of packages when we came home. She had me get the key from her purse and unlock the door, and then she told me to key in the number so we wouldn't have sirens going off."

"You knew where the keypad was."

"Of course. I'd seen them use it to activate the system, and to deactivate it."

"And she told you the number?"

"I couldn't just press buttons at random, could I? She told me the number, and later on she explained the significance, that it was their anniversary."

"And that helped you remember it."

"Actually, it was the other way around. I'd never known the date of their anniversary, but the number stuck in my mind, and that's how come I know when their anniversary was."

"She didn't mind letting you know the number."

"Well, I don't think she thought I was likely to rob the place."

"No, of course not. But they had that alarm system for how long, twenty years? Something like that? And the odds are they picked that number early on, and never changed it. As a matter of fact, it's probably not the only thing they used it for. I wouldn't be surprised if it turns out to be the PIN number for their bank accounts and credit cards. People aren't supposed to do it that way, it's a bad idea from a security standpoint, but life's a lot easier when you've only got one number to remember."

"I use . . . well, the same number for everything."

"And it's probably either your birthday or the last four digits of your Social Security number."

It was one or the other, from her reaction, but at least she didn't tell me which one. "It's my AOL password, too. I guess I'd better change it."

"As far as your aunt and uncle's alarm system was concerned," I said, "anybody could have let that slip. A burglar is as good as his research, and the smart ones learn to use people who don't even know they're being used. Repairmen, delivery boys. Maybe they had someone doing work in their house, building bookshelves or rewiring the top floor, and he needed to be able to get in and out in their absence. They knew they could trust him."

"And he never told anybody," T J said, picking it up smoothly. "Only he mentioned to his wife that these people were so sentimental they used their wedding anniversary to get in and out of their house. And she told her son, so he'd know that it wouldn't be a good idea to forget his parents' wedding anniversary, and then the kid got into drugs and wound up on Rikers Island, and somebody brought up the subject of burglar alarms, and he knew these people who used their wedding anniversary as a password. If the right person heard it, all he'd need to do was find out when those people got married, and how hard would it be to get that information?"

"Or Kristin could have let it slip," I said. " 'My parents are so sentimental . . . ' and if the right person's listening . . ."

She nodded, taking it all in, then frowned. "They got in the front door," she said. "They must have had a key."

"Do we know they used the front door?"

"They would have had to, wouldn't they, to turn off the alarm in time?"

"They'd have forty-five seconds or a minute, depending on the system. That's enough time if you know what you're looking for. But you're probably right, they probably went in the front door. That doesn't mean they had a key."

"Wouldn't it show if they broke in? And wouldn't my aunt and uncle have seen the door was forced, and not gone in?"

"Same answer to both questions," I said. "Maybe and maybe not. A skilled burglar can pick a standard pin-and-tumbler lock without leaving obvious signs. It takes a few minutes, it's not as easy as they make it look in the movies, but you don't have to be Houdini. If you're not up to picking a lock, there are any number of ways to force a door without leaving it in splinters. Would there be any signs of forced entry? Probably, but you might need good light and a magnifying glass to spot them. Returning to your own house after a brief absence, with no reason to think anyone might have paid you a visit, you might not look too closely."

We went over it some more, and she kept nodding and fussing with her hair and emitting soundless whistles. "I was just making something out of nothing," she said. "I should have called you and told you not to come. I dragged you up here for nothing."

T J pointed out that it wasn't as though we'd flown in from London. "Rode up on the One train," he said. "Not a big deal."

And I told her it wasn't for nothing. "You had suspicions, and they weren't entirely groundless. There were questions in your mind that you couldn't put answers to. How do you feel now?"

"A little foolish, I guess."

"Besides that."

She thought about it, then nodded slowly. "Better," she said. "Kristin's all I've got left of my aunt and uncle, and at the funeral I couldn't look at her without thinking, well, uncomfortable thoughts. I just hope she didn't get any sense of what was going through my mind."

"She probably had other things to think about."

"Yes, of course."

We talked some more, and she and T J said something about someone with a French name, probably from the course they were taking. Then she reached for the check, but I already had it. She protested that the least she could do was pay for our meal. Or, failing that, for her own.

"Next time," I said.

We were at 122nd and Broadway, and the IRT stops at 116th, then comes up from underground and stops again at 125th. We were three blocks closer to the elevated platform at 125th Street, but it goes against the grain to walk opposite from the direction you're headed. I don't know why it should, you wind up catching the same train either way, and if it had been pouring I suppose we'd have worked it out logically and walked uptown to catch our downtown train. But it was a nice enough day, cooler and drier than it had been, and we felt like walking. At 116th Street we looked at each other, shrugged, and kept going.

Someone made a TV documentary a few years ago about a walk the whole length of Broadway, from the foot of Manhattan to the island's northern tip. Or maybe they didn't stop there, because Broadway doesn't. There's a bridge over the

Harlem River and the street keeps going on the northern side, through Marble Hill (which is technically part of Manhattan, although there are people living there who think they're in the Bronx). If the TV people went that far, they probably pushed on through Kingsbridge and Riverdale to the Westchester County line, but if they'd wanted to they could have stayed on Broadway clear to Albany.

It's a great street, following an old road and thus cutting across the rectilinear grid of Manhattan. It had been a long time since I'd walked this stretch of it, and I was enjoying it.

Aside from reaching for the check at coffee shops, walking's about the only exercise I get. Elaine goes to the gym three mornings a week and takes a yoga class a couple of times a month, and every other New Year's I resolve to do something similar, and invariably give it up, whatever it is, before January's out. But they say walking's the best exercise of all, and I hope they're right, because it's all I've got.

Uptown-downtown blocks run twenty to a mile, so we'd covered something like a mile and a quarter when we got to Ninety-sixth Street. "Case you getting sick of this," T J said, "this here's an express stop."

"We need a local anyway," I said.

"How you figure?"

"Columbus Circle's not an express stop," I said. "On the D or the A, yes, but not on the IRT."

"Seventy-second's an express stop," he said.

"Seventy-second?"

"Ain't that where we goin'?"

"Seventy-fourth, you're thinking about."

"So?"

"No real point in going there."

"So you want to catch the local and go on home?"

We had walked a block past Ninety-fifth while we were having this conversation. No harm, there's another entrance at Ninety-fourth, and it saves you an extra two flights of stairs, one down and one up.

I said, "Ninety-fourth to Seventy-fourth, that's what, twenty blocks?"

"I could work that out, but I do believe I left my calculator in my other pants."

"We walked this far," I said. "We could walk the rest of the way, if you're up to it."

"If I up to it," he said, and rolled his eyes.

SEVEN

Cost aside, Elaine and I never even considered buying a house. We both preferred apartment living, with a doorman to receive packages and screen visitors, and porters and handymen on staff to fix plumbing leaks and replace blown fuses, to put out the trash and clear the walk of snow. When you owned a house you didn't have to do all that yourself, you could hire people to do it for you, but it was still your responsibility to see that it got done. In our well-run building, everything was magically taken care of. We never had to give it a thought.

You get more room in a house, but we had all the room we needed, and more than we were used to. From the time I'd left the house in Syosset, I'd been perfectly content in a little coat closet of a hotel room, and Elaine had lived and worked in a one-bedroom apartment on East Fiftieth Street a block from the river. To us, our big two-bedroom felt as spacious as Utah.

Still, standing across the street from the Hollander brownstone, I could understand the satisfaction of living in it. It was a fine architectural specimen, of a piece with the houses on either side. The location was hard to beat, with the park a block and a half away and a choice of two subway stops almost as close. You couldn't see it from the street, but there was sure to be a garden in back. You could keep a grill there and barbecue, or just sit outside on a nice day with a book and a pitcher of iced tea.

It had been twelve days since the murder, and just a week since they'd found the two dead men on Coney Island Avenue. The case had finally disappeared from the papers, if not from the collective consciousness of the neighborhood. I couldn't see any yellow Crime Scene tape on the front entrance, or any official seal on the door.

I crossed the street and mounted the steps for a better look. T J, tagging along, asked what we were doing.

"Snooping," I said.

The drapes were drawn, and the front door was windowless except for a frosted fanlight above the lintel. I put my ear to the door, and T J asked me if I could hear the ocean. I couldn't, or anything else. I stepped back and gave the doorbell a poke. I hadn't expected a response, and didn't get one.

"Nobody home," T J said.

I looked at the lock. I could have used more light, but if there was evidence of tampering I couldn't see it. No gouging around the jamb, no fresh scratches on the face of the cylinder. Of course the cylinder itself might have been replaced since the incident. If you were going to occupy the premises, or even if you weren't, changing the locks would be the first order of business.

The ground-floor antique shop was closed, the gates drawn and locked. A card in the door announced the shop's hours, Monday to Friday, noon to six, or by appointment. A decal warned that the premises were protected by an alarm system, and threatened an armed response.

"If we was burglars," T J said, "that'd have us shaking in our boots. 'Armed response.' Not just cops, but cops with guns."

"It's a comforting thought for a lot of people."

"A cop with a gun?" He shook his head. "They best hope they never meet one. You want to break in upstairs? Keypad's in the coat closet, and the password's ten-seventeen."

"Maybe another time."

"You just scared of that armed response."

"That's it."

"If we going to Brooklyn, tell you right now I ain't walking."

"Why would we go to Brooklyn?"

"Coney Island Avenue," he said. "See where the cops kicked the door in."

"I don't think so," I said. "I want to go home. We can take the subway."

"We this close," he said, "we might as well walk."

Elaine fixed a light supper, pasta and a green salad, and I watched the fight on HBO. Afterward I took a hot bath before I went to bed, but I was still a little stiff and sore the next day from all that walking. We left the house around two and walked up to Lincoln Center, where we had tickets for an afternoon concert of chamber music at Alice Tully Hall. There was a string quartet, with a clarinetist joining them for one selection.

They played Mozart and Haydn and Schubert, and it certainly didn't sound like jazz, but there's something about chamber music, and especially string quartets, that puts me in mind of a jazz combo. The intimacy of it, I suppose, and the way the instruments feed off one another. And it feels improvisational, even when you know they're playing notes written down a couple of centuries ago.

We stopped for Thai food after and got home in time for her to watch **Masterpiece Theatre.** It was Part Three, and she'd missed Parts One and Two, but it didn't matter; she'll watch anything on television where the performers have English accents. I was in the kitchen, fixing her a cup of tea, when the doorman rang up on the intercom to announce a Mr. T. J. Santamaria.

I brought her the tea and told her we had a guest coming up. She said, "Santamaria? Eddie was on the door when we came in. I guess Raul must have relieved him at eight."

We've never managed to learn what T J's last name is (or his first name, come to think of it), but it's a safe bet it's not Santamaria. Somewhere along the way one of the guys working the door insisted on a last name before he would call up and announce him, so he became T. J. Smith. He used that name some of the time, switching now and then to Jones or Brown, or Mr. Smith's partner, T. J. Wesson. ("He sort of an oily dude," he explained.) If the doorman du jour had a discernible ethnic identity, he'd pick a handle to fit, and on occasion he'd been announced as T. J. O'Hanrahan, T. J. Goldberg ("Whoopi's kid brother"), and, as now, T. J. Santamaria. For a few months we'd had a guy from St. Kitts with perfect posture and a piss-elegant manner, and T J'd delighted in making the poor bastard announce him as T. J. Spade.

He came in carrying a file folder with a stack of paper half an inch thick. "Printed out everything that made the papers," he said, "plus some wild-ass shit off an Internet site. Funny how the **Times** missed out on the connection between the Hollanders and the death of Sharon Tate."

"That sounds reasonable," I said. "Charles Manson had as much to do with the death of the Hollanders as their daughter Kristin did, which is as much as anybody did outside of those two losers out in Brooklyn." He held out the folder and I took it, saying, "What's the point? There's nothing here for us. We spent an hour or so yesterday taking a load off your girlfriend's mind."

"Not my girlfriend."

"Just a friend. I stand corrected." I hefted the file folder. "Why do I need to look at all this?"

"Why did we need to look at the house where it all went down?"

"Curiosity," I said.

"Killed the cat," he said. He pointed at the folder. "Kill a few more," he said, and headed for the elevator.

Monday morning I called Joe Durkin and asked him if he'd like to do me a favor. "It's the real reason I come to work every morning," he said. "What I do for the city is beside the point."

I told him what I wanted.

He said, "Why, for God's sake? What are you, turning into a writer? You plan on writing it up for one of the **True Detective** magazines?"

"I hadn't thought of that, but it would be a good cover sometime."

"Guys would expect to see clips. Seriously, Matt, what's your interest? And don't tell me you've got a client."

"How could I? They lifted my license."

"Way I heard it, you surrendered it voluntarily. And what difference would that make? You worked years without one."

"That was my point, as I recall."

"One of them," he said, and something hung for a moment in the air between us. He asked who hired me and I said I honestly didn't have a client. He said, "The daughter? How much closure does she need, for Christ's sake? The bastards who did it are dead. What's she need with you nosing around?"

"I haven't even met the daughter," I said, "and I don't have a client. My interest is personal."

"You're a public-spirited citizen and you want to see justice done."

"I gather it's already been done," I said. "Did I mention that Elaine and I were at dinner with the Hollanders the night they were killed?"

"It seems to me you did. You were at separate tables together, the way I remember it. You know, there was an elderly gentleman beaten to death on the G train just last month, and G's my father's middle initial, but I never felt the need to get together with the guy who headed up the investigation. Of course it might have been different if I had a client."

"If I had a client, any kind of a client," I said, "I'd have work to do, and I'd be too busy to waste my time bothering with a case that's already been closed."

"That's reason enough to wish you had your license back," he said. "You're serious, aren't you? Lemme make a phone call, see what I can do."

He got back to me twenty minutes later with a name and a number. "I don't know this guy," he said, "but the word is he's straight-up and thorough, though not necessarily the very man you'd want Regis to call for you if you couldn't remember the capital of Ethiopia."

"I hope you were as complimentary when you told him about me."

"I said you probably wouldn't steal a hot stove, and the morals charge was dismissed when the boy's mother withdrew the complaint. I know, you don't know how to thank me, but don't worry. You'll think of something."

The fellow who'd stayed at the curb to make sure Kristin Hollander got into her house okay had a cell phone, and he'd used it to call 911. A car from the Twentieth Precinct responded, and the uniforms reported back on what they found, and within the hour two detectives from the precinct were on the scene. It was their case, but the next day someone in charge saw what a media circus it was going to be and shuffled the cards, and a special unit was set up with a detective from Manhattan North Homicide in charge of it.

"You never like to have a case taken away from you," Dan Schering said. "Ego aside, though, we were better off, because you can't put as much into an investigation if you have to stop once an hour to hold a press conference. The guy from Homicide knew how to play the media, and we went ahead and pursued the investigation, and we cracked the damn thing. Before the stink came through the door out in Brooklyn, we already had a name and a description. All we had to do was pick the bastard up, and the only thing that stopped us from doing just that was he was dead."

Joe had suggested Schering wasn't the sharpest knife in the drawer, but he seemed bright enough to me. There was a stolid, Midwestern quality about him, and that might have been enough to lead a New Yorker like Joe Durkin to label him slow. But he reminded me of an Ohio cop I knew named Havlicek, whom I'd liked and respected enough to stay in touch with. There was nothing slow about Havlicek.

Schering hailed from Albert Lea, Minnesota, where he'd played high school football and basketball before going to the University of Minnesota. He played freshman football but didn't make the Golden Gopher varsity, and didn't even bother trying out for basketball, where everybody was six-five or taller.

His girlfriend was a theater major, and after graduation he followed her to New York, where she waited tables and went to auditions. He was riding the subway to his entry-level office job when he saw a recruiting ad for the NYPD. He sailed through the entrance exam and never looked back.

The relationship didn't last and he didn't know what had become of the girl, whether she was still in New York or had gone on to L.A. or back to St. Paul, and didn't care enough to find out. When I asked him if he ever missed Minnesota he looked at me like I was out of my mind.

They'd known Ivanko was right for it before the DNA evidence came along to lock it up, he told me, because they'd recovered a partial thumbprint from the fireplace poker. It was just one print, and a partial one at that, so it hadn't led anywhere until they acted on the tip and got hold of Ivanko's sheet.

"It was a match," he said. "Forensics pegged it at something like sixty percent, so it wouldn't stand up in court as an absolute certainty, but it was as sure as you could get given the amount of the thumbprint left on the poker. In other words, **we** were a hundred percent certain, and it turned out there was nothing we had to sell to a judge and jury. And if we had to, well, we had the DNA. His semen, his pubic hair at the scene, plus Brooklyn Forensics found trace evidence on one of the bodies."

"Trace evidence?"

"Put it this way," he said. "Our boy Carl didn't have time to shower."

It had been exciting when the tip worked out and the case started to break, and slightly anticlimactic when the cops in Brooklyn walked in on Bierman and Ivanko before the Manhattan team could track them down. But he was just as glad it turned out the way it did.

"For the victim's sake," he said. "Not the actual vics, they were past caring, but the daughter. Sooner the better for someone in her position. And the two of them being dead means she's spared weeks of a trial and tons of media hype and it's over now instead of six months from now, or six years from now, or never because for the rest of her life they're calling her every few years to testify at a parole hearing. It's never really over no matter what, because losing your parents like that is something that never goes away, but at least she can close the books on it, same as we can."

He sympathized with the girl, as anybody would have done, but that hadn't kept him from taking a good look at her. "Because that's got to be the first thing enters your mind," he said. "The parents killed in their own home, the daughter discovers the bodies, first thing you wonder is did she make it happen. Because there's cases all the time, one just four months ago in Astoria, high school girl, her parents didn't approve of the boy she was dating, and she shows them how mistaken they are by teaming up with him and shooting them both dead."

I remembered that one. "They didn't do too good a job," I said.

"She stole her father's gun," he said, "and gave it to the boyfriend, and he shot the old man. Then he made the girl shoot her mother, or it was her idea, depending who you listen to. And then he goes out and steals a car and makes a drive-by shooting out of it, pumping three, four shots through the front window. And she's in the house when this happens, and she calls it in, all hysterical, and she's even got superficial cuts on her hands where she's presumably hit by flying glass from the drive-by. Which would be a nice touch except there was no flying glass, the bullets went right through, knocked out a little circle and that's all.

"And when you play **What's Wrong with This Picture?** the answer comes up **Everything**. The two bodies are in the front room, where they supposedly got shot from the drive-by, but there's blood spatters in the kitchen and other evidence indicating that at least one of them was killed there and dragged into the living room, including one slug that went through and wound up in the kitchen wall. And the bullets fired from the passing car, the trajectory's all wrong, they wound up in the living room ceiling, and with the woman, the mother, not only is the angle wrong but the wound's got powder burns. That's a neat trick, leaving powder burns around a wound inflicted from outside the house."

So he could hardly avoid taking a careful look at Kristin Hollander. He wasn't hard on her, because chances were she was innocent, in which case the last thing anybody wanted to do was add to her pain and suffering. But he watched her reactions and he checked her alibi, and he kept an ear cocked for any false note.

And there was none. "Anybody claims he's a hundred percent human lie detector, well, he's full of crap. But you develop an instinct. You were on the job yourself, so you know how many times a day you get lied to. Bad guys just lie all the time, even when they got no reason. They got a reason, they'll tell six different lies one after the other, hoping that'll sweeten the odds and you'll believe one of them. 'That bag of dope? I never saw it before in my life, Officer. That bag of dope? It ain't dope, it's talcum powder, case I meet a baby needs his diaper changed. That bag of dope? Hey, man, where'd that come from? Must be you planted it on me.' You're laughing, but that's how it plays out."

"I'm laughing because the routine hasn't changed in thirty years."

"It never will. You don't tamper with a classic. And each of them thinks he's the first one to run this crap by you. Each one's a criminal genius in his own mind. But you're completely used to it and you know the body language that goes with it, and you can tell the lie's on its way before the first words are out of his mouth."

And Kristin wasn't lying, he was positive of it. You couldn't fake a reaction like that, couldn't go pale on cue, couldn't have your voice climb to the top of its register without even being aware that it had done so. She'd been in shock, that's what the doctor had called it, that was the medical condition she'd manifested, and you couldn't act your way into it.

Plus her alibi stood up a hundred percent. She was with people the whole evening, some who knew her well and others, like the one who drove her home, whom she'd met that night for the first time. No way they were all lying, and their statements overlapped, covering her for the entire evening.

Of course she wouldn't have had to be on the scene when her parents came home. She could have let the burglars in earlier, or she could have supplied them with a key and the keypad code and made sure she was elsewhere when the shit hit the fan. But there was no reason to suspect her, no evidence they could find of any conflict between her and her parents, no screaming fits, no simmering resentments. Nor was there any motive in sight but the admitted value of the house and whatever else she stood to inherit, and she already had the use of the house, she lived in it, for God's sake, and she didn't have any special need for money, so what would motivate her to do something so thoroughly monstrous?

EIGHT

You'd think Coney Island Avenue would run to if not through Coney Island, but it doesn't. It begins at the circle at the southwest corner of Prospect Park and extends due south until it winds up in Brighton Beach a few yards from the Boardwalk. I got there on the D train, and got off at Sixteenth Street and Avenue J. I'd have saved myself a few blocks if I'd stayed on one more stop to Avenue M, but I wasn't sure how the numbers ran.

I got my bearings and headed west on Avenue J, a commercial street that ran heavily to kosher restaurants and bakeries. The neighborhood was Midwood, and it had been solidly middle-class and Jewish in those days when pretty much all of Brooklyn was Jewish or Irish or Italian. From the signage it was still a Jewish neighborhood, but you didn't see the black frock coats and broad-brimmed hats you'll find in Borough Park and Crown Heights.

There was more ethnic variety on Coney Island Avenue, where a kosher dairy restaurant was flanked by a Pakistani grocery and a Turkish restaurant. I walked past used car lots and credit jewelers, crossed a couple of streets, and followed the house numbers down to the one I was looking for. I found it two houses from the corner of Locust, a little side street that angled off Coney Island Avenue midway between Avenues L and M.

The house where Bierman and Ivanko died was a squared-off box four stories tall. It had started life as a frame house, and I suppose that's what it still was, underneath it all, but someone had seen fit to improve it with aluminum siding. I understand that cuts heating bills and spares you the need to paint every few years, but the best thing you can ever say for a siding job is that it doesn't look like one, and this one looked like nothing else on earth. They'd done it on the cheap, simply encasing the house in siding without regard to any ornamentation or architectural details it might have boasted. Everything was squared off and covered over, and the siding itself was shoddy, or had been inexpertly applied, because it was buckling here and there.

"You're looking at it like you want to buy it."

I turned at the voice and saw a blue-and-white parked at the curb next to a fire hydrant. A fellow with a neat little mustache and a full head of dark hair was leaning out the window. He wore a Hawaiian shirt, and his forearms were tanned. "Ed Iverson," he said, grinning. "And you've got to be Scudder."

In the vestibule, there were eight buzzers, plus an unlabeled one off to the side. "Classy building," he said. "The super's got an unlisted number." He pushed the unmarked button, and when some static came over the intercom he said, "Police, Jorge. I brought somebody to see you."

There was more static, and a few minutes later the door opened to reveal a dark-skinned Hispanic. He was short and bandy-legged, and had the overdeveloped upper body of a weight lifter.

"Meet Mr. Scudder," Iverson said. "Your new tenant for One-L."

He shook his head. "Is rented."

"You're kidding, Jorge. You got a tenant in there already?"

"Firs' of the month, gonna be. Landlord tell me he sign the lease, mean I got to paint, got to clean up." He wrinkled his nose. "Got to get the smell out."

"Paint'll help with that."

"Some, but that stink's in the floorboards," Jorge said. "Is in the walls. What I think, maybe incense."

"Worth a try."

"But then you got the incense smell, an' how you get rid of that?"

"Hey, smoke some pot," Iverson suggested. "You want to show us the place, Jorge?"

"I tol' you, is rented."

"So Mr. Scudder'll see what he's missing. He don't really want to rent it, Jorge. He just wants to look at it. You gonna let us in or am I gonna kick that door in all over again?"

The smell's a lot better," Iverson told the super. "You're here all the time, you don't notice the difference one day to the next. You wash the floors down with ammonia, keep the windows open like you got 'em now, spray some air freshener around, nobody's gonna notice a thing."

"You can't smell it?"

"Sure I can smell it, but it's nothing like it was. Anyway, didn't you say some genius already took the place? What did he have, a head cold?"

"Took it over the phone."

"Guy can't be too fussy, rents a place without even looking at it. Just tell that lady across the hall to keep busy in the kitchen. She wasn't the one complained about the smell, was she?"

"Was somebody from upstairs."

"Smelled it all the way up there?"

"Passed by the door, you know, an' smelled it that way."

"Guess she wasn't cooking at the time, across the hall, or the smells woulda canceled each other out. What's she cook, anyway?"

"Cambodian food, I guess."

"Cambodian?"

"She's from Cambodia," Jorge said, "so must be Cambodian food, no?"

"I guess the national dish is Wet Dog with Garlic," Iverson said, "and her family can't get enough of it. Okay, Jorge, we'll take it from here."

"Take what?"

Iverson grinned. "Take a hike," he said. "Go on, go drink some steroids and do some bench presses."

"No steroids. All natural."

"Yeah, right."

"That juice is bad for you," Jorge said. "Shrink you balls."

"Like garbanzo beans," Iverson said. When the door closed he said, "You see the shoulders on that little fucker? All natural my ass. The little guys, they all want to be big, and there's a point where they try the steroid route, and it works, so how can they walk away from it? It **does** shrink your balls, and they're the first to say so, but they figure it's like lung cancer, it just happens to other people." He shook his head. "But we're all like that, aren't we? Figuring everything happens to other people. Otherwise we'd never get on a plane or drive home from a bar or smoke a cigarette or leave the goddam house."

"Or go to a concert," I said.

"Or anything. This is where it happened, and you can still smell it, can't you? Even if it's not as bad as Jorge thinks it is. And about all you **can** do is smell it, because there's not a hell of a lot to see. He cleaned up. Well, he had to, and there was no reason not to, once we cut the seals off the place. Forensics was done and we had the evidence bagged and the crime scene photos taken, and the case was essentially closed from the minute it was open, so why worry about preserving the integrity of the scene?"

He led me to the front room, then back through the kitchen where we'd entered to a third room at the rear. "Furniture's gone," he said. "Wasn't much to begin with, and God knows it wasn't worth keeping. Couple of Salvation Army chairs in the living room, and a TV sitting on top of a milk case. Card table in the kitchen, another chair or two. This here was the bedroom, but he didn't have a bed in it, just a foam mattress on the floor with a sheet over it. Was there a chest of drawers? I can't even remember. One thing I know there was, there was another TV, but it was right on the floor, so you could watch it from the bed without getting a crick in your neck."

"They thought of everything," I said.

"Including the importance of getting plenty of fresh air while you slept, because the mattress was over there by the window. The one mutt, Ivanko, was right about where you're standing, sprawled more or less facedown, half on and half off the mattress. You know what, we shoulda met at the station house and I could show you the photos, give you a better picture than you can get pacing around an empty apartment. Assuming they're still around the house, and assuming I could find 'em."

I told him Schering had shown me a set.

"So you just wanted to look around, get the feel of the place." He grinned. "Smell the smells."

"And talk to someone who was on the scene."

He nodded. "Well, if you saw the photos, you pretty much got it all. Shooter was in the corner opposite the bed, right there, in his shorts, which he messed up after he shot himself, which did nothing for the smell, believe me. I don't know why he took his shirt and pants off before he shot himself, or why he stopped when he got to his underwear, unless it was a sudden attack of modesty. His jeans were on the floor next to the television set, right about there, and his shirt, I don't remember where his shirt was. In here, anyway, and it had to be on the floor, because that's all there was."

"And he was seated in the corner?"

"Well, slumped there," he said. "He fell forward after he shot himself, so he wound up folded at the waist, more or less. So the first thing you saw was the exit wound in the back of his head." He walked over and pointed to a darkened area at the juncture of the walls, a couple of feet from the floor. There was a white circle in the middle, where a hole had been spackled. "Jorge scrubbed it down," he said, "and plugged up where they dug the bullet out, but he didn't get all of it. You might if the surface was a good semi-glossy, but with flat wall paint it soaks in. Doesn't matter, the paint'll cover it, even the cheap shit that's all landlords'll pay for. But you can see how it went down."

"Yes."

"First thing I thought, well, care to take a guess?"

"Lovers' quarrel."

"Got it in one. Two males, one mattress, and the one who did the shooting's in his shorts and nothing else. He killed his lover, realized what he'd done, and pretended his gun was a dick. Then the next thing I saw was an empty pillowcase, and then another pillowcase that wasn't empty, and I went back into the kitchen and there was a little walnut chest on the card table, with everything inside it including oyster forks. You don't get too many sterling silver oyster forks on Coney Island Avenue."

"Did you guess right off where it came from?"

He nodded. "All the press the case had, all the bulletins coming out of One Police Plaza, that was the first thing came into my mind. My partner, too, and I don't know which of us said it first. It gets your blood going, something like that. You can probably imagine."

"Sure."

"But there's a letdown comes about a minute later, because where are you gonna go with it? They're the ones did it, they're both dead, case closed, end of story. Of course you check it out to make sure, you check it out in detail, but nothing ever turns up to make you change your mind. What's funny is me and Fitz'll both wind up with commendations for this, and what the hell did we do besides look around and call it in?"

"The letter in your file's just as good whether you did anything or not," I said, "and it'll offset all the times you earned a commendation and didn't get one."

"You just said a true fact," he said. "It all evens out."

We talked some more as I walked around the apartment, getting the feel of the place, trying to imagine how it had all played out. Two men walk in the door, laden down with what they've stolen. They've just raped a woman, killed her and her husband, and they feel—how do they feel? How could I possibly guess how they felt?

They walk in, and moments later (or hours later, I didn't know the time frame here) one of them shoots the other. Then strips to his undershorts (unless he stripped first, before he shot his partner) and sits in the corner and eats his gun. Or, in Iverson's memorable imagery, fellates it.

I asked if they'd both lived here.

"Place was Bierman's," he said. "Signed a lease back in April, and, far as any of the neighbors knew, he lived here by himself. Clothes in the closet were his. Just one pillow on the mattress, and even if two people share a bed, wouldn't each one have his own pillow?"

"You'd think so."

"Maybe he brought Ivanko back so they could stash the loot, divvy it up, whatever they were going to do." He shrugged. "Maybe Bierman **was** queer for him, made a move and Ivanko didn't go for it. Bang bang, you're dead, bang again and **I'm** dead. If one of 'em lived through it we could ask, but they're both dead and we can't."

"You had to kick the door in," I said.

"Once again, if they were alive they could have opened it for us. But yes, we had to kick it in. Not me personally but the two uniforms who got here first. They must have known what they were gonna find. Nobody's on the job any length of time without getting a whiff of eau de corpse, and for the rest of your life you never mistake it for anything else, do you?"

"Was the super here when they got here?"

"Jorge? He was the one who called them. A neighbor complained and he went and called 911."

"He just let us in," I said. "Why couldn't he let the uniforms in?"

"Oh, I wondered where the hell you were going. The door was bolted from the inside."

"And the key wouldn't turn the deadbolt?"

"Not that kind of a bolt," he said. "This had nothing to do with the lock. It was the kind of gizmo you buy in the hardware store and screw onto the back of your door, half of it, and the other half onto the jamb. And you slide the bolt over and lock the door. Here, you can see the holes where the screws were. One more thing for Jorge to spackle before he starts painting, if he even takes the trouble. I saw the bolt itself when I came in, nice shiny brass thing. The door itself was intact, kicking didn't damage it, the inside bolt just pulled loose from where it was attached. Didn't the bolt show in any of the photos Schering showed you?"

"Maybe I didn't have a complete set." I walked around some more, looked out the bedroom window at the lot in back. There were four garbage cans out there, three upright and one on its side, with trash spilling out of it. There was a black Hefty bag alongside it, and it looked to have been gnawed open by a rat. The rat wasn't there to be seen, but I saw what might have been rat shit. The boys from Forensics could have identified it as such, and told me what the rat had for breakfast.

You could grow flowers back there, I thought, or cook on a barbecue grill, but you'd have to be out of your mind to want to.

"I wish I knew why he took his clothes off," I said.

"Bierman?"

"Was Ivanko undressed too?"

"No, just Bierman. It was warm, and you may have noticed that one of the things this place lacks is an air conditioner, or even a fan. They probably worked up a sweat, toting all that shit back from Manhattan. Bierman was wearing jeans and a long-sleeved shirt. He may have figured he'd be cooler without 'em."

"I guess."

"And maybe he just didn't like wearing clothes with blood on them."

"There was blood on his clothing?"

"Pants and shirt both."

"Ivanko's blood?"

He shook his head. "From the Hollander killing. Hers, I guess, but that'd be in the report. She got her throat cut, she's the one whose blood'd get on everything."

"Wasn't it Ivanko who cut her throat?"

"Did they decide for sure one way or the other? Does it matter? They both had blood on their clothes. You cut a throat, one thing there's plenty of is blood. Everybody can have some."

I said, "I wonder why they locked themselves in."

"They'd just killed two people and brought home a couple of sacks full of stolen goods. Maybe they didn't want anybody to walk in on them just then."

"Maybe."

"Or Bierman shot his buddy and wanted a few minutes of guaranteed peace and quiet before he went and joined him. But that's beside the point, isn't it? What you want to know is were they locked in, and they were, and from the inside."

Iverson had things to do, and he made sure the apartment was locked up again before he went off to do them. I don't know what he thought I could find to steal.

When he was gone I went down to the basement for a few words with Jorge, then went through the rest of the building looking for someone else to talk to. Half the tenants were out and most of the others either couldn't speak English or preferred to give that impression. I didn't learn anything, and I wasn't sure there was anything to learn.

I walked up to Avenue M, turned left, and realized when I got to the corner that I could have cut diagonally across Locust and saved myself some steps.

I had to laugh. If I'd wanted to save time, I could have skipped Brooklyn altogether. I walked a few more blocks, climbed the steps to the platform, and waited for my train.

NINE

He gets in the car and starts driving, with no destination in mind. He just feels like a drive, that's all.

And the car's so clean it's a pleasure to be in it. He's a neat person, he keeps his car neat, inside and out, and frequently runs it through a car wash. But he just recently had it detailed for the first time, and when he got into it he'd have sworn it was fresh from the dealer's showroom. It even smelled like a new car, and he's since learned how they managed that. There's this product, comes in a spray can, called New Car Smell.

They think of everything.

He's not paying attention to the route, because if you don't know where you're going, what does it matter how you get there? On Canal

Street he sees the signs for the Manhattan Bridge, and he crosses into Brooklyn and drives south on Flatbush Avenue, and now he knows where he's headed.

If you just wait, he thinks, you find out where you're going.

And you get what you get.

And isn't it traditional, returning to the scene of the crime? And he's done it before. Twice, since that evening, he's found himself walking across that block of West Seventy-fourth Street. He's slowed as he passed the house, but hasn't wanted to linger, hasn't cared to invite a second glance. Still, people will stare at the house for perfectly innocent reasons, won't they? With all the news, all the media coverage, the house has become a notorious site. It hasn't reached the point of tour buses cruising by, the drivers rattling off the gory details over their loudspeaker systems, and it wouldn't come to that, not in this city where there was always a fresh outrage to erase the memory of the last one.

Still, why tempt fate? On his second walk past the house, he'd been tempted to browse the ground-floor antique shop, maybe buy something for a souvenir. And what could be more innocent than to patronize a retail establishment? But no, he let it go.

He keeps one hand on the wheel, reaches to his throat with the other. Puts a finger inside his shirt collar, touches the thin gold chain around his neck.

The best souvenirs, he thinks, are ones you don't have to buy.

He turns right off Flatbush onto Cortelyou Road, turns left again on Coney Island Avenue. He drives to the house where it happened, and coasts right on by when he notices a police cruiser parked illegally two doors away. There's no one in it, and there could be any number of reasons to park a police car beside a hydrant on that particular block. There are a good many homes and apartment houses within walking distance, and a cop might have cause to visit any of them. There didn't even have to be a crime involved, or a complaint. He could just be visiting a girlfriend, or a favorite uncle.

He circles the block, parks legally a few doors down the street where he can watch the house. He's got his eye on it when the door opens and two men come out, the younger one looking Brooklyn-debonair in a boisterous Hawaiian shirt and dark trousers, the other older and more conservative in his dress. The two men shake hands, and then the younger man—and yes, he looks like a cop on vacation, a cop on his day off—gets into the police car and pulls away from the curb. The older man watches him go and heads back into the house.

The landlord, making sure he can rent out the apartment again without destroying evidence? Some city employee, some political functionary?

Or maybe the next tenant, concerned about building security. Except he looks wrong for the neighborhood.

The landlord, he decides. But it doesn't concern him, not really. He doesn't live here, and there's really no reason why he ever has to return to this neighborhood.

It's not like Seventy-fourth Street, where he has ongoing interests to consider.

TEN

Over the next several days I talked to ten or a dozen people, some on the phone, some face to face. I didn't have a client, or any real reason to be running an investigation, but I couldn't have been busier if I had.

I called a few lawyers I knew, including Ray Gruliow and Drew Kaplan, on the chance that somebody might know something interesting about Byrne Hollander. Ray had met a junior partner of his once, a fellow named Sylvan Harding, but remembered him chiefly because of his name. "Only man I ever met named Sylvan," he said, "and it was a constant struggle to keep from calling him Mr. Fields, because I absolutely could not get the phrase 'Sylvan Fields' out of my head. And still can't evidently. I'm not sure he'd even remember who I am."

"When did anyone ever forget Hard-Way Ray?"

"Well, you've got a point. If you want, I can call him and tell him to expect to hear from you. But I'm not sure if that'll smooth the way for you or just get him to keep his guard up."

"Just so it gets me past the reception desk," I said.

He made the call, and it got me past reception and all the way into Sylvan Harding's office. The first thing he did was apologize for the view. "If you're in the Empire State Building," he said, "you ought to be able to see three or four states, wouldn't you think? But we're on the seventh floor, and for all the view we've got we might as well be in the basement." He smiled in the right places as he told me this, and it had a very pat feel to it; I had the feeling every visitor got to hear the same little speech.

I was on a fishing expedition, looking for anyone who might have had something against the late Byrne Hollander, and I didn't get a lot from Harding. He couldn't come up with a single disappointed client or disgruntled employee, and seemed puzzled by the notion that anyone anywhere could actually harbor ill feeling toward a member of the legal profession.

I learned that Hollander had specialized in estate and trust work, which made it even less likely that a resentful client had sent Bierman and Ivanko to his door. In his line of work, his clients were dead and gone before any failings on his part became evident.

I asked about Bierman and Ivanko. Had Byrne Hollander ever represented either of them, or had any dealings that involved either man? Harding recognized the names and was shaking his head before I could finish asking the question. "Ours is an exclusively civil practice," he told me, and he didn't mean they were polite to one another, although I suppose that went without saying. "None of the partners or associates handle criminal cases."

"Even crooks draw wills," I said, "or get named in other people's. I'm trying to find a connection between either of the two killers and the Hollander family—or to rule it out."

"My feeling is that you can do the latter. Rule it out."

Just by force of will, evidently. "What I'd like you to do," I said, "is run a global search of Hollander's hard drive." I'd memorized what T J had suggested earlier, and I could rattle it off, even if I didn't entirely understand what I was saying. "Not just file names but within the files, looking for either of the two names, Bierman or Ivanko."

He swore he couldn't do that. The files were confidential, first of all, their contents subject to attorney-client privilege. On top of that, Hollander's computer files were protected by Hollander's password. I told him he'd obviously found the password or he'd be too busy to talk to me, with all of Hollander's unfinished work clogging the system. And I told him I didn't want to violate

attorney-client privilege, just to look for two
names. If he couldn't find them, it would be no violation to tell me so. If they showed up, he could
always tell me he'd changed his mind and I should
go to hell.

In the end, I guess it was easier for him to enter
a few keystrokes and click his mouse a few times
than to explain to me all that was wrong with my
reasoning. And, as I'd anticipated, he didn't have
occasion to strain his ethical conscience. Neither
name, Bierman or Ivanko, appeared anywhere in
Byrne Hollander's files.

When I talked to Ray Gruliow, I'd also made it
a point to ask him about the two killers. They
didn't strike me as likely clients for him, but you
never knew. If there was a way to paint the violation of the Hollanders as a political act, a blow
against the system struck from the left or right,
Hard-Way Ray could have done what he does
best—i.e., put the system on trial, confuse the hell
out of everybody, and win an acquittal for his
loathsome clients.

He'd never represented either of them, or so
much as heard of them until they turned up dead
on Coney Island Avenue. Drew Kaplan, who has a
one-man general practice in Brooklyn, hadn't had
any contact with them, either, but he said Bierman's name was familiar, though he couldn't say
why. "You ought to be able to find out who repre-

sented them in their court appearances," he said. "It's a matter of record. Whether the attorneys will feel free to talk to you is something else, but finding them ought to be easy."

I'd already worked that out myself. Ivanko had had Legal Aid lawyers the several times he'd been brought up on charges, and I called the one I could track down—one of the others had died and another had quit and moved out of state. She said she couldn't tell me anything, that a client's death didn't end privilege. Anyway, she said, there was nothing to tell me. She'd been the one who represented Ivanko on the attempted rape charge, when the witness blew it at the lineup, and she'd been on the scene and able to move for a dismissal, and got it. That was as much contact as she'd had with him, and I got the impression it was more than she wanted. The next time she drew an accused rapist, she volunteered, she'd switched with a male colleague. "Because I wasn't confident I could represent the client effectively," she said.

I called around, and had trouble getting Bierman's record. I don't think anybody was holding out; it was more that they didn't have the information on hand. I could understand that. By the time Bierman's name had come up, he'd already had a tag on his toe. He was down for two murders in Manhattan and a murder and suicide in Brooklyn, and he'd been dead for a couple of days, so how important was it to assess his prior record?

It had been of interest to the press, so what I did

know was what was in the papers—that he'd been arrested on a batch of minor charges, but had never drawn any prison time. He'd been held overnight on a drunk and disorderly charge, picked up and released during a raid on a Brownsville crack house, cited for jumping a subway turnstile, and all in all showed the typical profile of a low-level fuckup.

Burglary, assault, multiple homicide, murder—it was quite a step up. Of course Ivanko had been the rapist, Ivanko the artist with the fireplace poker, and it was very likely Ivanko who'd cut Susan Hollander's throat. But Ivanko certainly hadn't shot himself three times. That would have been Bierman's work, and it seemed reasonable to assume he'd also been the one to use the gun earlier, in the house on West Seventy-fourth Street. He'd fired three shots both times, before something made him send a seventh bullet up through the soft palate and into his brain.

It was the same gun both times, I knew that. A .22 auto, and what model was it? How many cartridges did the clip hold, and how many were left after he killed himself? Had he had to reload?

So many things I didn't know.

I stayed busy that week, even when I wasn't bothering cops and lawyers. I made a trip to the storage warehouse for Elaine, and spelled her at her shop one afternoon when she had an auction she wanted to go to. Didn't make any sales, but I didn't break anything, either, so we figured it was a wash.

I went to three meetings, two at St. Paul's and one noon meeting at the West Side Y. And Elaine and I got to two concerts, the second a Baroque ensemble that flew in from Bratislava. Elaine couldn't think of anyone she knew who'd been to Bratislava, and I told her I used to know a guy who'd been born there. I met him years ago at a meeting in the Village, but he'd come here as a child, and his earliest memories were of the Lower East Side, around Pitt and Madison. All those buildings were gone now, he'd told me, and it was just as well.

We didn't go to Bratislava, but walked out of the concert hall and cabbed down to the Village, where we caught an extended set at a basement jazz club off Sheridan Square. The audience was as respectfully attentive as the crowd at Lincoln Center, although they tapped their feet more and applauded at the end of solos. We didn't say much, and went straight home afterward.

At the kitchen table I said, "I had a dream the other night."

"Oh?"

"I don't remember how it started. Does anybody ever remember how dreams start?"

"How could you? Your mind would have to remember what it was doing before it started dreaming. Like remembering before you were born, although there are people who claim they can do that."

"Hard to prove."

"Or disprove," she said, "but I didn't mean to change the subject. You had a dream."

"Anita was in it. She was dying or she was dead, I don't remember which. I think she was dying at the start of the dream, struggling to breathe, and then it shifted and I realized that she was dead. She was looking at me, but I somehow knew she wasn't alive."

She waited.

"She was blaming me. 'Why didn't you do something? I'm dead and it's your fault. Why didn't you save me?' Those aren't the words, I don't remember the words, but that's what she was saying."

She stirred her tea. I don't know why, she doesn't put anything in it. She took the spoon out, set it in the saucer.

"Then she disappeared," I said.

"She disappeared?"

"She sort of faded," I said. "Or maybe she melted, like the Wicked Witch of the West. She just gradually wasn't there anymore."

"And?"

"That's it," I said. "I woke up. Otherwise I probably wouldn't have remembered the dream. I hardly ever do, you know. I suppose I dream, they say everybody does, but I don't often remember them."

"If we were supposed to remember them," she said, "we'd be awake when they happened."

"Sometimes," I said, "I'll wake up in the morning with the feeling that I dreamed, and the sense that I could remember the dream if I just tried hard enough."

"How would you go about trying to remember something?"

"I have no idea. It never works, I'll tell you that much. The dream never comes back to me. But that sensation of having dreamed, it can be very convincing."

"And you've had it a lot lately?"

I nodded. "And I have a feeling it's always the same dream."

"The one you had the other night, and did remember."

"That or a variation on it. I don't have any evidence of this, but I'm not sure 'dream' and 'evidence' belong in the same sentence to begin with."

"She dies and there's nothing you can do."

"She dies and there's nothing I can do, she's dead and I should have done something."

"Do you remember the feeling that went with it?"

"What you'd expect, I guess. Helplessness, guilt. A desire to do something and a complete inability to think of anything to do."

After a moment she said, "There really wasn't anything you could do."

"I know that."

"Or anything you should have done. You didn't

even know she was ill, and how could you? Nobody told you."

"No."

"But I suppose it goes back farther than that, doesn't it?"

"Thirty years," I said, "or whenever it was that I walked out."

"Still blame yourself?"

I shook my head. "Not really. I did all the crap they teach you in AA, I sorted it out, I made amends. I'm not proud of every decision I made during the drinking years, if you can even call them decisions. But I don't have trouble living with any of it, and I wound up in the right place. Sober, and married to the right woman."

"But sometimes you think you should have stayed married to the wrong one."

"No, I don't think that."

"Not that you'd be happier, or better off. But that it would have been the right thing to do."

"Maybe when I'm dreaming," I said. "Not when my mind's working. It's just . . ."

"Everything," she supplied.

"She died," I said, "out of the blue, and that was a shock, and then the funeral, and the happy horseshit afterward with Michael and Andy. Did I tell you about the bar where I met the two of them?"

"Bowls full of miniature Hershey bars."

"That's the one. I wanted a drink."

"I would have wanted a candy bar."

"I didn't have a drink," I said, "or think seriously about it. But the desire was as strong as it's
been in a while."

"Part of the deal, isn't it? And you didn't have a
drink, and that's what counts."

"I know."

"That's why you're looking into what happened
to the Hollanders, isn't it?"

"One way or another," I said. "I needed something to do. And if I were inclined to play amateur
psychologist—"

"Which God knows you're not."

"Which I trust God knows I'm not, I'd say I was
reenacting my dream, trying to save Susan Hollander when it was already too late."

"Just her?"

"Hell, make it both of them. I'm reliving my
childhood and trying to save both my parents. Do
you like that better?"

"I shouldn't have interrupted."

"Psychology aside," I said, "I let T J talk me
into going uptown to see that girl because I didn't
have anything better to do. And I needed something to do. We saw her and evidently put her
mind at rest, and you'd think I would have put my
own mind to rest in the process."

"But you didn't."

"I went and looked at the house," I said, "and
that didn't tell me anything new. And T J printed

out the news stories for me, and pulled some other stuff off the Web, and that didn't tell me much, either."

"But you stayed with it."

"I did."

"Because it was something to do."

"I guess so."

"And now you're done?"

"Not yet.

"You're staying with it? Because it's something to do?"

I shook my head. "Because it's something that ought to be done," I said, "and who else is going to do it? The cops closed the case."

"And they shouldn't have?"

"I'm not saying they were wrong," I said. "But I don't think they got the whole story."

ELEVEN

I called Iverson in the morning and left a message, and around eleven he called me back. "I was thinking about something you said," I told him. "How they carried everything back with them, the silverware and all."

"We recovered it," he said, "down to the last oyster fork."

"You happen to know how they made the trip?"

"Made the trip?"

"Did either of them have a car?"

"Not that Motor Vehicles knows about," he said. "You saw the apartment, remember? And I told you how it was furnished. Bierman was lucky if he had a spare pair of jeans. How was he gonna have a car?"

"So how did they get back to Brooklyn?"

"How'd you come out here? The D train, isn't that what you said?"

"Somehow the idea of those two carrying a couple of sacks of stolen goods on the subway . . ."

"No, though God knows it wouldn't be the first time somebody did. Always a chance they flagged a gypsy cab, although that's not so easy in Manhattan, is it?"

"No."

"So what's most likely is they stole a car. Hotwired one, if they knew how, or found one with the keys in it. Drove it to the job, so it was there waiting for them when they came out. Then drove it home."

"Did you recover a stolen car in the neighborhood?"

There was a pause, and he sounded a few degrees cooler when he said, "I don't believe so, no."

"I wonder what happened to it."

"If they left the keys in it," he said, "the odds are some other mope stole it, and drove it to some other precinct where it became somebody else's problem. Or how long did they have it, a couple of hours? Maybe they put it back where they found it, or close enough, and the owner never even knew it was gone."

"Maybe."

"You trying to make something out of this, Scudder?"

"I was just wondering."

"Yeah, and it's got me wondering myself. What are you trying to accomplish here, anyway?"

"Just trying to get a clear picture," I said.

"A clear picture. What it sounds like, you're poking here, poking there, next thing you're saying we fucked this up, we didn't look hard enough for the car."

"That's not what I'm saying at all."

"In the first place," he said, "it stopped being our case the minute we ID'd the chest of sterling. All the same, we went ahead and pursued our end of the investigation. You think we didn't look for the vehicle?"

"No, I think you probably did."

"You're damn right we did, looked good and thorough for it. And we checked stolen car reports. We did everything we were supposed to do, including things nobody would have blamed us if we hadn't done them, because the fucking case was over and done with. We did this a hundred percent right."

"That's exactly what I was hoping to hear," I said.

"How's that?"

"Suppose there was a third man," I said. "The driver, drove them to Manhattan, waited for them, drove them back."

"And?"

"And dropped them off in front of the house on Coney Island Avenue and then got rid of the car. Lost it in another part of town, if it was stolen. Or, if it was his own car, found a place to park it."

"Ran it through a car wash, if he had any sense."

"Meanwhile, Bierman and Ivanko are in the apartment, and Bierman shoots Ivanko."

"For reasons which remain to this day unclear."

He sounded a little like W. C. Fields, and his tone told me we were friends again. "And likely to remain that way," I said, "barring the discovery of a dying message."

"Morse code. Dots and dashes, gnawed into the floorboards by the dying Ivanko."

"Maybe that's why he bolts the door," I went on. "So the third man won't come back in the middle of things."

"Or he shoots Ivanko on impulse, and then he bolts the door while he figures out what he's gonna do next."

Or so the driver wouldn't walk in on him while he was doing it, I thought. Or bolting the door was automatic, something he always did when he entered the apartment, because he felt safer that way.

"A third man," Iverson said. "I see where you're coming from here, and it does a lot to explain the car we never found, but do you have anything to back it up with?"

"Not really. At this point all it is is a theory."

"Nobody saw a third guy on the scene in Manhattan."

"Not so far as I know. The trouble with a case that's closed—"

"Yeah, I know. There's things you would follow up otherwise. There was a guy visited Bierman a couple of times. Maybe it was the third man, the mysterious Mr. X."

"When was this?"

"Who knows? Bierman was pretty mysterious himself, far as his neighbors were concerned. Kept to himself, just went out to buy beer and pizza. Word is he had a guy who dropped in a couple of times, but nobody could say just when. We more or less assumed the guy was Ivanko."

"The description fit?"

"Description? 'Dude was wearin' a baseball cap. Or, hey, wait a minute, maybe he **wasn't** wearin' no baseball cap. Maybe it was some other dude was wearin' a cap.' "

"Maybe the third man gave them the gun."

"Hey, if it was his car, why shouldn't it be his gun, too?" He laughed. "I always more or less figured the gun was Ivanko's."

"Bierman didn't own one?"

"Not that anybody knew, but would they? My guess is it came from a burglary. That's the way most crooks get guns, especially small-time skells like these two. Some concerned citizen buys one for his protection, and there's a burglary, and that's the last he sees of it. Unless he's home at the time, the sad bastard, in which case the last he sees is it's pointed at him, and the last he hears is **bang**."

★   ★   ★

A little Italian twenty-two," Schering said. "Pellegrino ten-shot automatic. I bet you thought they only made soda water."

"Diversification is everything."

"Isn't that the truth? Gun was registered to a psychiatrist at 242 Central Park West, reported stolen in a burglary back in March. Shrink and his wife were at the theater, came back to find the place tossed, some jewelry and valuables missing. Well, this is cute."

"What's that?"

"In the list of what's missing—'two white linen pillowcases.' That tell you anything?"

"That the psychiatrist and his wife were lucky they didn't get home early."

"Sounds like Bierman and Ivanko, doesn't it? Pillowcases slung over their shoulders like they're on their way to do their laundry. Gun wasn't in the initial report."

"Oh?"

"Reported everything else, the jewelry, the pillowcases. Three days later he called back about the gun. It took him that long to think of it and remember the locked desk drawer he kept it in, and guess what? The drawer wasn't locked anymore, and the gun wasn't in it. Why keep a gun under lock and key?"

"For safety reasons, I guess."

"But why have it at all, if it's going to be that

complicated to get to it? A locked drawer in his office."

"The office where he saw his patients?"

I heard him shuffling paper. "It doesn't say," he reported, "but it makes more sense that way, doesn't it? He's seeing patients all day long, and they're not coming to him to have their tonsils out. Some of them have got to be real nut jobs."

"That must be the technical term for it."

"He's got someone coming in that he's a little worried about, he takes out the key and unlocks the drawer. Any problem, he can get to the gun in a hurry."

"It must be comforting for the patient," I said, "to have a shrink who can pull a gun on you if you start acting out."

Schering laughed aloud. "You're on the verge of this major breakthrough," he said. "Really getting in touch with your anger, or remembering what really happened when your uncle came into your bedroom that night. And you look up from the couch, and there's Dr. Nadler, and he's pointing a gun at you."

Dr. Nadler wouldn't talk to me, and I couldn't really blame him. Doctor-patient confidentiality aside, what did I expect him to tell me? That he'd had Bierman or Ivanko as a patient, stretched out on his couch for an hour every Thursday, reliving childhood trauma and recounting dreams? That he knew who broke into his apartment and stole his gun, but hadn't seen fit to mention it to the police?

I put the phone down and decided it was just as well he'd brushed me off. If he'd welcomed me warmly I'd have had to think up some questions to ask him, and I wouldn't have known where to start.

I kept finding things out, but what I learned was barely worth knowing. That's not an uncommon feeling in an investigation. You knock on a thousand doors and ask ten thousand questions, and the scraps of information you amass just pile up until something fits with something else. You learn to keep going, and you try not to listen when a little voice says the whole enterprise is pointless.

But this time the voice was hard to ignore. I didn't see how I could keep working my way around the edges, picking at loose threads here and there. I knew what I had to do.

I reached for the phone, then changed my mind and left it where it was. Rain, the forecast had said, and the skies looked dark enough. I went outside, headed uptown, and decided I should have taken an umbrella. It felt like rain, all right.

Well, maybe it would clear the air.

TWELVE

The ground-floor antique shop looked to be open. The lights were on, the window gates drawn back. But I couldn't see anyone inside. The door was locked, and there was a button to push for entry. I pushed it, and after a moment a woman appeared at the rear of the shop and squinted at me, holding her hand to her brow as an eyeshade. She gave a little shrug, as if it didn't matter whether I was a customer or a holdup man, and buzzed me in.

Her stock ran to small rural landscapes in elaborately gilded frames, French bronzes, mostly of animals, Royal Doulton figurines, Art Deco lamps. One shelf of an étagère was given over to cameos.

She was a dumpling, her hair an unconvincing red, her cheeks heavily rouged, her billowy print dress flowing. Her smile was guarded, and something about her stance suggested she was keeping close to whatever device she could use to summon help.

I said I had a few questions about what had happened upstairs.

She said, "You're a cop?" and her face relaxed for a moment, then tightened. "You're not a cop," she said, with such certainty she had me convinced.

"I used to be," I said.

She nodded. "That I can believe. You look like you used to be, but not like you are now. I used to be a teenager. I used to be skinny. What do you want from me, Mr. Used to Be? I wasn't here, I don't know anything, and I already told the whole megillah twenty times."

"Not twenty times," I said.

"So maybe it was nineteen. What can you ask me that nobody asked me already?"

Nothing, as it turned out. I asked and she replied, and I can't say that either of us was enriched by the experience. After a few minutes of this she said, "My turn. Where did you come from?"

"Where did I come from?"

"You don't live in the building, so you came from someplace. I don't mean where were you born, I mean today. Where did you come from?"

"Fifty-seventh Street," I said.

"East? West? Where on Fifty-seventh Street?"

"Fifty-seventh and Ninth."

"What did you take, a cab? The bus?"

"I walked."

"You walked all the way from Fifty-seventh Street and Ninth Avenue to ask me these questions?"

"It's not that far."

"It's not next door. And you didn't call first. What if I didn't come in today? What if I got a headache and went home early?"

"Then I'd have missed this wonderful conversation."

She grinned, but she was not to be sidetracked. "You didn't come all this way," she said, "just to waste your time talking to me."

"Maybe I'm not the only one here who used to be a cop."

"I raised four boys. They wouldn't dare lie to me, but sometimes they would leave something out." She glanced toward the ceiling. "You talk to her yet?"

"No."

"And the longer you spend talking to me, the longer it is before you have to go talk to her."

"Your sons didn't get away with much, did they?"

"They turned out okay. I'd tell you all about them, but you already wasted enough time on me. Go see if she'll talk to you."

"She's living here now?"

"It's her home. Where else is she going to live?"

"After what happened—"

"Listen to me," she said. "One day my husband gives me a look. 'I got heartburn,' he said, 'and I

bet anything you forgot to buy Gelusil.' And I
stalked out of the room, very proud of myself, and
I came back with a brand-new box of Gelusil in
my hand, the economy size, and he was dead. It
wasn't heartburn for a change, it was a massive
coronary, and his last words to me were he bet I
forgot to buy Gelusil."

"I'm sorry to hear that," I said.

"What sorry? You never knew him, you don't
even know me. There's a point to this, Mr. Used to
Be, and that's that I still live to this day in that
apartment. I still have the chair he was in when he
dropped dead. What am I going to do, move? Get
rid of a perfectly good chair? What do you expect
her to do, move out? Sell the house? And look
around for a building that nobody ever died in?"

And was she home now?

"You think I keep tabs on her? You want to find
out, go ring her bell. You weren't so shy about
ringing mine."

Kristin Hollander didn't look as though she'd
stepped out of a Kean painting, but then I hadn't
expected her to. I'd seen her face in the papers and
on television. She was tall, her figure athletic, her
dark hair becomingly short. Her blue eyes weren't
enormous, but they were large enough, and frank
in their appraisal.

I hadn't been able to see them when she took

her first look at me, through the peephole in the front door. I'd stood there while she looked me over, then showed her a business card, a driver's license, and a courtesy card from the Detectives' Endowment Association, the last a gift from Joe Durkin. It didn't mean anything, but civilians tend to find it impressive, or at least reassuring. It reassured Kristin enough to open the door.

She led me down a hallway past a darkened room. "The living room," she said, not glancing in that direction. "I don't go there. I'm not ready yet."

There were lights on in the tiled kitchen, where a radio played softly, tuned to an easy-listening station. Two red-painted ladderback chairs with caned seats were drawn up on either side of a pine table. One of them had a Snoopy mug in front of it, half full of coffee, along with a book that had been turned facedown to keep her place. She pointed to the other chair and I took it.

"I hope you don't need milk in your coffee," she said. "I'm afraid there isn't any." I said black was fine, and she brought it to me in another Snoopy mug, this one with a beagle stretched out on top of his doghouse. On her mug he was standing beside his food dish, his ears perked up.

She topped up her own coffee, sat down, marked her place in the book, and closed it and set it aside. "It's a novel," she said, "set in the four-teenth century. I have no idea how historically accurate it is. And what difference does it make? It's not as though I'm likely to remember what I read. Is your coffee all right?"

"It's fine."

"I didn't ask you if you wanted sugar."

"I never use it."

"Or artificial sweetener?"

"No, thanks."

"Well," she said expectantly. "Now what happens?"

"I guess I offer an explanation for coming here and ringing your doorbell."

She nodded, waiting.

"First of all, I should tell you I'm not a police officer. I was for some years, but that was a while ago. I've worked since then as a private detective, but I have no official standing in that capacity, either. I had a license, but I surrendered it a couple of years ago."

"I see."

"I was at Lincoln Center the night your parents were killed. At the patrons' dinner and at the concert afterward. I didn't know your parents and I didn't meet them that night, but my wife and I were there."

"I've heard from quite a few people who were there that night."

"Maybe that got my attention," I said. "Maybe I've just got too much time on my hands these days. I don't know." I'd leave out her waif-eyed cousin, at least for the time being. "For one reason or another, I found myself conducting an unofficial investigation of my own."

"An investigation of . . ."

"Your parents' death."

She frowned. "But it was only a couple of days before they found the bodies in Brooklyn, and once that happened there was nothing to investigate."

"That's when I started," I said.

"I'm confused. The case was closed, wasn't it?"

"Yes."

She leaned forward. "You found something, didn't you? What did you find?"

"I went to Brooklyn," I said. "I'd seen the crime scene photos, but I went and saw the crime scene itself, walked through it with one of the investigating officers. I think it was staged."

"What do you mean?"

"The police had to kick the door in because the door was bolted from inside. They found the two men in the bedroom, one shot three times, twice in the torso and once in the head."

"The same way my father was shot."

"And with the same gun. They found the other man in the corner of the same room, dead of an apparently self-inflicted wound. Again, the same gun."

"He shot his partner and then committed suicide."

"That's how it was supposed to look."

"But you don't think that's what happened?"

"No, I don't," I said. "I think someone else killed both of them."

She looked at me, then down at her coffee cup. She said, "Caf and Decaf."

"I beg your pardon?"

"The coffee cups," she said. "One he's wide awake, the other he's zonked out on his doghouse. My father called them Caf and Decaf."

"Oh."

"Not that either cup ever had decaf in it. Both my parents thought of decaffeinated coffee as a crime against nature."

"They wouldn't get an argument from me."

"I've always thought there was something wrong with it. The solution. It was too quick, too easy. But then I'd have to think that, wouldn't I? That there was more to it than showed on the surface, because these were my parents, and I saw them in the morning and the next time I saw them they were dead." She leaned forward. "My reasons are personal, they come from inside me, from my need to believe things happen for a reason. Have you heard of a book called **When Bad Things Happen to Good People**?"

"I've heard of it. I haven't read it."

"Well, you're welcome to a copy. Three different people sent me copies of it, can you believe it? I tried one of them but I didn't get very far. Maybe I should try the other two. But for now I think I'm

better off in the fourteenth century. What makes
you think the death scene was staged?"

Because it felt wrong, I thought, and maybe she
wasn't the only one with a need to believe. But I
picked something specific.

"The door was bolted," I said.

"From within, you said."

"With a two-dollar bolt from the hardware
store."

"And that means someone **outside** did it?"

"The bolt was shiny," I said.

"I don't follow you."

"I never saw the bolt," I said, "but the cop I
talked to did, and he described it down to the
gleam of its brass finish. That meant it was new,
because the painters who slap a coat on apartments
like that one don't paint around the trim. They
never heard of masking tape, they paint over
everything—electric cords and outlets, switch-
plates, hardware, everything. If that bolt had been
there when Jason Bierman moved into that apartment, it would have been painted the same
washed-out white as the walls and windowsills and
ceiling."

"But it wasn't."

"No."

"Which means what, exactly?"

"Which means Bierman would have had to buy
it himself, and I can't see him doing it. The guy
lived in a dump and made zero improvements to

the place. He slept on a mattress on the floor. He
didn't have anything that anybody might want to
steal. Once he'd bought the bolt, he'd have needed
tools to attach it. I just can't see him taking the
trouble."

She thought about it. "You didn't actually see
the bolt," she said. "Maybe the cop just said 'shiny
brass bolt' because you think of them that way,
even if this particular one was painted. I mean—"

"It hadn't been installed when the place got its
last paint job," I said. "I saw where it had been,
with the screw holes, and there was no interrup-
tion in the paint like you'd get if there'd been
something there that was painted over. There had
been a bolt there, that's why they had to kick the
door in, and it had been installed during Bierman's
tenancy."

"And you say he had no reason to install it."

"None."

"So someone else installed it."

"I think so, yes."

"Bought it and installed it so that it would look
like murder and suicide. But actually you're saying
it was two murders."

"Yes."

"Someone else killed both of them. I'm not going to say their names."

"All right."

"I'm just not going to, not for the time being.
They killed my parents, and somebody else killed

them." She frowned. "They **were** the ones who killed my parents, weren't they?"

"One of them was." She hadn't said I couldn't say their names. "Carl Ivanko. I'm not sure about Bierman."

"The one who had the apartment."

"Right."

"And who shot the other one, and then killed himself, or at least that's what we were supposed to think. Wouldn't we have thought that anyway, even without the bolt?"

"Yes."

"Because if you find two men dead like that, and it looks as though one of them shot the other one and then committed suicide, you'd think that, wouldn't you?"

"Yes. The bolt was just to be cute."

"Cute?"

"Showing off," I said. "Gilding the lily."

"I see. If he did it that way, though, killed them both and locked and bolted the door—"

"Then how did he get out?"

"That's what I was wondering. Through the window?"

I nodded. "The windows were closed, but this was the ground floor. It wouldn't have been terribly difficult to climb out a window and close it after yourself. You couldn't engage the window locks, assuming they worked, but I don't think there's any way to tell whether the windows were locked or not. The first thing the responding patrolmen would have done was open all the windows."

"Are they supposed to do that?"

"No," I said, "definitely not, but they were in a small apartment with two dead bodies that had been in there for several days, and I don't know a lot of cops who wouldn't have opened a window without thinking twice."

"So the locked bolt was supposed to prove one thing," she said, "and instead it proves another."

"Prove's the wrong word," I said, "because it doesn't really prove anything. It suggested something to me, but I was probably pretty suggestible. I went in there looking for something to be wrong."

"And the bolt was it."

"The bolt was part of it."

"What else?"

"The way Ivanko was shot. Two in the torso, one in the head."

"The same as my father."

"Yes and no."

"What do you mean?"

"I don't want to be too graphic here," I said.

"I walked in," she said. "I found them. You can be as graphic as you want."

I said, "Your father was shot from the front. Two bullets in the chest from a couple of feet away, then a third fired point-blank into his temple."

"He was probably already dead by then."

Maybe, maybe not, but let her think so.

"Ivanko was shot from behind. Two bullets, one of which got the heart, both shots leaving powder burns on his shirt. Then the killer knelt down next to him and put a third bullet in his temple."

"So?"

"The killer didn't want Ivanko to know what was coming. He deliberately took him by surprise, followed him into the bedroom and shot him in the back. That doesn't sound like somebody who just had a sudden attack of conscience, or a mental breakdown."

"Suppose he decided he just wanted to keep everything for himself?"

"The score wasn't big enough to make anybody kill his partner in order to hog it all. The killing was done in a calculated manner, but it wasn't the act of a calculating man. And the ritual of three bullets, two in the back and one in the temple, was an obvious signature, but there was no real reason for it **except** as a signature. Why just two shots in the back? Why not empty the gun into him? The only reason that jumps out is that he'd shot your father twice in the chest. He wanted to establish a pattern."

A third man," she said. "It sounds like a mole in a British spy novel. Or wasn't there an old movie with that title? An Orson Welles movie?"

"That's the song," I said.

"I beg your pardon?"

" 'The Third Man Theme,' " I said, and hummed a couple of bars. "It's been running around in my head for days now and I couldn't think what it was or how it got there."

"A message from your subconscious."

"I suppose so. Of course I'd had the phrase in my mind for days. I'd gotten used to thinking in terms of a third man."

"Still, there must be something the song's trying to tell you. Not to get sidetracked, maybe. To trust your own reasoning."

"That's possible. Or maybe the only way I could get the song out of my head was to remember what it was."

"Maybe. If there was a third man . . ."

"Yes?"

"Were there three of them here that night?"

"No, I don't think so."

"Because the witness, the woman who thought they were going to do their laundry—"

"Only saw two men."

"Yes."

"Eyewitnesses get things wrong," I said. "But in this case I think she got the number right. There were just two men."

"And the third man was waiting for them? Wait a minute, he was the driver, wasn't he? He was waiting for them in the car, and drove them back to Brooklyn, and . . ."

Her words trailed off. I said, "Finish the thought. The three of them walk into the Coney

Island Avenue place. The third man shoots Ivanko three times, then kills Bierman in a way that looks like suicide, first getting him to strip to his underwear."

"His underwear?"

She hadn't known about that part, so I had to go back and fill in. Then I said, "It would be awfully hard to manage. I think I might be able to come a little closer to what actually happened."

She finished her coffee, put the cup down, sat up straight in her chair, and folded her hands on the table in front of her, waiting for me to explain.

THIRTEEN

Bierman was never in the house, I told her. Never on West Seventy-fourth Street, never anywhere near Manhattan the night of the murder. Bierman never left the apartment on Coney Island Avenue, and in fact he couldn't leave, because he was already dead.

Sometime late that afternoon the third man pays Bierman a visit. He's been there before, and this time he brings along a bolt from the hardware store and the tools he'll need to install it. First, though, he manages to catch Bierman unawares.

He overpowers him, or simply knocks him out. He strips Bierman down to his underwear, props him up in the corner of the room where he'll be least visible to someone entering the apartment, presses the butt of a little Italian automatic into his hand, sticks the business end of the gun in his mouth, wraps his own hand over Bierman's hand, and gives the trigger a squeeze.

It's just one shot from a small gun, and there's not much likelihood anyone'll take any notice of it. It's a pistol, not a revolver, so he could even have a suppressor on it. But even without a suppressor it's not all that loud, and both their hands are clutching it, his and Bierman's, and that should muffle the report some. And it's not like it's a whole string of shots, and there's nobody screaming, no doors slamming. It's just one little gunshot, about as noisy as blowing up a paper bag and smashing it with your fist. But it's enough to kill Bierman.

You'd think he'd be in a hurry to get out of there, but you'd be wrong. He's pleased with himself, exhilarated by how well it went with Bierman. First thing he does is put on Bierman's shirt and pants. It might be messy later on, in fact he'll want to make sure it's messy later on, and wearing Bierman's clothes serves a double purpose, keeping his own clothes clean and providing some solid physical evidence for the cops. He leaves his own clothes in Bierman's closet, where they'll be handy later on.

If Bierman's body is discovered before he can get back to the apartment, well, that'll be inconvenient, but nobody's going to look twice at his clothes in Bierman's closet. They'll look twice, or even three times, at the body in the corner, an obvious suicide, you'd think, but what happened to the gun? Maybe they'd decide it wasn't suicide, maybe they'd figure someone else wandered in, found Bierman dead, and walked off with the gun.

But the odds are nobody's going to find the body. He'll be back in a matter of hours, and then he'll be ready to return the gun to Bierman's hand.

Until then, though, he has a use for it.

But first he has that bolt he bought earlier, and a drill or an awl to make holes for the screws, and a screwdriver. It doesn't take him long to mount the bolt, and when he's finished he takes his tools with him and walks out the door, leaving the bolt unfastened and locking the door with the key—he's got Bierman's keys now, and he's wearing Bierman's shirt and jeans, and no neighbor's going to give him a second glance.

Then, as arranged, he goes to meet Ivanko.

Ivanko has never met Bierman, doesn't know Bierman exists. Ivanko knows he and his friend are going to pull a job, and there's money in it, and an opportunity to have some fun.

The friend, the third man, drives. He has a car, although he may tell Ivanko it's stolen. He drives, and finds a place to park.

He has a key to the house on West Seventy-fourth Street. As soon as he's inside he opens the closet door, where he keys in the code to deactivate the burglar alarm. They go through the house, and he guides Ivanko, tells him where to look, what to take. Meanwhile he holds the pillowcases so

Ivanko can drop in the loot. That way he's not touching anything, not leaving his prints anywhere. He encourages Ivanko to be messy, dumping drawers, pawing through their contents, because he doesn't mind if Ivanko leaves prints here and there. But Ivanko's not entirely unprofessional, and may even be wearing surgical gloves. That's annoying, he'd like a print or two left behind, but for the time being it can't be helped.

Then they're done, and waiting for the Hollanders to return. Now he has to keep Ivanko eager to stick around for the last part. They've got two sacks of money and valuables, and Ivanko would have to feel the natural impulse to get out while the getting's good, to take the money (and jewelry and silver) and run.

She's pretty and she's hot-looking, he tells Ivanko, and you can have her and do anything you want to her. Anything you want, anything at all.

Knows what to tell him, knows how to keep him right at the end of his leash.

Then the Hollanders come home. . . .

And it's really not that difficult. He killed earlier that day, killed Bierman, and that went just as smooth as silk. He didn't mind doing it again. Sort of looked forward to it, actually, had been looking forward to it all along. Nothing tricky this time, no gun in the mouth, no hand clamped over Hollander's hand, because this is supposed to look like what it is, a murder committed by burglars. And so he shoots Byrne Hollander twice in the chest. For insurance (and perhaps because he likes it, pulling the trigger, feeling the little gun buck in his hand) he fires a third round into Hollander's temple.

Smooth as silk, easy as pie.

And it's time to let Ivanko off his leash. Take the gloves off, he tells him. You want to feel everything, don't you? Wearing gloves, be as stupid as wearing a rubber. You don't think you're going to catch AIDS from her, do you? Nice respectable married lady?

Except Ivanko still doesn't leave prints, he's ripping cloth and grabbing skin, nothing that will take a print. Oh, he'll leave his DNA, but a set of prints would be so handy. If they knew who it was before they found the bodies . . .

Don't forget the best part, he says, and hands Ivanko the fireplace poker. Imagine it's burning hot, he says. Go ahead, he says, you know what you want to do.

And Ivanko takes the poker. It's metal, it ought to take a print.

And how'll he finish up? Shoot her? He'd reloaded after killing Bierman earlier, had a full clip when the Hollanders walked in, but he's used three bullets on Hollander and he'll need more when they get back to Brooklyn. He has a spare clip in the car, he could always reload, but how would that look?

Besides, Hollander hadn't bled much, and it would be good to have some blood now. Blood on him, blood on Ivanko.

He'd brought the knife from the kitchen, just in case. Wicked-looking thing. Let Ivanko do her? He'd probably enjoy it, the pervert. On the other hand, he'd probably fuck it up. You wanted something done right, you did it yourself. And he didn't mind doing it himself, might find it interesting, might even get, oh, not a thrill, but a certain sort of satisfaction out of it. . . .

Done.

He'd had the presence of mind to pick up the three ejected cartridge cases while Ivanko was thrusting into the woman. Picked up Ivanko's gloves, too. Now what? Reset the burglar alarm? No, that made no sense. Just walk out the front door and pull it shut after you. Stroll off without a care in the world, two roommates looking for a coin laundry. Young men on the way up, putting in long hours, stuck with doing their wash in the middle of the night.

He drives to Brooklyn, while the woman's blood dries on his shirt and pants. He's careful not to get any on the upholstery, and hopes Ivanko exercises similar care.

Maybe he should have shot Ivanko and left him at the scene. Would have been easy, the way he was grunting and straining like an animal. He never would have seen it coming, could have died in the act. Wasn't that how men were always saying they wanted to go?

Shoot him and leave him and what message are you leaving? Bierman got disgusted and killed his partner? And then went all the way home and got depressed enough to kill himself? And, if you shoot Ivanko in the act, what do you do with the woman? Shoot her? Cut her throat? You were so disgusted with Bierman that you killed him to keep him from raping the woman, and then you were so disgusted with her that you cut her throat?

Better the way he'd done it, with the two of them driving to Brooklyn, where Ivanko knows there's a kindly old Jew waiting to pay them top dollar for the jewelry and sterling.

He gets there, he parks the car, he unlocks the door and ushers Ivanko inside. Does Ivanko wonder how come he has keys? No, because this is a friend's apartment, one he uses sometimes, and a handy place to sort their loot and divvy up the cash before they go to the fence's place, which is only a few blocks away.

They're inside, and he points Ivanko toward the bedroom. "Open a window," he says, steering him toward it, moving up behind him. Does Ivanko see Bierman's body out of the corner of his eye? Before he can turn, before he can do anything, there's a gun pressed against his back and two bullets fired into him.

And one more in his temple. How's that for symmetry?

The ejected cartridge casings roll around on the floor. They can stay wherever they wind up. No prints on them anyway. Should he press a finger of Bierman's to one of them? No, not worth the bother. He returns the gun to Bierman's hand, poses the stiffening Bierman just as he wants him.

Then, quickly, he returns to the kitchen, fastens the bolt he installed earlier. Strips off his shirt—Bierman's shirt, originally, and now Bierman's once more—and tosses it on the floor. Unbuttons Bierman's jeans, steps out of them, leaves them. The clothes smell of Bierman, the animal stink of his crotch and armpits, so they're probably swarming with his DNA, and wet with her blood. Perfect. Just perfect, nails the lid on tight.

He gets his own clothes from the closet and puts them on. Empties one of the Hollander pillowcases, puts the chest of sterling flatware on the table in the kitchen, strews the rest of the booty on the floor, wads the case itself and tosses it in a corner. Leaves the other pillowcase on the floor, its contents undisturbed.

Has he forgotten anything? Missed anything, left anything undone? He looks around quickly, sees nothing amiss. Still wearing his sheer surgeon's gloves, he raises the window in the bedroom, steps out into the rubbish-strewn back yard. Closes the window. By the time he is back on the street his gloves are off, tucked away in a pocket. Later he'll discard them, along with the brass cartridge casings he picked up from the Hollanders' living room floor.

The car's where he left it. He pulls away from the curb. Is there any reason to get rid of the car? He could, but it should be more than enough if he just takes it to the car wash, lets them give it the full treatment. Detail it, make it showroom-new.

Or maybe not. Trace evidence won't matter, not really. Nobody is going to look at his car, or at him. His crime is perfect, and brilliantly so, the case essentially closed before it can be opened. The criminals, tied inextricably to their crime by heaps of solid physical evidence, have already been punished. And he's nowhere near them, and in no way involved.

Perfect.

FOURTEEN

When I stopped talking she sat for a while, back straight, eyes lowered. I was starting to wonder if I'd unwittingly hypnotized her, or if she'd slipped into some sort of fugue state, when she looked up at me. She said, "If that's the way it happened . . ."

"It's just guesswork on my part," I said. "An educated guess is still a guess."

"I understand that. If, though. **If** that's how it happened, the burglary was just . . . incidental. The third man, the man who engineered it all, didn't even keep what he took from this house."

"He left it at the apartment in Brooklyn."

"As part of the stage setting," she said. "My mother's jewelry, the family silver. So the point wasn't what they could take from the house."

"Ivanko thought it was."

"But that was just to get him to play his part.

And the other one, did he even know there was going to be a burglary? No, there wouldn't have been any reason for him to know anything. He never even heard of my parents, never knew anything. He was dead before it started and now the whole world thinks he killed three people and committed suicide."

I thought about Bierman, whose criminal career peaked with subway-fare-beating. "I don't think he was much concerned about what people thought," I said. "Anyway, he's beyond caring now."

She nodded slowly. "This was very carefully planned," she said.

"If it happened the way I just sketched it out, yes. Very carefully planned."

"He had a key. They said he wouldn't have needed a key, that a skilled burglar could have gotten in without one."

"If there was a third man," I said, "I'm sure he had a key."

"Because he wouldn't have left it to chance."

"That's right."

"And he knew how to turn off the burglar alarm."

"I would assume so, yes."

"They said my parents forgot to set it. I couldn't believe that. They always set the alarm. When I was a teenager I went through an idealistic stage when I didn't even think doors should be locked, let alone protected by alarm systems. I thought it showed a sad lack of faith in one's fellow man." She shook her head ruefully. "I got over it, but it made my parents crazy while it lasted. They absolutely insisted I set the alarm when I left the house, no matter what other head-in-the-clouds crap I spouted. Believe me, they didn't leave the house without setting the alarm." She frowned. "But the code's a secret. Nobody knows it."

"One-zero-one-seven," I said, and her mouth fell open. "You'll want to change it, if you haven't already. Somebody told me, somebody who wouldn't be expected to know. There are always more people than you think who know our private codes and passwords. I don't know where he got the key and I don't know who gave him the four-digit password, but neither would have proved all that elusive to a resourceful man. And we know this man's resourceful."

"Who is he?"

"I don't know."

"And why? The only thing he accomplished was that they died. They suffered horribly and they died." She looked at me. "Was that the whole point of this? To make them dead?"

"It looks that way."

Always the beautiful answer that asks the more beautiful question.

"But . . . but **why?**"

"That's one of the questions I've been trying to answer. I came here today so I could ask you some of the questions I've been asking other people."

"Ask me anything," she said.

Always the beautiful questions. I asked the easy ones first, saved the harder ones for later on. Did her father have any enemies, anyone who might have felt justly or otherwise that he'd cheated him in a business deal, that he'd represented him ineffectually? Had he had a serious falling-out with an old friend or colleague? I found a dozen or two variations on the theme, looking for someone with something against either or both of the Hollanders, and if such a person existed, Kristin didn't know about it.

Then the questions got more personal.

She said, "Their marriage?" and frowned, giving the question some thought. "I guess it was what every marriage ought to be like," she said. "They loved each other, they cared for each other. They had private space in their lives, she had her writing and he had his work, his legal practice, but they spent most of their time together and they delighted in it. I don't know what else to say about it. Is that what you meant?"

"Was the marriage ever in trouble?"

"I think it was stressful for them when Sean died. I was thirteen and a half, so it was ten years ago this summer. It seems so long ago sometimes, and there are other times when it really does seem like only yesterday. I don't understand time."

"Nobody does."

"It was so totally senseless, what happened to Sean. Nobody gets killed playing baseball. The worst that happens is you pull a muscle, or skin your knee sliding into a base. It seemed completely unreal to me. And I kept seeing him."

"He would appear to you?"

"No, nothing like that. I guess that happens, I don't disbelieve in it, but it never happened to me. No, it was just my perceptions. I would think I saw him on the street, or in a crowd at school, any-where, and then it would turn out to be somebody else, somebody who didn't look like him at all. You're nodding. I guess that happens a lot."

"I was about the same age when my father died. Fourteen, I was. And it was sudden, too. He was riding between two cars on the subway and must have lost his footing."

"That's terrible."

"For a couple of years afterward I had the same experience you described. Certain I was seeing him, even though I knew it was impossible. Well, it's somebody who looks a lot like him, I'd tell my-self, and if I got close there'd be no resemblance there at all."

"I guess it's the mind's way of getting from de-nial to acceptance."

"Something like that. You said it was a strain for your parents. A strain on the marriage?"

"Neither of them ever moved out, and they didn't stop speaking. I was just the age to be super-aware of things without knowing what they amounted to. I was afraid that they were going to separate, to get divorced, but I think it was just that I'd lost my brother so now I was scared I was going to lose everybody else." Her eyes widened. "That's what happened, though, isn't it? It just took longer than I thought, but I'm all alone now."

She said the line entirely without affect, and I felt a chill.

I said, "Did either of them ever have an affair?"

"I've wondered," she said. "That's disgusting, isn't it? Wondering about your own parents that way. But I guess everybody does. Wonder, I mean. I don't know that everybody has an affair, although I gather most men do at one time or another."

That might have been provocative, flirtatious, if she'd lifted an eyebrow as she said it, or given me a look, or just put something extra into the words. But there was none of that. This wasn't about me, nor was it about the two of us.

"I'm not supposed to know this," she began, and then stopped talking and lowered her eyes to her clasped hands. I waited, and she took a breath and started in again. "My mother had an affair," she said. She spoke softly, and I had to strain to make out the words. "After Sean died. She was seeing someone. I knew it but I didn't know it, do you know what I mean?"

"Yes."

"I didn't know who it was," she said, "and I forgot about it. They were both fine, their marriage was fine, and if I ever thought about it I told myself I was mistaken. And then he died."

"The man who . . ."

"Yes. I was sitting quietly with a book and they must not have known I was in the room. This man had died, and he lived in Florida, and that's where the funeral was going to be. And my father asked my mother if she would have gone to the funeral if it was in New York. And she said she didn't know, she hadn't seen him in years, and would it bother my father if she went? Because she wouldn't go if he didn't want her to. And he said he didn't know how he would feel, and they both agreed it was all too hypothetical, and they dropped the subject and went into the other room, and they never did realize that I was there."

"And that was the man your mother had the affair with."

"Yes, I'm sure of it. From the whole tone of the conversation. But even if there was somebody else, a jealous husband or a vengeful lover, they'd know him, wouldn't they?"

"Who?"

"My parents. If he was the third man, if he was waiting here for them, they would recognize him. I mean, even if he wore a mask—"

"No, he wouldn't have been wearing a mask."

"Then wouldn't they know who he was?"

"He didn't intend to leave them alive."

"I know that," she said, "but what about his partner? If my parents walk in and my father says, 'Hey, Fred, what are you doing here?'"

"Ivanko would have to wonder," I agreed. "And that's the problem with the notion of the third man being an enemy, or anyone with a personal motive."

"They'd know him."

"Unless the third man was hired for the occasion," I said, and rejected the idea as soon as I'd spoken it. "No, this was no hired hand. It was expert, it was well-planned, but it wasn't professional."

"What's the difference?"

"A pro wouldn't have done anything that elaborate," I explained. "He might have tried to make it look like a burglary, but he wouldn't have brought a helper along, and certainly not an amateur. He'd have broken in, killed your parents the minute they walked into the house, and got out of there. He wouldn't bother setting up a couple of dead men in Brooklyn to take the rap for him, because all he had to do was go home. He'd be sitting in front of his big-screen TV in St. Louis or Sarasota while the police got nowhere investigating the killing."

"So it was someone who knew them," she said, "but someone they didn't know."

"Maybe it was someone you know."

"Me?"

"Is there anyone you could think of?"

"Anyone I know who would want to kill my parents?"

"A boyfriend whose attentions they discouraged," I suggested. "Anybody who might see them as standing in the way of a closer relationship with you."

"I'm not going with anyone," she said. "I haven't really been seeing anybody since Peter and I broke up."

"Peter."

"Peter Meredith. We broke up last fall. I was living with him on East Tenth Street and we were talking about moving to Brooklyn, but we broke up instead."

"Brooklyn."

"He knew some people, artists, who were going to chip in and buy a house in Williamsburg together. The building was a mess, and the idea was that everybody would work on the renovations together. There'd be three couples, and we'd each have a floor to ourselves and share the basement."

"On the order of an urban commune?"

"More like a do-it-yourself condo. I was intrigued at first. The neighborhood put me off a little, but not too much, because you knew it was getting gentrified in a serious way, with a steady stream of new people moving in. And prices were going up, too, so if we waited and tried to do the same thing a year later, well, we wouldn't be able to afford it, not in that neighborhood, anyway. They drew up papers and I brought them for my father to look over, and he said the numbers worked. He had a few minor changes to suggest, just so everything would be spelled out right from a legal standpoint, but he said basically it was all right. If it was what I really wanted to do."

"And it wasn't?"

She shook her head. "It's one thing to live with somebody in a rented apartment, his apartment, and another thing to buy a house together. That was much more of a commitment than I was ready to make. I liked living with him, and we'd have stayed together if it hadn't been for the whole business with the house. The way it worked out, I moved back here and Peter went in with his friends and bought the house."

"You weren't able to keep the apartment yourself?"

"It was his place to begin with. Anyway, I didn't like living there. It was all the way east in Alphabet City, and it's safe there now, not like it used to be, but it's so out of the way that it takes forever to get anywhere. I wanted to get my own place eventually, but why not live at home in the meantime and save up for something nice?"

"Did your parents get on well with Peter?"

"They liked him all right. Mom thought he was

a little head-in-the-clouds for me, and I suppose he was, but she liked him. They both liked him."

"And how did he feel about the breakup?"

"Relieved, I think, by the time I finally moved out."

"It took you a while?"

She nodded. "I didn't want to rush into the house in Williamsburg, but I didn't want to rush out of the relationship, either. For a while I thought we could work something out."

"How?"

"That's the thing, how do you compromise? Like when one person wants to have a child and the other one doesn't. You can't have half a kid."

"No."

"We went for couple counseling, and it was an interesting process, but we kept butting up against the same brick wall. He wanted to go in on the house more than he wanted to be with me, and I wasn't ready for that. I said buying a house was something married people did, and he said then let's get married, and I said you don't want to get married, you just want to buy a house, and anyway I don't want to get married, and if I got married I **still** wouldn't want to buy the house. And by the time we got through pointing this out to each other, well, we didn't really want to be together anymore. When I moved out it was a relief to both of us."

"Still, it had to be emotionally wrenching."

"I suppose so."

"Did he call you? Try to get you to come back to him?"

"No, nothing like that. I honestly think he was more relieved than I was to be out of it. And he was busy, first getting the money together and then moving in and doing all the work. If he missed me at all, that would take his mind off it."

"I see."

"And if it didn't, well, the other people in the house were all his friends. I'm sure they'd have been happy to fix him up with somebody who'd fit in."

"The way you didn't fit in?"

"You sound like the shrink, the counselor. And I guess I didn't fit in, because they all wanted something and I didn't want it. Anyway, what would I want with a house in Williamsburg? I have a house in Manhattan, all to myself."

Her voice broke on the final phrase, and she turned from me, rising and going to the sink for a glass of water. From the back I saw her shoulders rise and fall, but her sobbing was a silent affair. She drank a whole glass of water, and when she came back her brow was untroubled and her eyes were dry.

She hadn't heard from Peter, or of him, but he'd called after her parents were killed, called to express his sympathy and, like everyone else, asked if there was anything he could do.

"But what could he do? What could anybody do? People always say that, and there's never anything anybody can do."

"Your parents had met him," I said.

"Yes, of course, on quite a few occasions."

"He'd been to this house."

"Many times. Oh, no. I know what you're thinking, and it's impossible."

"You're sure of that?"

"You would be, too," she said, "if you knew him, or even knew anything about him. Peter is just about the gentlest person going. He's a vegetarian, he won't even wear leather shoes."

"Hitler was a vegetarian," I pointed out. Elaine, a vegetarian herself with a closet full of leather shoes, would not have been proud of me.

Kristin didn't seem to notice. "Peter would open windows to let flies out. We had cockroaches on Tenth Street, and he kept trying to find a nonlethal way to get rid of them. He wouldn't let me use glue traps because of the way they suffered, stuck there wiggling their little feelers. It bothered him. Does that sound like the man in your scenario?"

"Not really, no."

"And didn't the third man change clothes with the first person he killed? Didn't he wear his shirt and jeans and get blood on them?"

"I can't swear to it," I said, "but it certainly looks that way."

"The man he killed," she said. "The one who committed suicide. What did he look like?"

"I never saw him. From his picture in the paper—"

"Not his face, I saw the picture myself. I didn't want to look at it, but how could I avoid it? I saw both their pictures. What kind of build did he have, that's what I'm asking."

"Ordinary, medium height, medium build."

"Peter is five-nine," she said, "and weighs two hundred and sixty pounds. Do you think he could have buttoned that shirt, or even gotten it around his shoulders? Or squeezed into those jeans?"

"No."

"I haven't seen him in almost a year, so I suppose he could have lost some weight, but . . ."

"But not that much."

"I don't see how. His weight was something he was working on, but he'd been working on it all his life. Anyway, his shrink thought it was more important to get him to accept himself as he was than to sweat off a few pounds." She smiled gently. "And that was one time I agreed with him. Peter was a very sweet man, a very sexy man. He carried the weight well. But not well enough for him to fit into that man's clothes."

So Peter Meredith wasn't our mystery man, and there weren't any other candidates that I could see. Kristin wanted to know what was next.

"I don't know," I said. "I don't see how much

more I can do. I think what I probably **should** do is apologize for taking up this much of your time and then quit trying to make something out of nothing."

"That's not what it sounded like, something out of nothing."

"No," I said, "it sounds good, what I put together, but what is it besides smoke and mirrors? I certainly haven't got anything I could take to the cops. I still have a few friends on the force, and they'd take the trouble to hear me out, but I can't think of anybody who'd be inclined to reopen the case on the strength of what I've got."

"So you'll just give up?"

"Probably not," I admitted. "I've got a stubborn streak, and time on my hands. The best thing would be if somebody hired me to round up lost relatives for a family reunion. That would give me a good reason to stop poking around in a case that's not going anywhere."

"Is that what you want?" she said. "Because I'll hire you."

She was taken aback when I said she couldn't. Early on she'd sort of assumed that was what I was building toward, and it hadn't taken her long to decide to go along with it. And now that she'd come right out and made the offer, I was turning her down.

"I don't understand," she said. "It's what you

do, isn't it? And you've already been doing it, without a client, and not getting paid for it. Now I'm prepared to be your client, and you don't want to take the case."

"You'd be wasting your money, Kristin."

"So? You've been wasting your time. If you can waste your time, why can't I waste my money?"

"I surrendered my private investigator's license," I said.

"Why would you do that? Did you decide to retire?"

She might as well know; maybe it would help dissuade her. "They were threatening to take it away from me," I said. "I was helping a friend, and I had to cut some corners. That got a few official noses out of joint, especially since the friend I helped is a career criminal."

"Really? A career criminal?"

"Oh, very much so," I said. "A certifiable bad guy."

"But he's your friend."

"Yes."

A light came into her eyes. She said, "There's no conflict of interest here, is there? I mean, your friend's not the third man, is he?"

"He stands about six-four and outweighs your friend Peter," I said, "so I don't think Bierman's shirt would fit him."

"That's reassuring. But I still want to know who killed my parents. If I can't hire you, who should I hire?"

FIFTEEN

I started to tell her she'd have trouble finding anybody to take her case," I told Elaine, "but I stopped myself when I realized it wasn't true. Ray likes to say that there's no case so bad you can't find some lawyer who'll take it, and God knows that's true of private detectives. If you'll write out a check, someone will be happy to accept it."

"And did she write out a check?"

"I told her cash would be better. She gave me a thousand dollars, and I said I'd let her know when that ran out, but that it probably wouldn't unless I got results or incurred heavy expenses. When it's over I'll tell her if I think I have more money coming, and she can pay it or not, depending on how she feels about it. And I gave her an assignment. I told her to go through the articles the police returned to her and see if anything's missing."

"Not because you think some cop took a bracelet home to his wife."

"They generally don't, not in a major murder case. No, I thought the killer might have kept a souvenir. Sometimes they do. What else? I told her not to expect written reports or expense accounts, and suggested that she'd be better off not expecting anything. I wasn't working for her, I said, just doing her a favor, just as she'd be doing me a favor by giving me a gift of a thousand dollars."

"Same as in the old days."

"Pretty much. It was okay for a while there, having a license, being respectable, keeping books and making out bills. But I think I like it better this way."

"Well, it suits you. But that's a pretty small advance, isn't it?"

"I don't know, it strikes me as a pretty handsome gift. Hundred-dollar bills, ten of them."

"Not very much money, though. A thousand dollars."

"There was a time when you could buy a decent car with it, and there'll probably come a time when that's the price of a decent cup of coffee. But right now you're right, it's not very much."

"The work you've already done," she said. "How much would that be worth?"

"Not a red cent," I said. "I didn't have a client."

"If you had."

"I don't know. I put in some hours here and there."

"More than a thousand dollars' worth."

"Maybe."

"It's not as though we need the money," she said.

"No."

"Though we can always find a use for it."

"We always do."

"Matt? You're not going to fall in love with this one, are you?"

"I'm already in love." She didn't say anything, not out loud, anyway, and I said, "No, I'm not going to fall in love with her. She's decent and bright and pretty, and she's forty years younger than I am, and she couldn't be less interested. And, to tell you the truth, neither could I."

"That's interesting," she said. "But let me ask you another question, and you can take all the time you need answering it." She tilted her head, licked her lip, lowered her voice. "Is there anything you could be interested in? Anything you can think of?"

I thought of something.

Later she rolled over and propped herself up on an elbow.

"Thirty-nine," she said.

"On a scale of one to what?"

"Silly man. That wasn't a rating, it was a correction. You're thirty-nine years older than she is, not forty."

"Well, I have tell you," I said. "I feel younger already."

SIXTEEN

He is five feet eleven inches tall, and his weight has remained between 165 and 170 pounds for the last fifteen of his thirty-seven years. That makes him the same height and weight as the late Jason Paul Bierman, but that is less of a coincidence than it might at first appear. It might have been coincidental if circumstances had thrown him and Bierman together first, if their roles in the human drama had preceded his awareness of their superficial resemblance. But no, it was the other way around. He had picked Bierman out of the great sea of humanity, noting his height and weight, his build. Why, he'd thought, they could wear each other's clothes.

(Bierman, appearing in court, charged with trying to sneak under a subway turnstile. Charges dismissed, Bierman leaving the courtroom, looking vague, uncertain. He catches him

as he hits the street, takes him by the arm. Bierman cringes, no doubt assuming he's being arrested again. "Mr. Bierman? Jason? Relax, my
friend. I think perhaps I can help you." Bierman
trying the couch, choosing the chair. Closing his
eyes, sharing his hopes and fears. Learning the
gospel. "Jason, what do you get?" "You get what
you get, Doc.")

And so he'd selected Bierman. Good luck for
him. Bad luck for Bierman.

Or was it bad luck? Bierman had been one of
life's losers, a man who asked little of life and
got less. You never got more than you asked for,
he liked to tell people, and there was nothing
wrong with asking for all you wanted. You may
go to the ocean with a teaspoon or a bucket, he
liked to say; the ocean does not care.

Bierman took a teaspoon, and held it out to
the ocean—upside-down.

So his life had never amounted to anything,
and in death, in addition to serving as a part of a
Grand Design (which, to be fair, would have
meant precious little to Bierman, even if he'd
been aware of it, which he manifestly was not),
in addition to that, why, Bierman had achieved
in death what he had never achieved in life.

The sad bastard was famous.

He is at his computer now, scanning a newsgroup he has taken to visiting lately, alt.crime.
serialkillers. There's been a spirited exchange
of posts recently between someone who has an

unwholesome amount of information to share about the Green River killer and someone else, similarly well informed, who claims to be the Green River killer. The likelihood that there's any truth in the claim strikes him as somewhere on the low side of infinitesimal, but that doesn't make the posts any less interesting to scan.

And yes, there are some new additions to the string of posts about Bierman. Technically, of course, Bierman is a far cry from a serial killer. Three corpses, all of them slain in a single night and in connection with a single crime, do not a serial killer make. You'd have to knock off unrelated individuals over a span of time, though just how many it takes is a matter of some dispute, and indeed is perennially disputed on alt. crime.serialkillers.

If Bierman's anything, he's a mass murderer, like the disgruntled postal employees who bring an automatic weapon to work and lose it big time. Three, though, is on the thin side. You might need a little more in the way of mass in order to make it as a genuine mass murderer.

(As a matter of fact, Bierman is no killer at all, and probably lived out his brief span without so much as giving anyone a bloody nose, but none of these people know that. They all assume Bierman killed the three victims credited to him, and some of them, mirabile dictu, are willing to add other victims to his string.)

He reads the post, nodding, smiling, shaking

his head. The minds of the various members of the newsgroup, revealed in their posts, never fail to fascinate him. Some write with evident admiration of the notorious murderers of our time, comparing the tallies and techniques of Bundy, of Kemper, of Henry Lee Lucas. Others take a strong moral stand, draping it over a fierce desire to punish; they're death penalty enthusiasts, and rejoice whenever it's applied to one of the subjects of newsgroup gossip. And, of course, there are those in both camps who are deliberately striking a pose, playing a part, feigning contempt or admiration for reasons one can only guess.

He never posts. He's tempted sometimes, when he's inspired with just the words to tweak these clowns. But what, really, is the point? He doesn't post, he lurks. To post is human, to lurk divine.

Bierman, he thinks, I've made you immortal. Living, you were a walking dead man. Dead, you live!

His wristwatch, set to beep not on the hour but a precise ten minutes before it, tells him it's 12:50. He reads the last of the Bierman posts, clicks Mark All Read, and signs off. His screensaver comes on, showing a city skyline at night, forever changing as lights go on and off, on and off.

He sits back, stretches. His shirt is unbuttoned at the throat, his tie loose. He reaches under his collar and produces a mottled pink disc an inch and a quarter in diameter, perhaps an eighth of an inch thick, holed in the center. It's stone, rhodochrosite, and cool to the touch, and it hangs around his neck on a thin gold chain. He rubs the smooth stone between his thumb and forefinger, savoring the feel of it.

He tucks it inside his shirt, buttons the top button of his shirt, tightens his tie. He checks the knot in the mirror and it's fine, perfect.

And he can feel the pink stone disc, smooth and cool against his chest. . . .

Time to go to work.

SEVENTEEN

So we got us a client," T J said. "Damn! We on the clock, Doc."

"Well, it's barely ticking," I said. "I think the main reason I took her money was to keep her from giving it to somebody else."

"You clever, though, way you work things out. Girl wants to hire us, thinks her cousin did this bad thing. You put her mind at rest, pat her on the head and send her on her way. Then you turn around and get the rich cousin to hire us. We gonna work for one of the cousins, might as well be the one with the money."

"That's right, I almost forgot. Our client started out as the designated suspect."

"You happen to tell her that?"

"It slipped my mind."

We were at the Morning Star. I'd slept later than usual, and Elaine had left for the gym by the time I'd shaved and showered. There was coffee left, and I poured a cup and called T J. "If you haven't had breakfast," I said, "why don't you meet me downstairs in ten minutes." He'd been up since six, he said, when a couple down the hall had a louder-than-usual drunken argument, and he'd gone out and eaten, then went home and booted up his computer and got on-line. But he'd gladly keep me company.

I was working on an omelet, and he was keeping me company with a side of home fries and a toasted bagel and a large orange juice. He dabbed his lips with a napkin and said, "Slipped your mind. Probably a good thing. There any case left, now that we on it?"

"It's hard to know where to go with it. I wish there was someone with a motive. It's a lot of trouble to go through for no reason."

"Stole some stuff," he said.

"More like borrowing it. Moved it from Manhattan to Brooklyn, where the cops recovered it."

"All of it?"

"There's a thought," I said. "He might have held on to something, our mystery man."

"Might be why he did the job in the first place. Say he wants one thing, but he doesn't want anybody to know he took it."

"Like what?"

"How I know, Beau? Something real valuable, some diamond, some priceless painting."

"It would be on the insurance schedule," I said, "and it would be evident it was missing."

"Something else, then. Some legal papers, some photos or letters, kind of thing people kill to get back."

"Why not just take whatever it was," I said, "and go home? Why kill the Hollanders?"

"To keep everybody from finding out you took whatever it was."

I thought about it. "I don't know," I said. "It sounds too complicated. Whoever did this, he put it together carefully and didn't mind killing four people to carry it off. I can't think what the Hollanders could have had in the house that would have warranted that kind of effort."

"Guess you right," he said. "Just came to me is all."

"I wish something would come to me," I said. "Looking at the victims doesn't seem to lead anywhere. They led a blameless life, everybody adored and respected them, and they loved each other. I wonder."

"Wonder what?"

"Maybe I've been looking at the wrong victims."

"Only victims we got," he said.

"I can think of two more."

It didn't take him long. "In the house in Brooklyn," he said. "Bierman and Ivanko. You sayin' he went through all that to waste those two dudes?"

"No, they weren't the point, just the means to the end."

"Use 'em and lose 'em. But he had to find 'em first—that what you gettin' at?"

"There has to be a connection. Not so much with Bierman, whose role was essentially passive."

" 'Bout as passive as it gets," he said. "All Bierman did was get hisself killed."

"Bierman may not have known him at all."

"Dude comes to the door, tells Bierman he's the exterminator, come to spray for roaches. Bierman lets him in and it's a done deal, Bierman's chillin' in the corner and the dude's out the door, wearin' Bierman's shirt an' pants."

"But Ivanko was in on the play," I said. "Even if the last act came as a surprise to him."

"Dude comes to Ivanko, tells him he's got a deal lined up."

" 'Big profit, low risk, here's the key, here's the alarm code . . . ' "

"Can't have that conversation with a dude 'less you know he be down for it. How's he know that about Ivanko?"

"He did three years in Green Haven for burglary. Maybe that's where they met."

"You think the dude's an ex-con?"

I thought about it. "Somehow I don't," I said. "You pick up a few things in prison, but one you tend to lose there is the sense that the law can't touch you, because it already has. The guy who orchestrated all this still thinks he's bulletproof."

"Might have got his hands dirty, though."

"I don't think this was the first time he broke the law. Whether or not he's done time, he could know people who have. Ivanko's got no living relatives, as far as I can tell, and his mother's old apartment's his last known address. He must have been living somewhere when he broke into the Hollanders', but the police found him in Brooklyn before they could find out where he was staying."

"An' then they stopped lookin'."

"That might be a place to start," I said. "If we're looking at Ivanko, you know who we ought to talk to?"

"If you thinkin' same as me, it's too early to call him. He be sleepin'."

"Danny Boy," I said. "It's his neighborhood, too. Poogan's is two blocks from the Hollander house. I'll go see him tonight."

"And between now and then?"

"The gun," I said. "Somebody stole it from a Central Park West psychiatrist's office."

"Maybe the gun was ready to be stolen."

I gave him a look. "The way it appeared on the surface," I said, "Bierman was the shooter, so it seemed logical to assume he brought the gun. Which meant either he stole it himself or someone else stole it and sold it to him."

"But all Bierman really got," he said, "was the bullet."

"Right, so somebody else supplied the gun, and it wouldn't have been Ivanko or it would have been in his hand during the burglary and not his partner's."

"Ivanko coulda had two guns. Didn't need both, so he kept one and gave the other to the mystery man."

"Ivanko didn't have a gun on him when they found him," I said, "but the killer could always have taken it off his body on his way out. Simplest explanation, though, is that there was only one gun, and the man who used it is the man who brought it along."

"The dude himself. Where'd he get it? From the shrink's office?"

"That's where it came from, and he must have been the one who took it."

"Why couldn't he buy it on the street? Not the hardest thing in the world to do, if you know your way around."

"The pillowcases," I said.

"Forgot about them. Same deal in both break-ins, at the shrink's and at the Hollanders'. Stripped the pillows, used the cases to carry off the goods."

"It's a fairly natural thing to do," I said, "and it saves hunting in the closet for tote bags, but when it pops up in both burglaries—"

"Likely the same person done both."

"Seems that way."

"If it was Ivanko, well, ain't burglary what he went away for? Maybe that's something he always did, strip the pillows an' turn the cases into sacks for Santa."

"Full of toys for girls and boys. I can't see Ivanko picking that apartment to break into. It's a doorman building facing the park. Ivanko was street-smart, but street's all he was. How would he get past the doorman?"

"Or even know about the shrink's place to begin with?"

"The burglar knew about the gun. That's the only thing he took from the office, and he took it out of a locked drawer. And he did it without making a mess, because the shrink didn't even miss the gun until a couple of days after the burglary."

"Burglar knew the shrink."

"I think so."

"Knew the office, knew how to get past the doorman. Knew about the gun."

"That's probably what brought him. He wanted a gun, so he broke in and took one."

"From the drawer where he already knew the shrink kept it. He knows the office, then he most likely knows the shrink."

"Stands to reason," I said.

"You tried with the shrink, didn't you? Called him or something?"

"I think a more imaginative approach might yield better results."

"Well," he said, "you imaginative, when you puts your mind to it. That what you gonna do today?"

"I think so."

"I disremember the doctor's name. Keep thinking Adler, but that ain't right."

"Nadler."

"Nadler. There was an Adler 'round the time Freud started the whole thing. What's the matter?"

"Nothing, why?"

"The look on your face. You didn't think I knew that, did you?"

"It's surprising, what you know and what you don't."

He nodded, as if he could accept the truth in that. He said, "Psychoanalysis. Anything to it, you figure?"

"You're asking the wrong person. I think they've gotten away from that approach nowadays, though. Easier to write out a prescription than listen to neurotics all day long."

"Listen to Prozac instead. You don't need me to see Dr. Nadler with you, do you?"

"I think that might be counterproductive."

"All you had to say was no. What I'll do, I'll go to Brooklyn, take a look at that house."

"Really?"

"Talk to people, see what's shakin'."

"Maybe you'll find something I missed," I said. "You want the D train to Avenue M, incidentally. I got off a stop too soon."

"Wrong house. I was thinkin' I'd see how the boyfriend's doin' in Williamsburg. She tell you the address?"

"I didn't ask."

"Not like you. She at least mention the street?"

I searched my memory. "No," I said, "I'm pretty sure she didn't. She'd have to know the street, and probably the house number as well. She was thinking about moving there."

"Boyfriend's name's Peter Meredith?"

"Yes, and he's the original Mr. Five-by-Five and wouldn't kill a cockroach. Where are you going?"

"Don't go nowhere," he said. "Be right back."

He was gone long enough for me to drink another cup of coffee and call for the check, and I was waiting for change when he came back. "I had half of a half a bagel left," he said. "You eat it?"

"The waiter took it."

"Damn," he said. "How I look?"

He'd been wearing knee-length camo shorts and an oversize sweatshirt with the sleeves cut off, and he'd changed into the pants from a black pinstripe suit and a white shirt with short sleeves and a button-down collar. No tie. His black shoes were polished. There were four pens in his shirt pocket, and he was carrying a clipboard.

"You look like a city employee," I said.

"Buildings Department."

"They're usually older," I said. "And thicker through the middle."

"And lighter-complected."

"For the most part. The ones I ran into over the

years all looked as though their feet hurt them some."

"I 'spect mine will," he said, "by the time these shoes take me to 168 Meserole Street."

"What did you do, call Brooklyn Information?"

"Takes too long. They got to answer the phone, and then all they'll tell you is the number. You still got to look it up in a reverse directory or else call it and trick the address out of whoever answers. Who's got time for all that shit?"

"Your time is valuable," I said.

"I got on the Net," he said. "Typed in 'Peter Meredith, Brooklyn,' and got the address, the phone, the zip code. Took two seconds an' I didn't have to talk to nobody."

"Except the address is wrong."

"Say what?"

"Meserole's in Greenpoint, not Williamsburg. The two neighborhoods run into each other, but Meserole's in a part of Greenpoint that got gentrified a while ago. That's not a place to find a low-priced fixer-upper."

"That's Meserole Avenue. They on Meserole Street."

"There's two Meseroles?"

"You'd think one'd be enough," he said. "Look hard, you can probably find some cities don't have any." From the back of the clipboard he produced a sheet of paper showing a map of a few square miles of North Brooklyn. "Printed it out just now," he said, anticipating my question. "See? Here's Meserole **Avenue**, up in Greenpoint, an' this here's Meserole **Street**, runnin' over towards Bushwick Terminal."

I looked at the map. Both Meseroles, street and avenue, crossed Manhattan Avenue, the two intersections a mile and a half apart. It was the sort of thing that drove UPS drivers crazy.

Ray Galindez, a police artist I know, had bought a house in Williamsburg a couple of years ago, and I'd taken the L train out to visit him. The same train would get you close to Meserole Street, but you'd have to stay on an extra three stops. I didn't know the neighborhood—I hadn't even known the street existed—but I could guess why Kristin Hollander thought she'd rather stay in Manhattan.

"I didn't know you could do this," I said. "Print out a street map of Brooklyn."

"Man, you could just as easy print out a street map of Samarkand. You gotta get on-line. You missin' out."

We'd had this conversation before. "I'm too old for it," I told him, not for the first time, and he told me about a man he'd exchanged e-mails with, eighty-eight years old, living in Point Barrow, Alaska, and surfing the Net for hours every day.

"Why would anyone that age live in Point Barrow, Alaska?" I wondered. "And how do you know he's telling the truth? It's probably some nineteen-year-old lesbian posing as an old man."

He rolled his eyes.

"I'm sure I'd have a wonderful time surfing the Net," I said, "and I'd be a better person for it, too. But I don't need to because I've got you to do it for me."

"And to chase out to Brooklyn for you." He looked down at himself, shook his head. "Good thing it out in the middle of nowhere. Don't want nobody I know seein' me lookin' like this."

"Not to worry," I said. "They'd never recognize you."

EIGHTEEN

I should know better, but I tend to form mental images of people I haven't met. I'll hear a voice over the phone and think I know what the person's going to look like.

With Seymour Nadler I'd had his voice—low in pitch, professionally calm—to go by, along with his name and address and profession. I found myself preparing to meet a big bear of a man, balding on top, with a mane of dark hair flowing down over the collar of his open-necked corduroy shirt. His beard, as black as his hair, would need trimming.

Nadler turned out to be about my height, trimly built, clean-shaven, and wearing a gray glen plaid suit and a striped tie. His hair was brown and neatly barbered, and he still had all of it. His eyes, behind horn-rimmed glasses with bifocal lenses, were a washed-out blue. He had a small, thin-lipped mouth, and the hand he offered me felt small in mine.

His office was on the tenth floor, agreeably furnished with older pieces. There was a couch, of course, but there were also several comfortable chairs. The carpet was Oriental, the paintings American primitives. Next to his desk, a computer perched on a black metal stand, the room's only contemporary note. The windows looked out on Central Park.

"I can give you twenty minutes," he said. "My next appointment's at two, and I need ten minutes to prepare."

I told him that would be ample.

"Perhaps you could tell me exactly why you're here," he said. "My claim for losses incurred in the burglary has long since been settled. It took you people long enough, and I can't say I was happy with the amount, but it didn't seem worth going to court over." He smiled. "Although I considered it."

He evidently thought I was working for his insurance company. I hadn't quite said that, but I'd certainly done what I could to create that impression.

"Well," I said, "it's in connection with the gun."

"The gun!"

"Twenty-two-caliber Italian pistol," I said. "Stolen from a desk in your office, if my information's correct."

"I never even reported the loss of the gun."

I paged through my notebook, trying to look puzzled. "You didn't report it to the police? The law requires—"

"To the police, yes, of course, but I'd already submitted my claim to you people before I missed the gun. It wasn't that expensive, and I'd never listed it on my inventory, so I didn't bother to amend my claim. If I'd known you people were going to nickel-and-dime me on the value of my wife's jewelry, you can be sure I would have put the gun on the list."

I held up a hand. "Not my department," I said. "Believe me, I know where you're coming from. Don't quote me on this, but our claims adjusters pull that crap all the time."

"Well," he said, and gave me a sudden smile. We were on the same side now, and I felt pleased with myself for having successfully used psychology on a psychiatrist. "Well, then. What about the gun?"

"It was used recently in a home invasion."

"Yes," he said, frowning. "Yes, I actually did hear about that. A genuinely horrible incident, and it happened not far from here, I believe."

"On West Seventy-fourth Street."

"Yes, not far at all. Two people killed."

"And two more in Brooklyn."

"The perpetrators, yes. Murder and suicide, wasn't it? Interesting. That seems to happen sometimes, you know, with people who run amok and kill people. They conclude the drama by killing themselves." He put the tips of his small fingers together, pursed his lips. "I'm not certain of the mechanism. The conventional wisdom is that they're suddenly struck by the enormity of their actions and commit suicide to punish themselves. But I wonder if it isn't simply that they've run out of people to shoot and still feel the need to go on. So they turn the gun on the only person available, their own self."

His waiting room held several framed diplomas and certificates, but that speech did more to convince me he was a board-certified psychiatrist than a whole wall full of sheepskins.

"Well, that's just speculation," he said, after I'd admired the theory. "But why are you here? Surely the gun's not likely to be returned to me."

"No, I believe it's going to have to stay in a police evidence locker for a long time."

"It can stay there forever," he said. "I certainly don't want it back."

"Did you replace it?"

He shook his head. "I bought it for protection. I never expected to use it, and indeed I never had occasion to remove it from the locked drawer where I kept it." He stroked his chin. "When it was gone, I wondered if I might not have **wanted** it to be gone. Perhaps my distaste for the weapon had somehow contributed to its having been taken away by the burglars."

"How would that work, sir?"

"There's a principle that nothing happens entirely by accident. Some element of unconscious design is involved. This doesn't mean that the victim is always at fault, that's nonsense, but sometimes there's a contributory element. In this instance, the burglars confined themselves to our living quarters. The gun was absolutely the only item removed from my office. That's why it took me as long as it did to know the damned thing was missing."

"So you think the way you felt about the gun . . ."

"It may not have literally induced the burglar to come in here and get the gun," he said. "I can see where you might find that a bit of a stretch, and so might I, truth to tell. But the whole business, well, I certainly didn't feel inclined to go out and buy another damned gun."

I said, "You kept it in your desk."

"That's right."

"That desk you're sitting at?"

"Yes, of course. Do you see another desk in the room?"

"And which drawer would that be?"

He looked at me. "Which drawer? What possible difference can it make which **drawer** I kept it in?"

"Probably none," I said.

"And once again, just why **are** you here? I regret profoundly that a weapon I once owned was the instrument of several people's deaths, but I can't see that it's any of my responsibility."

"Well, that's just it."

"I beg your pardon?"

"There's a question of legal responsibility," I said. "It's possible that the owner of a weapon could be held accountable for the results of the use of that weapon by another party. In other words, someone injured by a bullet from your gun could sue you for letting the gun fall into criminal hands."

"But that's ridiculous! Why not go all the way, why not sue the gun's manufacturer, for God's sake?"

"Matter of fact," I said, "that's been done a couple of times. Made a product-liability case out of it and got a judgment against the weapons manufacturer. It's likely to be overturned on appeal, but—"

"Are you saying somebody who was shot with my gun is going to sue me?"

"Well, in this case the primary victims are all deceased. If a suit were brought, the plaintiff would be an heir of one of the victims."

"That couple's daughter . . ."

I certainly didn't want him calling Kristin, trying to head off a mythical lawsuit. "In this instance," I said, "our concern is that one of the other parties might bring suit."

"You don't mean one of the criminals? Someone breaks into my home, steals my personal property, including my lawfully registered pistol, and kills several people with it, himself included, and you're saying some relative of his is entitled to sue **me**?"

"Dr. Nadler," I said, "anyone can instigate a lawsuit, and some lawyer will always turn up to take the case."

"Ambulance-chasing shysters," he said.

"No suit has been brought, and in the unlikely event that one is, it's almost certain to be dismissed, or resolved in our favor. I'm just here to gather information that will help us nip such a legal action in the bud."

It had been surprisingly easy to stir him up, and it wasn't as easy to calm him down again. I didn't want to waste time, either; he kept looking at his watch, and I knew he'd send me on my way at ten to two.

I asked him again which drawer had held the gun, and had him show me how it was locked and unlocked. The desk was an oval kneehole desk, mahogany, with a tooled leather top. There was a center drawer with three drawers on either side, and the gun had been kept in the second of the three drawers on the right. He was right-handed, he explained, so that would be most convenient, if he were at his desk and needed the gun.

All of the drawers were fitted with locks, although the locking mechanisms on two of them had failed with age and rust. The small skeleton-type key was in the center drawer, with a piece of red yarn tied to it, I guess to make it easier to find.

"During the burglary," I asked, "were all the drawers unlocked? Or only the one with the gun?"

"It was the only one locked in the first place."

"Who knew about the gun?"

"Who knew about it?"

"That you owned it," I said, "and where you kept it."

"No one."

"Your wife? Your receptionist?"

"My wife knew, yes, knew that I owned it but not where it was kept. My wife is somewhat phobic about guns and was opposed to my obtaining one in the first place." He frowned. "I suppose that's one reason I didn't amend the insurance claim. As for Georgia, my receptionist, she wouldn't even have known the gun existed, let alone where it was kept."

Georgia was a middle-aged black woman with cool eyes and a warm smile, and I had the feeling she didn't miss much. I let that pass and asked about his patients. Had he ever had occasion to show the gun during a session?

"Absolutely not," he said. "I never so much as opened that drawer with a patient in the room. I never even unlocked—no, that's not true. Twice, with a patient who was going through a critical time, I prepared for the session by unlocking the drawer. Because of my own anxiety, you see. But in the event I never even opened the drawer, let alone showed the weapon."

"And that patient . . ."

His face clouded. "Took his own life, I'm sorry to say. Lived in a second-floor apartment, rode the elevator up to the roof and threw himself off it. He left a note, said he was afraid if he didn't do this he might kill someone. So perhaps my anxiety hadn't been entirely misplaced."

"And this happened recently?"

"His suicide? No, it was last winter, the week between Christmas and New Year's. Not an unusual time for it."

"Before the gun was taken, then."

"Oh, yes. Months before."

"The two burglars," I said. "Their names were Jason Bierman and Carl Ivanko."

"Yes."

"Was either a patient of yours?"

He didn't even hesitate. He might have refused to answer if he'd thought I was a cop, but he wouldn't hold out on a guy from the insurance company looking to head off a lawsuit. "No," he said. "The first I heard of either of them was when I read about them in the newspaper."

"Of your other patients," I said, "can you think of any who might have served time in prison?"

He shook his head. "My patients are middle-class professionals," he said. "Two-thirds or more of them suffer from depression. Several are young women with eating disorders. I have a blocked writer, the author of five novels. The fifth was his breakthrough book, a bestseller. It was published nine years ago and he hasn't been able to finish anything since. I have patients who are unhappy in their marriages, patients who feel their careers have dead-ended."

He came out from behind his desk, walked over to the window, looked out at the park. With his back to me he said, "When I was in medical school they talked admiringly of dermatology. The skin game, they used to call it. 'Nobody ever dies, nobody ever gets well.'" He turned to face me, one hand holding the other. "You could say that about what I do, dabbing ointment on psoriasis of the psyche. Of course it's not really true of a dermatologist. Some of his patients do recover, certainly, and some die of melanoma. And many of mine are better for having treatment. Their depression is lessened, their neuroses less debilitating. And, of course, now and then one flings himself off a roof."

He returned to his desk, picked up a letter opener, brass, with a handle of green malachite. "I had a patient who molested all four of his children, three girls and a boy," he said. "I had another who embezzled a quarter of a million dollars from his employer to finance an enthusiasm for sports gambling and cocaine. Neither of them went to jail. I suppose the work I do might benefit a criminal, an ex-inmate, but none has ever come to me." He started to add something, then drew himself up short and looked at his watch.

"It's ten minutes of two," he said. "I really

can't spare you any more time. No one could have known the gun was there. No patient of mine ever saw it. If there's nothing else . . ."

"You've been very helpful," I said. "I'm sorry to have taken so much of your time. Unofficially, let me just say that I don't think you have anything to worry about."

"Then I won't," he said, and gave me a wintry smile. I can't say he looked too worried. We shook hands, and he showed me to the door.

NINETEEN

It was drizzling when I left Nadler's office, but not enough to make me sorry I'd left the umbrella home. We had a concert that evening and I wanted to fit in a meeting first, so I walked through the raindrops to Broadway and took the subway down to the Village. There's a storefront on Perry Street that's been leased to an AA group for twice as long as I've been sober. Back when I came in they used to hold two or three meetings a day there, and now they run pretty much continuously from early morning to late at night. I got there halfway through one meeting, went out for coffee when it ended, and came back for a little more than half of the next one. I heard a lot of the neurotic self-absorbed drivel that Seymour Nadler had to listen to all day, and I wasn't getting paid, either. But when I walked out of there I was sober.

T J called in, reporting that no one had questioned his performance as a deputy inspector for the Department of Buildings, City of New York, Borough of Brooklyn. He'd had no trouble finding the house on Meserole Street, but said he'd have felt more comfortable in that part of town if he'd stayed with the camo shorts. There were Dumpsters here and there and a lot of renovation going on, so the neighborhood was evidently in the process of improving, but it looked to him like it had a ways to go.

He'd met Peter Meredith, and three of his four housemates, and he'd report at length face to face, but for now he'd summarize it by saying Meredith might not have gained weight since Kristin saw him last, but it didn't look as though he'd lost any, either, and he wasn't about to fit into Jason Bierman's shirt and jeans. And two of the other people he'd met were women, and the other man was black, and, while we'd never actually spelled it out, he more or less assumed our mystery dude was of the Caucasian persuasion.

That left one member of the team he didn't get to see, I told Elaine, and another visit from the same buildings inspector might arouse suspicions. But he had the name of the missing man, and we could figure out some way to check him out.

"I know it's never a complete waste," she said, "but it sounds as though he had a long trip for nothing."

"That's what I said. He said it wasn't that long a

trip, and he got to see a part of town he hadn't known before. Besides, it wasn't for nothing."

"Because you get to rule these people out."

"That's only half of it. He got paid. They believed he was a genuine buildings inspector, and evidently they'd had dealings with the breed before, or knew someone who had. So, when he kept hanging around, wanting to look at one thing after another to no particular purpose, Peter Meredith took him aside and slipped him a hundred-dollar bill."

"And of course T J took it."

"If he hadn't," I said, "I don't know what I would do with him. Yes, of course he took it. It would have spiked his whole act to turn it down, and on top of that it would have contravened a fundamental principle."

" 'When they give you money, put it in your pocket.' "

"That's the one."

We ate at home and walked up Ninth to Lincoln Center. It was raining in earnest by the time we set out, so we might have taken a cab, but the rain made it impossible to get one. It was only half a dozen blocks, and we both had umbrellas, and stayed dry under them.

The concert featured a Belgian pianist who performed on a Mozart piano, which was evidently some intermediate stage in evolution between a harpsichord and the modern piano. The program notes told me more than I cared to know about the differences and similarities involved. The Mostly Mozart orchestra provided accompaniment, and what they played was certainly easy to listen to.

And, in my case, easy not to listen to, because I couldn't keep my mind on it. I kept playing different conversations through my mind—with Nadler, with Kristin Hollander, with my police contacts in Brooklyn and Manhattan. I ran switches on the scenario I'd spun out for Kristin ("Scudder's variations on the Third Man Theme") until they became a dream I couldn't wake up from, or a song I couldn't get out of my head.

At intermission Elaine asked me if I wanted to go. "You're not squirming in your seat," she said, "but your mind's miles away, isn't it?"

I said I'd stay. The festival had only a week to run, and we had tickets for two of the remaining concerts. She'd be taking a friend to one of them, and then there'd be the last night, and eleven months before we did it again. It was early, and Danny Boy's day was just starting. It wouldn't hurt me to sit back and let them play beautiful music for me, whether I listened to it or not.

A Ninth Avenue bus pulled up just as we were leaving. The rain had lessened and she said she'd walk, and I said either she'd take the bus or I would walk with her.

She said, "And then turn around and walk all the way back to Seventy-second Street?"

"So take the bus," I said, and she did.

Poogan's is on Seventy-second east of Broadway, a dark little hole in the wall with precious little to recommend it, as far as I'm concerned, aside from the frequent presence of Danny Boy Bell. I've known him for years—Elaine was sitting at his table the night I first laid eyes on her. I'd say he hasn't changed, that he looks exactly the same, but I know that can't be true. He was around twenty-eight when I met him, and looked much younger. He still looks young for his years, but there are more of them, and it shows.

Back then he looked like nobody else in the world, and that hasn't changed. He's African-American, a term I don't tend to use much, but it fits him better than "black," which doesn't fit him at all. Danny Boy's a true albino, his skin whiter than white, his hair colorless, his eyes pink and light-sensitive. Even in the summer, he manages to see about as much daylight as an overly cautious vampire.

Nights, he generally holds court at one of two places where the lighting and sound are both muted. Mother Blue's, farther uptown, has live music and a more upscale salt-and-pepper clientele; Poogan's, with a tasteful if eclectic jukebox, is a little more raffish. At either place he takes his usual table and waits for people to come join him. Some bring him information and others take information away with them. If this is the Information Age, Danny Boy's up to date—information is his stock in trade.

I nursed a Coke at the bar while he chatted with a woman who looked too chubby to be a working girl, but who, dressed and made up as she was, could hardly be anything else. She was an over-stuffed kewpie doll fresh out of a Stephen King novel, but any sense of malevolence was dispelled by her obvious jollity. She laughed with good humor, and at the conclusion of the interview she stood up, leaned over, and kissed Danny Boy smack on the mouth. She laughed again and strode out of the place, and when she passed me I got a whiff of her perfume. It was as demure and understated as everything else about her.

When I got to his table Danny Boy was dipping a white handkerchief in vodka and wiping his lips with it. "Becky has a lovely mouth," he said, "but God only knows where it's been. It's good to see you, Matthew. It's been too long."

"Time flies," I said.

"When you're having fun," he said, "and also when you're not." He cocked his head, looked me over. "You're looking well," he announced. "Sobriety evidently agrees with you. I can't think it would agree with me."

He put his handkerchief away and took a big sip

of vodka, churning it in his mouth like Listerine, then swallowing it down. "Germs," he explained, "though I'm sure she tidies up after every little adventure. Still, better safe than sorry." At both Mother Blue's and Poogan's they leave the bottle for him, and he took it from the ice bucket and filled his glass. "The only thing wrong with your sobriety," he said, "is you don't get to the bars as often."

"I'm turning into a homebody," I said.

"And how is the fair Elaine?"

"Fine. She sends her love."

"And give her mine." He picked up his glass, took a sip. He could still drink like a man twice his size and half his age. They say in the rooms of AA that it's just a question of time, that nobody gets away with it forever, but I'm not sure they're right. Some friends of mine seem to do just fine.

He swallowed and closed his eyes for a moment, and I could just about feel the drink going down. He opened his eyes and said, "I'd miss it," to himself as much as to me, and thought about that for a moment. Then his eyes found mine and he said, "Well, Matthew? What brings you here?"

When I got home Elaine was in the living room, reading a Susan Isaacs novel and drinking a cup of tea. She was barefoot and wore a silk robe that left a lot of her uncovered. I looked her over and made some appreciative noises, and she told me that men are swine. "It says so right here," she said, and tapped the book. "How's Danny Boy?"

"The same. He sends love."

"That's sweet. Michael called."

"Michael?"

"Your son."

"He never calls," I said, remembering the last call I'd had from him. "What did he want?"

"He must have called while we were at the concert. The message was on the machine when I got home. He wants you to call him, and he left a number. His cell phone, I think he said. The message is still on the machine."

I went and played it. Without preamble he said, "Dad, it's Michael. Could you give me a call? Anytime, it doesn't matter. I don't know where I'll be, so call me on my cell phone . . ."

I jotted down the number and went back to the living room. "Whatever it is," I said, "you don't get a clue from his tone of voice, do you? It's perfectly neutral."

"There's probably an easy way to find out what he wants."

"It's almost midnight."

"Which is what, nine in California?"

"If that's where he is."

"If he's in Paris," she said, "it's six in the morning."

"Wherever you go," I said, "it's always sometime. All I have to do is pick up the fucking phone, but I don't seem to want to."

"I know. But it might be good news, honey. Maybe June's expecting another baby."

"I don't think that's it," I said, "and I don't think it's good news. But whatever it is, I might as well hear about it."

Dad," he said. "Thanks for calling back. Listen, are you at home? The number I called before?"

"Sure, but—"

"Let me call you back. I'm getting an echo on this piece of crap."

He broke the connection, and I hung up myself and waited for the phone to ring. I suppose I ought to have a cell phone, but there's not a day goes by that I'm not glad I don't.

Elaine said, "What happened?" and I was starting to tell her when the phone rang.

"Sorry," he said. "Listen, did Andy call you?"

"No," I said. "Why?"

"I didn't think he would. He said he wasn't going to, but I thought he might have changed his mind. But I guess he didn't."

"Michael . . ."

"I'm sorry, Dad. He's got himself in a mess, that's all. He wouldn't call you, and he didn't want me to call you, but I felt I had to."

"What kind of a mess?"

"There's no great way to say this. He took some money."

"Stole it, you mean?"

"Technically, yes. I don't think he thought of it that way, but when you take money from your employer that you can't pay back, I guess that's stealing."

A whole slew of questions came to mind. I reached out and picked one. "How much money?"

"Ten thousand dollars."

"From his employer."

"From the company he works for, yes."

"I don't even know who he works for," I said, "or what he does."

"They're an independent auto parts wholesaler. Andy's a sort of branch manager of the Tucson operation, services some accounts, does some back office work."

"It doesn't sound like a business that would handle much cash."

"No, it's all checks. The way he did it, I don't know the details, but he evidently set up some dummy accounts and cut company checks payable to them. Then he set up a bank account where he could deposit the checks, and wrote checks from that account and cashed them through his own account."

That's one way to do it, and it always works like a charm until they catch you.

"His boss found out, and—"

"They always do."

"I know, I can't believe he was that stupid. Anyway, his boss gave him a choice. If he pays the money back before the end of the month he'll let it go. Otherwise he'll press charges, and Andy'll go to jail."

"And ten thousand's the amount he took?"

"That's what it rounds off to, and that's what he has to pay back."

"And he called you asking for the money."

"I'm the one he calls," he said.

"This has happened before."

"Not exactly."

"Not exactly? Meaning what, it wasn't auto parts and it wasn't in Tucson?"

"It was never this serious. He calls me, I don't know, every once in a while. Once or twice a year, I guess. Whenever it's him on the phone, I know he's in some kind of a jam."

"Like what?"

"He's broke, he needs money, something didn't work out. His car died and he has to get it fixed. He borrowed money from people who break your legs if you don't pay. It's always something."

"I didn't know anything about this, Michael."

"No, I'm always the one he calls."

"And you bail him out?"

"Well, he's my brother."

"Sure."

"And, like I said, it was never this serious. It's usually a thousand dollars. Sometimes it's less, and the most it ever was was twenty-five hundred."

"He calls and you send the money. Does he ever pay you back?"

"Every once in a while I'll get a check or a

money order in the mail, part of what he owes me. And he's very generous at Christmas. Since Melanie was born, there's always an expensive gift for her, at Christmas and on her birthday. But as far as how we stand, well, you don't like to keep accounts with your brother."

"But you have to know where you stand."

"Well, I keep track, you know?"

"What's he into you for?"

"Something around twelve thousand dollars."

"Twelve thousand," I said.

"I feel funny saying it. June doesn't know how much it comes to. She knows I give Andy money from time to time, but not what it adds up to."

"I had no idea. I knew he was drifting, taking his time finding himself, never staying in one place too long. But it sounds like he's a fuckup."

"He's Andy, Dad. He's charming, he's funny, everybody likes him. But yeah, I don't like to say it, but he's a fuckup."

"Where does it go, Mike? Gambling? Cocaine?"

"He was betting basketball games for a while, I remember that. But I don't think he's a serious gambler. I know he's done coke from something he said once, but just in the sense that he'll take some if he's out partying, more or less to keep going. I gather there are a lot of people who do that."

Otherwise all those other people wouldn't be getting rich selling it.

"He took the ten thousand because he had this investment opportunity. I forget what it was, some new business he could buy a half-interest in if he could come up with ten grand. As a matter of fact he called me, wanted me to invest in it. I didn't pay attention to the details because I never considered it for a minute. We don't have a lot of extra dough to invest, but when we do it goes in an index fund. No glamour there, but I like that a lot better than the idea of waking up one morning and the money's gone."

"He couldn't borrow from you, so he borrowed from his boss."

"That's how he saw it."

"And he made the investment?"

"No, the deal fell apart."

"And what happened to the money?"

"He pissed it away."

"Nice."

"He was depressed because he had high hopes, you know. He's always got high hopes. But he was down, so he got to drinking, and he decided he had to spend some money to cheer himself up. He took a girl to Cancún, he traded his car for a new one."

"And now he pays up or goes to jail."

"That's right."

"What did you tell him?"

"Dad, I didn't know what to tell him. 'Mikey, I swear this is the last time, I learned a big lesson here.' What am I supposed to say, you're full of shit and I know you're full of shit? 'Mikey, you'll get it back.' Yeah, right. I work my ass off, June works as hard as I do, we got the kid, we got the house . . ."

"I know."

"Could I give him ten grand? Yes, I could. I'd have to sell some securities, take out a loan, but I could do it. Am I going to?" He paused, as if considering the question anew. "I said it was too much. I said I could manage half of that."

"What did he say?"

"That wouldn't do it. His boss told him if he presses charges, then his insurance company covers the loss. So if the guy settled for half he'd have to eat a five-thousand-dollar loss, and he's not willing to do that. Andy said if all I can send him is half I should just wire it to him, because what he'll do is take the money in cash and run with it. I told him I didn't think that was such a good idea."

"It may be the worst idea he's ever had in his life," I said, "although I'm beginning to realize that covers a lot of ground. The last thing he wants to do is make himself a fugitive from justice."

"That's exactly what I told him."

"You say you're willing to send him half."

"Five thousand dollars. And I told him that's it, the well just ran dry. Next time you're in trouble, call somebody else."

I said, "When was your mother's funeral? Two weeks ago?"

"Something like that."

"He seemed the same as always. A little subdued, given the occasion, but not like somebody with this hanging over his head."

"That was before his boss figured out what was

going on. Andy never expects trouble until he's in it. So he was feeling fine, and then he got back to Tucson and the roof fell in."

"And he called you."

"Uh-huh. Day before yesterday. I sat around all day trying to figure out what to tell him."

"Did you talk about it with June?"

"No. I called him and told him what I told you I told him, and I said he should call you for the other half of the money. And he said he didn't want to do that."

"So you're calling on his behalf."

"No, he didn't want me to call you. But I'm calling you anyway."

"And what do you want me to do?"

"I don't know."

"Of course you do. You want me to kick in the other half."

"I don't even know if that's true," he said. "Maybe that's what I want. Or maybe I want you to turn him down, so that I'm not the only one turning him down, you know? I don't want my brother to go to jail."

"No."

"Or be—what was the phrase you used? A fugitive from justice? I don't want that either."

"No. Mike, can't he sell something? Didn't you say he just bought a new car?"

He snorted. "He owed more on the old car than it was worth. He used a few thousand dollars of what he stole to swing a down payment. Now the old car's paid off and he owes more on the new car than **it's** worth, so he's got no equity in it whatsoever. If he sold everything he owns, he could maybe scrape up a thousand dollars. If that."

"A real American success story. I suppose he's run out of friends to borrow from."

"You know Andy. He makes friends real easy. Then he throws 'em away and gets new ones. What do you want to do? I don't even know what your financial situation is. Could you come up with five thousand dollars in a hurry?"

"I could," I said. "I want to sleep on it, Michael. How about if I call you tomorrow?"

"Tomorrow's okay," he said. "He's got until the end of the month."

TWENTY

I'd told him I wanted to sleep on it, but I didn't get all that much sleep. Elaine and I were up talking until late, and when she got up around seven she found me in the kitchen with a pot of coffee.

"It's not the money," I said.

"Of course not."

"Except in a funny way it is. The amount's a factor. If it was five hundred dollars, I'd write out a check and put it in the mail. I wouldn't have to think twice."

"Uh-huh."

"And if it was fifty thousand dollars, well, I still wouldn't have to think twice, because it would be out of the question. But five thousand's right in the middle, small enough to manage but big enough to notice."

"We can afford it, baby."

"I know we can afford it."

"We wouldn't have to liquidate assets, or tighten our belts. We've got it in the bank."

"I know."

"But then again, you just said it. It's not the money."

I drank some coffee. I said, "He's the one that looks like me, you know."

"I know."

"Michael takes after his mother. He's heavyset, too, like the men in her family. Andy looks like his father."

"He could do worse."

"I think he drinks like his old man, too. I wonder how many DUIs he's had, how many cars he's cracked up. I don't know what the hell I should do."

She poured herself some coffee, sat down across the table from me.

"If he had to take after me," I said, "it's a shame he didn't go all the way and get on the cops. Then he could steal with both hands and not worry about the consequences."

"You were never a thief."

"I took money that wasn't mine. I generally found a justification for it, but people generally do. Look at Andy. He was just borrowing it, he was going to pay it back. You know, all I do is keep going around in circles. I don't want him rotting in an Arizona jail, and I don't want to buy his way out of it, either."

"It's tricky," she said. "But it's your call."

"What if it were yours?"

"That's hard," she said, "because it's not, and it shouldn't be."

"What would they tell you at Al-Anon?"

"Not to be an enabler," she said without hesitation. "That I'd be doing him no favor by getting him out of a jam. That all I'd really achieve would be to keep him from getting the lesson. That he'd never be able to change his behavior until he experiences the consequences of it. That, wherever he was supposed to go, he'd get there faster without my help."

"So there's your answer. You wouldn't send him the money."

"No, I'd send it."

"You would? You just said—"

"I know what I said. But there's another principle, and that's that every dog gets one bite. He may have done this before, but this is the first time he's come to you."

"He didn't come to me. He told his brother—"

"He told his brother not to call you, but at the same time he put his brother in a position where he **had** to call you. So in that sense he came to you."

"So you would send him the money."

"And I'd tell him it was the last time."

"He'll fuck up again."

"Of course he will."

"And next time you'd turn him down."

She nodded. "No matter what. Whether he'd go to jail or get his legs broken, I'd turn him down."

"But this time you'd send the money." I drank some more coffee and said, "You know, I think you're right."

"I'm right for me. What's right for me isn't necessarily right for you."

"This time it is. I'll call Michael."

But not just then; it was, as she pointed out, four in the morning in California. I didn't ask her what time it was in Paris.

I was relieved to have the decision made, but I felt less sanguine about the whole business as the morning wore on. My mind kept fussing with it like a kitten with a ball of yarn, and I had to remind myself over and over that I'd made up my mind.

And I was forever checking my watch, wishing it was time to make the call, anxious to get it over with. But I kept putting it off, first reluctant to chance waking him, then deciding against calling while they were at breakfast. It evidently wasn't something he wanted June to know about, so why make him take the call in another room? I could wait and reach him at the office.

T J came up around eleven, wearing khakis and a polo shirt but carrying yesterday's clipboard. He'd made notes on his trip to Williamsburg and went over them with me. The house was a three-story brick rowhouse sheathed thirty or forty years ago in garish asphalt siding. "Musta been some salesman," he said, " 'cause everybody on the block went for it. Made it a real Neighborhood Uglification project."

The siding had been stripped from the lower two floors at 168 Meserole, and they were working on the top floor. The brick underneath was going to need repointing, and a good deal of repair work, but even in its present state it looked better than what had covered it. They were doing a similar kind of work inside, deleting the improvements of previous owners and tenants, tearing out the partitions that had divided the original floor-through apartments into smaller units, pulling off the pressboard paneling and dropped-ceiling tiles, taking up the worn linoleum. The plaster was scheduled for removal from the exterior walls, to expose the brick. The three apartments would be loftlike open-plan layouts, but some half-walls were planned, to hold bookshelves and display paintings.

"Be nice when they finish it," he said. "They artists, so they need their work space. They all workin' together. Time I got there, Peter was down on the first floor, scrapin' ugly wallpaper off one wall they fixin' to keep, an' two of the others was up in Peter's place on the third floor, workin' on the brick. They got these little masks over their mouths an' noses, keep the dust out of their lungs, an' they got plaster dust coverin' the rest of them. Looked pretty comical, but I figured a buildings inspector be seein' that all the time, so I held back and didn't laugh."

Peter had the third floor to himself, he said, and he wondered if they'd put him up there because they figured he needed the exercise. He was fat, no question, but it didn't seem to slow him down any. He went up and down the stairs without getting out of breath, and he didn't have that apologetic manner that so many fat people seemed to have.

"You see him," he said, "and you say to yourself, man, this is one fat dude. You around him a little while, an' what happens is you forget he's fat. It slips your mind. And then later on, like, you spendin' time with one of the others an' then you see Peter again, and you're like, Damn, he's fat! Like you never noticed it before, 'cept you did."

I knew what he meant. I'd observed the same phenomenon with several other people, not all of them overweight. One is blind, for example, another missing an arm. The common denominator, I think, is self-acceptance, and the result is as he described it. Because they accept it, whatever it is, you stop noticing it.

Peter Meredith's therapist may not have been able to save his client's relationship with Kristin, or to trim him down to a size 42, but it sounded as though he could claim a certain degree of success.

Marsha Kittredge and Lucian Bemis had the second floor. She was a blond Wasp princess from Beaufort, South Carolina, and he was a tall gaunt black man from South Philadelphia. She was a painter, he a sculptor, and T J had decided that, once upon a time, her great-grandfather had owned his great-grandfather.

The ground floor's occupants were Ruth Ann Lipinsky, another painter, the only native New Yorker in the group, short and dark and intense, and Kieran Eklund, a painter and printmaker, who'd been doing something unspecified in Manhattan during T J's visit. T J'd thought he might stick around until Eklund got back, so he could get a look at him, but it turned out the others were going to meet Eklund in the city. They'd been anxious to clean up and get out of there, which may have prompted Peter Meredith to give T J a hundred-dollar handshake.

"Made me suspicious," he said. "Man gives you money, you got to figure it's so you'll look the other way. Started to wonder what I wasn't meant to see. Then I remembered who I supposed to be."

"A city employee."

"You right, Dwight. Man in my position, they got to pay you even if they ain't done nothin' wrong." He sighed. "Good business to be in," he said, "if only the uniforms wasn't so lame."

When I finally picked up the phone and called him, Michael was in the car, on his way to a client. "I'll make the check out to you," I said, "and put it in the mail this afternoon. For five thousand dollars. You write your own check to him, or better yet—"

"I was thinking of making the check payable to his employer."

"That's exactly what I was about to suggest. Not because we don't trust him, but because the canceled check will be proof of payment."

"That's a good point," he said. "I can even say as much to Andy if he takes offense. But to be perfectly frank about it, as far as I'm concerned it's because I don't trust him."

I got out the checkbook and wrote out a check for five thousand dollars payable to Michael Scudder. I looked up his address, addressed an envelope, and folded a sheet of notepaper to wrap the check so that it wouldn't be visible through the envelope. I don't know why, I can't imagine that a lot of postal employees hold envelopes to the light, looking for personal checks they can steal.

And it seemed to me I ought to write something on the sheet of paper. I sat there trying to think of something to say. Everything that came to mind struck me as redundant or foolish or both. I decided to face the fact that I didn't have anything to say to my boy, to either of my boys, and I wrapped the check in the piece of paper and tucked it in the envelope, sealed it and stamped it and held it out and looked at it.

T J was sitting on the couch, turning the pages of an art magazine. He hadn't said a word in a while.

"I'm sending five thousand dollars to my son in California," I said.

He didn't look up from the magazine. "He probably be glad to get it," he said.

"It's not for him. It's for his brother in Tucson. Andy, his name is. He embezzled money from the company he works for and if he doesn't pay it back he'll go to jail."

He didn't say anything

I picked up the envelope, held it in my hand. It didn't weigh much. One stamp would carry it all the way across the country. I said, "I could get the money from the bank, squirt lighter fluid on it and set it on fire. It'd make about as much sense."

"Blood," he said.

"Blood?"

"Thicker'n water."

"So they tell me. Sometimes I wonder." I got to my feet. "I'm going to drop this in the mail," I said. "You want to wait here?"

He shook his head, closed the magazine, stood up.

I mailed it in the box on the corner, thinking what an act of faith I'd just performed, expecting the post office to transport it three thousand miles and actually deliver it to its intended recipient. Yet it seemed far more likely that the letter would get there than that the check inside would do any good.

We got two Cokes and two slices of Sicilian pizza at the corner of Fifty-eighth and ate our lunch standing up. My Coke tasted cloyingly sweet, and I asked the counterman if he had a wedge of lemon. He gave me one of those little plastic packets of lemon juice, and I decided that would only make things worse. I looked into the glass and said, "Thicker than water."

"So they say."

"You have any family, T J?"

"Not since my gran died."

I knew she'd raised him. He'd said as much once, and that her death was the last time he'd cried.

We finished our slices and looked at each other, and I motioned to the counterman for two more. We worked on them, and T J finished his Coke. I told him he was welcome to the rest of mine, but he didn't want it. We'd both been silent for a while, and not just because we were busy eating.

And then he said, "I could have a daddy. No way to know."

I didn't say anything.

"My mama came home an' had me," he said, "an' then she sickened and died. I don't remember her at all. I wasn't a year old when she passed. Gran told me about her, showed me pictures of her, said how she loved me, which maybe she did an' maybe she didn't. Far as my daddy, my gran said all she knew about him was he was dead. He was killed, she said, but as to whether or not that's true, I couldn't tell you. Gran coulda made that up, or maybe it was what my mama told her, but Mama made it up."

On the sidewalk, a man walked by having a spirited telephone conversation. He didn't have a cell phone, however. The mouthpiece he was half-shouting into was that of the receiver of a pay phone, a foot-long strand of cable still attached to it. I'd seen him before, wearing the same mismatched pants and suit jacket, the pants several inches too short for him, the jacket's sleeves too long. He walked around like that all the time, carrying his private phone, telling whoever was at the other end of it all about the KGB and the CIA and the hidden truth about the Oklahoma City bombing.

Nobody was paying the slightest bit of attention to him.

"I'd say he was a black man," T J said. "Bein' as I'm what you could call medium dark. Other hand, my gran was a good measure darker, and my mama, best I recall from the pictures, she was dark like my gran. So my daddy coulda been more on the light-skinned side. But it ain't like mixin' paint. You never too sure what's gonna come out. Could be he was as dark as my gran. Could be he was white. No way to know."

"No."

"Could be my mama herself didn't know," he said. "Gran didn't say she was wild, but she was real young, an' I'd guess she was wild. Could be she was a workin' girl, could be I was a trick baby. No way to tell."

Later we were sitting in the park going over what he'd learned in Williamsburg—which, all in all, wasn't much. None of the people he'd seen were physically right for the part of the third man. Kieran Eklund was still possible, but only because he hadn't been ruled out yet.

But you could just about rule him out on the grounds that people who work day and night restoring a neglected house, digging out old mortar, scrubbing bare brick with muriatic acid, scraping walls and sanding floors, are just plain not the type to create elaborate charades leading to multiple homicide. Putting that kind of effort into a house in the shadow of Bushwick Terminal and equidistant from two low-income housing projects might cast doubts on their judgment, but it still made them all extremely unlikely killers.

"And he's not just nuts," I said. "He's calculating. I wish there was money in this."

His eyebrows went up. "Last I heard, we had a client."

"I don't mean money for us. Money for him. Nobody puts something like this together for revenge, or out of bloodlust. The whole thing's too cold. There's got to be a pot of gold at the end of this rainbow."

"That's what Lia thought. You startin' to think she was right?"

"No."

"Didn't think so. Only money's the house, right? An' it goes to Kristin, and she our client, so we know she ain't guilty."

I'd had guilty clients in the past, but I didn't have one now. But how did we know the house was the only asset? And how did we know everything went to Kristin?

TWENTY-ONE

As before, she checked me out through the peephole before she opened the door. This time, though, I didn't have to show any ID. I introduced T J as my assistant, and he switched to the speech pattern that served him well on the Columbia campus. He was already dressed for the part.

She led us into the kitchen, and we all three took seats at the pine table. At first she was confused at the idea of a monetary motive for her parents' death. That had been the original line of thought, that the incident had been a burglary gone wrong, a burglary that turned spontaneously into something much worse.

But hadn't I explained that the burglary was only there to mask a purposeful murder?

"What I'm wondering," I said, "was if it could have been murder for gain. Who stood to gain financially from the death of your parents?"

"Well, I did," she said without hesitation. "I get pretty much everything."

"If it's all the same to you," I said, "I'm leaving you off the list of suspects."

She managed a smile.

"I assume you inherit the house," I said, "and I know it's a valuable piece of property." I didn't mention that her cousin Lia had already given us a rough appraisal. "Is that essentially the whole of the estate?"

"No, there's more. There's the contents of the house, the furniture, the paintings on the walls. And things like Mom's jewelry. Oh, you asked me to do something and I forgot. You wanted me to look through the goods the police returned and see if there's anything missing, and I just haven't gotten to it yet."

"There's no rush on that."

"I was going to do it, and then it slipped my mind. But there are so many other things in a house this size. I don't have any idea what it's all worth, though I think one or two of the paintings might be fairly valuable. I suppose I'll have to have everything appraised for estate tax purposes. Oh, I'm terrible. There's coffee, and some ginger ale in the fridge, and I think some beer." We said we'd pass, and she said, "Well, I could use some more coffee," and filled a cup for herself.

"Then there's my father's stock holdings," she said. "Well, they owned everything jointly, but he was the one who decided what to buy and sell. And there was also his retirement account. Together it comes to something like one and a half million dollars."

I wrote down: **stock—1.5 mil.**

"Plus insurance," she said. "There was a million-dollar policy with my mother as the beneficiary, with me listed as contingency beneficiary, or whatever they call it. And there was another policy through the firm, slightly less, I believe the death benefit is eight hundred thousand. That was supposed to be three-fourths payable to my mother and one-fourth to me, but now it all comes to me. And there was a small policy, a hundred thousand dollars, payable to me. The big policy, the million-dollar policy, has a double indemnity clause in it, so that makes it worth, well, two million."

I wrote down: **insurance—3 mil**.

"And debts?"

She shook her head. "Credit card balances. They don't amount to much, he paid everything off right away."

"A mortgage?"

"They paid it off years ago. The house is free and clear."

I wrote down: **real estate—3.5 mil.**

"And there'll be something from the law firm," she said. "A share of the current cash assets, something. I don't know how it works." She looked at my notes, and I turned the pad so she didn't have to read upside-down. She said, "What is that, eight million dollars? I don't know what the rest adds up to, the artwork and jewelry, or what's coming from the law firm. Or what other assets they might have had that haven't come to light yet. There's a key to a safe-deposit box, but I haven't even gone yet to see what's in it. You have to open it in the presence of someone official. I don't know what's in it." She closed her eyes, and didn't say anything for a while. Then she opened them and said, "So I guess I'm rich."

"Bill Gates and Warren Buffett wouldn't think so. But a lot of other people would."

"I never thought of my parents as rich," she said reflectively. "I knew my father was well established, I knew he made a good living, I knew we were comfortable. But we weren't rich. The house, well, it was just the place we lived. It never used to be worth so much."

"No."

"And the stocks were savings, so that they could be comfortable when he retired. They were going to travel, they wanted to go everywhere." She set her jaw, stopped any tears that might have been about to flow. "And the insurance was in case anything happened to him, so that she would be able to maintain the same standard of living. So they really weren't rich. But for me to have all that money at my age—I guess I'm wealthy. Rich. I don't even know what to call it, but that's what I am."

"And it all comes to you?"

"Yes," she said. "Well, essentially all of it."

"Essentially?"

"One of my dad's partners went over the will with me. Except for a couple of small bequests, I'm the sole beneficiary."

"Do you remember any of the small bequests?"

"Well, let me think. I didn't pay close attention, and I don't have a copy of the will around. Is it important?"

"Probably not. Just tell me what you can remember."

"Well, there were about two or three dozen charitable bequests. Most of them were in the five-thousand-dollar range, but I think I remember twenty-five thousand each to the New York Philharmonic, Carnegie Hall, and the Met. The opera, I mean. The Metropolitan Museum was in the five-thousand range, along with MOMA and the Whitney and, oh, there were a lot of museum bequests."

It added up, and some of those outfits certainly pursue donations aggressively, but somehow I couldn't see any of them killing for it.

"And some charities," she went on. "Goddard-Riverside, the Coalition for the Homeless. Meals on Wheels."

"Any bequests to individuals?"

"Several small bequests of one or two thousand dollars. To the woman who cleans for us twice a week, to a nurse who took care of my grandmother toward the end. And some larger bequests to relatives." She named several, names I didn't know and didn't bother taking in, and then I snapped to when she said, "And twenty thousand dollars to my cousin Lia."

I thought T J might react visibly, but the street is a good teacher. I could only hope my face stayed as opaque as his. I said, "That's more substantial, isn't it? Were your parents particularly close to your cousin?"

"They added a codicil," she said. "Within the past year. Lia's a sweet kid, she's on full scholarship at Columbia, and my mother liked to have her over for dinner. Lia's mother and my mom were sisters, and Aunt Frankie made a really bad marriage and things never really went well for her. She and my mom pretty much lost touch, so with Lia here in New York, Mom welcomed the chance to do something for her. Plus Lia's really nice, so it was pleasant to have her around."

"So your father would have added the codicil . . ."

"I guess the idea was this'll be enough to see Lia through college. Her tuition and dorm rent was covered by the scholarship, but the kind of budget she was on, well, let's see, will I replace that worn-out pair of panty hose or will I have lunch?"

"So your mother was helping her out."

"Well, you know. 'Lia, this was on sale and I thought how nice it would look on you and I just couldn't resist it.' Or after dinner, 'Here, it's late, I insist you take a cab home,' and giving her twenty dollars, and how much is the cab going to run? Maybe eight dollars?"

"Have you seen Lia since—"

"Since it happened? Twice. No, three times. I was in shock the whole first week, you know. Looking back, it's as though I was walking around with a concussion. I guess that's protective, the psyche walling itself off, not letting much information in. And I think Lia was in the same state, though of course not as intense. She couldn't look at me, and then I remember once I glanced over at her, caught her off-guard, I suppose, and she was staring at me. But a lot of people stare at you when something like this occurs."

"I can imagine," I said. "Do you suppose Lia knows about the codicil?"

She shook her head. "I just found out myself when I went over the will with Mr. Ziegler. I haven't seen her since. I suppose I should call her and tell her. It's not a fortune, but in her circumstances it could really make a difference over the next couple of years."

"That's true," I said, "but why don't you wait and let the lawyer notify her?"

"You think that's better?"

"Yes," I said. "I'd have to say I do."

Later she said, "I was just thinking. About something Mr. Ziegler said."

"You mentioned him before. He's your attorney?"

"Well, he was my father's partner. Is he my attorney? I suppose that's what he is." She furrowed her brow, considering the concept, and T J asked her what the man had said.

"Oh," she said. "He asked me if I had a will, and I said of course not, what did I need a will for, and he said, well, now I'm a woman with a substantial estate, and I should think about executing a will."

"I suppose he's right."

"Except I don't see what's the hurry. I know anything can happen at any time, believe me, I know that. But it would be one thing if I had someone it was very important for me to leave it to. But what happens if I get hit by a bus tomorrow? It wouldn't all go to the state, would it?"

"Only in the absence of living relatives."

"So it would go to them?"

"One way or another. I'm not sure how it would be apportioned, and someone you hardly know might get more than someone you're close to, which might not be the way you'd do it if you had a will drawn."

"I'm not even sure it ought to be up to me to decide," she said. "I mean, it doesn't feel like my money." She leaned forward, looked at me. "What do you think?"

"I think it's your money."

"No, I don't mean that. Do you think I have to be in a rush to get a will drawn?"

"No," I said. "No, I don't think so."

TWENTY-TWO

He sits in his car across the street from the house. The living room drapes are drawn. So are the curtains on the higher floors, but these are not light-tight, and he can see that there are lights on upstairs.

She's at home. He's fairly certain of that.

He came here yesterday, parked where he could watch the house. He was still sitting there, calm, patient, when she opened the front door and descended the steps to the street. The shopkeeper on the ground floor, the dyed redhead, spotted her and opened the door, called her over for a few words. Then the old hen retreated into her jumble shop and the Hollander girl turned to her left and walked west. Seventy-fourth was an eastbound street, so his car faced Central Park West, and he had to turn around in his seat to watch her proceed a half block to the corner of Columbus and disappear around the corner.

The very route he and Ivanko had taken on that fateful night, pillowcases slung over their shoulders like laundry bags. Heavier than laundry bags, though, and the weight had thrown Carl's balance off, exaggerated his limp.

Couple of fags off to do their wash together, he'd thought, but he hadn't risked saying as much to Carl. And there'd been no chance to mention it later on, because he hadn't wanted to wait, hadn't dared wait, and as soon as he got the chance he'd drawn the gun, and it bucked twice in his hand, just a little thing, not much recoil, but it bucked and Carl went sprawling, and it bucked once more and Carl lay still, forever still.

He'd waited in his car, one arm over the back of his seat, peering through the rear window and remembering it, replaying the memory, and then she came back into view, headed for the house once more, a white plastic grocery bag in hand. He turned around, not wanting to be caught staring, and watched her out of the corner of his eye as she reached the house and mounted the steps again.

Key in the lock, he thought. Now turn and push, that's right. And don't forget the alarm. . . .

Now, a day later, he is not sure what he wants

to do. Twice this morning he was on the verge of calling her. He tried out a variety of conversations in his head, deciding in the end not to make the call. Sitting here, knowing she's home, he considers ringing her doorbell, explaining that he was in the neighborhood. Or would it be better if she thinks he made a special trip to see her? Perhaps he should say he was just in the neighborhood, but in such a way that she infers he came especially to pay his respects and offer counsel.

But is it a good idea? Perhaps, as he so often advises people, perhaps it is necessary to give time time. Sometimes the best action is to take none. Sometimes one can but wait. And what is it Pascal wrote? Something about all of man's ills growing out of his inability to sit alone in a room.

He sits alone in a car. . . .

And what's this? Two men, appearing as if from out of nowhere. One is middle-aged and white, the other much younger and black. And they are mounting the steps to her house, and the older one rings the doorbell.

They could be anyone, he thinks. Jehovah's Witnesses, come to forecast the end of the world. An unlikely pair, an old white man, a young black man. First thing comes to mind, a combination like that, you figure they're gay. White guy's a john, black guy's a hustler.

The door opens, and she lets them in.

Maybe they'll come out with laundry bags, he thinks. Couple of fags heading for the laundromat. But they're in there for a long time, the better part of an hour. His watch beeps at ten minutes before the hour, and he tells himself he ought to go home.

But he doesn't. Something keeps him there, some quiet certainty that this is important, that these two are more than casual visitors.

He keeps his eyes on the door, and he's looking at it when it opens and the two men emerge. It closes behind them and they descend the flight of steps, and he shrinks back into the shadows, not wanting to be seen. It's ridiculous, he's on the other side of the street, he's in his car. No one can see him, and he realizes that he's hiding because he has something to hide.

Hide in plain sight, he tells himself, and wills himself to sit forward, to turn and take a good look at the two of them.

And shrinks back in spite of himself, because he's seen the older man before. He didn't recognize him until this minute, perhaps because he didn't take a good look at him earlier, but now he does, and he recognizes him.

What about the black youth? Has he seen him before?

Well, honestly, how can you tell? It is not that all young black males look alike, he knows better than that. It's that one sees them that way, one simply registers Young Black Man mentally and lets it go at that. Deliberately, he inventories this one's facial features, determined to know him when he sees him again.

Assuming that he will in fact see him again. . . .

They're on their way west. It's the same as yesterday, when she went out for groceries. He's parked facing the wrong way, he has to turn around to watch them. As they near the corner it comes to him with perfect certainty that they play an important role in all of this, that it's a mistake to let them walk out of the picture so easily.

He doesn't hesitate. He gets out of his car, locks it, and starts off after them.

And now, he thinks, they'll turn the corner and get in their car, leaving him on foot. Or they'll hail a taxi. Well, if there's one cab there'll be two. With luck his taxi can follow their taxi.

But they don't get in a car, or hail a cab. They turn down Columbus Avenue, and the young one whips out a cellular phone and makes a call, talks, then hands the phone to the older man, who's done talking by the time they cross Seventy-second Street. The young one puts the phone away and they walk west another block, disappearing into the subway entrance at the corner of Broadway and Seventy-second.

It's remarkably easy to follow them. The station's poorly designed, and there are separate

turnstiles for the uptown and downtown plat-
forms, but he's lucky, he's close enough to see
them go through the uptown turnstiles, and he
follows in their wake and picks a spot a dozen
yards from where they're standing. He positions
himself so that he can watch them out of the
corner of his eye, but they will only see him in
profile, with his body largely screened by others.

Not that they're looking around, not that they
suspect a thing. He could probably stand right
next to them without arousing suspicion.

He considers it, thinking it might be interesting to know what they are saying.

If it were just the one man, the older man, and
if there were fewer people on the platform—
well, that sort of thing happens all the time,
doesn't it? You stand close, waiting, timing the
approach of the oncoming train, then give a
sudden lurch, a shove, and, if you are clever
about it, you can even make it appear to anyone
watching as though you are trying to save the
person, trying to grab hold of the fellow you've
just sent hurtling into the train's path.

Ridiculous even to think about it. But he has
to acknowledge that his hands are tingling, as if
anticipating their role.

Interesting, what you learned about yourself. . . .

An express train comes. They board it and so
does he, entering the same car by a different

door. They stand, their hands a foot apart on the overhead rail. He sits, watching them without being watched in return.

One stop to Ninety-sixth Street. The doors open. They get out, talking, paying no attention, and he follows. Again he plants himself ten or a dozen yards away, and follows them onto the Broadway local when it arrives.

TWENTY-THREE

On the street I said, "I hope I was right."

" 'Bout her not needin' a will?"

"Uh-huh. She's sitting on what, nine or ten million dollars? This may be hard to believe, but there are cases on record where people have killed for less than that."

"Some for as little as twenty thousand."

"Just what I was thinking."

"She didn't know about it, though. Lia."

"That's according to Kristin. No way of telling what Aunt Susan might have let slip, along with the combination for the keypad."

"Coulda known about it," he allowed. "Coulda thought it'd be more. Can't quite see her as the Third Man, though."

"Does she have a boyfriend?"

"Never mentioned one. Don't mean she don't have one." We were walking as we talked, and as we neared the corner he said, "Here's what don't make sense. If she's involved, what she wants is what happens—the cops wrap it up an' close the case. Otherwise why stage it that way?"

"So why does she say anything to you? Why let on she's suspicious of Kristin?"

He nodded. "That's what don't make sense."

"Twenty thousand's not really all that much," I said. "Not as a payoff for an operation like this. Maybe she was expecting more."

"Like how much?"

"I don't know, pick a number. A hundred thousand? She sees how the Hollanders live and they look to her like they've got more money than God, and Aunt Susan says she's made a provision for her to see her through college, and who knows what kind of dollar-sign sugarplums start dancing in her head? Then she finds out it's twenty thousand dollars and that seems like nothing. On the other hand, if Kristin's implicated, she can't profit from her parents' death. And the whole pie gets chopped up among the surviving relatives."

"So what's she get?"

"How many relatives did she name before, eight or ten? Say there are more she didn't mention, say a total of twenty, and say they all get equal shares. What is that, half a million dollars?"

"More'n twenty thousand."

"A lot more," I said, and pictured the ash-blond waif, the see-through skin, the big soulful eyes. "But I can't believe she was involved. Not knowingly."

"What you lookin' for?"

"A pay phone," I said. "Do you see one anywhere?"

"Got a free one," he said, and took his cell phone from his pocket. I said I didn't suppose he remembered Lia Parkman's number, and he rolled his eyes. "Don't need to remember it," he said. "Got her on my speed dial." He punched some numbers, flicked a lever, and held the contraption to his ear. After a moment he said, "Lia? T J. Hold on a second."

He covered the mouthpiece with his hand. "You really oughta get one of these," he said, and handed me the phone.

We rode up on the subway, meeting her at the Salonika, the same place as last time. She was waiting for us in a booth, an iced tea half finished in front of her. I said I'd have the same, and T J ordered a Coke. The waitress didn't seem to mind that no one was having any food. It was an off-hour, and if we weren't there the booth would be empty.

Lia had been surprised to hear from me. I'd done such a good job of setting her mind to rest that she'd never have guessed I was following up on the inquiry she'd set in motion. Her first reaction was one of alarm. She didn't want to make trouble for Kristin, that was the last thing she wanted, and now that the initial shock had worn off she couldn't imagine what had ever led her to have such a crazy idea in the first place. She'd seen Kristin since then, and Kristin was completely rocked by the death of her parents, and . . .

I assured her that Kristin wasn't a suspect. But, I said, there were some unanswered questions in the case, some possibility that the burglary had been arranged, that the killers had had inside help.

"The burglar alarm," she said.

"The burglar alarm code, the front door key, the Hollanders' schedule. I was just wondering if someone could have wormed any pertinent information out of you."

"Out of me?"

"Well, you or your boyfriend."

"Well, I don't have a boyfriend," she said, "so that's not it. And nobody even knew about my aunt and uncle or where they lived or anything. So I can't think how anybody could have gotten any information from me."

There was something she wasn't telling me. I could feel its presence there, parked on the edge of thought. I tried a few approaches, and then I said, "How about the key? Did anybody borrow it?"

"No, of course not."

"But you did have a key, didn't you?"

"Aunt Susan gave it to me."

"You didn't mention it before," I said. "You and

your aunt came home one day, and she had her arms full of packages, so she gave you the key and had you open the door. Then she told you the key-pad code so you could turn off the alarm."

I hadn't meant to scare her, but I did. She looked like a waif caught in the headlights.

Gently I said, "Isn't that what you said?"

"Yes. That's what happened, but the way you said it just now—"

"If you had your own key, why did your aunt hand you hers?"

"I didn't have a key then. Later on she gave me one. In case I needed to get in when nobody was home, she said. And she reminded me I already knew how to deactivate the alarm. Just be sure to set it again before I left, she said."

"And did you have much occasion to use your key?"

"I don't think I ever used it," she said. "Until you mentioned it just now, I more or less forgot I had it. And nobody else knew I had it, and I certainly never let anybody borrow it."

"Do you have it with you now?"

She fished in her purse, brought out a ring of keys, identified one as being the key to the Hollander house. "So even if somebody took it when I wasn't looking," she said, "which wouldn't make sense because nobody even knew I had it, but if somebody did, and he took it, well, he couldn't have, because here it is."

"That just means he gave it back."

"Don't you think I would remember? Especially after what happened, don't you think it would get my attention if someone gave back a key to the house where my aunt and uncle were murdered?"

T J pointed out that he could have returned the key the same way he took it, without her knowledge. "And it wouldn't have had to be after the break-in," I added. "He wouldn't have kept the key for long, wouldn't have wanted to chance your missing it. He'd just need it long enough to have a copy made. It's not a hard key to duplicate. Any neighborhood locksmith could do it in five minutes."

She was silent for a long moment, then announced she had to go to the bathroom. She took a step away from the table, then came back for her purse.

"She 'fraid we might look through it," T J said.

"And didn't want to let us know she was thinking that, but didn't want to leave the purse, either."

"Hidin' something."

"Feels that way to me, too."

When she came back to the table I fed her a few easy questions, ones it wouldn't disturb her to answer. They were designed to make our relationship feel a little less adversarial. Then I asked her if there was anything else she could think of, something she might feel reluctant to mention. I could feel her wrestling with the question, deciding whether or not to give it up.

"No," she said at length. "I'm sorry, but there's nothing."

Back on Broadway, T J said he didn't suppose I felt like walking all the way home again. I didn't, and we headed for the subway.

"Thought you'd keep at her," he said as we walked. "Thought you'd get her to open up."

"I thought about it."

"Just handed her a card. 'Call me if you think of anything, however far-fetched or unimportant it might seem.'"

"When you go fishing," I said, "and you get a bite, you have to know when to give line and when to reel in."

"I didn't know you liked to go fishing."

"I don't," I said. "It bores me to death."

"So you gave Lia some line."

"I gave her an easy way to change her mind," I said. "She knows something, or thinks she does, or is afraid she does. Now she'll go home and think about it, and she'll feel guilty, because she lied to me and I acted as though I believed her. And maybe she'll pick up the phone." I was silent for a moment, and then I added, "But it's all guesswork, you know. If she makes the call, then I guessed right."

Not exactly, as it turned out. She made the call, but that didn't mean I'd played it right.

TWENTY-FOUR

Lia!

He is on the street in front of the coffee shop, squinting through the plate glass window, and they are in a booth with their backs to him. He wouldn't be able to pick out either of them, just seeing the backs of their heads from this distance, but the combination, black and white, makes it easy to spot them. And, across from them, a blond girl sits, and she is instantly recognizable.

And what business do these two have with Lia Parkman? How do they even know she exists?

Kristin Hollander, of course. They went to Kristin Hollander's house, she let them in, they stayed for the better part of an hour, and they left, made a phone call, and here they are, sitting across a table from Lia Parkman, Kristin's cousin.

What are they talking about?

What is she telling them?

She can't tell them too much. She doesn't really know anything. But she knows him, and she could conceivably put them on his track.

He doesn't want that. Whoever they are, whatever they're after, he doesn't want that.

His hand goes to his throat. He's not wearing a tie today, nor a jacket, just a blue shirt with the collar open and the sleeves rolled up for comfort. He lifts out the rhodochrosite disc, feels its smoothness, tucks it away beneath his shirt.

His own fault. He knew she was a loose end, dangling invitingly, waiting for someone to grab hold and give a tug. But, because everything went so smoothly, he let himself believe it was all right to leave a loose end.

He mustn't stand here, staring in the window. They can't see him, but what's the point of drawing attention from anyone? He walks fifty yards south on Broadway, where there's a bus stop. No one thinks you're loitering when you do so at a bus stop.

And it provides a fine view of the coffee shop entrance.

His own fault, but it wasn't just simple carelessness. Because he'd found himself itching to tie off that loose end, and he'd been suspicious of his motives. His hand remembers the way the gun had bucked in it, remembers gripping the

knife, cutting that throat with surgical precision.
And his whole being remembers the way it felt.

Thrilling?

Well, perhaps. But he doesn't much care for
the word. Roller-coaster rides are thrilling.
Drugs are thrilling. Breaking rules is thrilling.

What he'd done was . . . what?

Satisfying?

Whatever you called it, he had wanted more
of it. And so he'd overruled the impulse to tie off
this loose end, talked himself out of it on the
grounds that he'd be running a risk to no real
purpose.

Instead, he'd run a greater risk by leaving the
deed undone.

There is a lesson here, he thinks, if one can
but find it. There is almost certainly an important underlying principle. He will have to think
about it.

What's the best that can happen?

She's in there, sitting with them (whoever
they are, Mr. Salt and Mr. Pepper, whatever it is
they really want). Well, the best thing that can
happen is that the only questions they think to
ask lead to answers that have nothing to do with
him. In which case the only harm done by this
meeting in this dubious restaurant will be to
their respective digestive tracts.

Conversely, what's the worst that can happen?

The worst that can happen is not that dire. She can tell them she met with a man named Arden Brill. That's the name he gave her, and it is manifestly not his own. If they look for Arden Brill, they will search in vain.

Still, it was incredibly stupid to give her that name. Why not John Smith, for God's sake? Why not John Doe or Richard Roe, or, hell, anything properly anonymous and uninformative? He was being cute, calling himself Arden Brill, and to what purpose? Making little jokes only he himself could appreciate? That was ego in action, setting traps into which he alone could fall.

Stupid.

God, he loathes and detests stupidity! He finds it annoying in others, though unquestionably useful at times. But he just plain hates it in himself.

She can tell them his name, Arden Brill's name. She can furnish a description of Arden Brill. She can't provide a photograph of him, can't supply anything his fingertips have touched. He never spilled any DNA anywhere near her—though, he has to admit, she's physically attractive, and that aching vulnerability adds to the strength of the attraction.

Not that it should make any difference. He's not going to make love to her. He doesn't want to, and even if he did, it's not something he would permit himself to do. He would not be quite that stupid, thanks all the same.

What he is going to do—and the sooner the better—is kill her. And why on earth should it be any more satisfying to kill a pretty woman than a plain one?

But it is. He knows it, knows it in his tingling hands, knows it in his surging blood.

Knows it in his bones.

The two men are first to leave. Side by side, youth and age, black and white, they walk uptown on Broadway, headed away from him, looking like a poster for National Brotherhood Week. Well? Shall he follow them?

No, his business is with Lia.

Shall he seize the moment? Stride into the restaurant, do a plausible double-take. Lia, my goodness, I've never seen you in here before. Do you have time for a cup of coffee? No? Well, which way are you headed? I'll walk with you. . . .

No, too visible. People around, and someone might remember something. There's no Bierman handy to take the blame. This is going to be murder by person or persons unknown, so best to stay unknown, and out of sight.

Anyway, she's leaving the restaurant. Now what? Shall he follow her?

Without his willing it, his hand moves to his throat, touches the disc of mottled pink stone. So smooth, so cool to the touch. Different minerals have special properties, that's why men have chosen to wear them since time immemorial. It's not just for adornment. Amethyst is supposed to make you immortal, especially if you dissolve it in brandy and drink it. He doesn't know the traditional properties of rhodochrosite, but it seems—seems—to clarify thought.

Because it's suddenly all quite clear to him. She's bound for home. She may stop somewhere en route, may go home directly. It doesn't matter. He needn't follow her if he knows where she's headed.

First, he has to do something about his car. It won't do to leave it parked where it is, across the street from the Hollander house. And he'd better figure out just what he's going to do about Lia Parkman, and what tools the job will require.

How they met:

Excuse me, but aren't you Lia Parkman?

Yes, and you're—

Arden Brill. You don't know me, there's no reason why you should know me. But . . . well, let me plunge right in. Someone told me you're related to the writer Susan Hollander.

She's my aunt.

By marriage, or . . . ?

My mother is her sister.

And you, uh, you know her?

Well, sure. She's my aunt.

I'm sorry, I must be coming off as very silly. You see, I happen to think she's an outstanding writer. One of the best of her generation. As a matter of fact . . .

Yes?

Well, she's the subject of my dissertation.

You're doing your master's on her?

A doctoral dissertation, actually.

Oh, a doctorate. I'm impressed.

I'm the one who's impressed. Susan Hollander's niece. Could I buy you a cup of coffee? Because I have a million questions I'm dying to ask you.

Well, sure. And if you want . . .

Yes?

Well, I could probably introduce you, and—

No, you're wonderful to offer, but I don't think that would be a good idea.

Oh.

Academic distance and all that. I think I'd be compromising my objectivity if I actually met the woman. But to meet her niece, I think that lies well within the bounds of the permissible.

I see.

Especially when the niece in question is so charming. . . .

She lives on Claremont near La Salle, in an apartment house purchased years ago by the university for student housing. She shares a fourth-floor apartment with three other female students. There's a large living room with a Pullman kitchen, and a long hallway with four small bedrooms off it, and a bathroom at the end of it.

When he moved the car, he went into his office and got a ring of keys from his desk. There are three keys on the ring and they are all shiny. One of them fits the front door of the house on West Seventy-fourth Street, and it has been used only once since he had it made. The others, made the same day by the same locksmith, have not been used at all, so he can't be entirely certain that they will work.

He waits until there's no one around, then picks one of the keys and tries it in the front door. It works perfectly. He turns the key and walks in, crosses the bare lobby.

There's an elevator, but he passes it up and takes the stairs to the fourth floor, walks the length of an empty hallway to the door he knows is hers. He puts his ear to the door, listens, hears nothing.

Ring the bell?

No.

He slips the remaining key in the lock, turns it slowly, eases the door open. The living room is empty, but there's music playing behind closed doors elsewhere in the apartment. He walks quickly down the hall to the last door before the bathroom. He listens, hears talking within.

The door's closed, but not shut tight. He nudges it open an inch or so. She's on the phone, and, incredibly, he hears her say his name.

Well, not his name. Arden Brill's name.

"You have the number if you want to call me. I'm sorry I didn't tell you this before but I had to think about it. I'm sure it's nothing and I don't want to make trouble for anybody but I thought you should know. I just thought—"

And she stops, just like that. She can't see him, but did he unwittingly make a noise? Has she somehow sensed his presence?

He pushes the door open.

Her reaction is remarkable—mouth wide open, eyes big as saucers, hands rising of their own accord, about tit-high, palms out, as if to ward him off.

Her cell phone's on the dresser top, the mouthpiece shut. The answering tape ran out, he realizes. That's why she stopped herself in midsentence. When the machine cut out, she broke the connection.

"Lia!" he says, refusing to react to her reaction, letting her know how glad he is to see her, taking it for granted she's just as delighted to see him. "Lia, where've you been? I've been trying to reach you."

He keeps talking as he strides across the room toward her, and she can't say anything, can't do anything, because it would mean interrupting him in the middle of a sentence, and how can a well-brought-up girl like Lia do anything of the sort? Besides, she's hypnotized, frozen, she's the bird and he's the snake, and it's just delicious looking at her and knowing that she knows that she doesn't have a chance.

He has the little Mace canister in his hand. It's the size of a disposable lighter, and he's had it for weeks, he'd been ready to use it on Jason Bierman, but it hadn't been necessary. It probably isn't necessary now, but she might try to scratch him, she might cry out, and why take the chance? Besides, he'd really like to see just how this stuff works. He's read descriptions, but he has never seen it in action.

He presses the little button, hits her smack in the face with the spray.

And it puts her right on the ground. It's remarkable, really. She's rolling on the floor, her eyes clenched shut, her hands to her face, rubbing her eyes with the heels of her hands—

He feels a great surge of emotion. It takes him by surprise, just as the Mace took her, and the effect is almost as dramatic. He has all of this feeling for her, a feeling rather like love, or, more accurately, like what he imagines love must be like.

Eyes welling with tears, he drops to his knees and reaches for her.

★   ★   ★

The tricky part is getting her into the bathroom. It's only steps away, but someone could be out there in the hall, could see him carrying her. He can't run that risk.

Easier to finish her in her room. Tear strips from a bedsheet, fasten a noose, hang her from an overhead pipe. She's despondent, sad about her aunt's death. Why not?

Or just smash her skull with the lamp base. Someone broke in, robbed her, killed her.

But he's already put her to sleep with a choke hold, already cracked the seal on the pint of vodka and forced a few ounces down her throat.

Stay with the plan, he tells himself.

He opens her door, checks the hallway. He steps out alone, knocks on the closed bathroom door, opens it when there's no response. The room is empty.

He comes back for her. Using a handkerchief, he wipes down the room for fingerprints. That done, he gets her to her feet, checks the hallway again, then half-drags, half-carries her out of her room and into the bathroom. As soon as they're inside he closes and locks the door.

He puts the stopper in the tub, turns the faucets. While the water runs he stretches her out on the cold tile floor, kneels beside her. He undresses her, strips her to her skin, delighted as her slender body reveals itself to him. Like a

Christmas present, he thinks, and sees himself as a willful child, smashing and discarding his toy before he or anyone else has a chance to play with it.

He smiles at the metaphor.

When she is naked and the tub full to a depth of about ten inches, he slips one arm under her thighs and the other under her shoulders and lifts, then lowers her into the tub. He grabs her blond hair with one hand, puts the other on her chest, his fingers spread out so that he is touching both her small breasts at once. He presses down, holding her head under water.

Her eyes are open, staring up through the water. Can she see him? Does she know what's happening?

Does it matter?

He holds her like that, drinking in the sight of her, until bubbles come out of her mouth and nose. He presses down on her chest and more bubbles emerge, float to the surface. And her eyes change. Something has gone out of them.

He takes a deep breath, lets it out. He lets go of her hair, and her head remains beneath the water's surface. He gives her breasts a last little squeeze, lets his hand trail down to her loins. He parts her thighs, slips a finger just the tiniest bit into her, then withdraws it, wondering briefly what impulse prompted the act.

No matter. He folds her clothes, stacks them neatly on the closed commode. He uses his handkerchief again, wiping any surfaces he may have touched.

He sees no one on his way out of the apartment. He takes the stairs again, and passes no one on his way through the lobby. There are a few people on the street, but nobody gives him a second glance.

It is not until he is on the elevated platform again, waiting for the train, that he takes the business card from the breast pocket of his blue shirt. He found it on her dresser, next to the cell phone, and read it then, but he reads it again now.

Matthew Scudder, he reads, and nods to himself, and puts the card back in his shirt pocket.

TWENTY-FIVE

If I'd gone straight home I might have been there when she called, but maybe not. It's hard to say.

And it's moot, because I didn't go straight home. I stopped across the street, watching CNN while T J booted up the computer and searched for Jason Bierman. There were already several Web sites devoted wholly or in part to the massacre on West Seventy-fourth, and he read out several bits of arcana to me, including the report of one incisive fellow who'd paced off the precise distance from the Hollanders' home to the spot in front of the Dakota where John Lennon was shot.

I said, "How many more steps to the grassy knoll? That's what I want to know."

"Here's somethin' else," he said. "His mama says he didn't do it."

So had Oswald's, I told him, and how was that for coincidence? On the TV, Lynne Russell smiled bravely through a report of bad news from the Balkans and worse news from the Middle East. I turned her off when they went to a commercial and called Elaine at her shop. We arranged to meet for an early dinner at Armstrong's. I asked T J if he wanted to join us, but he said he had things to do.

I left him hunched over his Mac and went across the street. I collected the mail and took it upstairs, sorted it, and didn't find anything exciting. I checked the messages, and there was one from Lia Parkman, a disjointed, rambling riff in which she apologized for not having told me earlier that she could recall a conversation involving her Aunt Susan. It had been with a graduate student who was doing a doctoral dissertation on her writing. His name was Arden Brill. She went on to say I could call her, that I had her number, and then the machine cut her off in the middle of a sentence.

But I didn't have her number, T J had her number, and when I called him his line was busy. I tried his cell phone and he picked up, checked the number, and read it off to me. I dialed it and it rang four times, and then a recorded voice told me I'd reached Sprint voice mail, and invited me to leave a message for—and another recorded voice, hers, said, "Lia Parkman."

I decided I'd try her later, and rang off without leaving a message.

I took a shower and decided I didn't need to shave again, and after I got dressed I tried Lia's number again, with the same results. I watched the news some more, tried Lia a third time on my way out the door, and walked a long block west to Tenth Avenue, where Jimmy Armstrong keeps a saloon. I went in and got a Perrier at the bar, turning when I heard my name called. The man on his feet beckoning to me was Manny Karesh, a friend from the old days, when Jimmy's joint was on Ninth Avenue, just around the corner from my hotel.

Manny was at a table with a couple of nurses fresh off their shifts at Roosevelt. They were drinking Margaritas and he was nursing a beer—a Dos Equis, he said, to fit the Mexican theme of the girls' drinks. Perhaps, he suggested, I might want to switch to some Mexican brand of bottled water.

One of the nurses said they had a woman on the ward who'd gone to Mexico on vacation, and drank the water. Manny asked how she was doing. "We're all sort of waiting for her to die," the girl said.

Elaine showed up and we got our own table. "I'd apologize for being late," she said, "but maybe I ought to apologize for showing up at all. You looked as though you were doing just fine."

"Yeah, right," I said. "They take one look at me and they think 'Geriatric Ward.'"

"That might not be so bad," she said. "Maybe you could get them to give you an enema. Anyway, if they've got one eye on the calendar, what are they doing with Manny? He's twenty years older than you."

"He's got the heart of a boy."

"In the body of a dirty old man," she said, and reached for the menu.

She had the avocado salad and I had a bowl of chili, and while we waited for the food I told her I'd sent the check to Michael. "All I did was write a check," I said, "and that seems like too much and not enough, both at once."

I explained how I'd made the check payable to Michael, and he'd write a single check for the full amount payable to the employer. She asked if he'd know half of it was from me. I said, "His boss? He won't care who it's from. Oh, that's not what you mean, is it?"

"Michael said he could only send five thousand, so will he say where he got the rest?"

"We didn't discuss it," I said. "He can do what he wants."

When we got home there were three messages. The one from Lia was still on there, joined by a message from Danny Boy, who suggested I might want to drop over to Mother Blue's anytime after nine.

The third message said, "Will the party who receives this message please call Ira Wentworth." There was a number to call, and nothing else.

I found Elaine and asked her if she knew anybody named Ira Wentworth. She didn't, and when she asked why I played the message for her. She said, "Guess what? We just won a free trip to inspect a time-share resort on beautiful Grand Cay-

man Island. Except he doesn't sound like a telemarketer. You know what he sounds like? A cop."

I played it again, and I knew what she meant. I
dialed the number, and it rang a long time. I was
on the point of hanging up when a woman picked
it up and said, "Squad room, this is McLaren."

I asked for Ira Wentworth and she said he was
out. Did I want to leave a message? I said I was
Matthew Scudder, returning his call. Did I want to
leave a number? "He must have it," I said. "He dialed it."

Did I know what this was in reference to?
"Well, I figure he'll know," I said. "He called me."

"You were right," I told Elaine. "He's a cop, according to somebody named McLaren. Who's also
a cop, or she wouldn't be answering the phone,
though I can't say she sounds like one."

"I wonder what he wants."

"No idea. She didn't even say which precinct,
she just said 'squad room,' and I didn't think to
ask."

"You could call back."

"I could also say the hell with it," I said. "I'm
going to see what Danny's got. While I'm at it I
can ask him what he knows about Wentworth and
McLaren."

"Wentworth & McLaren. It sounds like a team
of architects. Or maybe a design studio."

"They're cops," I said, "first and foremost, and
design's strictly a sideline. Look, if he calls, see if
you can find out what it's about, will you?"

★   ★   ★

When I got to Mother Blue's, the house rhythm section was working its way tastefully through "Walking," the Miles Davis tune. I joined Danny Boy, and when the number ended the drummer and bass player left the stage and went to the bar, and the pianist played a Thelonious Monk composition. Danny and I both recognized the tune, but neither of us could come up with the title. When the number ended the pianist joined his fellow musicians at the bar, the jukebox kicked in, and Danny poured himself an inch of vodka and said that everybody had the same thing to say about Ivanko and Bierman.

"Which is that it's a good thing they're dead," he said. "The consensus seems to be that they're the sort of people who give crime a bad name. Especially Ivanko, who they all figured would do something like this sooner or later. Of course that's hindsight talking, but in this case it spoke with rare conviction."

"And Bierman?"

"Now that's what's interesting," he said, "and the reason I called. Nobody had much of anything to say about Bierman. If they were just as glad he was dead, that's because they knew him as Ivanko's partner in this particular outrage of the week. The one exception is Jason Bierman's mother."

"According to T J," I said, "she's all over the Internet."

"All over New York, too. She flew into town to clear her boy's name."

"Bierman's not from New York?"

"I don't know where he's from," he said, "or her either, originally, but she lives in Wisconsin these days. The city's one I never heard of before, and it's got ten or twelve letters and half of them are O's. Not that it matters, because she's not there anymore. She's here."

"In New York."

"At the old Hotel Peralda, known to the cognoscenti as the Paraldehyde Arms."

"Just west of Broadway in the Nineties," I said.

"Ninety-seventh Street," he said, "and what a pesthole it always was. Babies crying and bullets flying, and the only quiet rooms were the ones where the tenants were dead. Some hotel chain bought the place, if you can believe it, and they've converted it to a budget hotel for respectable travelers. I just hope they tented it first and fumigated the daylights out of it."

"And that's where she's staying?"

"If she hasn't gotten herself killed yet, or reinvented herself as a transvestite hooker, or hopped a freight back to Ocomocoloco. She swears her son was a good boy, and he couldn't possibly have done what they say he did. According to her, Jason was a fall guy for a player to be named later."

"Either I'm as crazy as she is," I said, "or the woman's right."

He poured himself some more vodka. "You were made for each other," he said. "She's been talking some to the press, from what I hear, but the only ones who want to bother with her are from the supermarket tabloids, and what they really want her to do is tell how young Jase used to pull the wings off flies and use stray cats for scientific experiments. When she insisted on making him sound like a choirboy, they lost interest. And of course the cops don't want to hear from her. They make some rookie take her statement, and then they just shine her on."

"Can't blame them."

"No. So what she's doing, even though she doesn't have a pot to piss in, and God knows the Colonial Inn expects you to bring your own—"

"That's the new name of the Paraldehyde?"

"Yes, and it's wonderfully descriptive, as long as your idea of a colony is Devil's Island. What the woman's doing, and why I couldn't wait to call you, is she's looking for a private detective to represent her interests and clear her poor boy's reputation. Made for each other, the two of you. Made for each other!"

If that had been one of Danny's nights at Poogan's, I might never have met Helen Leich Bierman Watling, the twice-widowed mother of

Jason Bierman. I'd have thought of calling her at her hotel, and I might have looked at my watch and decided it was too late for a phone call. If I'd failed to find a working pay phone, intending to call when I got home, I'd have been that much more likely to decide it was too late and let it go until morning.

By then I'd have heard from Ira Wentworth (of Wentworth & McLaren) and a call to a dotty old lady from Wisconsin would no longer have ranked high on my list of priorities. In any event, I'd have had to call her by nine that morning, because that was when she was leaving to catch an eleven-A.M. flight to Milwaukee, the airport of choice for those living in Oconomowoc.

But Mother Blue's is on Amsterdam in the Nineties, just a few minutes from the Colonial Inn, late the Paraldehyde Arms. I didn't even call, I just walked there, and a clerk who looked too well-scrubbed for the rest of the lobby confirmed that Mrs. Watling was a guest of the hotel. I picked up a house phone and he put through a call to her room.

I said, "Mrs. Watling, my name's Matthew Scudder, I'm a private detective. I'd like to talk with you about your son."

"Oh, my," she said. "You people really come out of the woodwork, don't you?"

"I beg your pardon?"

"I guess you smell money," she said. "I'm sorry to disappoint you, but I'm afraid I can't possibly afford the fees you charge."

And she rang off.

"I think we got cut off," I told the clerk. "Could you put me through again?"

When she picked up I said, "Mrs. Watling, you couldn't hire me if you wanted to. I already have a client, and I happen to believe your son is in fact innocent, that he was set up and killed by a man as yet unidentified. I'm downstairs in the lobby, I walked over here to talk to you, but if you hang up on me again I'll go home, and you can go to hell."

I said all that in one breath, wanting to get the words in before she broke the connection, and maybe that's why my finish was a little more forceful than I'd intended. For a moment I thought she had in fact hung up, because I didn't hear anything from her, and then she said, "Oh, dear. I **finally** act in an assertive manner, after being so namby-pamby ever since I **got** to this city, and I guess I picked the wrong man to hang up on. Are you still there?"

"I'm here."

"Do you want to come up here?"

NO VISITORS ALLOWED IN ROOMS, a sign announced. "I don't think I can," I said. "There seems to be a rule against it."

"Do you suppose they think I'm a prostitute? Well, it doesn't matter, there's no room for two people in here anyway. There's not really room for one. This is the worst excuse for a hotel I've ever seen in my whole life, let alone stayed in, and they're charging me ninety-five dollars a night, and tax is extra. And people tell me it's a bargain!"

Welcome to New York, I thought.

"I'll have to get dressed," she said, "but it won't take me a minute, and then I'll be right down."

It was more than a minute, but no more than five, before she emerged from the elevator, wearing a beige pantsuit and a bright yellow blouse. "I'm dressed all wrong for New York," she said. "You don't have to tell me."

"I wasn't going to."

"Well, I am, and I know it, but I'm not going to run out and buy a lot of black clothes just so I can fit in. And I don't think I would fit in even if I did."

I wasn't inclined to argue the point. She looked like a suburban Midwestern matron, her light brown hair carefully styled, her lipstick neatly applied, her wrinkles the kind they call laugh lines. She wasn't the stereotypical mother I'd envisioned, but she seemed to fit the role she'd fashioned for herself, or found forced upon her—the mother determined to salvage a dead son's good name.

Except it wasn't all that good a name to start with, she told me, after we had settled into a corner booth at the Ninety-sixth Street equivalent of the Morning Star, or the Salonika. "Nothing ever really worked out for Jason," she said. "His father was about the handsomest boy in our high school class, and the most fun. But fun was all he cared about, and fun meant drinking, and drinking meant . . . well, he took off when Jason was four years old. I never heard from him, and I was told I could divorce him **in absentia,** or have him declared legally dead after seven years. But I didn't know that I wanted to do that, either of those things, and then I didn't have to, because he turned a car over somewhere in California and there was a card in his wallet of who to notify in the event he died, which he did."

Jason didn't do well in school, she said, and then when she remarried he didn't get along with his stepfather, who was, she had to admit it, a hard man to get along with. And Jason sort of drifted, and he wasn't too good at staying out of trouble, but he was never what you'd call bad. There was nothing hurtful about him, nothing mean-spirited. They said he'd been arrested for sneaking under a subway turnstile, and she could imagine him doing that, or even shoplifting from a supermarket or department store, but what they'd said he'd done . . .

I told her how I was investigating from the other direction, trying to find someone with a motive specific to the Hollanders. If I could find some common element, someone in her son's life who was in any way linked to Byrne and Susan Hollander, then I might be able to connect the dots.

She thought it over while she spread butter on her toasted bran muffin ("one thing that's definitely better in New York, I'll grant you that") and took a little bite. She sipped some iced tea, ate more of the muffin, drank more of the tea, and looked up at me and shook her head.

"I just don't know who he did or didn't know," she said. "He would call me just about once a week, he was good about that. He called collect, of course. I told him to, he didn't have the money to pay for his calls. In fact I helped him out a little, I sent a money order every few weeks. I didn't send checks because it was almost impossible for him to find a place that would cash a personal check on an out-of-state bank, and of course he didn't have a bank account of his own to deposit it into. He didn't have anything."

Except, she said, he was beginning to find himself, to get his feet planted. Not to take charge of his life, that made him sound a little more capable than he had yet become, but at least to play an active role in his own life instead of watching passively as it unfolded before him.

"He was working," she said. "Three hours a day, Monday through Friday, delivering lunches for a delicatessen. They paid him in cash at the end of his shift each day, and it wasn't very much, but he got tips, too. And he worked nights, too, making deliveries for a package store."

I didn't know the term, and she said, "Don't you call it that? A store that sells packaged goods. Beverages, alcoholic beverages. What do you call it?"

"A liquor store."

"Well, that's New York for you," she said. "I guess we're more discreet in the Midwest, or maybe just more namby-pamby. We call them package stores. Now you didn't know that, and I didn't know there was anything **else** to call them, so I guess we both learned something, didn't we?"

Jason's life didn't sound like much, she knew. A couple of part-time subsistence jobs hardly amounted to a budding career. But when you knew him and where he'd come from, well, you could see that he was on the right track.

"The last time he got in trouble," she said, "they had him see a counselor, and I have to give New York credit for this, because Jason said the man helped him see things a little more clearly. How he was just getting in his own way time and time again, and how it didn't have to be that way. And from that point on, his life began to improve."

Some specifics might have helped. The name of the social worker, for instance, who might have known the names of some of the other people in Jason Bierman's new life. It would have been nice to know the names and locations of his occasional employers; she knew only that the deli was in Manhattan, which didn't narrow it down much. The package store ("or liquor store, I'll have to remember to call it that") might have been anywhere.

She finished her bran muffin and iced tea, and I decided I'd had as much of my coffee as I wanted. I picked up the check, and she took a wallet from her purse and asked how much her share came to. I said it was on me. She insisted she'd be happy to pay, and I told her to forget it. "You're a visitor," I said. "Next time I'm in Wisconsin, I'll let you pick up the tab."

"Well, that's very nice of you," she said. "And after I just about accused you of trying to drum up some high-priced business!" But she'd had audiences with several private detectives, she said, and one told her to go home, that she was wasting her time, and the others wanted substantial advances before they would undertake to do a thing.

"Two men asked for two thousand dollars, and one wanted twenty-five hundred," she said. "And there was another man who asked for two or three thousand, I can't remember which, and I said that was much too high, and he said, well, how about a thousand? And I hemmed and hawed, and he said if I gave him five hundred he could get started. And it came to me that he wanted whatever I could give him, and he probably wouldn't do a thing once he had the money in his hand."

I told her she was probably right. She apologized again, unnecessarily, and asked if I thought she should stay in New York. She was supposed to fly home in the morning but she supposed she could stick around for a few more days.

I told her there was no need. I gave her one of my cards and made sure I had her address and phone number written down correctly. And I walked her back to her hotel, even though she told me not to bother. I waited until she had collected her key from the desk and boarded the elevator, then went outside and looked for a taxi.

★   ★   ★

When I walked in the door, Elaine told me Ira Wentworth had called twice. He wouldn't say what it was about, just that I should call him as soon as I got in.

I tried his number and a nasal-voiced male said, "Squad room, this is Acker." I gave my name and said I was returning Detective Wentworth's call.

"He's not in," Acker said, "but I know he wants to talk to you. Will you be staying put for the next ten minutes?"

"I'm not going anywhere. He's got the number, but let me give it to you again."

He repeated it back to me and rang off, and I realized I'd missed my chance to ask the number of the precinct. I picked up the phone and had my finger on the redial button but didn't push it.

I had a feeling I knew which precinct it was.

I put the phone down while I checked my notebook, picked it up again, and tried a number I'd tried before, with no success. It rang once, twice, and then somebody answered but didn't speak.

I said, "Ira Wentworth?"

The voice I'd heard once before, on my machine, said, "Who the hell is this?"

TWENTY-SIX

Half an hour later the doorman called upstairs to announce a Mr. Wentworth. I said to send him up, and was waiting in the hall when he got off the elevator. He was in his late thirties, tall and broad-shouldered, with a square jaw and a high forehead. His dark hair was combed straight back.

He said his name and I said mine, and we shook hands. "I made a couple of phone calls," he said. "You were on the job yourself."

"That was a while ago."

"You had a gold shield."

I suppose that accounted for the handshake. You can't shake hands over the phone, but even if you could I think he'd have passed it up. He'd been wary earlier, thrown off-stride by my having called him on Lia Parkman's cell phone. He'd picked it up once they'd established there were no fingerprints but hers to be found on it, and he'd been carrying it around ever since.

That was how he'd called me. The phone logged recent calls, and all he'd had to do was find the last call she'd made and open the mouthpiece to redial it. He'd called me without knowing who I was. Thus his original message, requesting I call back without identifying me by name.

Then I'd called back and left my name, and he'd called again, twice, and left messages, and I called him, and Charlie Acker had managed to reach him, and he was all set to call me when the phone in his pocket rang. And it was me, asking for him by name, and confusing the hell out of him for a minute there.

Over the phone, he hadn't even been willing to confirm that she was dead. But I already knew that. I knew the minute I heard his voice instead of hers, and I may have known when I placed the call.

"This is a nice building," he said. "I've never been inside, but I've admired it many times from the street. You been here long?"

"A couple of years. I've lived in the neighborhood a lot longer."

"Nice," he said. "Walk to the park, walk to the theaters. Very convenient." He admired the apartment, too, as I led him through it to the kitchen. Elaine was in the bedroom with the door closed, but she'd made a pot of coffee first, and I poured us each a cup and sat down with him at the kitchen table.

He tried the coffee and said it was outstanding, and I asked him about Lia Parkman, and he said, yes, she was dead. Her body had been discovered shortly after five that afternoon by one of her roommates. She lived in student housing on Claremont Avenue, shared a unit with three other students, and two of them were home at the time, and one of them knocked on the closed bathroom door, got no response, and walked in to find her in the bathtub, drowned, dead.

"Cause of death's drowning," he said. "Water in the lungs confirms that, pending final results from the medical examiner. Open pint bottle of Georgi vodka on the dresser next to the cell phone. Her prints on the bottle, nobody else's. Initial impression, she had a drink or two, went to take a bath, passed out and drowned."

"I can't believe that's what happened."

"Well," he said, "neither can I, but probably for reasons that are different from yours. First off, there's marks on her neck suggesting she might have been choked. That's also pending word from the ME's office, but it gets your attention. Then there's the vodka. Just a couple of ounces gone, and you don't figure that's enough to make a healthy young woman pass out. Granted, different people react differently, and if the water in the tub's real hot it could be a contributing factor, but it's unlikely. Of course she could have had a couple of pops before she got home, or pills of some sort, and the last slug of vodka made the difference.

Once again, we'll know more when we get the autopsy results."

"Was she much of a drinker?"

He nodded approvingly. "That's where I was going next. According to the roommates, she hardly drank at all. Maybe a glass of white wine at a party, but the idea of her bringing a bottle back to her room, they couldn't see it. And then there's the prints on the bottle."

"Her prints, you said."

"Just her prints. What was the clerk in the liquor store doing, wearing gloves? Plus the prints are from her right hand, and she's right-handed."

"So?"

"Bottle's got a twist-off cap. You're going to open a bottle, how do you do it?"

I moved my hands in the air, working it out for myself. It had been a long time since I uncapped a pint of liquor, but I suppose any bottle would qualify, even salad dressing. "I think I'd hold the bottle in my left hand," I said, "and turn the cap with my right."

"If you're right-handed," Wentworth said, "that's how you'd do it."

"Any prints on the cap?"

"None." He picked up his coffee cup, but it was empty. He didn't ask for more, but I got the carafe and filled both our cups, and he grinned. "I'll regret it," he said, "drinking a second cup this late at night, but the hell with it. Some sins are worth the punishment. You grind the beans yourself?" I said we did, and he said it made a difference. Then he said, "There's another thing, made a little alarm bell go off for me. Her clothes."

"Her clothes?"

"Toilet lid's down and her clothes are folded and stacked on top of it, neat as a pin. She came in, ran a tub, got undressed, and hopped in."

"So?"

"Where's her towel? They share the bathroom, the four of them, so they each have their own towels and keep them in their rooms. There's a hand towel there for everybody's use, but it's too small to use after a bath. How come she forgot her towel?"

"All that vodka," I said.

"Yeah, right." He ran a hand through his hair. "None of this is conclusive, but it makes me want to take a second look. Which I'd be doing anyway if the medical examiner comes up with anything interesting. But while we wait for word from him, I'm treating this as a homicide."

"I think you're right to."

"So you said, and I'd love to know why. I'd also like to know why you're the last person she called, and what your connection is to her in the first place."

"I'm doing some work for Kristin Hollander."

"Name's familiar."

"She's the daughter of Byrne and Susan Hollander."

"Couple killed in that home invasion end of July."

"That's right. Lia Parkman is Kristin's cousin, Susan Hollander's niece."

"Jesus," he said. "Now why the hell didn't anybody tell me that? The one roommate said something about she was depressed about a recent death in the family, but that wasn't just a death, it was a fucking bloodbath. But the perps are dead, aren't they? Murder and suicide out in Coney Island?"

"Coney Island Avenue," I said. "Which is actually in Midwood."

"Close enough. You're doing some work for the daughter, and I don't suppose you're putting a new roof on the house. You're doing what, investigating?"

"It's unofficial," I said. "But yes, I'm investigating."

"And offhand I can only think of one thing you could be investigating. Case is closed, right?"

"Yes."

"And the daughter thinks the whole story hasn't come out yet. Or you think that, or both. Which is it?"

"Both."

"And that's what put you on to the cousin? Help me out here. How does she fit in?"

I brought him up to speed, just hitting the high points—the front door key, the numeric code for the burglar alarm. "Lia Parkman had a key and she knew the keypad code," I said. "This afternoon I managed to sit down with her and ask her who might have borrowed the key or doped out the code. She said she couldn't think of anybody, but I knew she was holding something back."

"Sometimes you can tell."

"I could tell," I said, "but I couldn't do anything about it. Maybe I should have kept at her. I had to make a judgment call, and I decided I was better off letting her think about it. I gave her a card, told her to call me if she came up with anything."

"And she did."

"If I'd come straight home," I said, then broke it off. "But I didn't, and by the time I got here she'd called and left a message. I called her right back and got her voice mail."

"That's because her phone was turned off. When that happens the voice mail kicks in. You leave her a message?"

"No, what for? I figured I'd try her until I got her. And I did, a couple of times, with the same results. I didn't even know it was a cell phone, I figured it was the phone in her room and she was out."

"They rarely have actual phones in their rooms, the college kids. It's all cell phones. It's simpler, when you're moving all the time."

"Even if I'd left a message," I said, "she never would have received it. He must have already killed her by then."

"He must have been very fucking slick," he said. "Did I mention two of her three roommates were home when it happened? They were studying, they had music playing, but even so. He had to get in the building, get in the apartment, get into her bedroom, take her down, then drag her into the bathroom, strip her, hold her under until she drowns, and then get out of the place without bumping into anybody."

"If he's clever about it," I said, "and if his luck is running—"

"Oh, it's doable, no question. And he wasn't perfect."

"The towel."

"The towel is one. He probably just assumed towels are in the bathroom, you don't have to take one. But her bath towel was on a hook in her closet, and she wouldn't have left it there and then got in the tub. The vodka bottle's another. It's more plausible without the liquor—she stumbles, hits her head on the tub, whatever, drowns before she recovers consciousness. That's more plausible than an afternoon drunk on two ounces of Georgi with a girl who's not a drinker to begin with. Plus where's the bag?"

"The bag?"

"You ever buy a pint of booze and not have them put it in a paper bag for you? She'd have left the bottle in the bag until she got home, not tossed the bag on her way home. And the fingerprints. He was cute, wiping the bottle, getting her prints on it, but he used the wrong hand and didn't bother with the cap. That's not enough to hang him, but it's plenty to make a person take a second look."

"You think so? Most people wouldn't even notice."

"Well, I noticed."

"But you're pretty good at this," I said. "A little smarter than the average bear."

He colored, surprised by the compliment. "I don't know about that," he said. "If I was that goddam good, I'd be able to tell you who killed her."

"According to Lia," I said, "his name is Arden Brill."

Hell," he said. "It sounds more like Arden than anything else, doesn't it? Could you play it one more time?"

I had gone into the bedroom to fetch the answering machine, but Elaine woke up while I was unplugging it and insisted I leave the machine where it was and bring Wentworth in. She disappeared into the bathroom, and emerged during the second playing of the message, wearing a robe and fresh makeup. Since then we'd heard the message another half-dozen times, and were getting less certain with each hearing.

"Arden," he said. "Isn't that a place? The Arden Forest?"

"In Shakespeare," Elaine said. "I don't think there's a real forest."

"No? It's just made up?"

No one was entirely sure, and he pointed out

that either way, it was an unusual first name. A last name, sure. Elizabeth Arden, for example. Elaine recalled Eve Arden, the actress, who was before Wentworth's time. I pushed the button and we listened to the message again.

"It could be Auden," he said. "Like the poet?"

"Or Alden," I suggested, "or maybe Alton. They're both occasionally used as first names."

Elaine checked the phone book. There were several Brills, but none with the initial A. "Of course that's just Manhattan," she said. "And who knows where he lives, or if his phone's listed."

"It's probably not his name," I said.

"Well, here's the way I see it," Wentworth said. "If it is his name, he's probably not the guy."

Elaine said, "Wait a minute, I must be missing something. If there actually **is** an English scholar named Arden Brill, that means the girl was lying? That doesn't make any sense."

Wentworth shook his head. "Let's assume she wasn't telling a story," he said, "because why would she? No, she was telling the truth. A guy told her his name was Arden Brill and he was doing a thesis on her aunt. Now if there really is such a person, then not only was she telling the truth, but so was he. His name really is Brill and he really was doing a paper, a thesis, whatever. So he's legit."

"And if there's nobody by that name—"

"Then he's a phony," I said, "and he got close to Lia so that he could copy her key and find a way around the burglar alarm. So if Brill is real, somebody else had a reason to want Lia Parkman dead. And if there's no such person as Brill, then he's the one."

"And a lot of good it does us to know that," Wentworth said, "because we've got no idea who he is."

After he left, promising to get back to us when he knew something, Elaine said there was another possibility. "There could be a man named Arden Brill, and he could even be a doctoral candidate in the English department. But that doesn't mean he's necessarily the man who got in touch with Lia Parkman."

"Don't stop there."

"Well, say I want to win your confidence. I make up this story about my thesis and your aunt, di dah di dah di dah. But suppose you check? So I pick a name of somebody who really exists, some scholar she wouldn't ordinarily run into in a million years, and when she checks, yes, there is an Arden Brill in the English department, as a matter of fact he's hard at work on his doctorate, which is probably on bird symbolism in the poetry of Robinson Jeffers and nothing to do with Susan Hollander, but nobody's going to tell her that. You see what I mean?"

"Yes, sure."

"Does it make sense?"

"Maybe."

"Because here's what **doesn't** make sense otherwise," she said. "If his name's **not** Arden Brill, why would he make up such an unusual name?"

TWENTY-SEVEN

I was shaving when the call came. An Officer Tillis from the Twenty-sixth Precinct, and could I come in so they could take my statement in the Lia Parkman case? I said I could, and drank a cup of coffee before I caught the train to 125th Street.

The station house is on 126th Street, a block and a half west of Broadway. I walked there and wound up sitting at a metal desk in a room that was otherwise empty, except for a framed photo of the mayor on the wall over the desk. Above it, someone had taped up a headline cut from an American Express magazine ad: DO YOU KNOW ME?

They gave me a yellow pad and let me use my own pen, and I wrote out a sort of **Reader's Digest** version of my connection to Lia Parkman. I hadn't told Wentworth about my first meeting with the girl, or her initial suspicions of her cousin. Why add to the confusion? With that exception, my statement was reasonably complete. I read it over and signed it, and they told me I could go home.

There's an Episcopal church across the street from the Two-six, and if the doors had been open I might have gone in. Instead I went back to the subway entrance, then kept on going to La Salle and west for a block to Claremont. I didn't know which building was Lia's, but I didn't have to ask too many people before the sleepy-eyed attendant at a coin laundry pointed out the apartment house on the corner. I stood across the street and looked it over, a six-story brick cube with mock-Tudor trim. I didn't go in, didn't try to locate any of her roommates. An official investigation was in process, and I had no business getting in everybody's way. I just wanted a closer look, and I decided this was close enough.

I headed back to Broadway. There was a West African restaurant a few doors up La Salle, and I made a note to try it sometime. Meanwhile I thought of the Salonika, just two blocks away. I was hungry, I hadn't had anything but that one cup of coffee, and I could eat there as well as anywhere else, but I decided I didn't want to share my table with a ghost. I didn't blame myself for her death, I blamed the son of a bitch who'd killed her, but I couldn't help wondering whether the hand might have played out differently if I'd been a little firmer with her the previous afternoon.

And if I had, and if she'd told me in person

what she later told my answering machine? Wouldn't she still have gone home, and wouldn't he still have paid her a visit? And wouldn't it have all come out the same?

I rode downtown and had my breakfast at the Morning Star.

When I got home there was a message to call Ira Wentworth, and this time I didn't shortcut the process by ringing Lia Parkman's cell phone. I called the precinct, and he answered his own phone. I told him he was putting in a lot of hours.

"I stayed at it pretty late last night," he said, "and I came in early this morning, because I wanted to see if I could goose the ME's office a little. I got the report. Injuries to the throat are consistent with a choke hold. Cause of death is definitely drowning, water in the lungs, et cetera. Blood alcohol is close to zero. Small amount of vodka in the stomach, unabsorbed into the bloodstream because she died so soon after ingesting it. He was being cute with the vodka, and it's three different kinds of a wrong note."

He'd been cute before, with the brass bolt he'd attached to the inside of Bierman's door.

"And you'll like this," he said. "Skin tissue on the face reveals traces of—and there's a chemical name a yard long I'm not even going to try to pronounce, but it's identified as a propellant frequently added to chemical Mace."

"That's how he took her down."

"Maced her and choked her," he said, "and then took her and drowned her. Must have been quick."

"And quiet."

"Well, it had to be quiet, with her roommates just a few yards away. Poor kid."

"She was on full scholarship," I said. "Taking a summer school course on the French Revolution."

"Maybe she had a classmate named Arden Brill. Wouldn't that be handy?"

But there was no Arden Brill. Wentworth called an hour later to tell me as much. There were no Brills at all registered at Columbia, none at NYU or CUNY or any other colleges he'd checked.

Phone directories for the city and the surrounding tristate area showed a fair number of Brills, about the same number proportionally as we'd found in the Manhattan book. None with Arden for a first name, though, and nothing close—no Alden, no Alton, no Auden. He had a couple of officers on the phones, working their way through the Brills, trying to find an Arden Brill. It was a thankless task, stupefyingly dull, and he didn't expect it to yield anything useful.

"He made up a name," he said, "and she passed it on, and got killed for it. It proves one thing, though it wouldn't prove it in court."

"Oh?"

"Proves you were right about the Hollanders.

Case never should have been closed, though you can see why they closed it."

I asked if he was going to try to get it reopened.

"Call up somebody I don't know and tell him he fucked up? That's no way to win friends and influence people."

"It might help get police protection for Kristin Hollander."

"The cousin. You think she needs it?" He answered his own question. "Both parents and a cousin, I guess somebody ought to keep an eye on her. Reminds me, she's on my list of people I'd better talk to."

"Has she been notified?"

"Not by me. Next of kin's her mother, and nobody's been able to reach her yet. Roommate ID'd the body."

"I'll notify Kristin," I said, "and I'll tell her to expect to hear from you."

"Appreciate it."

"And not to open the door for anybody else."

"I'll make sure I'm the one contacts her," he said. "And as far as reopening the case, for now all I want to concentrate on is getting this guy. Once he's good for Parkman, we can add the Hollanders to his tab."

"Plus two in Brooklyn."

"Yeah, I forgot those. What's that come to, five in all? He's beginning to look like a poster boy for the death penalty, but I wouldn't count on it. Still, five life sentences should keep him on ice for a while. Now if only we had some idea who he is and where to find him."

"You'll find him," I said. "He's good, but he's too cute to stay hidden."

"You know," he said, "I got the same feeling myself. There's one more thing he did, besides the vodka bottle."

"What's that?"

"Well, you gave her your card, didn't you? Your business card?"

"Yes."

"And she must have had it out to dial your number. So where is it?"

"Gone, I gather."

"And it didn't walk off by itself. One more thing to confirm what we already know, which is that she didn't just slip beneath the water's surface and drown of her own accord. Of course there's something else it tells us."

"What's that?"

"Well, he picked up the card. He knows who you are."

Kristin hadn't looked at a paper or listened to the news, so I got to tell her that her cousin was dead. It might have been gentler in person, but I was more interested in saving the time it would take to get from my place to hers. So I didn't see her face when I gave her the news.

"He tried to make it look like accidental death,"

I said, "but he didn't do a very good job of it, and there's a damn good cop running the investigation. His name's Ira Wentworth, and he'll be in touch with you."

"He'll want to talk to me?"

"Definitely."

"But I don't know anything," she said. "What can I tell him that he doesn't already know?"

Probably nothing, I allowed, but he'd want to establish that for himself. I told her he might be getting someone higher up to authorize police protection for her, and that she should accept a police guard if he offered it. "I don't think you're in danger," I said, "but I didn't think your cousin was in danger, either, and it turned out I was wrong. In the meantime, I don't want you to open your door to anyone but me or Detective Ira Wentworth." I described him, and told her to make sure he showed some ID in that name. "And can you screen your calls? I'd advise you to do that, if only to avoid the press. It's a miracle they haven't learned yet that Lia was your cousin, but they'll get the word before long, and they'll start calling and turning up on your doorstep. Don't talk to them and don't answer the door."

"I won't."

"I mean it, Kristin. It's not just that they'll upset you and waste your time. There's also the fact that one of them could be the man who killed your cousin."

"And my parents."

"Yes."

"I won't let anyone in. Oh."

"What?"

"Well, I'm expecting someone this afternoon."

"Who?"

"His name's David Hamm. He's the man who gave me the ride home the night I found . . . the night it happened."

He'd waited at the curb, making sure she got in all right.

"It couldn't be him," she said, anticipating my thought, "because he was there all evening, at my friend's house. And the police investigated him thoroughly before they found the two dead bodies in Brooklyn."

"Whose idea was it for him to come over this afternoon?"

"Well, he called. I invited him. He called once before, after the funeral, all concerned, and . . ."

Her voice trailed off. I said, "Call him now and tell him something's come up, you won't be home, you can't have company."

"All right."

"If he calls back, don't take the call, and don't return it."

"But . . . all right."

"Call him now, and then call me back."

"All right."

He was probably perfectly all right. He couldn't have been in two places at one time, and the police would have checked him inside and out during the early stages of the investigation. I didn't give a damn. I didn't want him getting close to her, him or anybody else.

I was just starting to wonder what was taking so goddam long when the phone rang and she said it was all taken care of, and was there anything else?

"Yes," I said. "As a matter of fact, there is. Do you know anyone named Arden Brill?"

"Arden Brill."

"Yes. Does the name ring a bell?"

"No, should it?"

"Did anyone ever get in touch with you, recently or in the past, with the explanation that he was doing a doctoral dissertation on your mother?"

"On my mother?"

"On her writing."

"Gosh, no," she said. "I can't imagine that anyone would. I mean, she was serious about her work, and I think she was a fine writer, but she wasn't important to the extent that anyone would write a thesis about her."

"But someone could have been interested in her work."

"Well, sure. I mean, she was an interesting writer, so why wouldn't people be interested?"

"Could you see if she had any correspondence from Arden Brill?"

"Is that who—"

"I don't think he exists," I said, "but I think that's one name that he used."

"I could check her files," she said. "She filed all her correspondence in a cabinet in her studio, and there's a pile of miscellaneous papers, and I could go through those. And I could check her computer, too, and see if his name comes up. First name A-R-D-E-N, last name B-R-I-L-L? I'll call and let you know if I find anything."

I'd tried T J a couple of times earlier but he was out. The second time I remembered to try him on his cell phone—it's never the first thing I think of—and it rang unanswered. I took another shot when I got off the phone with Kristin, and this time he picked up right away.

He already knew about Lia. He'd been on the Columbia campus, and there were a lot of conflicting stories going around—that she was the latest victim of the man the tabloids had dubbed the Dorm Rapist, that she had killed herself, that the boyfriend of one of her roommates had killed her accidentally in some sort of rough sex play involving water.

"The last part's right," I said. "The part about the water." I filled him in, then asked if he was home.

"You just called me," he said, "and I picked up. Where else I gonna be?"

"You could be anyplace," I said. "I called you on your cell phone, didn't I?"

"Oh," he said. "So you did."

"I think I did, but I suppose—"

"No, must be you did," he said, " 'cause here I be, talkin' on it."

"You didn't answer when I tried you before."

"Had the sound turned off when I was in the classroom. Professors get all hinky when they're in the middle of a sentence and some fool's phone goes off."

"But you're home now. Don't go anywhere, I'm on my way over."

"Can't wait."

"Force yourself," I said. "And while you're waiting, start looking for Arden Brill."

There was an Alden Brill in Yreka, California, and an Arlen Brill in Gadsden, Alabama, and their names popped up without much effort on his part. I was impressed, but he frowned and shook his head.

"Ain't gonna find him this way," he said. "Even if we do, we don't be findin' nothin'. This ain't about some dude flew in from California an' killed a bunch of people. Guy we lookin' for is home-grown."

"That's true, but—"

"An' his name ain't Arden Brill, neither."

"Still," I said, "it's a place to start, and it's all we have."

He was nodding. "What you said before," he said, "that Elaine said. Why'd he pick a name like Arden Brill?"

"That's the question."

"Maybe that's where we ought to go."

"How?"

"Let's see something," he said, bending over the keyboard. "This here'll take a minute. Y'all just talk amongst yourselves."

I put the TV on but muted it so the sound wouldn't distract him. When I found myself trying to read Judy Fortin's lips I gave up and turned it off. I reached for a magazine and got one called **MacAddict**, which wasn't, as I might have guessed, for people who filled up regularly on Happy Meals and Egg McMuffins, but for users of Macintosh computers. I was trying to find an article I could make head or tail out of when he said, "Arden Brill."

"You found something?"

"Coulda called himself Abe," he said, "'less he thought it was too ethnic. Or AA, only then you'd likely go lookin' for him at a meetin'."

"What are you talking about?"

" 'Bout Arden Brill. Coulda called himself Carl Young, an' then we never woulda got nowhere 'cause we never woulda knowed how he spelled it. You don't see what I'm sayin', do you?"

"Not a clue."

"Thing is," he said, "I heard the name Brill, an'

I knew it was familiar. But there's this Steven Brill, started Court TV and all."

"I think we can rule him out."

"Yeah, well I know that. But there was another Brill naggin' at my mind, but 'tween Steve an' Arden I couldn't get him sorted out. An' when I typed in Brill on Google I got about a million hits, and most of 'em had to do with Contentville, which is this Web site he started. Steven Brill, I'm talkin' about."

"And?"

"Let me print this out," he said, "and you can read it for yourself."

"If it's as crystal-clear as this magazine—"

"No," he said, tapping keys. "It's real simple. You'll see."

He switched on the printer, and in less than a minute a sheet of paper scrolled into the tray. He picked it up and handed it to me.

I read:

BRILL, Abraham Arden, 1874–1948. Born in Austria, came to United States alone at age 13, resided in New York City. Graduated NYU 1901, MD Columbia University 1903. Studied in Switzerland with Carl Jung, returned to US in 1908. An early and outspoken advocate of psychoanalysis, Brill was one of the first to translate Freud and Jung into English, and did much to

make their theories accessible in the United States. He taught for years at NYU and Columbia; publications include Psychoanalysis, Its Theories and Application **(1912) and** Fundamental Conceptions of Psychoanalysis **(1921).**

"Could be a coincidence," he said.

"No."

"You still see his books on reading lists. That's what rang a bell. Arden, though, that kept the penny from dropping. It's usually A. A. Brill, or Abraham Brill."

He'd dropped the hip-hop speech patterns, and sounded like someone who'd know about Freud and Jung, and Abraham Brill.

I said, "It's not a coincidence."

"It really couldn't be, could it?"

"He picked the name because it meant something to him, and he was confident it wouldn't mean anything to her."

"To Lia, you mean."

"No one else was ever supposed to hear the name. He went to Lia's dorm and killed her to keep her from repeating it. He was too late, but not by much. 'Arden Brill' were two of the last words she ever spoke."

"Good thing you had your machine on."

"If I'd been home to take the call—"

"Good thing you weren't."

"How do you figure that?"

"Because she'd have said she thought of something, that it might be important. And you'd have said, 'No, not over the phone, I'll meet you in twenty minutes at the Salonika.' Only you'd have been waiting a long time at that restaurant, because she'd be floating in the bathtub, and you never would have heard the name Arden Brill."

I thought about it, agreed it was possible.

"Or," he said, "she hears your voice, and she gets flustered and hangs up."

"She could just as easily have hung up on the answering machine."

"But she didn't," he said.

"If I'd questioned her a little more intensively at the Salonika—"

"Maybe she'd have said then and there."

"Maybe."

"And maybe not," he said. "Maybe she'd have clammed up tight, and not made a phone call later, because of how hard you pressed her."

"Maybe."

"And he would have shown up right on schedule," he went on, "and she'd be just as dead as she is now, same as if we never even made the call and went up there yesterday in the first place. This way we got a name, Arden Brill, and otherwise we wouldn't have a thing."

"Arden Brill," I said.

"Figure it's him?"

"It pretty much has to be."

"Yeah," he said. "I guess."

"I suppose," I said, "when you turn around and take a good long look at it, it all becomes very obvious. But I was right in the room with the son of a bitch and it never even occurred to me. For Christ's sake, it was his gun. The son of a bitch used his own gun!"

TWENTY-EIGHT

He sits, watching the lights of the city go on and off, on and off. It's the middle of the afternoon, but on his computer it is forever night, and his screensaver is tireless. Office and apartment lights wink on and wink off, and gradually buildings change their shapes, adding floors, losing floors, becoming wider or narrower. The idea, of course, is that each tiny subsection of the monitor will have its turn to be dark, and thus no single high-traffic spot will burn out ahead of the others.

Is this a real problem? Do computer screens ever burn out? With the relentless march of technology, does anyone actually keep a piece of equipment long enough for wear and tear to affect it?

Probably not. Every year—every six months—

the new computers are faster and more powerful, and cost less than the previous generation.
Soon he'll replace his own computer. There is
nothing wrong with it, it does everything he
could possibly require of it, but he'll replace it
with one that is newer-better-faster . . . and
he'll dutifully install his screensaver on his new
hard drive.

All so he can watch lights wink on and off. . . .

He lowers a finger, touches a key, and the
screensaver is gone. He touches more keys, clicks
his mouse, and in no time at all (though the next
machine will do it even faster) he's on-line.

He checks his e-mail, hurrying through it,
deleting the garbage, the junk mail, answering
one message that needs to be answered, keeping
the rest for later. Pulls down the Favorite Places
menu, selects Newsgroups: ACSK.

And his newsgroup comes on-screen, alt.
crime.serialkillers. He scrolls down the list of
new messages. There are four in the Jason Bierman thread, and he reads them, and there's
nothing very interesting. He's seen this happen
time and time again in a thread. After a few days
the whole point of the topic gets lost, as people
post responses to someone else's off-topic me-
andering, and as others, the Johnny One-Note
element, ride their individual hobby horses—
for/against capital punishment, say, or warning
of government intrusion and the New World
Order. There is a way to screen out messages

from the most obnoxious members, you add their names to your killfile and their messages never appear on your screen, but he hasn't done that yet. Soon, perhaps.

There's nothing about Lia Parkman.

Well, how could there be? If all has gone well, they think the little darling had too much to drink and forgot you needed gills to breathe underwater. That may not hold up, it depends how good the medical examiner is and what kind of a day he's having. If they're good, if they look closely, they may well guess that she had help.

Eyes staring up through the water . . .

But even if they work it out, he realizes, they won't know who did it. That's fine, that's the way he wants it, and yet, well, there is a slight downside.

Bierman's not getting credit.

Bierman's going to drop off the edge of the newsgroup's consciousness. He doesn't really belong there, he's barely a mass murderer and by no means a serial killer. He has three victims, all killed the same day, one miles apart from the others, to be sure, but all slain as part of a single extended episode.

So it's quite proper that he fade and be forgotten.

But there's a real serial killer involved, and nobody even knows. Nobody has a clue!

Call him—well, just for now, call him Arden

Brill. It was an error, borrowing a name from that musty old Freudian, but let it go. Unless the investigating officer has a side interest in discredited psychoanalytic claptrap, the name will set off no alarms. So why not use it, if only in the privacy of one's own mind?

Arden Brill has killed not three people but five. He killed twice on West Seventy-fourth Street, twice on Coney Island Avenue (at intervals several hours apart, making them, really, two separate incidents), and now he can claim a fifth victim, on Claremont Avenue.

And no one knows!

He scans the computer screen. At the bottom of the newsgroup window is a button that reads New Message. He clicks on it , and there's a new screen, all set up to receive a message for alt.crime.serialkillers.

On the subject line he types: **BIERMAN INNOCENT VICTIM.**

No, only the worst idiots use all caps like that. It's the newsgroup equivalent of shouting. He deletes it, tries again: **Bierman innocent victim.**

Better.

He looks at the screen, then begins to type:

Jason Bierman never killed anybody. He was artfully set up to take the rap for a killer none of you know anything about. That man's name is Arden Brill.

He deletes the last sentence and goes on:

. . . I am that man, and you may call me
Arden Brill. I have killed five times. Bierman
was my first victim, the Hollanders numbers
two and three. Carl Ivanko was fourth. You
have credited Jason Bierman with all of
these killings, and he never even met or
heard of a single one of his purported victims!
My fifth victim is Lia Parkman, and you
have never heard of her, but you will. I
drowned her in a tub of water, held her by
her tits and watched her fight for life.

But she hadn't struggled. In fact he was not
altogether sure she ever regained consciousness.
Her eyes were open, but did that necessarily
mean she knew what was going on? Maybe he
should change that last sentence:

. . . I drowned her in a tub of water, held
her by her sweet little tits and watched the
bubbles rise to the surface as the life went
out of her.

That was better. That, in fact, was exactly
how it had happened. Calling her tits sweet and
little was not exactly clinical, but no one could
fault him for veracity.

. . . I do not kill for the thrill of it. I have a motive, and it is perfectly logical. I shall profit enormously from my crimes.

No, not crimes. He deleted "crimes," resumed:

. . . profit enormously from my actions, which may disqualify me as a serial killer. Still, for all that my work is undertaken for profit. I cannot deny that the act of killing is satisfying to me in ways I would never have anticipated. I enjoy it before the act, during the act, and after the act has been completed.

He pauses, forming his thoughts:

I have killed both men and women. Killing men, I would say, provides me with more of a sense of accomplishment. On the other hand, for sheer pleasure, there's nothing like killing a woman.

No, amend that slightly:

. . . nothing like killing an attractive woman.

He sits there, looking at what he has written, nodding his approval. His watch beeps, signaling that it is ten minutes before the hour.

He moves the mouse, poises the cursor over the Post button.

Oh, no. No, I don't think so.

He shifts the mouse, clicks on Cancel. The message, unsent, vanishes from the screen. A few more clicks and he's off-line, and his screen-saver is back in place, lights winking on and off, on and off. . . .

TWENTY-NINE

Let's go over it again," Wentworth said. "Doc's name is Nadler?"

"Seymour Nadler."

"And he's a psychiatrist, is that right?"

"Board-certified," I said.

"A disciple of Sigmund Freud."

"That I wouldn't know."

"And maybe of Brill," he said. "A. A. Brill. Studied with him, maybe."

"The dates are wrong," I said. "Brill died in 1948."

"Was Nadler even born then?"

"No," I said. "He's around forty."

"And the gun was his, the murder weapon."

"Yes."

"Registered, and he had a permit for it."

"For his office and residence. He didn't have a carry permit."

"He bought it when, sometime last year? Did he give a reason?"

"According to him," I said, "he had a patient he was worried about."

"Makes sense," Wentworth said. "I got a patient worries me, I want a gun so I can shoot him. Why dick around with medication? I don't suppose he ever had occasion to shoot this patient."

"He said the man committed suicide."

"Shot himself?"

"Went out a window, or maybe it was off a roof."

"Story check out?"

"About the patient? I have no idea. He didn't furnish the name, and I didn't see any reason to ask it."

"You didn't suspect him."

"No, not at all. Of what, killing three people with a registered weapon and leaving it at the scene? The man had diplomas on the wall, I figured he had an IQ at least as high as his body temperature."

He started to say something, then stopped. At the corner, a vendor of soft ice cream had parked his truck, and the Mister Softee music was playing relentlessly. Wentworth said, "Excuse me," and got to his feet, striding off toward the ice cream truck.

"Man hears that music," T J said, "he just got to have it. What it is, he was conditioned as a child." He glanced across the street, raised his eyes about ten floors. "You got any trouble with the concept, Dr. Nadler be glad to explain it all for you."

We were on a bench on the east side of Central Park West, directly across the street from Seymour Nadler's building. There was a five-foot stone wall behind us, and on the other side of it was the park. I'd left word for Wentworth at the precinct, and he'd called me right after he left Kristin's house. He'd interviewed her at length, and had reinforced the advice I'd given her—don't take any calls, don't open the door for anyone. He hadn't been able to arrange police protection yet, but he had a request in, and expected it would be approved before long.

I looked over and saw Wentworth in conversation with the Mister Softee man. After a few moments the truck pulled away from the curb, crossed the intersection, and kept going for another block. Wentworth returned empty-handed, but with a look of triumph on his square-jawed face.

"Told him to take it down the road," he said. "What's the point of having a gold shield if you can't kick Mister Softee's ass off your block?"

"Who I wanted to be," T J said. "When I grew up."

"Who, Mister Softee? Or a guy with a gold shield?"

"Mister Softee. You like the Pied Piper, ring that little bell an' all the boys an' girls come runnin'."

"You'd like that, would you?"

"Thought so, when I was young. Everywhere you go, they be happy to see you."

"Not their parents," Wentworth said. "Not anybody who's trying to concentrate. Imagine sitting in the truck all day, listening to that music for hours on end." He shook his head. "Guy didn't want to move. 'But this is my spot,' he kept whining. Like nobody'll be able to find him a block away. 'This is **my** spot,' I said. He got the point."

"It's a small victory," I said, "but at least it goes in the win column."

"Damn right," he said. "Look at me, I put the fear of God into Mister Softee. You figure that's his wife's pet name for his thing? Jesus, let's hope not."

On the sidewalk in front of us, a girl in her early teens whizzed by on Rollerblades. "They're not supposed to skate on the sidewalk," he said, "but I'll let her go this time. I already filled my quota with Mister Softee. You want to get back to your boy Nadler?"

"Sure."

"He bought the gun last year, kept it locked away in his desk drawer. March, he and his wife are out, he comes home and there's been a burglary. He makes a report, files a claim with his insurance company. Right so far?"

I nodded.

"Then two, three days later he opens the drawer and the gun's gone. Did he say what made him look?"

"Not that I remember."

"It's not a stretch. He's at his desk, he's thinking about the burglary, thinks, Jesus, suppose I was here, what would I do, would I go for my gun? So he looks for the gun and it's missing. And he reported it, right?"

"Right."

"But didn't add it to his insurance claim."

"He didn't want the aggravation of amending the claim," I said. "And he wasn't sure it would be covered, as he'd never included it on the schedule. It didn't seem unreasonable."

"No, and it still doesn't. Plus there's the embarrassment factor. 'I bought a gun to protect myself and my family and the burglars took it away with them.' The law requires him to inform the police, but nobody says he has to put in a claim. That's up to him."

"Right."

"So we fast-forward a few months," he said, "and it's the end of July, beginning of August, and the Hollanders are killed, and the two in Brooklyn."

"Bierman and Ivanko."

"And the gun's left at the scene, as it more or less has to be if it's going to look like suicide, and a ballistics check reveals the gun is the very same twenty-two-caliber pistol stolen from the good Dr. Nadler. Was it a twenty-two? Did I get that part right?"

"Yes."

"Okay," he said, "run it by me. The gun was never stolen in the first place, right?"

"Right."

"How about the burglary? He fake the whole thing?"

"Probably not," I said. "But it's not impossible. He rides down to the lobby with his wife, then remembers he left the tickets on the dresser."

"So he goes upstairs, turns some drawers upside down, scoops up some jewelry, and what? He doesn't take it along to the theater."

"He's got it in two pillowcases he stripped off the bed," I said. "He ducks into his office, stows them both in a closet, and goes back downstairs to the lobby."

"And off to do the town. Comes home, reports the burglary. It's possible, but you don't think he did it that way."

"My guess," I said, "is the burglary happened just the way he said it did in his initial report. They went through the residence, took whatever he said they took, and carted it off in pillowcases. And two days later he realizes he's been trying to figure out how to get hold of a gun that can't be traced back to him, and here's the perfect way. He reports his own gun as stolen, and, when it **is** traced back to him, they say oh yeah, right, it was taken in a burglary, it was reported stolen months ago."

He nodded slowly, thinking it through. "What I like about it," he said, "is it's cute, and we already know our guy's got a weakness for being cute." To T J he said, "You ever decide to become a crook, don't be cute, okay? Three guesses what you wind up stepping on."

"On my Mister Softee," T J said.

"You think that's why he bought the gun in the first place? You think he planned it that far ahead?"

I'd wondered about that point myself. "It's possible," I said. "Say he decided he wanted a gun. He's an Upper West Side shrink, he's not going to have access to the people with unregistered guns to sell. He could cross a couple of state lines and pick up something at a gun show, but would he even think of that?"

"So he's got a use for the gun planned all along."

"If so," I said, "then he faked the burglary, because he couldn't just sit around and wait for someone to turn up right on schedule and knock off his apartment. Unless he didn't have the details worked out yet, especially the part about the suicide. If there's no weapon recovered, he doesn't have to worry about it being traced back to him."

"And then the burglary happens, and it's a gift from on high."

"What I think," I said, "is that he knew who he was going to kill and why he was going to kill them. But he didn't know how, and the burglar who knocked over his place supplied that part for him."

"Turned his registered gun into a possible murder weapon, and gave him the idea of faking a burglary to cover the killing."

"And even showed him what a burglary looked like. Using the pillowcases, for example. I thought it was a coincidence when the same MO turned up in both jobs, Nadler and Hollander. Then I thought, well, Ivanko knocked off Nadler's place, and he kept the gun, and he had it with him when he knocked off the Hollander house."

"A burglar hits him," Wentworth said, "and he borrows the guy's MO when he stages a burglary of his own. Then he uses his own gun because he's managed to turn it into an untraceable weapon. Jesus, he really is cute, isn't he?"

THIRTY

Peter," he says, beaming, stepping back from the doorway. "Come in, come in. You're right on time."

"Compulsive," Peter Meredith says, grinning.

It's a reference to a joke he told the five of them several months ago in a group session. Analysts, he said, divide their patients into two categories, based on the time they arrive for their appointments. The ones who are chronically early are anxious, he explained, while the chronically late are hostile.

And then he'd waited, knowing someone would ask the question, and it had been Ruth Ann, predictably enough, who'd obliged him. What about the ones who are on time? she'd wondered. They're compulsive, he'd assured her.

He grins back at Peter, steps forward and

gives him a hug. The man's girth is considerable. He hasn't lost a pound, he will never lose a pound, but his progress in every other respect is enormously gratifying.

Teach a man to lose weight, he thinks, and he will love you until he gains it back. Teach a man to love himself, however much he weighs, and he will love you forever.

And isn't that the whole point?

"Well now," he says. "Couch or chair? What do you think?"

"No, no," says Peter, always obliging, donning a Viennese accent, his thumb and forefinger caressing an imaginary beard. "Nein, Herr Doktor. Not vot do I zink. Vot do you zink?"

They laugh together, and he says, "The couch, I think. Yes, the couch today, Peter."

Peter sits on the couch, slips off his shoes, then stretches out and puts his feet up. He looks at Peter and wonders fleetingly if the couch will hold the weight, then realizes the illogic of his concern. The couch is designed so that three people may sit on it at once, three people whose total weight might be twice that of Peter Meredith. And that couch has held Peter's weight regularly for many months. He has not grown appreciably heavier, or the couch less sturdy. And yet he, the couch's owner, reacts with the same unwarranted anxiety every time Peter uses it.

Fascinating, the human mind. And one's own is no less an object of interest than anyone else's.

"Well, Peter. You're comfortable?"

"Very comfortable, Doc."

"It's relaxing, isn't it, to lie down, to close your eyes. Cares and concerns rise up and float away."

His voice is soothing, comforting. He is not hypnotizing Peter, although he has done so in the past, but still there is something hypnotic in his tone, his cadence. It won't put the man under but it will help him to relax, to open up.

"So," he said. "How is the house coming?"

"Ah, the house," Peter says.

Ah, indeed. They are working night and day on the Meserole Street house, and Peter can talk about it for hours on end. It's not really necessary to listen. One of the nasty little secrets of the profession is that one does not always listen to one's patients. Sometimes, even with the best will in the world, one drifts off on wings of tangential thought, or even falls asleep. Nor can he imagine any greater exercise in futility than fighting sleep. Better to give in gracefully and gratefully, soothed into sleep by the neurotic drone.

Because, along with the nasty little secret, is the happy little truth—what is important is that the patient say it, not that the therapist listen. Of course he might contribute just the right in-

sight, might steer the patient in just the right direction, but who is to say he/she might not get
there as well on his/her own?

It reminds him of a woman who'd been told to
give up her dog because of allergies. She'd been
to an allergist, suffered through a series of shots
and the rigors of an elimination diet, and all to
no avail; her eyes would tear and her nose run
and her throat shut down whenever she went
near the animal. She'd come to him in the hope
that it was all in her mind, and that he could do
what the allergist could not.

And what he did, of course, was solve the
problem. He had her bring the dog to his office,
explaining that he knew just the person to give
the animal a home, a good friend of his who was
relocating to Wyoming. The dog would have
acres of countryside to romp in, and, best of all,
he'd be a couple of thousand miles away, where
she wouldn't be tempted to visit, or, God forbid,
take him back.

The dog was a King Charles spaniel, with
alert, expressive eyes and a proud carriage. As
soon as she was out of his office he gave the little fellow a man-sized shot of morphine and put
him out of everyone's misery. Then he stuffed
him into a small overnight bag and took him for
a last walk in the park. He set the bag down and
wandered off to watch the ducks, and when he
returned, why, wouldn't you know it? Some en-
terprising young man had made off with the

suitcase. And what a nice surprise he'd have for himself when he forced the locks!

Then he sent the woman to FAO Schwarz to pick out a teddy bear. She could shower it with the same affection she'd lavished on the dog, and could imagine her love was reciprocated—with about as much validity as with a real pet. She didn't have to walk it or feed it, didn't have to clean up its messes, and, by God, the thing was guaranteed hypoallergenic.

And now she has a houseful of stuffed animals—no surprise there, and you can have all the stuffed pets you want without the neighbors complaining of the noise and the smell—and she thinks he's a genius, and who's to say he's not?

And she loves him.

And, he asks himself a second time, isn't that the whole point? You can't do this for the money, because there's just nowhere near enough of it. People think you've got a license to coin money, getting a hundred dollars an hour to listen (or not listen) to dreams and fears and childhood memories. As if it's a fortune, and as if you're stealing it!

But how many patients can you see, fifteen a week? Twenty? And how many actually pay a hundred dollars an hour? Peter and his chums, for example, paid sixty dollars each for their individual sessions. In group therapy, when he works with all five of them, he charges them each twenty-five dollars, so he does in fact take in $125 for that particular weekly hour.

But, for heaven's sake, you have to knock yourself out to drag down a hundred thousand dollars a year, and how far does that go in New York in the twenty-first century? Any other medical specialty is almost certainly more lucrative. Forget the plastic surgeons, the anesthesiologists. Why, storefront family practitioners can see as many patients in an hour or two as he sees in a week.

A hundred thousand. The big law firms are offering $150,000 to kids fresh out of law school! No, forget the money. You can't do what he does for the money. You have to do it for love.

And that, of course, is where the real money is.

There is an awkward moment when he realizes that Peter has stopped talking, that there is an expectant quality to the silence. Has he been asked a question?

"Hmmm," he says, leaning forward, clearly giving the matter some thought. "Peter, do me a favor. Say that again, word for word, with the same inflection you just used. Can you do that?"

"I can try," Peter says.

And he does, bless him. And it is a question, just as he'd sensed, and Peter, having voiced it a second time, then proceeds to answer it himself.

A breakthrough, thanks to his own inspired inattentiveness.

They think he's a genius. And, really, who is he to say they're wrong?

Peter," he says, "I've been thinking about Kristin."

"Oh."

"I'm sure you've been thinking about her yourself."

"Some."

"Have you had any further contact with her?"

"I called her after what happened. I think I told you about that."

"Yes, I believe you did."

"And I'm glad I did, Doc. It was the decent thing to do. I wanted to, but at first I was, well . . ."

"Afraid?"

"Yes, sure, let's call it by its right name, huh? Fear. I was afraid."

"Would you like to sit up now, Peter?"

"Yes, I think so."

"Good. Take the chair. You were afraid to call, but you called, and you're glad you did."

"Yes."

He got to his feet, put his hands together, rocked back on his heels. "Peter," he said, "when two people relate in a certain way, when there's a

particular magic that they create between themselves, it's really a rather remarkable thing."

"I know."

"I always sensed that magic with you and
Kristin."

"So did I, but . . ."

"But you separated. You went to Williamsburg and she returned to her parents' house."

"Right."

"And that was inevitable. You were committed
to the others, to Marsha and Lucian and Kieran
and Ruth Ann."

"And to you, don't forget."

"Well," he says. His smile is gentle, self-
effacing. "To me insofar as I embody in your
mind your own best interests. You and the others shared a goal, and what we determined together was that Kristin did not share that goal."

"Not the way everybody else did."

"The five of you," he says, "are a family, Peter."

"Yes, we are."

"The house is perfect for you. You have a
floor, Marsha and Lucian have a floor, Ruth Ann
and Kieran have a floor. But you work together,
you create this space together."

"Yes."

"As a family."

Family is the magic word; delivered with the
right cadence, it can bring Peter almost to tears.

"Kristin had a family of her own," he says, "and she was not ready to change one nest for another. You made the right decision, Peter."

"I know."

"And she made the right decision, too."

"I know that now. I wasn't sure at first, but now I know you're right."

"But her situation has changed."

"Because—"

"Because she lost her family."

"It was a terrible thing."

What a way with words the fellow has! "A terrible thing," he echoes. "What do we get in life, Peter?"

"What do we get?"

"You know the answer, Peter."

"We get what we get."

"Exactly. We get what we get, and what we do with it makes it good fortune or bad. You and Kristin belong together."

"That's what I always thought."

Thought, he notes, rather than think. What's this?

"I think you should call her," he says, pressing. "I think you should visit her, I think you should be with her in her hour of need." Did he really say that? No matter. "You have broad shoulders, Peter, and that's what she needs right now, even as she needs once again to be part of a family."

"But—"

He waits. His hand goes to his throat, and his

fingers find the rhodochrosite disc. He strokes it, feels its cool smoothness.

"There's this woman I sort of met, she's a sculptor? She lives on Wythe Avenue in Northside Williamsburg? She's really nice, and her values are the same as mine, as ours, and, and I thought maybe . . ."

The words trail off. He touches the pink stone disc again, thinks: Clarity. He waits a beat, then says, "Rebound."

"Pardon?"

He's on his feet, pacing, spins around to face Peter Meredith. He says, "Rebound, Peter! You're on the rebound! That's all this is."

"You really think so?"

"I know so. Stand up. Up! Yes. Face me, yes. Now close your eyes. Now hold out both your hands, palms up. All right. Are you ready?"

"Uh, I guess."

"Put your feelings for Kristin in your right hand. Feel the weight, the substance. Do you feel it?"

"Yes."

"Now put whatever it is you feel for this sculptor in your other hand. There! Do you feel the difference?"

"Yes."

"Open your eyes, Peter. Which hand is heavier?"

"This one."

"The body doesn't lie. It feels the weight of

one, the lack of substance of the other. Tell me, then. Where is your destiny?"

"With Kristin?"

"Are you asking me or telling me?"

"It's with Kristin."

"What's with Kristin?"

"My destiny."

He goes to him, embraces him. "Peter," he says, "I'm so proud of you. Do you know how proud I am?"

When the door closes he turns the bolt, sighs deeply. He could have killed Peter Meredith, could have reached out and killed him. A sculptor, playing with fucking clay in a Wythe Avenue shithole, someone to share his fucking values.

You have to lead these people every step of the way. Every step of the way!

THIRTY-ONE

"What'd be nice," Ira Wentworth said, "is a shred of evidence. Something I could take to a judge and come back with a warrant."

"You want everything handed to you," I said.

"That's me," he said. "Give me the easy ones every time. I remember when my father taught me to play pool. 'Son,' he said, 'always pocket the easy balls. Leave the bank shots and combinations for the boys with rich fathers.'"

"Sound advice."

"Yeah," he said, "but I didn't hear it from my old man, who as far as I know never picked up a pool cue in his life. I heard it from a guy I was playing pool with, right after I missed this three-ball combination." He shook his head ruefully. "It was so pretty I couldn't resist it."

"And you never got over it," I said.

"Never," he said, getting to his feet, "but I'm

still young. There's hope. I'm going to start digging, see what I can find on this shrink. Maybe we'll get lucky and there'll be a sheet on him. Maybe I'll ask him where he was yesterday and he'll turn beet-red and blurt out a confession."

We shook hands all around, and he walked off, heading uptown. "He's pretty good," I told T J.

He didn't say anything. I turned and saw him gazing across the street, holding up a hand to shade his eyes against the afternoon sun. "Thought I saw somebody," he said, "but it ain't him."

"Nadler?"

"Ain't never seen him, so how would I know?"

"Then how do you know it's not him?"

"Huh?"

"Never mind," I said. "I'm going home. What about you?"

"Guess I'll go up around Columbia," he said. "Hear what they sayin' 'bout Lia."

I took my time walking home, trying to think of something useful I could do, and when I got there Elaine told me I was just in time.

"To go to the movies," she said. "I got bored and closed early. I decided I wanted to go to a movie in the middle of a weekday afternoon. It's the most decadent thing I can think of."

"What a sheltered life you've led."

"That's it exactly," she said. "Wanna keep me company, big boy?"

"What do you want to see?"

"There's an Adam Sandler movie at Worldwide Cinema."

"You've got to be kidding," I said.

"C'mon, it'll be fun. And it's only three dollars. That's our reward for missing it the first time around."

"Missing it was its own reward," I said.

She looked at her watch. "We've got seventeen minutes. Do you think we can get to Fiftieth and Eighth in seventeen minutes?"

"Yes," I said. "I'm afraid we can."

When we got home there was a message from Kristin. Could I call her? I called, and when the machine invited me to leave a message I identified myself and said I was returning her call. "Please pick up if you're there," I said. "Otherwise call me back when you get this message. I should be home the rest of—"

The evening, I would have concluded, but she picked up and said, "Mr. Scudder? Sorry, I was in the other room. The reason I called, well, I suppose I shouldn't have bothered you . . ."

"What is it, Kristin?"

"Well, I had a call earlier. From Peter."

"Peter Meredith?"

"Yes, that's right. I was standing right next to the machine when the call came in, and I thought, really, what's so terrible about picking it up?"

"And did you pick it up?"

"No, because you said not to."

"Good."

"But I felt really strange about it, you know? I mean, there have been all these calls from people I don't know, like newspaper reporters, and I just delete the message and that's that. I don't give it a second thought."

"There's no reason why you should. They'll keep pestering you, but they'll pester you less if you don't give them any encouragement."

"I know that. But Peter's different." She paused for breath, then said, "He wants me to call him back."

"I don't think that's a good idea."

"Why?"

I gave her an answer, but it might have sounded more convincing if I'd had a reason. I just didn't want her talking to him, and I couldn't explain why. It's not as though I thought Nadler could morph into a handful of electrical impulses and shoot through the phone lines at her, but I still didn't want her on the phone with an old boyfriend or anyone else.

"Well," she said at length, and I didn't know what it meant. Ultimately, of course, it was up to her. Unless I had her phones ripped out, I couldn't stop her from taking whatever calls she chose to take.

"That policeman was here," she said. "Officer Wentworth?"

"Detective Wentworth."

"Oh, is that a faux pas, calling him officer if he's a detective? Not that I did, I don't think I called him anything. He's nice."

"He's a good man," I said.

"He said he would assign some police officers to watch the house, but that I wouldn't even know that they're there. So of course I keep going to the window and peeking out from behind the curtain, and I can't see anybody, but then he said I wouldn't be able to. So maybe they're there and maybe they're not."

"You'll be fine."

"I guess I'm not expected to give them milk and cookies," she said, "so I don't suppose it matters if they're there or not. I mean if I **know** if they're there or not."

"I know what you mean."

"Thank you. It's a little weird being cooped up like this. I wanted to order a pizza, but I didn't know if I should, because you said not to open the door. Is it okay to open the door for a pizza delivery boy?"

I was beginning to understand what a pain in the ass it must be to guard somebody in the Witness Protection Program. While I was thinking up an answer she said, "Never mind, there's plenty of stuff in the house. I must be driving you crazy. Am I? Tell me if I am."

"No, of course not. I know it's tough for you."

"It's just being cooped up with nothing to do

but listen to my own head. Oh, I know what I
wanted to tell you!"

"What?"

"I almost forgot. Remember I was supposed to
see if there was anything missing? Anything taken
in the burglary and not returned?"

"And is there?"

"I think so," she said, "but I don't know if it
means anything. I mean, it's not valuable or anything. So if it is missing, that doesn't mean anybody took it. It could just be lost."

"What is it, Kristin?"

"Do you know what rhodochrosite is?"

"A gemstone?"

"Well, I guess they call it semiprecious. Or
maybe not even that. It's sort of a rosy pink,
but . . . you know what? Why don't you come over
here and I'll show you?"

"If it's missing," I said, "how can you show
me?"

"It's an earring," she said.

"Oh."

"And that's how I knew it was missing, because
there's only one of them left."

"Yes, of course." I looked at my watch. I'd been
thinking of going to a meeting, but the hell with it.
"I'll be right over," I said. "And make sure it's me
before you open the door."

"I will. Oh, Mr. Scudder? Do you think . . . no,
never mind, it's silly."

"Say it anyway."

"Well," she said, "do you suppose you could pick up a pizza?"

I'd seen the stone before, in shop windows, but I'd never known what it was called. It was rhodochrosite, she told me, and it wasn't valuable, it was too soft and too fragile, but she thought it was pretty.

"Very pretty," I agreed, and turned the earring over, examining it from different angles. The stone was smooth, cool to the touch, the clip silver.

"I bought them for her," she said, "while I was still at Wellesley, but I bought them here in New York, in a little shop on Macdougal Street. They're not there anymore, I guess they went out of business. They weren't expensive. Maybe thirty-five dollars? Under fifty, certainly. I gave them to her for her birthday."

"And she still had both of them when . . ."

"As far as I know. But, you know, it's real easy to lose an earring. Especially clip-ons. She'd had her ears pierced, and most of her earrings were for pierced ears, but these only came with clips, and I thought they were pretty, and she liked clips sometimes. But they're easier to lose. And she might not have wanted to say she lost one, because I gave them to her, you know? Or maybe she just didn't get around to mentioning it."

We were in the kitchen, a pizza box open on the table between us. She'd already eaten two slices and was working on a third. "When you want pizza," she said, "nothing else really does it."

It wouldn't have been my first choice, but I hadn't eaten anything since breakfast, aside from a few handfuls of the popcorn Elaine bought as an accompaniment to Adam Sandler. It wasn't bad pizza.

I said as much, then held the earring to the light. "May I take this?"

"Yes, of course. Do you think . . ."

"That he took it? Probably not. But if we pick him up wearing it, it'll be interesting to hear him explain it."

THIRTY-TWO

I called Wentworth as soon as I got home, and was assured that he'd get the message. I don't know when he got it, but it was the next morning when I heard from him.

There was something in his voice I hadn't heard before, but I chalked it up to the hour and gave him my news. He was silent for a beat, and then he said, "An earring."

"One of a pair. Maybe it's nothing, and then again maybe he wanted a souvenir."

"Nadler, you mean."

"Of course."

" 'Of course.' Thing is, there's a problem. Nadler didn't do it."

"What do you mean?"

"I mean Seymour Nadler's a perfectly respectable psychiatrist who never even got caught jaywalking."

"That's not surprising, is it? We know he'd have to have a respectable front, and—"

"He's also got a respectable alibi. I spoke to him yesterday, couple of hours after I talked to you."

"And?"

"I would have liked to talk to him face to face. **Mano a mano,** you know? But I didn't figure my lieutenant would authorize the plane fare."

"What plane fare?"

"To Martha's Vineyard, which is where he and Mrs. Nadler have been for the past eight days. I had one hell of a time getting the number there from his fucking service. I guess I must have sounded crazy enough to be one of his patients, but eventually I convinced them I was worse than that, I was crazy enough to be a detective with the New York City Police Department."

"He's been there all this time?"

"Since a week ago yesterday. They go up every year, him and his wife, the last two weeks in August. Most shrinks take the whole month, he said, but he just takes two weeks in August, and then in February he spends two weeks in the Caribbean."

"He came back," I said. "He must have. He caught a flight to New York, killed Lia Parkman, and caught the next flight back."

"You know, believe it or not I thought of that possibility. I didn't think it made much sense, but it was worth a couple of phone calls. There's this little airline, has a schedule of flights between Teterboro Airport and the Vineyard. They're very cooperative, I don't think their employees have a whole lot to do, and they checked the passenger manifests for me. Nadler and his wife flew up right when he told me they did, and they're scheduled to fly back a week from now. And that flight up a week ago yesterday is the only one he's been on."

"Unless he used another name."

"They want to see photo ID these days, even the little puddle-jump operations. And there can't be more than eight people in total who work for this outfit, so how could you fly on it a couple days apart under two different names?"

"Then he found some other way to get to New York," I said.

"Because he must have."

"Yes."

"Because he's the one who killed Parkman, and you happen to know that for a fact."

I didn't say anything.

"It sounded very good," he said, "when you were spinning it all out for me, with the kid on hand to nod in all the right places. It sounded so good it wasn't until I'd established that he couldn't possibly have done it before it hit me that there was no real reason to suspect him in the first place. What did you do, tie him to the gun? For Christ's sake, there was never any question that it was his gun. We knew that all along."

"Now wait a minute—"

"No, you wait a minute. What somehow slipped my mind is the fact that there's never been a damn

thing to tie him to the people he's supposed to have
killed. Why should he pick on the Hollanders? Because they've got money? He's got money himself,
he's doing fine. Two weeks on the Vineyard, two
weeks in Virgin Gorda—the guy's not living hand
to mouth."

"That doesn't mean he doesn't want more."

"Still, make the connection for me, will you?
Did he know the Hollanders? Did he know the two
mopes in Brooklyn, I forget their names . . ."

"Bierman and Ivanko."

"Well, did he? Did he know Lia Parkman?
Somebody did, somebody knew all those people
and had some kind of reason to kill them, but I
don't see any reason to figure it was Nadler. Because he picked a dead shrink's name for an alias?
And only a shrink would do that, and he's a
shrink, so it's gotta be him? Am I getting through
here at all?"

Loud and clear, I told him. I didn't ask him
what he wanted me to do with the earring. I was
afraid he might tell me.

Every once in a while Elaine and I rent a car and
drive somewhere, and the last time we did that I
picked up a Rand McNally road atlas. Usually I
forget and leave that sort of thing in the car, but I'd
kept this one, and I found the Massachusetts map
and looked at Martha's Vineyard, right off the

coast alongside Nantucket. It struck me that a person wouldn't have to fly there. You could take a ferry to the mainland and pick up a car.

Because it had to be him, didn't it?

I put the atlas back and got a fresh cup of coffee. I couldn't get past the fact that Wentworth's objections were perfectly sound. There had to be a connection, there had to be something that had led Nadler to select the Hollanders. Money was the motive, I was almost sure of that, but why **their** money? What made him look at that particular brownstone and translate it into dollars? What made him think he stood a chance to get it for himself?

I reached for the phone and called Kristin. She must have been standing right next to it, because she picked up almost as soon as I said my name.

"He called again," she said, before I could get a word out.

I had nobody but Nadler on my mind, so what I said was, "From Martha's Vineyard?"

"Huh?"

"I'm sorry," I said. "Who called again?"

"Peter, and he called from Brooklyn. I felt really mean, listening to him leave a message and not picking up. In fact I thought it was him just now."

And would she have picked up the phone if it had been? I left the question unasked, perhaps because I was afraid what the answer would be.

Instead I said, "I may have asked you this before, but I want you to think about it. Do you know a Dr. Nadler?"

"That name's familiar," she said.

"Take your time, Kristin."

"Oh, I remember, and yes, you did mention it. He's the original owner of the gun, right? The gun they used."

"And that's the only time you heard the name?"

"The only time I can remember. Why?"

"I don't mean to be intrusive," I said, "but did you ever have occasion to see a psychiatrist? Did you ever have any psychotherapy?"

"I had a consultation my freshman year at Wellesley," she said. "I was screwing up in one of my courses, and they had a policy where you had to see the school shrink to stay off academic probation. But it was a woman, and her name wasn't Nadler."

"What about your parents? Did either of them consult a psychiatrist?"

"Not that I know of. I suppose they would, if they felt the need. And I know my mom had something prescribed for her after Sean's death. Antidepressants or tranquilizers, I don't know what they gave her. But I think that was just our family doctor."

I found other ways to cover the same ground, and got nowhere. Then she asked again about Peter, and whether she could talk to him.

That sent me off in another direction. "The

person you went to for counseling," I said. "Remember the name?"

"At Wellesley? I can't possibly remember her name, and what difference—"

"No, the person you and Peter went to."

"Oh, him. I can't remember his name. I know it wasn't Nadler, though."

"You're positive?"

"Absolutely. What **was** his name? Peter just called him Doc. I could call Peter and ask him."

"No, that's all right. Was his office on Central Park West?"

"No, nowhere near there. It was this office building on Broadway and about—oh, I don't know. Somewhere below Fourteenth Street. We walked there from where we lived, and we were in Alphabet City, so it was a fairly long walk, but it wasn't like walking all the way to Central Park West."

"I see."

"I can't remember his name," she said, "**or** his address, but I'm sure Peter would know them both."

"Never mind," I said. "It's not that important."

But of course I remember you," Helen Watling said. "You're the man who paid for my bran muffin."

"I guess it's even better than ginkgo."

"Better than . . . oh, for memory! Well, as for what a bran muffin's best for, let's not even go there."

That was fine with me. "Let's try your memory," I said. "You mentioned that your son was seeing a counselor."

"Well, he **saw** a counselor. I don't know that it was ongoing."

"But it helped him."

"Well, that was certainly the impression I got. I honestly think he was getting back on the right track. Of course as a parent you want to believe that, but—"

"I wonder," I said, "if Jason ever mentioned the counselor's name."

"The counselor's name."

"Or if you had any correspondence from the man."

"Well, on the last point, I certainly never did. But I'm sure Jason mentioned the man's name. And I do take ginkgo, as a matter of fact, but evidently I don't take enough of it, because I just can't come up with that name."

"If Jason wrote it down in a letter—"

"Oh," she said, "don't I wish! No, Mr. Scudder, I don't think Jason ever wrote me a letter from the day he left Wisconsin. The only way I ever heard from him was over the phone."

"So that's how he would have told you."

"Yes, that's right."

"Maybe you could try to call up the sound of his

voice, Mrs. Watling. He's talking to you on the phone, telling you about his counselor . . ."

"Oh, now you're going to have me crying, Mr. Scudder."

"I'm sorry."

"I can just about hear his voice. I was going to say before that I wish he had been the sort to write letters, because it would be so nice if I had a letter from him, but do you want to know what I really wish I had? A tape recording. I wish I could actually hear the sound of his voice, and not have to imagine it."

I don't know where it came from, but I had a lump in my own throat. I swallowed it down and asked her if Jason had ever mentioned a Dr. Nadler.

"Dr. Nadler," she said solemnly.

"Seymour Nadler."

"Seymour Nadler. No, that's definitely not the name Jason told me."

"You're sure."

"Oh, there's no question in my mind. The name's on the tip of my tongue, Mr. Scudder, and I can't quite spit it out, but one thing I can say for certain is it's not Seymour Nadler."

"But it's right on the tip of your tongue."

"Well, I **think** it is! But what good is that if I can't say it?" She sighed, exasperated with herself. "It was a cheerful name," she said.

"A cheerful name?"

"I remember thinking that. Not that the name

was cheerful, but that the person sounded cheerful, and since all I knew about him was his name . . ."

"It must have been a cheerful name."

"Well, it stood to reason."

"Like Happy or Lucky? What kind of a cheerful name?"

"No, not like that. Oh, I'm terrible, aren't I? I'll bet you're sorry you wasted your time calling me."

"Not at all, Mrs. Watling."

"It was a positive name, that's all. An optimistic sort of a name. I'm sorry, listen to me, I'm just making it worse. And this must be costing you a fortune, calling all the way from New York."

"That's all right," I said. "Look, you wait and see if the name comes to you. Sometimes if you stop trying to think of it . . ."

"I know exactly what you mean."

"Well, if it comes to you, just call me." I gave her my number, although she assured me she had kept my card. "And I'll call you in a couple of days if I don't hear from you," I said. "Just to check."

A cheerful name, an optimistic name. What the hell did that mean?

THIRTY-THREE

The woman is driving him crazy.

She is the type of patient he ought to culti-
vate. She comes twice a week, Tuesdays and Fri-
days, at ten in the morning, an hour that is
generally hard to fill. And she pays full price,
one hundred dollars an hour, two hundred a
week, ten thousand a year, and, most remarkable
of all, she pays him in cash. Always a fresh new
bill with Benjamin Franklin's avuncular portrait
beaming out at him. She's a dominatrix, and gets
paid in cash herself, by the men she abuses ver-
bally or physically.

She seems oddly cast for the role, a small,
slightly built woman of forty-two, who tends to
dress down for her appointments, often turning
up as she has today in sweats and sneakers, often
capping her session with a run around the Central Park Reservoir. She wears no makeup and

her long black hair is pulled back in a ponytail and secured by a fuzzy yellow elastic.

On the job, she has told him, she wears a lot of black leather.

You would think, given her occupation, that she would have interesting stories to tell, but no. Her voice is grating, and impossible to ignore, or fall asleep to, and she is hopelessly neurotic, incapable of making the most trivial decisions without agonizing endlessly over them. She whines, she drones, she repeats herself. And, God bless her, she adores him, and is sure he's saving her life, and perhaps he is.

He is, after all, quite good at this.

When his watch beeps he gets to his feet, signaling that time is up. She breaks off in the middle of a sentence, as well trained in obedience as her own clients. In no time at all she's out the door, and he tucks a crisp hundred-dollar bill— green love, he likes to call it—into his billfold.

Ten minutes to eleven. His next appointment isn't until two. He turns to the computer, turns away from it, reaches for the phone.

P eter," he says, "I'm at a loss here. I don't understand."

"I left a message, Doc."

"You left a message."

"On her answering machine. I asked would

she please call me, I said I really wanted to talk to her. But she hasn't called back."

"And this was yesterday that you left this message?"

"Yes, yesterday afternoon."

"And she hasn't called back."

"No. I think maybe she's out of town."

"I rather doubt that, Peter."

"Oh."

"I'm sure she's in town, and in her house, and feeling very lost and alone."

"Oh."

"And most likely depressed, and overwhelmed, all of which are entirely appropriate responses to her situation. She's had some devastating losses. And she's only now beginning to feel the enormity of the first loss of all."

"The first loss of all?"

"The loss of your love, Peter. The two of you separated, for reasons that may have been inevitable at the time, and in due course all of her misfortunes followed."

"Oh."

"Do you see what I mean?"

"I think so."

"You have to break through her resistance, Peter. You don't call once. You call until you get a response."

"You want me to keep calling?"

"I think you must."

"Then I will, Doc."

"What do you get, Peter?"

"You get what you get."

"Precisely. You take the action and accept the result. But the way you take the action determines the result. Peter, when her machine next invites you to leave a message, I want you to visualize Kristin standing right next to the machine. And this time don't speak to the machine. Speak directly to Kristin. Picture her taking in every word even as you are speaking to her."

"I will."

"Tell her to pick up the phone. Get her to pick up the phone."

"Yes, Doc."

"And call me back after you've spoken to her."

He's on the computer when the phone rings. There's nothing interesting at alt.crime. serialkillers this morning, but he's found several Web sites dealing with various aspects of the topic, and he's visiting one of them. What he's reading is interesting, fascinating really, and he's tempted to let the machine take the call, but knows that it's Peter Meredith.

And of course it is, and he's calling to report success.

Success and failure.

"I did what you said, Doc," he begins, "and it worked. Instead of talking to the machine I talked to Kristin, as if she could hear every word I was saying. And I didn't stop, I went right on talking as if we were having this long one-sided conversation, and I said some of the things we talked about yesterday, about family and destiny and, well, I just kept talking."

"And?"

"And I wore her down, I guess. She picked up the phone and we talked."

"When are you going to see her?"

"I'm not."

"What's that?"

She doesn't want to see him, Peter says. She has good feelings for him, good memories of their time together, but it's a closed chapter for her. She has her life to live, and he has his own life, at the house in Williamsburg, and she wishes him the best of luck in that life, but she doesn't want to share it with him.

"And Doc," Peter says, "I'm so glad you made me make that call. You always know just what's right for me."

"Oh?"

"Because I am so relieved. Doc, I'm over her now, for the first time. When she said there was nothing there, that she had zero interest in getting back together again, I just felt completely liberated. Like I could get on with my life in a way I couldn't up to now."

You fucking idiot, he thinks. But he says, "That's wonderful, Peter. I'm proud of you."

"You did it, Doc."

"No, you did it, Peter," he says automatically, thinking, Yes, you did it, you fat oaf. You stepped in it with both feet.

"Everything you said, about destiny and all? It was like those were my own inner thoughts, but I didn't even know it until I said them and she shot them down. And that released me from them. I think . . ."

"Yes?"

"I know you said it was just rebound, but Caroline—"

"The sculptor."

"Yes."

"On Wythe Avenue."

"Yes."

"You want to pursue that."

"Unless you think it's a bad idea."

God, he feels tired. "I think it's worth exploring, Peter. If it's a failure, well, every failed relationship is preparation for a successful relationship." He takes a deep breath. "Now you'd better get back to work on that house of yours, hadn't you?"

The shower pelts down on him. Great water pressure in this building, much better than the last place. He lets the spray hit him in the back of the neck, feels the tension drain away. He showered on arising, he showers first thing every morning, but it's not rare for him to take a second or even a third shower in the course of a day, and it seems very much in order now.

You get what you get.

Physician, heal thyself. Is the catchphrase he feeds his patients any less applicable to himself? You get what you get, and whatever comes your way is an opportunity.

You can go to the ocean with a teaspoon or a bucket. The ocean does not care.

Peter is all wrong for Kristin. That had been his first reaction when he met the woman for the first time. This preppy goddess, this daughter of privilege—what was she doing with this jovial fat man?

And so he'd engineered their separation, only to see it in the fullness of time as a mistake. They should be together. While Peter toiled on that sow's ear of a house in Brooklyn, Kristin languished in a silk purse of a brownstone, worth more every day in New York's dizzying real estate market. Now if her inconvenient parents were out of the picture, so that the house and everything else were Kristin's, and if Peter were then to make himself once more available . . .

He gets out of the shower, pats himself dry. Applies deodorant, dabs a little cologne on his cheeks.

How interesting, he thinks, the way the mind has reasons that the mind knows nothing of.

He'd arranged everything for Peter, so that the fellow could win the fair maiden and occupy the castle. (And Peter would be grateful, of course, and would love him more than ever. And, when the castle was Peter's alone, why, he'd show that gratitude in the most concrete way.)

But why go through all that? All along—and he must have known this, albeit unconsciously— all along he has been preparing this banquet not for Peter but for himself. It is he who will win the maiden, he who will own the castle.

How could he ever have thought otherwise?

He puts on all clean clothes, choosing a deep-toned blue shirt, a red tie. The tie is knotted and he's reaching for his jacket when he remembers the amulet, the talisman, the disc of rhodochrosite that so sharpens his perceptions and boosts his mental clarity.

Shall he be angry with himself for having forgotten it at first, or shall he congratulate himself on having remembered? The choice is his—the ocean does not care.

Congratulating himself, he puts down his jacket, loosens his tie, unbuttons his shirt collar, and fastens the gold chain around his neck.

He looks up a phone number, dials it. The voice of his destiny: "No one can take your call right now. Please leave a message at the tone."

And what a tone, hers, not the machine's—cool, regal, but promising so much.

He dials another number. A man answers, and he recognizes the voice as Lucian's. "It's Doc," he says. "Is Ruth Ann handy?" And, learning she's gone to the hardware store, "That's all right, you can give her a message for me. Tell her I'm canceling my appointments for the rest of the day. She's down for two o'clock, so just tell her to call me and we'll shoehorn her in some other time."

On the way out the door he strokes his cheek, holds his hand to his nose, breathes in the smell of his cologne.

W hat a splendid house it is!

He has come on foot this time, and stands on the opposite side of the street, looking at his future home. And it's nothing new for him to think of it in those terms. Within its walls, watching the barbarian Ivanko spilling drawers, tipping over tables, he'd wanted to caution him against doing any damage to the house and its furnishings.

And, when he cut the woman's throat, didn't it bother him to think of her blood spoiling the carpet?

Well, no, he admits. At the time he never gave it a thought, he was too utterly involved in the act itself to give a thought to its consequences. Afterward, though, he had time to regret that blood, spoiling that carpet.

His carpet.

How circuitous his original plans seem now! A reunion of Peter and Kristin, and a wedding, and Peter moves in, and then, after a suitable interval, something unfortunate happens to Kristin. And Peter, wanting only to get back to his beloved friends on Meserole Street, makes the house over as a gift of love to him, for the foundation he will establish.

Or, if that won't fly, then Peter, despondent over the tragic death of the love of his life, takes his own life—after having willed everything he owns to the man who has always been there for him.

Well, the hell with all that. He'll marry the girl himself. He'll have to do some artful management of Peter's emotions, but by then he'll see to it that Peter is so mad for the Wythe Avenue sculptor as to banish any particle of potential resentment. The five of them could be wedding guests—six, if you included the sculptor, and why should she be left out?

And then there will be no rush to close the account, either. Kristin will be an ornament, her mind an interesting one to play with. Only when he tires of her will anything need to happen to her, and death, when it comes, will clearly be the result of natural causes. Nature, in her bounty, has provided no end of natural sub-stances that can bring on wonderfully natural death.

He crosses the street, a smile on his lips. He mounts the steps, faces the door. His fingers touch the knot of his tie, checking its shape, and one slips inside his shirt for the quickest touch of the mottled pink disc. He extends a finger, rings the bell.

Stands there, waiting.

Waiting . . .

He slips a hand into his pocket, draws out a ring of keys. He finds the right one and slips it into the lock, and it goes right in, a perfect fit, but it won't turn.

Well, that's understandable. There's been a burglary, after all, and the brutal murder of both her parents. She's had the good sense to change the locks.

The bitch. The fucking cunt.

His eyes widen at his reaction. He feels the rage and steps off to one side, weighing it, as-sessing it. It's completely disproportionate to the fact of the changed lock, a fact he had al-ready accepted intellectually as logical and to be expected. Ergo it has nothing to do with the lock, or the fact that no one has come to answer the doorbell.

Pressure. He's under pressure, and needs re-lease.

Fortunately, that's easily arranged.

★　★　★

The massage parlor is on Amsterdam Avenue, one flight up over a nail parlor. Both establishments are owned and staffed by Koreans. He climbs the stairs, and a balding Korean behind the desk takes a pair of twenty-dollar bills from him and points at a door.

The girl is short, slender, flat-faced, with a mole on either side of her little mouth. One would be a beauty mark; two, so symmetrically arranged, cry out for a plastic surgeon. If she were a patient of his . . .

But it is in fact he who is her client, and as he undresses she takes his clothes and hangs them in the metal wardrobe. She's wearing a red-orange shift, easy-on easy-off, and she doesn't seem to understand when he asks her to take it off. He mimes the request, and now she understands, and, smiling, shakes her head, and points toward the table.

He gets on the table on his back and she leans over him, kneading the muscles of his shoulders and upper arms. Her hands are small, her arms spindly, and he doubts there's much strength in them. The girl couldn't give a genuine massage if her life depended on it.

Interesting turn of phrase, that. . . .

Her touch turns light, lingering, and she strokes his chest and stomach. He's engorged, and her fingers flutter ever so lightly over his erection.

"So big," she says, and sighs. She touches him again, feather-light, and says, "You wan' spesho massa'?"

"Special massage," he translates. "Yes, that's what I want."

"Fi'ty dollah."

"All right."

"Fi'ty dollah now."

He gets up from the table, goes to the wardrobe, takes his billfold from his pants. He gives her the crisp hundred he just received from the dominatrix—what goes around comes around—and stops her when she starts looking for change. Through a combination of words and pantomime he indicates that she is to keep the whole hundred dollars, and that he wants her to take off her dress.

And, in a single motion, it's off. She's got a young girl's body, hairless but for the tiniest tuft between her legs. Little baby-doll titties.

She reaches out, touches his amulet. "You still wearing," she said.

"Yes."

"Pity."

That confuses him for a moment, until he realizes she's saying that it's pretty. He lifts it over his head, settles it around her neck. The rhodochrosite disc floats just above and between her breasts.

She giggles, delighted.

And now he gets back on the table, and, with skill beyond her years, she performs as required. She uses her hands, and, at the end, a Kleenex tissue. His orgasm is powerful, his ejaculation abundant, but for all of that he is curiously detached from it all. He is, in a sense, off to the side watching, and without a great deal of interest.

He gets up from the table and she hands him his clothes, watches him dress. Before he buttons his shirt he holds out a hand, pointing to his amulet.

She giggles, clasps both hands over the pink stone circle, hugs it to her heart. She says, "Keep?"

He shakes his head, and she giggles again. She never really expected him to give it to her, and she's not surprised when he reaches to take it from her. She's still smiling and giggling, in fact, as his hands position themselves on her throat.

THIRTY-FOUR

I had a dream that night, an awful one. I dreamed I was asleep and Michael called, waking me out of a sound sleep to tell me that his brother Andy was dead. **That** woke me, and I sat up in bed with the same awful uncertainty that characterizes an awakening from a drunk dream: Yes, I know it was a dream, but did I really drink? Is my son really dead?

I'd only slept an hour or so at that point, and I was tired, so I went back to sleep, and kept drifting into one variation after another of the same fucking dream. What I guess I wanted to do was go back into the dream and fix it, so that it resolved itself in some way I could be comfortable with, but that's not what happened.

I wound up sleeping late, and when I finally did wake up I knew it was a dream. I knew, too, that it indicated nothing more than that I was anxious about my younger son, and perhaps that my second piece of pizza had not been a good idea. But I couldn't shake the feeling of foreboding that was the nightmare's legacy. It stayed with me, through breakfast, through a second cup of coffee. I set it aside while I watched the news and then when I read the paper, but it hung around. It never left the room.

I picked up the phone, called Kristin. The line was busy. A busy signal's irritating, and I guess they must intend it to be or they wouldn't make it sound the way it does. This one irritated me more than usual, because her line wasn't supposed to be busy. She wasn't supposed to be on it.

But of course the busy signal didn't necessarily indicate she was talking to someone, as I realized after my irritation subsided. It could mean that someone was leaving a message on her answering machine—Peter Meredith, for example, telling her fifty reasons why he needed to talk to her. Or it could be that she'd tired of media types calling all the time, and had taken the receiver off the hook. I didn't really want her doing that, I wanted to be able to reach her if I had to, but I hadn't said anything to her about it. If I'd given her any more orders, you'd have thought she was working for me. . . .

I tried the number again, got a busy signal again. I went into the bathroom, checked myself in the mirror. I didn't really need a shave, but it was something to do.

★ ★ ★

The next time I tried Kristin's number it rang through, and the machine picked it up on cue. I listened to her announcement and said, "Kristin, this is Matt Scudder. Please pick up the phone. I need to talk to you." I waited and nothing happened, and I said essentially the same thing a second time, and went on repeating myself for a while. Then I gave up, told her to call me, gave her my number, repeated it, and cradled the receiver.

I went into the kitchen to make myself another cup of coffee, and decided that was the last thing I needed, and thought about having it anyway. I said the hell with it and walked back into the living room, and when I got there the phone rang.

I picked it up, and it was Michael. I had a very bad moment, but only a moment, and then he was saying he just wanted to let me know that everything had gone according to plan, that Andy's boss had accepted his check and even returned the quit-claim Michael had thought to enclose, and that Andy had packed up and moved out of Tucson, not as a fugitive from justice, thank God, but as a young man looking to better himself in a more propitious location.

"I just hope he doesn't run out of locations," Michael said.

"Does he know where the money came from?"

"I didn't tell him."

That didn't quite answer the question, but I let

it go. I asked about June and Melanie, and he asked about Elaine, and we were left with nothing to say to each other. I wished I could have talked to him about my work, and for all I know he wished he could have talked to me about his. Instead we told each other to take care, and be well, and give my love to so-and-so, and said goodbye and rang off.

A few minutes later I realized that Kristin hadn't called back. But then how could she, while I was on the phone with Michael? I called her number again and got the machine again, and asked her a couple of times to pick up if she was there.

When she didn't, and when five minutes went by without a call from her or anyone else, I decided that something was wrong.

I'm not sure how rational that was. I don't know how much of it derived from circumstance and how much from a combination of the dream and Michael's phone call. But I was sure something was wrong, and that I'd damn well better do something about it.

I called Wentworth, and for a change I got him at his desk. "Scudder," I said. "I just wanted to know if you've got men on Kristin Hollander."

"The order went in," he said.

"I know the order went in. What I wanted to know—"

"Just a minute," he said, and went away. I stood there, shifting my weight from foot to foot, and he came back and said the order was still awaiting approval.

I started to say something but I'd have been talking to myself. He was no longer on the line. I got a dial tone and tried Kristin one more time, but before the machine could pick up I cradled the receiver and got the hell out of there.

I got a cab right away. The driver may have been the only cabby in the city to brake for yellow lights, so it took a little longer getting there than it might have, but I made myself sit back and take it easy. By the time we turned into Seventy-fourth Street I'd cooled down enough to realize I was overreacting. We pulled up and I paid off my cabby and went up and rang her bell.

It didn't take her long, although it probably seemed longer than it was. Then I heard the cover of the peephole snick back, and I said my name, just in case age and anxiety had rendered me unrecognizable. And then she opened the door.

I felt a great rush of relief, and at the same time felt like an alarmist and a damned fool. I was on the point of apologizing—I'm not sure what for—but she beat me to it.

"I'm sorry," she said. "You were afraid something happened to me, weren't you? That's why you're here."

"You didn't answer."

"Oh, God," she said, and sagged against me. She was sobbing, and I held her for a moment, then took hold of her by her upper arms and set her upright. "I'm sorry," she said again. "Just give me a minute."

She turned and disappeared through a doorway, and when she came back a minute or two later the tears were gone and she'd regained her composure. "I did something I wasn't supposed to do," she said. "Peter called, it must have been the third or fourth time, and he talked right through the machine to me. It's as if we were having this conversation, except he was doing all the talking, and I hadn't picked up the phone."

"And then you did pick up."

"I couldn't help it," she said. "I tried to walk away but I couldn't, it would have been like hanging up on a person, except somehow worse. I don't know, it doesn't make any sense, but I picked up the phone."

"Don't worry about it."

"He was going on and on about destiny, and how he wanted to be there for me, how all of them wanted to be there for me, and I just couldn't take it."

"Destiny," I said.

"And I knew the only way to end this was to end it, so I told him to forget about destiny and forget about me, because I had to make a life for myself, and the life I had in mind didn't have room for him in it." She frowned. "That sounds terribly cold and cruel, doesn't it? If anybody talked to me like that I'd probably want to stick my head in the oven. But that's not how he took it."

"Oh?"

"He said he was really grateful to me for telling the truth about how I felt. He said it helped cut through a lot of illusions. He said it was liberating."

"You think he meant it?"

"You don't know Peter. If he didn't mean it, he wouldn't say it."

But the conversation took a long time, she said, and that must have been when I was getting the endless busy signals. Then when she got off the phone she felt exhausted, and decided she wanted to sit in the tub with last month's **Vanity Fair** and just wallow in somebody else's misery. She was just ready to get into the tub when the phone started to ring, and she thought it might be Peter, and she didn't want to talk to him again, and if it wasn't Peter it was probably some reporter, and whoever it was she wasn't supposed to answer it, so she just got in the tub.

And while she was soaking and reading about the murder of a Connecticut socialite, still unsolved after thirty years, the phone rang again. And again she let the machine get it, and stayed right where she was.

"And then I got out and got dressed and came down here and played the messages," she said, "and they were both from you, and you sounded really upset, and I grabbed the phone and called your number, but all I did was get your machine."

"I'd left the house by then."

"And you're here, and you made the trip for nothing, and I'm really sorry."

"Forget it. I was as much to blame as you, and it got me out of the house, and that's not the worst thing that ever happened to me."

"Oh?"

"I had a bad dream last night," I said, "about one of my sons. It was groundless, and everything's fine, but sometimes you can't really shake off that sort of thing without a change of scene."

"I know what you mean."

"Yes, I'm sure you do."

"Well," she said, a little awkwardly. "Well, you were wonderful to come rushing over, but fortunately I'm fine, and, uh, actually I was going through some papers upstairs. And I know you've got things to do, and, well . . ."

"You're right," I said. "I'd better be going. It's just that I'm a little leery of leaving you here."

"Even if I promise not to answer the phone? Unless it's you, in which case I promise to answer right away? Remember, I've got a couple of guardian angels posted outside."

"Oh?"

"My police protection," she said. "I still haven't been able to spot them, but it's good to know they're there."

Should I let her go on believing that? And what if she waltzed out the front door, confident her guards were there to protect her?

I said, "I spoke to Wentworth. He hasn't been able to get authorization."

"But I thought it was just a formality."

"I guess some precincts are more formal than others," I said, "and some precinct commanders, or whatever deadhead's in charge up there. May I use your phone?"

"Of course," she said, and grinned suddenly. "I can't, but you can."

I have four numbers for Ballou, and at that hour I wasn't at all confident he'd be at any of them. But he picked up the phone at the third one I tried. I told him what I wanted in about five sentences, and all he wanted to know was the address.

"A friend of mine," I told her. "He'll stay here in the house with you, and God help anybody who tries to get through the door." And I told her a little about my friend Mick Ballou, and watched her eyes widen.

We were sitting in the kitchen, waiting for him to ring the doorbell, when she said, "Oh, I almost forgot. At least I managed to do something right when I talked to Peter."

"If you cooled his ardor for keeps, I'd say you did a lot of things right."

"Besides that. I found out his name." My confusion must have shown in my face, because she said,

"No, not Peter's name. Remember you wanted to know the man we saw for couple counseling?"

"You said Peter called him Doc."

"They all called him Doc. I asked Peter what Doc's name was, and he couldn't believe I didn't remember. Doc played a much bigger role in Peter's life than in mine. Anyway, it turns out his name is Adam, and I swear I never knew that. I just remember him being introduced as Doc."

"Adam."

"And what did you say Dr. Nadler's first name was? Sheldon?"

"Seymour."

"Well, I was close. But not Adam, anyway."

"No," I said. "You said they all called him Doc. All his patients?"

She shook her head. "Peter and his friends. Maybe his other patients, too, but I don't know about them, just Peter and the four artists we were going to be sharing a house with in Williamsburg."

"They all knew Adam?"

"They were all patients of his. I think they all met each other in group therapy, or something like that."

"Really."

"When Peter was talking about destiny," she said, "and everything else he was saying, you could tell he was just parroting something he got from Adam. That was another reason I was sort of relieved when we broke up. Adam was good for Peter, I guess he was good for all of them, but I could picture the five of them all turning into little Adam Breit clones."

"Adam Breit."

"Yes."

"Describe him, would you?"

"Oh, gosh," she said. "I only met him at the counseling sessions, and Peter and I spent most of our time looking at each other. Or not looking at each other. Let's see. He's about your height, and maybe a little slimmer, and, well, sort of ordinary-looking. This isn't helping much, is it?"

"I need to use the phone again," I said, and went and picked it up. I found the number I wanted in my notebook, and dialed it, and caught her in. I said, "It's Matthew Scudder again, Mrs. Watling. About the name of that therapist."

"I'm afraid it hasn't come to me," she said. "I'm so ashamed of myself."

"A cheerful, optimistic name, you said."

"Yes, but I can't—"

I wasn't in court, no one was going to accuse me of leading the witness. I said, "Could it have been Adam Breit?"

"Yes!"

"You're sure? I don't want to—"

"Yes, that's it! I couldn't swear to the Adam part, but the Breit part is absolutely right. Bright and sunny, bright and cheerful, bright as day, bright as a new copper penny. I don't know **why** that name wouldn't come to me. It seems so obvious now."

I thanked her and told her I'd let her know how things worked out. Then I took a chair and we waited for Mick Ballou.

THIRTY-FIVE

Smile in place, he emerges from the little room, saying, "Bye-bye, see you soon," as he draws the door shut. He nods and smiles his way past the expressionless Korean minding the desk, and keeps the smile on his face until he is down the stairs and out of the building. He walks quickly to the corner, turns, and maintains a brisk pace, but not so brisk as to draw attention.

No great need to hurry. No one will open her door, not right away. They'll wait for her to come out on her own. And, when they do lose patience and knock, and open the door when the knock goes unanswered, all they'll see is an empty room. She must have come out unnoticed, they'll think, and gone to the bathroom.

Eventually, of course, someone will open the metal wardrobe, where he stuffed her body, along with her slippers and her red-orange dress.

No one notices him, and in return he notices no one; waiting for the light at Columbus Avenue, he's so involved in his own thoughts that it changes twice before he remembers to cross the street.

He's had a revelation, and he has to get it written down. It may have some scientific merit, but that's almost beside the point.

At his building, he smiles at the doorman, smiles at a tenant stepping off the elevator. A nod here, a smile there.

As the elevator wafts him upward, his fingers find their way to the cool pink stone he wears around his neck.

He sits at his desk, looks at the screen of his computer, where the endless evolution of the New York nightscape continues. But he doesn't have time to watch it now. He presses a key, and the screensaver vanishes.

He doesn't log on, but opens his word-processing program and selects New from the menu. A blank page fills the screen. He stares at it for a moment, remembering the feel of the girl's hands on him, remembering the feel of his hands on her.

His fingers move, and words begin to fill the screen:

In respect to that type of serial murderer whose actions are motivated by a desire for the thrill of the act itself, the presumption has long existed that a distortion of the sexual impulse is present, and probably causative. The person in question cannot perform normally, and the thrill he finds in the act is the thrill of sexual fulfillment.

My research would indicate that this is not necessarily the case.

Let us consider a young man whom we will call A. Just recently, A confided to me that . . .

He stops, frowns at the screen. Later, if he decides to publish, he can tart it up like that. For now a more straightforward approach will serve better to get the words and thoughts down. He deletes the paragraph that begins Let us consider and resumes:

Earlier today, I felt a need for sexual release and went to a professional establishment where what I sought was offered for sale in a carefree and presumably hygienic environment. In the guise of a masseuse, a girl-woman of Asian extraction gave me a commendably skillful hand job. I was rock-hard as soon as she touched me, and the orgasm I attained was powerful. My performance (if such a word is appropriate, considering that all I did was lie on the table with my eyes shut, not even bothering to look at the body I'd tipped her extra to unclothe, not troubling to reach out a hand to touch her ivory skin)—my performance, indeed, left nothing to be desired. I had arrived in that room with a fierce desire—a need—for sexual release, and I had achieved that release.

And it was satisfying. The sopping-wet Kleenex she so casually flipped into the bucket was mute testimony to my satisfaction.

Yet I was not satisfied. The orgasm might as well have happened to someone else. I might be sexually sated, but something else within me was entirely untouched.

I didn't even know what I was going to do until I did it. I had almost finished dressing when the impulse came, and I knew instantly that this was what I craved, what I required, what had brought me to this dingy little room in the first place. And so I put my hands around her neck and squeezed.

She never made a sound. I cut off her air before she realized what was happening, lifted her off the ground. Her little feet kicked in the air, and one of her slippers went flying. Her eyes stared into mine, and,

even as I watched her die, I felt something—
kundalini? the life force?—enter through my
hands and race up my arms, filling my entire
being.

I did not, while this was happening, experience any sort of feeling I can characterize
as sexual, nor did my body respond sexually.
I did not get an erection, did not feel a stir-
ring in my loins.

On the other hand, I was left with a feeling of satisfaction, of fulfillment, infinitely
greater and more abiding than my orgasm
had provided. This, clearly, was what I had
been seeking, although I had not known it
consciously until I reached out and took the
little darling by the throat. I was not depleted, as one sometimes is by sexual release, but rather reinvigorated, able to
think clearly and act decisively. To wit: I not
only tidied up, stuffing her body where it
would not be quickly noticed, along with
her dress and the slippers she'd kicked off
in her struggles, I also had the presence of
mind to use her dress to wipe away fingerprints, and to retrieve from her change
purse the $100 I'd tipped her. (Indeed,
there were three twenties and a ten along
with my $100, and I took them as well. I'd
paid $40 at the door, so I made a $30 profit
on my visit, which, given the time involved,

**compares not unfavorably with my profes-
sional rates!)**

He smiles at that last line. When it's time to
publish his findings, and he knows he'll want to
do so, considerable editing will be required. It
will be some anonymous patient who's confiding
all of this to him. And yet, isn't there some
value in presenting the material directly and
authentically? As it stands, his report provides
first-person testimony by one who is himself a
professional in the field. Aren't his perceptions
all the more valuable because of his professional perspective? And won't they be undercut
for being disguised as those of some unnamed
analysand?

He needs to give this some thought. Perhaps
there's a way to post it as written on some appropriate Internet site. Of course he can't
e-mail it from this machine, or through an exist-
ing account. But what's to prevent him from
dropping in at an Internet café, say, and logging
on to AOL with a stolen password (not too hard
to come by, certainly) and posting it that way?
They can trace it, they have the technology to
trace anything these days, but there'll be nothing to point them in his direction.

Meanwhile, he'll want to work on this, shape
it, refine it. Maybe add a little more detail to the
report, make the whole process of her dying a

little more vivid. First, though, a word or two of summary:

There is a line to be drawn, it would seem, between Eros and Thanatos. The two can walk side by side, yoked in harness, plowing a double furrow. There is surely some overlap. Part of the pleasure of killing is sexual, just as part of the pleasure of the sex act lies in imposing one's will upon another. But when all is said and done . . .

His watch beeps.

And that's a good place to leave it, right in the middle of a sentence, so he'll be able to recapture the thought train when he returns to the work. Now, though, he has other duties calling him. He's canceled his afternoon appointment, but that doesn't mean he lacks for things to do.

He moves the cursor, clicks the mouse. Night falls in the form of his screensaver. Lights come on and lights go out.

He gets to his feet. Does he have time for a shower, a change of clothes? Surely he does. And, on his way out, might it not be a good idea to leave his suit at the dry cleaner?

He wears a camel's-hair blazer with leather buttons, dark brown flat-front trousers, a white shirt, a tie with half-inch stripes of tan and royal blue. On the way to her house, he stops at a florist, wonders what's appropriate. Surely not roses, but what?

He leaves empty-handed, deciding that the occasion does not call for flowers at all. But one wants to bring something. Candy? Does anyone come calling with a box of chocolates?

Inspired, he walks on down to Seventy-second Street, where there's a wonderful place for pastry. I passed this shop, he hears himself saying, and I couldn't help myself. He selects an éclair, a napoleon, and a couple of tartlets that look appealing. Does she even care for pastry, his future bride, chatelaine of his castle?

There is so much still to be learned about her. . . .

The little white box tied up with string and tucked under his arm, he walks the two blocks to Seventy-fourth Street. He is within two houses of hers, striding merrily along, when her front door opens and a man emerges, turning for a last word, then turning again and pulling the door shut.

And it's that man again, the man whose card he took from Lia Parkman's room. Scudder, Matthew Scudder! It's him, coming down the steps, and what's he supposed to do now? Stop short and invite attention? Maintain his pace and walk right into the man?

He stops, turning his head, feigning a glance

at his wristwatch. Scudder reaches the sidewalk, and he wills the man to turn to his right, away from him. But no, the son of a bitch turns left and walks right toward him, a look of grim determination on his face.

He maintains his own pace now, averts his eyes, but somehow can't resist a quick glance at Scudder as they come within a few feet of each other. And Scudder looks right at him!

And looks past him. Scudder doesn't know him at all. And they pass, and Scudder keeps heading west, and he himself walks on past the Hollander house and halfway to the corner before he dares to turn around.

Scudder's nowhere to be seen.

And, he realizes, no one to be feared. Oh, he's involved in this, the son of a bitch. And now he knows why he looked familiar, and where he saw him before. In Brooklyn, on Coney Island Avenue, when he drove past the house where it had all started. He'd been driving along, and he'd seen two men emerge from the house, two men who didn't look right for the neighborhood. The younger man wore a Hawaiian shirt and looked like a cop, and the older man, Scudder, looked like the landlord or someone who worked for the city.

Now he knows his name and where he lives, and that's all he knows about the man. But whenever you turned around, he turned up. Was it time to do something about him?

Just now, if he'd had a gun, he could have dropped him in his tracks and kept walking. Or a knife, a sharpened hunting knife in a leather sheath on his belt, and he'd draw it in a single motion and thrust forward in another, swift and silent.

Where could you buy a hunting knife? In the rest of the country, certainly, but in New York?

Well, it will wait. He has a castle's walls to breach, a maiden to rescue.

He mounts the steps, rings the bell. If she's not answering the door these days, well, he'll do as he told Peter to do. He'll keep ringing the bell, and he'll talk to her through the door, as if the door's not there.

And, whatever her intentions, she'll open it.

His finger moves to the bell, and he's just about to give it another poke when the door opens. And there's a giant of a man planted in the doorway, filling the doorway, glowering at him. Christ, will you look at him—unforgiving green eyes in a face like a chunk of granite. He looks as though bullets would bounce right off him.

"What do you want?"

A rough voice—no surprise there—with a trace of brogue.

He can't think what to say.

"What are ye, then, some fucking reporter?"

He hesitates, nods.

"Then you're not wanted here, so why don't you fuck off?"

The door closes in his face. He scampers down the stairs, turns right, heads toward the park. At the corner he drops his white string-wrapped pastry box in a trash can.

THIRTY-SIX

I said, "Here we are. Adam Breit," and spelled it. I'd been looking for Bright, as in bright as day, because no one had told me how he spelled it, and why would they? Neither Kristin nor Helen Watling had seen the name written down.

I was in T J's hotel room, where we were going through the phone books, I the White Pages and he the Yellow. I'd had no luck in the residential section, but I'd found a business listing for Breit, Adam, with a 255-number and no address.

I dialed the number, and a recorded voice told me it was no longer in service.

I called information, and did what you had to do to talk to a living human being. I'd have done as well with a recording. I identified myself as a police officer, invented a name and a shield number to go with it, and told her I needed an unpublished address. I gave her the name and phone number, and she put me briefly on hold and came back with the news that the number was no longer in service.

I said I knew that, but that I needed to know the address where it had been in service, once upon a time. She said she didn't have that information. I asked if there was a new listing for that name, Adam Breit, published or unpublished, and she checked and told me there wasn't.

I hung up, and T J said, "Ain't that a crime, Sime? Sayin' you a cop when you ain't?"

"It is," I agreed, "and by using criminal methods I'm revealing myself as no better than Adam Breit."

"Adam Breit, Arden Brill," he said. "Subtle pattern here?"

"Maybe. If we could find him we could ask him."

"You want to make some more calls," he said, "use this." He handed me his cell phone and did something with his computer, and it made that weird sound they make when they hook up somewhere in space with all the other computers in the world. Then a friendly voice told him he had mail, and he said, "Yeah, well, it'll have to wait," and set about tapping keys and frowning and making nerdlike clucking noises with his tongue.

I picked up a Classic Comic version of **A Tale of Two Cities**—required reading for his French Revolution course, no doubt—and was getting reintroduced to Madame Defarge and her knitting needles when he said, "Seven twenty-four Broadway."

"What about it?"

"Goes with that phone number."

"What have you got there, a reverse directory?"

"Sort of an everything directory," he said. "An' I didn't have to lie to no operator."

"She said he had an office on Broadway," I remembered. "Down below Fourteenth Street. That sounds about right."

"Just a minute," he said, and came back with the information that 724 Broadway would be somewhere around Waverly Place. I asked if he could find anybody else at the same address, and he wanted to know who we were looking for. Anybody who might know where Adam Breit had gone, I told him.

I wound up with a dozen phone numbers. Five went unanswered when I called, and the others were about as useful; four of the people I reached had never heard of Adam Breit, two recalled the name vaguely, and one said he'd moved, but couldn't say when or where to.

I said, "You're near Waverly Place, right?"

"Between Waverly and Washington," he said, "but I'm on my way out, pal, so there's no point coming over."

"That's all right," I said. "I've got no further use for you."

"Well, the hell with you too," he said, and hung up.

* * *

TJ had some other ideas of how to find Breit, so he stayed at his computer while I caught a subway downtown. I came up to the surface at Broadway and Astor Place and walked a block and a half to a narrow building with a cast-iron front. Most of its eight stories of commercial loft space had been turned into residential units. All the mailboxes had names on them, and Breit was not among them, but that was no surprise.

A sign directed me two doors south to the super, and I managed to find him in the basement, a light-skinned black man with a long oval face, a pencil-line mustache, and just a trace of the West Indies in his speech. I said I was looking for a man named Adam Breit, and he laughed as if that was the funniest thing he'd heard in days.

"It would be very helpful if he left a forwarding address," I said.

"Oh," he said, "that would be helpful for everyone, wouldn't it? When he left here Mr. Breit had the better part of two years to go on his lease, and he was a full three months behind in his rent. The landlord would be very happy to know where he is, and so would Mr. Edison and Mrs. Bell."

"Mr. Edison and—"

"Mr. Conrad Edison," he said, enjoying himself, "and Mrs. Alexander Graham Bell, best known as Ma. He didn't pay the light bill or the phone bill."

"When did he move out?"

"Now there's a question. It seems to me it was sometime after the first of the year when his absence became evident, but as to when he quit the premises, I don't really know. The landlord was after him about the rent, and finally brought a locksmith over to open the door, and it was Old Mother Hubbard all over again."

"How's that?"

"When she got there, the cupboard was bare. He took his clothes, left his furniture, and lit out for the Territories."

"Just like Old Mother Hubbard."

"Exactly."

"Furniture worth anything?"

"He owed money on it, and it must have been worth something, because the firm that sold it to him sent people to fetch it back. What's your business with him, if I may be so bold?"

"That's a good question," I said. "Speaking of business, was he running one here?"

"Speaking of business," he said, "I was busy minding my own, so I'd be hard put to say. He lived here, and people came to see him during business hours, and during nonbusiness hours as well, but who's to say what a man's hours of business may be?"

"Who indeed?"

"I don't think he was trafficking in illegal substances, if that was going to be your next question."

"It wasn't."

"And you never answered **my** question, now that I think about it, aside from declaring it a good one. Did our Mr. Breit owe you money, too?"

"No," I said, and I could have let it go at that, but something about this gentleman made me want to say more. "I can't be a hundred percent sure," I said, "but it looks as though he killed five people."

"Oh, my," the man said. "Five, you say?"

"It looks that way."

"Well, that's just terrible," he said. "Why on earth would he want to go and do something like that?"

I went back the way I'd come, on the subway, and when I got to the Northwestern T J was downstairs, in what passes for the lobby. He said, "Thought I'd save you a trip upstairs. I been all over the Internet, and the man don't exist."

"Adam Breit."

He nodded. "Spelled either way, E-I-T or I-G-H-T. He a psychiatrist, a psychoanalyst, a psychologist, any damn kind of a shrink, he gotta be listed somewhere."

"You couldn't find a thing?"

"Oh, I found all kind of things," he said. "Broader you make your search, more useless shit you turn up. Put in 'Adam Bright' an' you get some news story, some politician predictin' 'a damn bright future for the farmers of Schuyler County.' You narrow it down enough to be useful, ain't no Adam Breit to be found."

"Well, he's not at Broadway and Waverly," I said, and told how Breit had pulled up stakes and disappeared.

T J said, "Maybe he did light out for the Territories. Or he was the first person killed."

"The man we're looking for killed Adam Breit and took his identity."

"You don't like that?"

"Not a whole lot," I said, "since you've just established he didn't have an identity to take."

"Slipped my mind."

"And he's still around, because Peter Meredith and his friends are still seeing him. I gather he's some kind of guru, the spiritual leader of their little commune."

"The Buddha of Bushwick," he said. "You want to find him, you start right there."

"On Meserole Street? I don't know. If they think he's the closest thing to God, how much are they going to give out about him? All we'd do is run into a brick wall."

"An exposed brick wall," he said.

We needed a place to start, and I didn't think Meserole Street was it. I thought for a minute and said, "Seymour Nadler."

"You think him an' Breit the same person? He sets up this other identity, goes down an' lives on Broadway an' Waverly an' meets with Peter

Meredith an' the rest of them, an' then—" He stopped, shook his head. "That don't make no sense," he said.

"That's not where I was going."

"Good thing, too."

I said, "The burglary. When we figured Nadler was our guy, there were two possibilities. He faked the whole burglary, or it was legit and a day or two later he made a false report about a missing gun."

"One or the other."

"But if Nadler's in the clear—"

"Then the burglary was legit, an' the burglar took the gun."

"Right. And how did Adam Breit wind up with it?"

"He was the burglar."

"Right again," I said, "which would explain the similar MO in both burglaries. They were similar because one man committed both of them."

"Now that we know that," he said, "what do we know? The burglar did it, but are we any closer to finding him?"

"Think about it."

He thought about it. "He did it to get the gun."

"That's my guess."

"How'd he even know the gun was there?"

"There you go," I said.

Some years ago, back when I lived in the room that is now T J's, a couple of computer hackers,

David King and Jimmy Hong, spent an evening on my behalf deep in the innards of the phone company's computer system, digging out records that were supposed to be unobtainable. They've gone on to bigger and better—and far more legitimate—things, but one legacy they left me was a lifetime of free long-distance calls. I don't know exactly what they did or how they did it, but out-of-state calls made from that telephone never showed up on a bill.

I suppose stealing is stealing, whether it's the phone company or a blind newsboy you're ripping off, and I'm sure moral relativism is philosophically unsustainable, but what the hell, nobody's perfect. If I had to call all over Martha's Vineyard looking for Seymour Nadler, I was just as happy to do it from T J's room, secure in the knowledge that nobody was ever going to have to pay for it.

When I finally got him I said, "Dr. Nadler? I'm sorry to disturb you. I believe you spoke yesterday with Detective Ira Wentworth?"

"Yes?"

"I have a follow-up to that interview, Doctor. I wonder what you can tell me about any connection you might have had to a man named Adam Breit."

"I can't talk about patients," he said. "I'm sure you're familiar with the principle of doctor-patient confidentiality, and—"

"As I understand it," I said, "that would only apply if Adam Breit were a patient."

"If he's not a patient," Nadler said, "then why are you calling me?"

"We thought he might be a colleague."

"A colleague."

"A psychiatrist, or therapist of some sort, and—"

"Breit!"

"You know him, then?"

"Adam Breit," he said. "He's not a close friend, we never worked together, never studied together. But yes, I know him. Not well, but I know him."

"How do you—"

"In the most casual way, yes, I know him. Adam Breit. A pleasant enough young man. What about him?"

"How did you happen to know him?"

"Didn't I just tell you that? Casually, very casually. I smile, he smiles. I say hello, he says hello. One day we get to talking, and I say, 'Breit, you're a good fellow. You must come over for drinks. Bring your wife.' 'I don't have a wife,' he says. 'So bring somebody else's wife,' I say, which is of course intended as a joke, and he laughs, showing he has a sense of humor."

"And he came over for drinks?"

"Yes, and by himself, needless to say. Very personable fellow, told some wonderful stories. I don't know what exactly his field is, but I suppose you would class it as reality-oriented therapy. He told about a patient of his, oh, it was a charming story, how she was allergic to dogs so he had her switch to stuffed animals instead, with perfectly satisfactory results." He chuckled. "I suppose a traditionalist like myself would want to know first **why** she was allergic, but Breit seems to have found an effective and humane solution."

"That's interesting," I said. "But I must have missed something. I don't think I understand how the two of you happened to meet."

"We bumped into each other."

"At a conference or—"

"In the lobby. The lobby of our building."

"You live in the same building?"

"Well, where did you think we lived? Breit moved in, oh, sometime around Christmas. You know Harold Fischer? The paleontologist?"

"I don't believe so."

"Brilliant man. He's on sabbatical, a full year in France, poking around in caves. Breit's subletting his apartment."

"He lives in the same building."

"Didn't I just say this?"

"Yes, of course. Was he at your apartment only the one time?"

"Maybe twice. No more than that. He was pleasant company, but we didn't have that much in common."

"Did he know about the gun?"

"The gun? What gun are we talking about?"

"The one taken in the burglary."

"This was before the burglary," he said, "so how could he know about it?"

"Did he know the gun existed, Dr. Nadler?"

"Oh," he said. "Oh, now I see what you mean," and laughed heartily. "Oh, have you got the wrong number, Detective."

"How do you mean?"

"He was afraid to touch it."

"You showed him the gun?"

"I **tried** to show him the gun. I took it out of the drawer, I held it out to him, you'd have thought I was trying to hand him a coral snake. It wasn't loaded, he knew it wasn't loaded, and still he wouldn't touch it."

"How did you happen to show him the gun?"

"I don't know. The subject came up. Is there anything else? Because we have guests, and I'd like to get back to them."

THIRTY-SEVEN

Harold Fischer's phone was listed, his Central Park West address the same as Nadler's. I tried the number and it rang four times before the machine picked up. An uninflected male voice repeated the last four digits of the telephone number and invited me to leave a message at the tone.

"If you were leaving the country for a year," I asked T J, "and if you were subletting your apartment, wouldn't you turn off the phone?"

"I don't, could be I come home to a nasty phone bill."

"Maybe Fischer told them to cut it off," I said, "and Breit told them to turn it back on again."

"Said he was Fischer, you mean."

"Maybe. I wonder if Fischer even knew he was subletting his apartment. Maybe he closed it up and Breit moved in."

"Best for Breit if he leave before Fischer come back from France."

"Best for Fischer, too." I tried the number again, got the machine again. "He's not home," I said.

"Then what we waitin' for?"

The doorman took a lot of convincing. I showed him a letter from Harold Fischer, advising anyone concerned that one Matthew Scudder was hereby authorized to enter his premises at 242 Central Park West. The letterhead bore two addresses, the permanent New York address on the left, and a temporary address on the Rue de la Paix in Paris on the right. T J had cobbled it up, letterhead and all, on his computer, and I'd signed **Harold P. Fischer** in a hand any paleontologist would be proud of.

In the past, when a fellow needed phony letterhead, he had to go to a printshop for it. Now anyone can make his own at home in five minutes. Desktop forgery, T J calls it.

After the doorman had a good look at the letter, I had three more things to show him. I led off with my Detectives' Endowment Association courtesy card, and followed with a photocopy of my New York State private investigator's license. It had long since expired, but I kept my thumb over the date. In case these items were insufficiently impressive, I finished up with a pair of fifty-dollar bills. "For your trouble," I murmured. "Mr. Fischer wanted to show his appreciation."

"I could get in trouble," the man said.

"In the first place, you're authorized," I told him, "and in the second place nobody's going to know."

"Suppose he comes in while you're up there?"

"He's in Paris," I said, "and I'm acting on his behalf in the first place, and—"

"Not Mr. Fischer. The new man, Dr. Breit."

"Just send him up," I said. "I'd love to meet him."

In the end he sorted through a drawer and came up with a set of keys to the Fischer apartment. "Anybody asks," he said, "you went and grabbed these out of the desk on your own. You didn't get them from me."

"We never met," I agreed.

We took the elevator to the fourteenth floor, found Fischer's apartment. There was a bell to ring and I rang it, and knocked on the door as well. No response. I tried the key in the lock, opened the door, and walked in, with T J right behind me. I called out, "Harold? Harold Fischer?" and walked through the large high-ceilinged room with its windows overlooking the park. There was a couch and a couple of chairs, and a desk with a computer on it. T J went straight to it, while I checked out the rest of the apartment. In the bedroom, the bed was made, the drapes drawn. In the bathroom, one towel was still damp.

T J called to me, and I went back to the living room and found him hunched over the computer, his eyes on the screen. "Something here you better look at," he said.

Ira Wentworth read the two-page printout a couple of times through, pausing now and then to shake his head. He looked up when he was done and said, "Tell me again where you got this."

"Off the Internet."

"You know what this is, don't you? This is a murder happened just hours ago. Did it even make the news yet?"

"First we heard of it," T J said, "was readin' this-here on the Web. Went to this site I been watchin', has a lot of shit about the Hollander murders. People speculatin', offerin' their own theories 'bout the case."

"Buffs," Wentworth said, the way a man might look around a kitchen and say **cockroaches**. He looked at the papers he was holding, shook his head again, and said, "This is the man who killed that girl. Amsterdam and Eighty-eighth, earlier today, did it just the way he says he did it. Different precinct, but everybody's talking about it, because you don't get just one of these. Maniac's out there, he's gonna do it again."

"This one's done it before."

"Yeah, that's clear, isn't it? But there's nothing here about the Hollanders, nothing about Parkman. Nothing saying who he is, either, far as that goes."

"He implies he's a mental-health professional."

"He's a mental-health case, is what he fucking is. You say his name's Breit?"

"Adam Breit."

"And how do you tie him in? You told me, but tell me again."

I said, "He met Kristin Hollander when he did couple counseling for her and a former boyfriend. He still sees the boyfriend and his little circle professionally. He was a counselor, court-appointed or self-appointed, I don't know which, for Jason Bierman."

"Mope who had the place in Coney Island."

Midwood, I thought, but the hell with it. "He's subletting an apartment in the same building with Nadler," I said, "and Nadler had him over for drinks and showed him the gun."

"Which was later stolen, and used at the Hollanders' and out in Brooklyn."

"Right."

"Makes him look awfully good for it," he said. "You know what we got? We got everything but evidence."

T J said, "He posted this. Every chance in the world he used his home computer, an' if he didn't erase it . . ."

"Even if he did," Wentworth said, "there's geniuses who can recover stuff after you erased it.

But we can't seize his computer without a warrant. We can't even walk in his door without a warrant."

"It's not his apartment."

"He's subletting it, isn't he?"

"There's some question about the legality of that. There's a chance he moved in without informing the apartment's owner."

"And the owner?"

"Is in France and can't be reached," I said. I pointed to the paper he was holding. "Isn't that enough to obtain a warrant?"

"This? How can you tell where it came from?"

T J pointed to the upper left corner of the first page, where a Web address appeared in a different typeface from the rest. "Person runnin' the site could ID the account of the person made the post," he said.

"Take forever, wouldn't it?"

"Take a while."

"And you'd have to get cooperation, and those people out on the Web aren't always in a hurry to cooperate."

"That's a fact."

"But that's what we did," Wentworth said, "and we reached the guy, and got the confirmation from him over the phone. Of course, there's some judges who'd want to see proof of that before they issue a warrant." He grinned. "But there's some who won't."

★   ★   ★

By the time we got there, armed with a warrant
authorizing a search of Apartment 14-G at 242
Central Park West, City of New York, County of
New York, State of New York, our party had
grown to include Dan Schering from the Twentieth Precinct, two detectives named Hannon and
Fisk from the Two-six, and two more from Manhattan North Homicide whose names I never did
get. There was somebody from the crime lab as
well, equipped with a camera and whatever gear
he'd stuffed in his backpack. The same doorman
was on duty downstairs, but we were careful not to
recognize one another. Wentworth showed him the
warrant and he took us right upstairs.

"'Stead of a letter from Harold Fischer," T J
murmured, "I shoulda printed up a warrant. Save
you a hundred bucks that way."

"Next time," I said.

The doorman opened the door for us and stood
aside, and Wentworth led the way. I was ready to
point out the computer, but he saw it right away
and went straight to it, drawing on a surgical glove
so he wouldn't leave prints. "The New York skyline," he said, noting the screensaver. "Love it or
leave it. Now let's hope he liked what he wrote so
much he couldn't bear to erase it."

He extended a gloved forefinger and touched a
key, and the screensaver winked away, and there

was Adam Breit's last message. We'd left it right where we'd found it.

"Jesus," he said. He called the crime lab guy over and asked him if he could shoot a photo of the computer screen. There was a question of glare, I gather, but the fellow said the right filter might help, and he'd see what he could do.

He left him to it and came over to where the rest of us were standing. He stood there shaking his head. "This is almost too good to be true," he said.

I suppose he was right. It was a little bit too good to be true. But it was close enough.

The Web address on the printout we'd prepared for Wentworth was a real site, one T J had been keeping tabs on for the past week or so. And Breit might have posted his observations there or somewhere else, after he'd found a safe way to do so, but he hadn't, and we hadn't posted them for him. We'd considered it, T J thought he knew a way to make it work, but it would have taken too much time.

So we'd gambled that Wentworth would take what we showed him at face value, and T J had inserted the address in the appropriate spot of Breit's open file, printed it out that way on Breit's printer, then deleted his addition to the document and left everything as he'd found it.

Desktop forgery, part two.

★   ★   ★

One after another, the cops in the room put on gloves and used the phone, and as a result more cops and technicians began showing up at the apartment. One man dusted for prints, another bagged the clothes in the hamper, a third was going through the closet. In the bathroom, a man I didn't envy at all got to take up the shower drain and fish out a wad of hair and unidentifiable crud, all of which went into a plastic bag, and not a moment too soon.

"He said it right there," Wentworth said. "The bit about tossing the Kleenex into the bucket. Maybe he wiped away prints, maybe he took back his hundred bucks, but do you think he went through her scum bucket looking for the wad he just shot?"

"Somehow I doubt it," I said.

"According to him," he said, "he shot a big load. Oughta be enough DNA to convict him six times over."

"He said it was satisfying," I said, "but something else within him was entirely untouched."

"When the system's done with him," he said, "my guess is he won't be able to make that claim. I want to get an all-points out, and you know what we don't have? A picture of the son of a bitch. He's got an ego the size of Montana, how come he hasn't got any pictures of himself anywhere in the place?"

"Maybe he figures everybody knows what he looks like."

"Do you? Know what he looks like?"

"No, but the building staff must."

"That's a point. Have to get a description from the doorman, sit him down with a police artist. That way the papers can print something that won't look a bit like him, but what the hell. You got any idea where we'll find him?"

"I didn't know his name until earlier today. I couldn't even have proved he existed."

"I guess that's a no, huh?"

"I'd watch the Hollander house," I said.

"I've got men there."

"Oh? The authorization came through?"

He made a face. "I called in, told them to assign a couple of uniforms to sit in a car and stake the place out. If anybody approaches the house, they're to stop him and question him. As soon as I've got a description I'll give it to them, narrow it down a little."

"That's good," I said, "but tell them not to go inside the house. There's a man in there who'll take their heads off if they try."

"The Hollander house," he said. "Where else?"

"He had a place in the Village," I said, "on Broadway, but he got out of there when he moved in here. He left owing a lot of back rent. I don't think he'd be crazy enough to try going back."

"He got a girlfriend?"

"He had one at the massage parlor," someone

else chimed in, "and look what happened to her."

"What about this house in Brooklyn?" Wentworth said. "Anything there?"

"Coney Island," somebody said, and Dan Schering said, "No, Coney Island **Avenue**. House itself is in Flatbush somewhere."

"More like Midwood," I said.

"I don't want to buy it," Wentworth said. "I'm just wondering if the son of a bitch is likely to use it for a bolt-hole."

"It's rented," I said, "as of the first of the month."

"But it's empty now?"

"I believe so."

"Be a place for him to hole up," he said.

"There's a cop I talked with out there named Iverson," I said. "At the Seventieth Precinct."

"Somebody should call him," Wentworth said.

"I'll give him a call," somebody said. "Which precinct was that?"

"The Seven-oh," Wentworth said. "Is that right, Matt? The Seven-oh?"

"That's right," I said.

"I know that station house," one of the Homicide cops said. "That's on Lawrence Avenue, isn't it?"

"I don't know," I said. "I met him at the location."

"Sure, the Seven-oh," he said. "Ugly-looking station house."

"Jesus," Schering said, "that'd make it the only one of its kind in the five boroughs."

Wentworth said, "The boyfriend. You mentioned something about him."

One of the others said, "This asshole's got a boyfriend? Then what's he doing in a massage parlor?"

"Not Breit," Wentworth said.

"Not bright at all," the other said. "Fucking stupid, you ask me."

"Not the perp who had the boyfriend," Wentworth said. "Are you pulling my chain or what?"

"Would I do that, Ira?"

"All day long," Wentworth said. To me he said, "Hollander had a boyfriend, right?"

"Broke up over a year ago."

"But you said something about counseling, that that's how Breit met her."

"Yes."

"And he's still counseling the boyfriend."

I nodded. "He might go there," I said. "It's out by Bushwick Terminal."

Someone wanted to know why anyone in his right mind would go there, and someone else said Breit wasn't exactly in his right mind.

I said, "Maybe you already did this, but why not station somebody downstairs next to the doorman?"

Wentworth nodded. "Right. Because the most likely place for Breit to turn up is right here, and it would be nice if someone would point him out to us when he does."

THIRTY-EIGHT

It's not difficult to buy a hunting knife in New York City.

It's very difficult, prohibitively so, to buy a gun. You need a permit, and that's not the easiest thing in the world to obtain, and you need to show two pieces of photo ID along with the permit. A knife is easier, because the movement for knife control has not made much headway. There are, he learns, certain kinds of knives you can't purchase, because they're illegal. Switchblades, for instance, or gravity knives. It's possible, however, to buy a knife which can be converted into a switchblade, and the same dealer who sells it to you can also sell you a simple kit with which you can make the conversion. That's evidently legal—but, should you use the kit and convert the knife, you're then subject to arrest for possessing an illegal weapon.

A switchblade is illegal because, just by pressing a button, you can convert it into a weapon. But a regular hunting knife that doesn't fold to begin with already is a weapon. You don't even have to press a button. But it's legal.

On the other hand, you can't carry it on your person if the blade is over a certain number of inches in length. Then it's a deadly weapon. You can buy it, and play mumblety-peg with it in the privacy of your own home, or take it in the woods with you to skin out big game. But if you carry it around within city limits, you're breaking the law.

He is breaking the law.

The knife is a Bowie-type, ten inches overall, with a six-inch blade. The handle is wrapped in dark brown leather, and the sheath that comes with it is of black leather reinforced with steel. The design tooled into the sheath shows two crossed flags, one the stars and stripes, the other the Confederate stars and bars.

The sheath is now attached to his belt, and as he walks along, his arm at his side, he can feel its comforting presence. His jacket is long enough to conceal it, but it's easy to reach under his jacket, easy to get his hand on the handle. There's a little strap that snaps closed, securing the knife, but he can leave it unsnapped if he wants, to make it that much easier to get at.

It's a beautiful piece of workmanship. The manufacturer is located in Birmingham, Alabama, and much is made of this in the article's packaging. The clerk at the sporting goods store made a point of telling him the knife was American-made. Are the best knives those made in America? Or is it that customers for hunting knives like to support American industry?

He doesn't know, or much care. It pleases him to have the knife, even as it pleased him to have the gun. Long before he was ready to use it, almost from the day he took it from that Freudian idiot's desk, he'd enjoyed carrying it concealed on his person, in a pocket or wedged under his belt, where he could touch it whenever he felt like it.

It's very satisfying, walking about armed, carrying a concealed weapon. You know something no one knows. You're empowered, secretly empowered. Sitting in a subway car, you look at the man opposite you, knowing you can draw your gun and shoot him dead and there's nothing, nothing at all, that he can do about it.

Once, in a darkened movie theater, he'd taken out the gun and pointed it at the back of the neck of the person sitting directly in front of him. Bang, he'd thought to himself, and put the gun back in his pocket.

By the time he finally got to use the gun, on that fool Bierman, he'd anticipated the moment a thousand times.

And where shall he go now, with his beautiful new knife? He has the whole day to himself, to use as he wishes. Shall he collect his car from the garage and go for a ride in the country? Go home, stretch out, curl up with a good book?

He could return to the house. His house, his future home. The giant, the Irish thug, must have moved on by now. If not, he can see how the man does against six inches of steel, honed to razor sharpness and hardened to 400 on the Rockwell scale, whatever that's supposed to mean. It's evidently a selling point, as the manufacturer trumpeted it on the box and the salesman troubled to point it out.

No doubt it means it's hard, as you'd expect steel to be. He imagines the big man dismissing him, telling him to fuck off, then the green eyes widening at the sight of the knife in his hand.

Then again, he thinks, perhaps not. A knife blade, whatever its numerical degree of hardness, might snap like a twig against that one's rough hide. More to the point, he can envision the man's hand darting out, quick as a cat, and taking the knife away from him. . . .

He wants to try it out.

In a restaurant where he eats a sandwich and drinks a cup of coffee, he locks himself in the men's room and practices drawing the knife, practices thrusting at an imaginary opponent. There's a mirror, and he can watch himself as he goes through his moves. It seems to him that he has a natural feeling for the weapon. He'd been quick to master the gun (and, the job finished, sick at the thought of abandoning it) but it seemed to him that there was nothing to learn with the knife, or, more accurately, that his knowledge of the weapon was intuitive and innate, dormant and unsuspected for years, activated the moment he took the thing in his hand.

Perhaps he'd been a knife fighter in a previous life. Perhaps he'd been Jim Bowie himself, the man who'd invented the damn thing. Died at the Alamo, didn't he? Went out in a blaze of glory.

With a favorite knife in his hand? Why not?

Someone tries the door. It's locked. And if it were open? A man walks in, starts to apologize, sees the knife, tries to back away . . .

And he sees himself wiping the blade on the man's shirt, returning it to the sheath, and walking coolly out of the bathroom, drawing the door shut after him. Walking past the balding Korean attendant, down the stairs . . .

No, that was earlier, that was at the massage parlor. He's in a restaurant now, he's just eaten, just gone to the bathroom, and it's time to pay the check and leave.

On the street, he tells himself it was just imagination, that's all. A fantasy sideslipping into a memory. Nothing untoward in that, nothing to be alarmed about.

Now what? Another massage parlor?

The notion is shocking in the intensity of its

appeal. The only element he doesn't contem-
plate with delight, he realizes, is the massage
part. He doesn't want anybody touching him,
doesn't want to be aroused sexually. He just
wants to see the look in her eyes as the knife
slides home.

He's not thinking clearly.
That, at least, is clear to him. He has been
walking around, turning left, turning right,
walking into shops, looking around, walking out.
He's looking for something and doesn't know
what he's looking for, and he's not thinking
clearly, that's it in a nutshell, and in the process
he's placing himself at risk.

He reaches into his shirt, touches his amulet.

And knows what he has to do. He has to go
home and lie down, he has to take a Valium, he
has to get some rest. He has had a very busy day,
and his energy levels are depleted, and he's got
to allow them to replenish themselves. A hot
bath, a glass of Harold Fischer's excellent
single-malt Scotch, a Valium, and eight hours of
uninterrupted sleep. That's what he needs, and
what he's going to get.

He steps to the curb, holds up his hand, and
two taxis dart across several lanes of traffic, eager to take him wherever he wants to go.

He rewards the one who gets there first, gives
his address, sinks back into the cushions. He

touches the handle of his knife, touches the rhodochrosite circle.

Power and clarity. He's feeling better already.

On Central Park West, a block and a half short of his destination, the taxi stops for a red light. Without planning it, without any fore-thought whatsoever, he says, "I'll get out here," and takes money from his billfold. They're not at the curb, there's a lane of traffic to the right of his taxi, but no matter. He stuffs money into the pass-through compartment of the partition, ig-nores the driver's protest, and gets out. There's a red light, no one's going anywhere, and it's easy enough to walk between a couple of cars and reach the sidewalk.

Why, though?

There's a reason, he's certain of it, and so he keeps his eyes open and his wits about him as he proceeds north for a block on the side of the av-enue bordering the park. And, when he's covered half the distance, he knows why he didn't let the taxi take him to his door. He doesn't know what warned him, what subtle observation inspired that inner prompting, but he can hardly ques-tion it.

Because his building is swarming with police-men.

There are police cars parked all over the place—at a hydrant, in a bus stop, in a no-parking zone around the corner. Is there a fire truck on the scene? An ambulance? No, nothing but police cars. And there's a uniformed patrolman standing in the entrance, talking with the doorman. And there's a man who's not wearing a uniform, but might as well be.

Can he spot a film truck? Are there any barriers set up to hold back the crowd? They are forever filming things in this city, movies, television episodes, along with New York exteriors for shows ostensibly set here but actually filmed in Los Angeles, and much of what they film involves crime and the police. Walk into an apparent hostage situation and you're likely to spot Jerry Orbach, looking more like a cop than the cops do.

But Jerry Orbach's not here. No one's filming this.

It's all over, he realizes. He knows without the slightest doubt that he's the reason for the presence of all these policemen. And it's not one cop, come to ask him a few questions. It's a whole slew of them, several vehicles' worth, and that means they've been in the apartment, and yes, of course, they've read what's on his computer, they could hardly have failed to do so, and they'll have long since discovered the wretched little masseuse tucked in her wretched little cupboard, and, well, what is there to say? It's over.

And they're waiting for him, standing there waiting for him, and if he hadn't somehow known to get out of the cab when he did, he'd have waltzed right into their arms.

But he's been given a second chance.

He heads for the parking garage to collect his car.

You get what you get, he thinks.

And it's up to you what you make of it.

He thinks of alt.crime.serialkillers. He'll have his own thread, won't he? Have whole Web sites devoted to him and his exploits.

And how many cops will spend how many hours searching for him? There are no photos of him, he's seen to that. Family photos, high school yearbook photos, but he had another name then, and no one searching for Adam Breit will know that name, or have access to those photos. They can run all the sketches they please on America's Most Wanted. It won't do them any good. He'll watch the program with new friends in Spokane or St. Paul and shake his head and sigh with the rest of them. "What a sick son of a bitch," he'll say. "I wouldn't mind seeing him hang. I'd pull on the rope myself."

Waiting for a light to change, he drops his hand to his side and feels the knife, then reaches up to touch his amulet.

And thinks of the people who love him.

Christ, they're going to hear about this, and it's going to shatter them. Peter and Ruth Ann and Lucian and Marsha and Kieran, his whole little family, and what are they going to think? How are they going to feel?

He can't leave them like this.

He pulls out of line, wrenches the wheel all the way around, hears brakes squeal behind him as he makes a U-turn in front of oncoming traffic. Horns sound in reproach, but he scarcely hears them. He heads for Delancey Street, and the Williamsburg Bridge.

Is he in time? Will they welcome him with the love that is their greatest gift to him? Or will he walk through the door only to see fear and horror on their faces?

He brakes at the curb, leaps out from behind the wheel, dashes across to the front entrance. The door's unlocked and he flings it open, and there's Kieran and Ruth Ann, looking up from their work, and there's big Peter over to the side, chipping away at plaster. And what is it on their faces? Shock?

No, no, it's surprise, and of course they're surprised, because they were not expecting a visit from him. But it's a good surprise, he sees. They're delighted, their faces glow with love. "Doc!" they cry. "Doc, what are you doing here? Doc, it's so good to see you!"

He makes the rounds, embraces them in turn, and when he and Peter have finished their hug he hears footsteps on the stairs, and turns to see Marsha and Lucian, beaming, radiant, coming to join the party. Everybody's here, his whole family, and how could he have possibly driven off and left them, these five dear people who love him so? How could he even have considered it?

What was he thinking of?

THIRTY-NINE

When Wentworth called I was back home watching a ball game. Elaine was getting dinner ready and T J was at her computer, doing something that would enable her to perform more efficiently some task she'd lived all her life without doing at all.

I'd called the Hollander house earlier and told Kristin's machine I wanted to speak to Ballou. When he picked up I told him the police guard was in place, and he could probably leave if he wanted to. He said he'd long since spotted them through the window, and you could very likely march an army past them without getting their attention. He'd stay where he was, if it was all the same to me. The wee girl was a good cook, and she'd found a cribbage board, and he'd taught her to play.

I said, "Cribbage? I didn't know you played."

"There's much you don't know," he said.

I couldn't argue the point. I went back to the baseball game, where a Met pitcher was struggling. He was earning five million dollars this year, and so far he'd won two more games than he'd lost. I found myself wondering what kind of money Bob Gibson would get in today's market, or Carl Hubbell, or—

The phone rang, and it was Ira Wentworth, wanting to know if I was busy. I told him my wife was fixing dinner and I was watching a ball game. Why?

"You've been in on all of this," he said, "and I figure you earned the right to see the rest of it. But I have to say you're better off staying where you are."

"I don't follow you."

"I don't follow myself," he said. "You want to come, be out in front of your building in five minutes. I'll swing by and pick you up."

Elaine was planning to make pasta, and I caught her before the water boiled and told her she was cooking for one. "Then I'll just have a salad," she said, "and we can eat when you get home, if you're still hungry. Where are you going?"

I told her I didn't know. I got T J away from the computer and we went downstairs. A minute or two after we hit the pavement, a Ford about three years old made an illegal U-turn in the middle of the block and pulled up right in front of us. I opened the door and was about to compliment Wentworth on his driving, but the expression on his face stopped me. I got in next to him and T J got in back and the car took off before we had the doors shut.

He said, "I don't know why I'm in such a rush. Nobody's going anywhere."

"What is he, holed up somewhere?"

"In a manner of speaking."

"Does he have hostages?"

He laughed, but there was no humor in it. "Same answer," he said.

I didn't say anything, and he turned at Broadway, slowed down long enough at a red light to make sure there was no oncoming traffic, then coasted through the intersection. He drove like a cop, trying not to hit anybody, but otherwise unconcerned about the traffic laws.

At Times Square he switched to Broadway. As we approached Thirty-fourth Street he said, "You're not going to ask where we're going?"

"I figured you'd tell me sooner or later."

"Brooklyn," he said.

"Coney Island Avenue? He went back there after all?"

He didn't say anything. At Thirty-first Street two cars stood side by side at a red light, waiting patiently for it to change. Wentworth swung around them, shot across the intersection, cut back in. Somebody leaned on his horn.

"I don't know why the hell they do that," he said. "Hit their horns. Time they do that, I'm already out of their lives."

"If they had guns," I said, "they wouldn't have to honk."

"An armed driver is a quiet driver," he said. "What I'm doing, I'll cut over Houston to Forsyth or Eldridge. Whichever one's southbound. Take that to Delancey and shoot over the bridge."

"Wrong bridge," I said. "If you take the Manhattan Bridge it's a straight shot down Flatbush Avenue."

"Thanks for the geography lesson," he said, "but that's not where we're going."

I don't know how much of it I knew then. Enough, at least, to keep my mouth shut.

Heading east on Houston Street he said, "Somebody mentioned the boyfriend. I forget his name, if I ever heard it in the first place."

"Peter Meredith."

"Somebody mentioned him back at Breit's apartment, and I was going to call somebody in Brooklyn, see about getting a car and a couple of uniforms out there. But then I thought somebody else was gonna take care of it, and it was way down on the list, you know? They were patients of his, but he's a doctor, a therapist, whatever the hell he is, you figure he's got a whole file cabinet full of patients, right? What are you gonna do, go sit on each and every one of them on the chance he might show up?"

"What happened?"

"Fire," he said. "Place went up like a fucking film warehouse. Meserole Street? Couple of blocks from Bushwick Terminal? Isn't that where you said it was?"

"That's right."

"You don't recall the street number, by any chance?"

I was reaching for my notebook when T J said, "One sixty-eight."

"That's some memory, Tom Jones."

"He was out there," I said.

"When was this?"

"Few days ago," T J said. "Met all but one of them. They showed me what they doin', the renovations an' all."

"They just gave you the grand tour?"

"They under the 'pression I from the Buildings Department," he said. "They was doin' a whole lot of work on that house."

"That's nothing," Wentworth said. "You're not gonna recognize the place."

It had taken them a while to get the fire under control, but it was out by the time we got there, and the last hook-and-ladder unit was just pulling away as Wentworth angled in next to a red NYFD inspector's car.

I saw, but barely registered, the crowds of onlookers, the booted firemen walking around, the house itself with its windows gone and great holes chopped in its roof. We walked in, escorted by a fire inspector and a cop from the local precinct.

Crime lab personnel were on the scene, along with someone from the medical examiner's office.

We climbed stairs to the top floor and worked our way down. Most of the internal walls had been removed in the renovation, so we didn't have to go room to room; each floor was just one large room, and each room held its dead.

On the top floor, a large man lay on his side, one arm under his body, the other flung out to the side. He'd been pretty thoroughly roasted in the fire, and there wasn't enough of his face left to offer a clue of what he looked like.

"Stabbed twice, maybe more," somebody said. "They were all stabbed, though it's easier to tell with some of them than with the others. There's empty drums of muriatic acid all over the place. You use it to get plaster residue off brick, and it looks as though he sloshed it over their faces. But we won't know for a while how much damage the acid did and how much was the fire, because everybody got a second dousing with accelerant before the place went up."

T J said the dead man was Peter Meredith, basing his identification on the corpse's girth. One floor down we found two more bodies, killed the same way, disfigured and burned the same way. T J was less certain, but guessed we were looking at all that was left of Marsha Kittredge and Lucian Bemis. They lay side by side, with the smaller figure nestled in the crook of the larger one's arm.

The fire had been a little less intense on the first

floor, at least at the front of the house where the two bodies lay. The man's hands and face had been bathed in muriatic acid, and his hair and most of his clothing had been burned away, but it was easy to spot the stab wounds in his chest.

"Kieran Eklund," T J said. "Never did meet him, but that there's Ruth Ann Lipinsky. Just about enough left of her to recognize."

She lay a few feet away, her face eroded by the acid, her hair burned away in the fire, her throat slashed. Blood had gouted from the wound and pooled around her, and big bloody footprints, still distinguishable after the fire, led diagonally across the floor to a stairway at the rear.

"He went out the back," I said, but the fire inspector shook his head.

"He didn't go anywhere," he said.

The stairs down to the basement had mostly burned away. A portable metal ladder, marked FDNY, had been laid down over what remained of it, and we made our way down it one at a time. The cellar floor was a couple of inches deep in water, among other things.

There was a pile of rags at the foot of the stairs. Except it wasn't a pile of rags.

"Crispiest critter of them all," the fire inspector said, nudging the corpse with a booted foot. "That's a hunting knife next to him, and what do you bet it's the one made those cuts upstairs? I'd say the odds are good. You want to know what happened?"

"I'd love to know what happened," Wentworth said.

"I can tell you how we reconstruct it, based on preliminary observations. It's all subject to change when we've reached the stage where we're ready to release a full report."

"Understood."

"He went floor by floor, starting at the top. Killed the guy on the top floor, came down a flight, did the man and woman, one more flight and killed the last couple. Though how he managed to do all that without anybody resisting is something I'm glad it's not my job to figure out."

"They were patients of his," I said. "He was somewhere between a father figure and a cult leader."

"Maybe they drank Kool-Aid first," Wentworth said.

"Whatever," the fire inspector said. "He killed the last one and went upstairs again and did what he did with the muriatic acid, and then poured accelerant over the bodies and elsewhere on the various floors. It looks as though he had all kinds of accelerants to choose from and it looks as though he used them all. Paint thinner, turpentine, joint compound, different kinds of solvents. They were artists, and between their art supplies and what they were using for renovation, they had enough accelerant to burn down Mount Everest. Worked his way down killing, worked his way down a second time with the acid and the accelerant.

"Time he got down here he was running low on accelerant, or maybe it was beginning to dawn on him that he better move his ass before the place went up like a torch. So he went a little light on the accelerant, and he stepped in the blood, and tracked it across the floor."

"Sloppy," somebody said.

"Down here," the inspector went on, "is what he was saving the rest of the accelerant for, and his instincts were good, because fire burns up, not down. He splashed shit all over the place, and then he did something you never want to do when you're fixing to burn your house down."

"Lit a cigarette?"

"Well, he could have, if he was dumber than shit. If he was not quite that stupid, my guess is he decided he needed a little more light, and he flicked that switch right over there. You flick a light switch, you're apt to get a little bit of a spark. You never see it and it doesn't amount to anything, unless you happen to be in a room full of volatile fumes, which he was. Boom—instant explosion, instant wall of flame, and we can only hope he knows better next time."

"Fucking electricity," someone said. "He shoulda used a candle."

"If only," the inspector said. "One other possibility, before you all clear out of here and go home to the dinners you've no longer got any stomach for. It's just as possible he knew what he was doing. If he figured it was all up and he wanted to join his fellow cult members in the next world, well, this way he'd go fast. It might not be much fun while it lasted, but it wouldn't last very long. Any questions, gentlemen?"

Wentworth said, "Anybody got a flashlight?" And, when one was handed to him, "Is it all right to turn this on? Is it safe?"

"I don't think you get a spark from a flashlight," the inspector said. "And you may not have noticed it, but they already had their fire here."

"Looks like something on that wall," Wentworth said, and flicked on the flashlight.

"I noticed that before," the inspector said. "I thought it was blood at first, but it looks like he used red paint."

" 'I came like water and like wind I go. Audrey Beardsley.' Who in the hell is Audrey Beardsley?"

"I think it's Aubrey Beardsley."

"Is that a B? All right, maybe it is. Same question. Who the hell is Aubrey Beardsley?"

"An illustrator," I said. "Around the turn of the century. And he didn't write those lines. They're from the **The Rubáiyát of Omar Khayyám**."

"Maybe Beardsley was easier to spell," someone suggested.

Wentworth said, "Arden Brill, Adam Breit, and Aubrey Beardsley. I guess he wanted to hang on to his monogrammed luggage." He pointed the flashlight at all that was left of our mystery man. He said, "Well? Does he look familiar?"

He didn't even look human. Then something caught my eye, and I reached for the flashlight. I stooped down and aimed it where I'd seen a glint of something, reached and picked it up.

A gold chain, its links melted and fused. And, hanging from it, an O-shaped disc of mottled pink stone.

FORTY

On Saturday Mostly Mozart had its final concert of the season. I went with Elaine, and we took ourselves out to a late dinner afterward. The festival had lasted just four weeks, and had served as muted accompaniment for more bloodshed than you get in your average opera. The death toll was pretty high—Byrne and Susan Hollander, Jason Bierman, Carl Ivanko, Lia Parkman, Deena Sur from the massage parlor, Peter Meredith and his four housemates, and, finally, Adam Breit or Arden Brill or Aubrey Beardsley, as you prefer.

That's an even dozen, but the count reached thirteen the middle of the following week, when Ira Wentworth told me he'd played a hunch, and had the ME's office run some checks on unidentified corpses they'd accumulated during the past eight or ten months. A floater, recovered from the Hudson in the spring after having spent a couple of months in the water, was now identifiable on the basis of dental records as all that was left of Harold Fischer. The distinguished paleontologist hadn't gone to France after all, and it was now clear how Adam Breit, unable to pay his rent at Broadway and Waverly, had suddenly been able to afford a handsome apartment in an elegant building on Central Park West.

I brought Wentworth into the kitchen and made a pot of coffee, and again he commented on how good it was. I asked what dental records or anything else might have had to say about the body in the basement, and he said, "It's got to be him, don't you think?"

"It'd be nice to confirm it. What about DNA? Can't they get it from a burned body?"

"They can get it from dinosaur bones," he said. "Remember **Jurassic Park?** They got plenty of DNA from him."

"And?"

"And there's nothing to match it to, that's the whole problem."

"What about the Kleenex in the massage parlor?"

"Somebody went through the bucket of tissues," he said. "You know, whenever I start whining that I've got the worst job in America, just remind me of that poor schmuck, will you? But they went through it and they didn't find anything that matched. Which might mean he's a fucking criminal genius who really did fish his own scum-soaked tissue out of the bucket, or it might mean that little scientific report we found on his computer was founded upon a lie."

"He never went to the massage parlor?"

"He never got off. He didn't come, and therefore there was no reason for her to use a Kleenex and no DNA to throw away. And that's why he killed her, but he didn't want to face the fact he was sexually inadequate, so he told himself that's not how it happened, here's how it happened, and wrote it all up."

" 'I may be a killer, but I ain't no limp-dick wuss.' "

"Something like that, yeah."

"Maybe," I said. "Of course there's another possibility we haven't mentioned."

"I don't even want to think about it."

"He faked his own death once already," I said, "and left a stooge behind in his place."

"Jason Bierman."

"Uh-huh. Fire inspector said there were two possibilities, either he accidentally touched off the explosion and fire before he could get out of the building, or he wanted to go down with the ship. I thought of a third one right away."

"So did I. You know what bothered me the most?"

"The bloody footprints."

"Got it in one. The fucking bloody footprints. Leading right straight to the cellar stairs, just so we'd know to look. You know the word that comes to mind? Cute."

"Which is something else he's done before."

"Every time he had the chance."

"What about dental records, Ira? Fire or no fire, he'd still have teeth in his jaw."

"Absolutely, but what are you gonna match 'em to? The floater in the Hudson had teeth, too, but we had to know to look at Harold Fischer's dental records before they told us anything. The problem with Adam Breit is we don't know who the hell he was before he became Adam Breit. He never lived in New York under that name, not that there's a record, except for a year and a half at Broadway and Waverly and eight months on Central Park West. He never went to medical school anywhere in America under that name, never joined any professional societies. Did he just fake the whole thing as far as his credentials as a therapist are concerned? It might not be the hardest thing in the world. You're never called upon to remove an appendix, or read an x-ray. You just nod your head every once in a while and say things like 'Well, how did that make you feel?' There've been impostors who posed successfully as doctors, as lawyers, and as the son of Sidney Poitier."

"And the daughter of the Czar of all the Russias," I said.

"Posing as a shrink," he said, "should be child's play in comparison, especially since you could make the case that half of them are unqualified to begin with."

I got the pot, refilled our cups. I said, "No fingerprints, I don't suppose."

"Are you kidding? There's barely fingers. And we did find some prints in the Central Park West apartment, but not a ton of them, and it's impossible to know which ones are his."

"Why's that?"

"Because no one set predominates. I think he wiped up a lot, and I wouldn't be surprised if he tended to be careful about fingerprints. Of the prints we did find, well, it stands to reason that the people from Meserole Street left some of them. They were there all the time for individual and group sessions with their fearless leader. And we can't get their prints for comparison, because the muriatic acid that didn't go on their faces went on their hands, and anyway they got burned up in the fire."

"What a fucking mess," I said.

"You got that right."

I drank some coffee. "How'd he get there?"

"Where? Brooklyn?"

"He didn't walk."

"Subway, I suppose. Unless you can find a cabby who'll go to Brooklyn. Nobody logged the trip, incidentally, which doesn't mean nobody made it."

"Did he have a car?"

"Not that anybody knows about. Nothing registered in his name at DMV."

"I think he had a car."

"Under another name? Could be."

"I think he used one when he and Ivanko took down the Hollanders. I thought that all along."

"Possible. Doesn't mean he drove it to Meserole Street."

"No."

"He wasn't carrying two pillowcases full of stolen goods this time, Matt. He could ride the subway and not get a second glance."

"That's true."

"Or he could have got a ride out with one of the Meserole Street people. He could have called them, told one of them to come pick him up. They stood around with their thumbs up their asses while he made the rounds and stabbed them. You don't think they'd run into the city and pick him up if he snapped his fingers?"

"I'm sure they would have."

"If he had a car," he said, "he probably went out there some other way that day. And left his car in a garage, or parked at a curb somewhere. And sooner or later it'll get towed, and wind up sold at an unclaimed property auction, and we'll never know, because it's registered under some other name."

"Uh-huh."

We were both silent for a while, and then Wentworth said, "But if he did take his car, it should have been parked out front."

"You'd think so."

"And it wasn't. Of course he could have left the keys in it, and then it could be anywhere by now."

"True."

"Or not left the keys in it, with the same result. That neighborhood, the kids learn to hot-wire a car before they learn how to drive it."

"Uh-huh."

"Where would he get a stooge at a moment's notice, will you tell me that? Just go out and pick one off the street?"

"Easier said than done."

"Exactly. And did anybody turn up missing?"

"I don't know."

"Well, neither do I," he said. "No reports, but how many people go missing and never get reported? Matt, I think it's him."

"So do I."

"Wallet was in his pocket, you know. It was a mess, what with fire and water damage, but there was some ID in it. A library card, one of those universal Student ID cards they make for you on Times Square. The kind of crap you have when you're using a false name."

"No driver's license?"

"No license, no registration. Which further supports the premise that he didn't have a car."

"Or that his license and registration were in another name, and he kept them separate. And made sure not to plant them on the corpse, because he might need them later."

"When he drove off into the sunset. He left money in the wallet, does that help convince you? I mean, who throws money away?"

"How much money?"

"A hundred and seventy dollars," he said, "which, to refresh your memory, is exactly the amount he boasted about walking out of the massage parlor with. His hundred-dollar bill plus three twenties and a ten."

"The exact amount."

"That's right."

"He walked around all day, and wound up having exactly that amount left in his wallet."

We looked at each other, and his eyes widened. "You know the word that comes to mind," he said.

"I think so, yes."

"Cute."

"That's the word."

"Oh, Jesus," he said. "Look, I'm not going to make myself any nuttier with this than I already am. That's him at the foot of the stairs unless I've got a real reason to think otherwise."

"I'm with you."

"He's dead," Wentworth said. "And if by some godforsaken chance he's not dead, at least he's out of here. And if he's out of here he's somebody else's problem and not ours. What did it say on that basement wall?"

" 'I came like water, and like wind I go.' "

"Well," he said, "all I can say is it's an ill wind."

★　★　★

It was about a week later that Elaine answered the phone and chatted enthusiastically for a few minutes, then covered the mouthpiece and said, "For you. It's Andy."

And indeed it was. He was just calling, he said, to let me know he'd moved again. He'd left Tucson, he said, and had knocked around a little, seeing something of the country, and now he was in Coeur d'Alene, Idaho, just up the river from Spokane.

"In a few months," he said, "I'll probably wish I was in Tucson, because everybody tells me they get a whole lot of winter here. But I have to say it's pretty nice so far." He had a job tending bar, he said, and a decent room a five-minute walk from where he worked.

"If I get loaded," he said, "I can make it home real easy. Don't even have to cross any big streets."

"Always a plus," I said.

"Speaking of loaded," he said, "I was out of line, what I said at Hershey's after the funeral. Plus I guess I was, I don't know, emotionally overwrought?"

"Don't worry about it."

"I guess what I'm trying to say is I apologize."

I told him he was forgiven and it was forgotten, and I wrote down his address and phone number, and we told each other we'd stay in touch. To

Elaine I said, "Well, that was nice, but as conversations go it was like an iceberg."

"Cold? It didn't feel that way to me."

"Invisible," I said. "Mostly underwater. He knows where the money came from."

"Michael told him?"

"Not in so many words. I'd say Michael told him without telling him, the way Andy just told me he knows, and thanks."

"He's in Idaho, he said."

"Tending bar across the river from Spokane, Washington. And living close enough to the job that he can make it home on foot no matter how drunk he is."

"Are you worried about him?"

"I've got no business worrying about him."

"That's not what I asked."

"It isn't, is it? I don't know if **worried** is the right word. I can't make myself believe that things are going to be different. People change, but only when they have to. Tucson's just one more thing that he got away with. The consequences would have been serious, but he didn't suffer them. He dodged the bullet, and a miss is as good as a mile."

"And next time?"

"There'll be a next time," I said, "and maybe a time or two after that, and all I can hope is he's alive and out of prison at the end of it. I have to care because he's my son, but I'm not really involved. I'm not his Higher Power. I'm not even his sponsor."

"Just his father."

"And barely that," I said.

Afterward I found myself thinking about a conversation I'd had with Helen Watling, Jason Bierman's mother. She was deeply gratified that her son's name had been cleared, that he was now known to have been not a multiple murderer but the first in a chain of innocent victims. Yet hers was a bittersweet victory. Her son was still dead, and he'd died a useless, senseless death. And the man she'd credited with helping him turn his life around had in fact betrayed him, and taken his life.

"But you know," she said, "I hate to say this, but I wonder if maybe he isn't better off this way. Because I don't think things were ever going to work out for Jason. But maybe I shouldn't say that, because we can't know that, can we?"

"No," I said. "We can't know that."

I'd had a couple of conversations with Kristin Hollander along the way, and then she called one afternoon to tell me I'd never sent her a final bill. I reminded her I didn't send bills, and that I didn't figure she owed me anything.

"That doesn't seem right," she said. "With all the time you and T J put in? And you must have had expenses, too."

"Nothing to speak of," I told her. "I didn't accomplish a hell of a lot."

"Oh? I'm still alive."

"Your cousin's not," I said, "and neither are those people in Williamsburg. You already gave me a thousand dollars, and that's plenty."

She tried to argue the point, but gave up after a while, and I figured that was the end of it. Then two days later the doorman called up to announce a delivery from Bergdorf's that had to be signed for. He sent the fellow upstairs, and while I was signing for it I told him the doorman was empowered to receive and sign for deliveries to us.

"This one, it had to be the addressee," he said.

I pointed it out to Elaine when she got home, and she started to unwrap it, then stopped to announce that it was for me.

I said, "From Bergdorf's?" They had a men's store, she said, and this was gift-wrapped, and the card had my name on it. I took it from her, mystified.

It was an alligator wallet, a beauty. There was no card, and I took it out of the box and looked for a note, and the thing was crammed with money, crisp new hundred-dollar bills. There were fifty of them, and a card that said "A Gift for You" and was initialed K. H.

I got her on the phone and she said, "You did me a favor and I gave you a gift. Isn't that how it works?"

When someone gives you money, you thank them and put it in your pocket. A cop named Vince Mahaffey had taught me that many years ago, and I'd learned my lesson well.

I gave half the money to T J, figuring he'd done half the work, and maybe more. His eyes got very wide for a moment, and then he took the money and thanked me, and folded the bills and put them in his pocket. He'd learned, too.

Elaine and I had had dinner one night with Ira Wentworth and his wife, and one afternoon he came over, explaining he'd found himself in the neighborhood and couldn't think of a better place to get a cup of coffee. We sat in the kitchen and talked mostly about baseball, and the chances of a Subway Series. "The rest of the country'll hate that," he said, "but you know what? The rest of the country can go screw itself."

And a little later he said, "You know, if you ever wanted to get your PI ticket back, there's a few of us'd be more than happy to write letters on your behalf."

"Thanks," I said. "I appreciate it. But I think I'm happy leaving things the way they are."

"Well, the offer's open," he said. "In case you happen to change your mind."

I had that conversation in mind after the gift arrived from Kristin Hollander, and it wasn't long before I found myself climbing the steps and entering the sanctuary at St. Paul's. The big room was empty, and I took a seat in a rear pew and just sat there for a while. Then I went to a side altar and lit a whole batch of candles, and then I sat down again and thought how things had changed, and how they hadn't.

On my way out I stuffed $250 in the poor box. Don't ask me why.

FORTY-ONE

There is so much to learn!

Take knives, for example. For the longest time all he knew about a knife was how to cut his meat with it. Then he bought a knife, a handsome one in a handsome sheath, paid fifty dollars for it, plus tax, and owned it for what, two, three hours?

Not that he regrets the cost. It's gone, that handsome knife, and he thinks of it fondly, but it doesn't owe him a penny. Oh, no. No, he got his money's worth out of that piece of sharpened steel.

His new knife looks rather like the last one. It too is a Bowie-type, with the same overall design. It is perhaps an inch shorter, and the blood groove is perhaps a shade deeper, but otherwise it looks no different to the uneducated eye.

It cost four times what the first one did. Two

hundred dollars—but there was no tax to pay, because no one collected tax at the knife and gun show where he bought it. He saw a knife quite like his for a little less than he'd paid, and he saw this one, right next to it, tagged $225, and he pointed to it and asked the bearded bear of a dealer why it was priced so high.

"Randall made it," the dealer said, and handed it to him. "It's bench-made, not factory-made. You ever owned a bench-made knife?"

He'd never heard of a bench-made knife. The dealer told him about custom knifemakers who made one knife at a time, the best of them working only on commission, and often booked up a year or two in advance. He drank in the information, and the man responded to his receptivity by bringing knife after knife out of his case, explaining the fine points, inviting him to hold the knives and feel their balance.

"You have a feel for these," the dealer told him. "You buy one of these, a year from now you're gonna have a whole wall cabinet full of 'em. I can tell."

He looked at dozens of knives and bought the first one that had caught his eye, the Randall. And now, weeks later and a thousand miles to the west, he sits on the edge of his motel bed and holds the knife in his hand, appreciating its lines, feeling its perfect balance.

He has two guns, too, both purchased at the same wonderfully convenient show. One is a .22, a pistol, very much like the one he used in New York, but this has a ten-shot clip, and he has three spare clips for it. The other is a five-shot revolver, and he has a box of .38-caliber shells for it.

He likes them, but he likes the knife better.

But, for all that he likes them, the guns and the wonderful Randall-made knife, they are, finally, just things. They exist to be owned, to be employed, to be appreciated, but they're things, and they come and go.

You get what you get.

You make what you can of it.

And then you move on.

It was sad to leave so many things behind. It was sad to leave his apartment, with its splendid view of the park. It was sad to leave all his clothes, including some perfectly fine shirts and ties. Harold Fischer had excellent taste when it came to shirts and ties.

It was sad to leave his house, to leave it before it had even come into his possession. He'd worked so hard for that house, he'd planned to thoroughly. . . .

It was gone. Let it go.

Oh, and saddest of all, he'd had to leave his friends, the people who loved him so. He remembers the joy with which they greeted him. "Doc! Hello, Doc! Doc, it's so good to see you! We love you, Doc!"

Lucian and Marsha appearing on the stairs. And, behind them, shy and wide-eyed, a college friend of Marsha's, who'd just shown up that afternoon, unannounced and unexpected, but welcome. And his name?

Isaac.

Could anything be more perfect, more of a sign from on high? But where is the ram for the sacrifice, father? The Lord will provide the ram for the sacrifice, my son, my beloved Isaac.

Gone now, all of them. Unforgettable, all of them, but replaceable, every one of them. Consider the knife. He'd loved that knife, loved the reassuring presence of it on his hip, the feel of it in his hand. It's gone—but now he has a better one!

He reaches into his open shirt collar, remembering the feel of the disc of rhodochrosite, remembering too the clarity it had provided. But one can absorb and internalize an amulet, he has come to realize. The rhodochrosite is gone, left behind in a city he need never return to, but the clarity it provided will be a part of him forever. He could get another amulet of the same mineral, it's neither rare nor costly, but, you see, he doesn't need to.

He draws out the stone he is wearing now, a crystal, almost colorless at its point, a deep purple at its broken end. He holds it, and feels its power.

★ ★ ★

He sits at the desk, boots up his computer, gets on-line. He liked the other computer better, liked the larger keyboard, liked his New York Night screensaver. This machine's a laptop, and he doesn't need a screensaver. He shuts it down entirely when he's not using it. He's less fond of it in many respects than his desk model, but he must admit it suits his lifestyle. When he's ready to put down roots again, that will be time enough to get a desk model computer.

And he'll be careful what he leaves on its desktop, too.

The cheery voice welcomes him, but does not tell him he has mail. He's just opened this account, and there's no one who knows of it, no one to send him mail.

He goes straight to alt.crime.serialkillers.

And catches up on the new posts in the several current threads centering on the late and variously lamented Adam Breit. Here again, he thinks, you can see the glass half empty or half full. On the one hand, Adam Breit is dead; on the other, Adam Breit lives!

Breit lives, indeed, as he had never lived before. Adam Breit has made a name for himself, a name with a long line of notches carved next to it. As he reads the new messages, he shakes his head at some of the comments. There are people out there who would credit Adam Breit with every dead massage-parlor whore from Maine to California, others who are sure he was personally acquainted with John Wayne Gacy. And, here and on the several Web sites devoted to Breit, there's a certain amount of speculation that Breit might somehow have survived, that the body burned beyond recognition might not be his, that he might have escaped to kill again.

Idiots.

Adam Breit is dead. Adam Breit will live on in memory, in legend, but in the flesh he has gone out in a blaze of glory, not unlike Jim Bowie at the Alamo. Another great knife-fighter, gone to his reward.

He won't be back.

Alvin Benjamin, on the other hand, is very much alive. Of course no one has heard of him.

But they will. . . .

His fingers find his new amulet, and he caresses the stone. The mineral is quartz, and its color marks it as the variety known as amethyst.

For immortality.